MY ADA MAE

KNOX COUNTY
BOOK 1

RACHAEL OGLE

AUTHOR'S NOTE

Dear Reader,

My Ada Mae deals with themes surrounding the death of a sibling, death of a significant other/partner, death of a parent, child abuse, addiction, and depression. Certain scenes and situations may be disturbing or triggering for some readers.

CAMPING

MARCH: ONE MONTH AFTER

CHAPTER ONE

ADA

The incessant knocking is back. For the past month, every few days, someone knocks on the door and I'm forced to open it. And the only person I would ever care to see on the other side of that piece of wood will never walk through it again. Thirty-four days ago, I stopped caring who walked through that door. Because thirty-four days ago, Cole walked out and won't ever be able to walk back in again.

Whoever's at the door knocks again. Three sharp raps. I know it's not Josie because she has a key. It's not Ingrid or Miles because they were both by a few days ago and they usually go about a week between visits. The visits from Cole's employees and their wives and girlfriends have started to dwindle. And if they do stop by, it's typically not until the evening, and a glance at the wall clock says it's barely past four PM. Maybe if I pretend no one is home, they'll give up and go away.

My phone dings and I reluctantly drag my eyes to it. Can't a woman just mourn in fucking peace? The name on the screen has me doing a double take. Why is Silas texting me?

Silas: Hey, Wednesday. Are you home? I saw
your car. I need to talk to you. Answer the
door.

What the fuck could Silas have to say to me? For twenty years, he's been nothing but cold and indifferent toward me. He's not come to see me or called or texted since the funeral. Why would he think I'd want to see him now? I type out a quick reply and hope it's enough to make him leave.

Ada: Go away, Ass. I'm not up to dealing with
you today.

Is my nickname for him juvenile, yes? Do I care? Not in the least. He is an ass. At least to me, anyway. My phone dings again and I heave a sigh.

Silas: I have some of Pap's shine. It's apple
pie. I also have marshmallow peeps—your
favorite. Cole's with me, too.

Damn him for baiting me with the only thing that would make me open the door for him: Cole. I knew his ashes were ready and Miles had picked them up, but I'm not sure I'd really considered what it would be like to have them. And knowing any part of Cole might be back with me, I jump off the sofa and fling open the door.

Unable to look at Silas's face, I let my eyes zero in on the black urn cradled in his arm and I swallow thickly, willing the immediate tightness in my throat to go away. I extend my hand to take it from him and he turns his body away so it's out of my reach. I bring my eyes to his and glare at him. He simply quirks a brow. "Invite me in, Wednesday. I'm not running a delivery service."

I don't say anything. I've spoken little since Cole died and I'm not about to waste words on Silas. Hoping that if I leave the door open and go into another room for a few minutes, he'll leave the urn and go, I turn and walk into the kitchen. I load the dishwasher and hear the front door close and once I finish, I head back to the living room, only to see Silas sitting on my couch like he doesn't have a fucking care in the world.

And knowing Silas, he's not going to leave until he says whatever he came here to tell me, so I sit on the other end of the sofa as he pulls the jars of amber liquid from a grocery bag. Spotting the urn on the coffee table, I lift and set it in my lap before reaching for one of the jars. He moves them out of my reach and I reward him with another silent glare. His expression is still the same placid indifference it always is. "I told you I needed to talk to you. You can have some after I'm done. You're probably going to need it."

Wishing I should shoot lasers from my eyes, I heave an exasperated sigh and lean back and fold my arms and wait. Silas opens one of the jars and downs a couple of healthy swigs and I feel my jaw clench in aggravation. Part of me wonders if he's simply doing it to get a rise out of me. Wouldn't be the first time. But I still refuse to waste words on him. He coughs with the strength of the moonshine before recapping the jar and blowing out a breath, the scent of the cinnamon liquor wafting in my direction.

"Cole sent me a package. It arrived this week." I open my mouth to ask one of the million questions that immediately come to mind, but then clamp it shut. Silas continues when he realizes I'm not going to say anything. "You know him; he was all about being prepared for anything. He's had a will and shit since, like, high school. He was a planner; you know that."

I sigh, hoping he'll get on with the rest of it. Whatever *it* is.

"There's a letter for you, too. And instructions." Confused, I furrow my brow and tap the top of the urn, hoping to glean some insight from its contents. "You're not going to like it, I'm sure. All I can say is, don't shoot the messenger. I'm simply following orders. Cole's orders. So, if you wanna be pissed, be pissed at him. None of this was my idea. I want to make that clear."

Frustrated with these dramatics, I roll my eyes and hold out my hand. He pulls a standard white envelope from his back pocket and my chest immediately aches at the thought of possibly having words from Cole. "I know I'm not your favorite person, but I want to honor my brother's wishes as best I can. So think about that before you balk, okay? I'll be back in a week. You've got that long to get ready. If you have questions before then, you know how to reach me." Silas doesn't hand it over and simply lays it on top of the jars of liquor. Annoyed, I lift my eyes to his face but can't look at him for more than a split second. It's too hard.

He rises without another word and before the door is even closed behind him, I've ripped the envelope to shreds. Having opened it, though, I can't bring myself to unfold the sheets of paper. Even after taking a few fortifying sips of Pap's shine, I can't make myself lay the pages flat. Seriously, why did I let Silas leave those jars? All I'm going to do is drink them and be massively hungover.

And then Silas's words hit me again. *I'll be back in a week. You have that long to get ready.* Get ready for what? I mean, if I read the letter I'll know, but knowing this is from Cole, I can only stare at the paper in my lap as it sits next to his urn. I pull the urn from its place on my legs and set it on the coffee table so I can glare at it. "What have you gotten me into, Cole? And did you honestly think it was the best idea to have *Silas* be the one to deliver whatever message you needed to get to me? You realize I would punch you if you were actually here, right?"

And even though I can't punch him, I still want to. For the fact that he's gone and left me in this apartment all alone. The apartment we moved into after I graduated from college. The apartment that's been our home for almost nine years. The two-bedroom apartment he showed me because it had north-facing windows that would be better for me when I work. The apartment that's ten minutes from his parents' house in Maryville since we spend so much time there. The apartment I've only left a couple of times since the funeral.

I'd want to punch him for the fact that I didn't even get to plan said funeral because he already had it planned out. At *thirty-one*. Seriously, who plans shit like that at our age? Cole, that's who. So, why was I shocked to see Silas had a letter? I should've predicted it. I should've counted on it. Being prepared has always been Cole's M.O. Yet, I feel like I've been sucker punched. I want to devour the letter, but what if it's the only one? What if this is the last thing I ever have with Cole's handwriting? What if this is the last thing I ever have from him?

But then something nags at me. Silas said he was following Cole's orders, so what does that mean? Could it mean that maybe Cole planned something? *Ada, stop speculating and read the damn letter.* My eyes flick back to the urn as if it had been his voice that had admonished me for stalling.

Taking a few more sips of the apple-cinnamon liquor, I blow out a breath. "Okay, babe, you win." I lean back on the sofa and hold the letter, still folded, to my forehead. As if I can magically absorb its contents through my skin. More likely, I'm hoping for some whiff of Cole's distinct scent. That earthy, grassy smell that always seemed to linger on his skin, no matter how many showers he took. It was as if the dirt, grass, and plants had embedded themselves into his DNA and permeated his very being. And part of me thinks he would have loved the idea of that. Unfortunately, the paper smells exactly like what it is: paper and ink. No grass or earth. No trace of the man I love. I pull it away from my face and tentatively unfold it.

But at the sight of his messy scrawl and the greeting of *My Ada Mae*, the tears immediately come and I can't do it. I toss it onto the coffee table and pick up the urn and go to our room— my room—and crawl into the unmade bed. I cuddle the ashes to my chest as if they're some stuffed animal and yes, I completely understand this is not a healthy coping mechanism in the least. I can't bring myself to care. My phone dings from the other room and I simply pull the covers up around me and let myself cry.

"Ada?" I'm jarred awake by a female voice and someone shaking my shoulder. I'd recognize the voice anywhere but can't muster more than a grunt of acknowledgment at her presence. "Ada, honey? It's Josie. I used my spare key. I'm sorry, I just wanted to come and check on you. I brought your favorite —Mom's chicken and dressing. Wanna come eat?" I simply pull the covers up around me tighter. "I'm not taking no for an answer. I'm under orders. If you don't at least shower and change clothes, I'll be forced to call in reinforcements and I think we both know you don't want that."

Peering above the blanket, I'm met with the sight of Josie standing with her arms folded next to the bed. Her brown eyes stare down at me with concern and affection. Brown eyes so much like her brother's, I can't hold them. "You and I both know Silas would get too much satisfaction from coming in here and turning the hose on you. You might as well let me help you." She scrunches up her nose. "He might've also mentioned there was a bit of a smell when he was here. And as much of an asshole as he is where you're concerned, he's not wrong, friend. You have smelled better. So, come on. Don't make me have to call Si; I'll never hear the end of it."

I want to ask her how she and Silas seem so... okay. Like their entire world hasn't shattered. Like their brother isn't *gone*. But I don't. I don't say anything. But I also don't protest when she turns the covers down. Her eyes fall to the urn in my arms and she doesn't even seem surprised. "I'll put this right on the nightstand, okay?" she asks, lifting it gently from my embrace.

Reluctantly, I let her coax me from the bed and tug me along to the bathroom. I let her start the shower and strip me down and push me under the spray. I let her wash my hair and don't even notice as she scrubs every inch of my body until I'm nearly raw. Of course, I'm not sure I'd notice anyway since I'm so emotionally raw, this physical discomfort doesn't even register.

She dries me off, helps me dress, and forces me to brush my teeth. Once she's satisfied I've done a fair job, she runs a brush through my hair and works it into a thick braid. And even though I know she's doing all these things, I can't speak or call forth any emotion other than numbness.

"Si also said he brought some shine from Pap's. Is that what's on the coffee table? Was that what he bribed you with to get to come in a couple of days ago?"

A couple of days? I slept for a couple of days? How is that possible? How is it, someone who should be as used to pain as I am isn't bouncing back like I always have before? *Maybe because the person who's always gotten you through your pain before is the one you're grieving for now.* How am I supposed to do this? How am I supposed to put one foot in front of the other and function like my existence isn't decimated?

Josie deposits me into a chair at the kitchen table and I don't even remember making the walk from the bathroom to the kitchen. She sets a plate in front of me. "Eat this." It's not a suggestion and neither is her tone. And because I don't have the wherewithal to even object, I pick up the fork and mechanically lift the food to my mouth. I chew and swallow without tasting what I know has to be a great meal, especially if Ingrid made it.

"Have you read the letter yet?"

I snap my eyes to where Josie sits across from me and she wears a knowing smile. The pull of her lips is almost exactly like I saw on Silas's when he was here, making me irrationally angry. "Thought that might get your attention. Have you?" I shake my head. "Why not?" I shrug. "Si mentioned you weren't talking. Have you suddenly decided to take a vow of silence?"

Rolling my eyes, I look back at the food I don't even remember eating more than half of. "So, what is it, then?" I shrug again. "All right. Well, Si also said you needed to be ready. And to do that, you have to read the letter. He'll be back here in four days, so you need to put on your big girl panties and find the ovaries to read it. You know he's not going to let it slide simply because you didn't have the balls to find out what Cole had to say. Whatever the big plan is, do you think he won't drag you kicking and screaming to complete it? Especially if it was something Cole wanted?"

My jaw clenches. I wish she'd stop saying his name like it doesn't hurt to hear it. I wish she'd shut up and go away and leave me to cope however I can right now. I don't want to read the letter. I sure as hell don't want to do whatever Silas has been roped into. I only want to dissolve and never have to live in a world that doesn't include the man I've loved since I was fifteen.

Come on, Ada Mae. You know you won't be able to stand it.

The not knowing. You can tell yourself you don't care all you want. We both know you're too curious a person not to be intrigued by what I might have to say.

Josie's hand covers mine and brings me out of my imaginary conversation with her brother. Her expression is softer than it was, as if she can sense how hard this truly is for me. "I know this is shitty. I wish this weren't something you had to endure. I know Cole has always been the person you lean on during hard times. It probably feels like the support you've always been able to rely on has been stripped away or the ground beneath your feet has dropped out. I get it.

"I know the love you and Cole shared vastly differs from the love our parents, me, or even Si had for him. I can't imagine how hard this is for you. But I know if he could put provisions in place—because let's face it, he was Cole. Why are we even surprised there'd be something planned? Whatever it is, it's likely to help. Somehow. Even if right now, it doesn't feel like it."

In theory, I know she's right. Cole was always the type of person who was good in a crisis. He was the one who checked on someone after a loss or tragedy. He organized meal trains and care tasks for friends in need. So, how much more would he do for me, the woman he loved? Am I brave enough to find out?

I heave a heavy sigh and nod slowly. "Yeah?" Josie asks, surprised. I shrug and then nod again and she gives me a small smile. "Okay. Well, I'm going to change your sheets and do some laundry for you before I leave. That okay?"

I shrug and she doesn't wait for me to answer further. I hear her practically running to my room. For those first few weeks, I refused to change the sheets because they still smelled like Cole. I know they don't anymore; I've wallowed all his smell away. Same with his clothes. He would've pitched a fit on me if he knew I pulled the last clothes he wore out of the hamper and wore them for days. Regardless of the fact they were sweat-stained and grimy from where he'd worked the day before. I didn't give a shit because they only smelled like him. They don't anymore.

Some undetermined amount of time later—it truly could be minutes or hours, I have no real concept of time anymore—Josie kneels next to my chair. She squeezes my hand and I slowly turn my head to look down at her. "Want me to tuck you in?"

I shrug and allow her to tug me up from my chair and guide me back to my room. I climb under the covers and she pulls them up around me. She sits on the edge of the bed and gestures to the nightstand. "I also set you up a little station here. I found your phone and plugged it up. There's also a jar of the shine and the letter." I squeeze my eyes shut and she pats my shoulder. "I didn't read it, of course; I just wanted it to be close at hand for you. Cole's also here, in case you feel like talking." She stands and leans down to press a kiss to my temple. "We all love you, Ada. Come back to us, okay? Mom and Dad miss you. Sunday dinner's not the same without you. I'll check on you in a day or two and Si will be here a couple of days after that. I'll close the door so you can rest, but I'll finish this laundry before I leave, okay?"

A few minutes later, the door opens and closes and I don't open my eyes again. At least, not for a long time. I'm not even sure how long has passed since it was dark when Josie shut the bedroom door and it's still dark now. I sigh and tap the screen of my phone and see it's four AM. I shouldn't be surprised. Cole and I would always get up to have our coffee together before he left for work around this time.

I stiffly pull myself up to sit and switch on the lamp, wincing when the light hits my eyes. Still in the same places she left them are the urn, the jar of shine, and the letter. And knowing I can't keep putting this off, I pick up the jar and paper and bring them over onto the mattress. I glance at Cole's urn and swallow thickly. "I swear, Cole Campbell, if I regret reading this letter, I will come to find you in the afterlife someday and punch you in your ghost face, you hear me?"

I open the jar and take three big gulps of moonshine. I welcome the burn and the cough that follows and replace the lid and set it back on the nightstand. *It's only paper and ink, Ada. It can't hurt you.* Maybe not physically. Blowing out a deep breath, I unfold the letter and steel myself to read.

My Ada Mae,

I know you're probably holed up in bed, not showering and not wanting to let anyone in. And if I was gonna guess, the only person you're talking to is me. Or rather, my remains.

I look at Cole's urn. "Haha. We get it. You know me." I picture his smug smile and want to scream at exactly how well he knows me.

I also know you're better than this, babe. I've seen you come back from worse. I know it doesn't feel that way, but you have. You'll come back from this, too.

Do you remember when we met? You were ten and it was Josie's birthday party. She'd gone on and on about this girl in her class and begged Mom and Dad to let her have you over for her slumber party. Usually, they would've said no since they didn't know your parents, but for some reason, they made an exception.

And I know Si and I tortured you that night. I blame it on your braids. Those two thick braids hanging over your bony shoulders. They were just too easy to yank. Hell, we tortured you every time you came over. I didn't know at the time it was because I had other feelings I didn't know what to do with.

Not then, anyway. But the day I saw you come into the school your freshman year, I knew exactly what it was. I hadn't seen you all summer and damn, you'd grown. Pretty sure my dick zeroed in on you before even my eyes did, babe. And that was it. I was gone for you. I've been gone for you ever since.

And you've made every single day of the last fifteen years worth living. You made me want to be brave despite my cautious nature and overanalyzing ways. You made me want to dream when I wasn't sure it was something I'd ever want to do. You were always my biggest dream. I wouldn't trade the time we've had together for all the money, margaritas, and Milky Way bars in existence.

Now, though, I need you to be brave. Believe me when I say I know what I'm about to ask of you is a lot. And if I know you, you'll want to yell and scream and have something or someone to punch. I'm sorry I'm not there to receive those blows; I genuinely am. But I also know you love me and you'll do this thing—these things—because I can't. Because they're my dying wishes. Yeah, I did go there. Sorry, babe, I'll pull out all my tricks —guilt included —to ensure these tasks get accomplished.

Do you remember when you were fifteen and we watched the movie about the two old guys who were dying in the hospital? One was rich and they decided to make a break for it to fulfill their bucket list. The one with Morgan Freeman?

I pull my eyes away from the letter for a beat. I swear, if I'm getting to read something about fulfilling some cheesy bucket list shit, I really will scream. Cole hated bucket lists. He believed every day should be lived like you were dying, to live a life without regrets. I blow out a breath and return my gaze to the page.

I know; I hate bucket lists. I think they're cheesy and an excuse for people not to live while they're alive. And that's not what this is, not really. Because most of these things aren't once-in-a-lifetime type things. They're everyday, ordinary things that were always a "someday" type of thing. You might not even remember some of them. But I do. I wrote them all down. Although, some of them are simply things I think you need to do or would enjoy.

And I know you think Si isn't your favorite person, but he is one of mine. I know it might even be hard to look at him since he looks so much like me. Except, in all honesty, we all know I'm the better-looking twin.

I asked Si to help you complete these things for a few reasons. Aside from you, he knows me best. He's got a flexible work schedule and can take the time to do the things I need him to do. And he's just enough of an asshole to not let you back out on the stuff I want you to do. We both know he'll drag you kicking and screaming if needed.

But the tasks are all on me; he's doing this because I've asked him to. He's just being a good brother and I hope you won't freeze him out. He's not so bad if you get past the crunchy exterior. Don't take your anger out on him. I mean, unless it's deserved. You know, if he drives terribly or chooses a shady place for burgers and you get food poisoning or he makes a terrible playlist. That kind of stuff is entirely valid. Bitch away about any of that.

True to my nature, everything is planned; you simply have to go. Si has all the details, but he'll only give them to you as instructed, so don't go bugging him for more than he gives up. We both know he won't crack.

I hope that by the end of this, you'll be in a better place. You'll have closure about my death and be able to move on. I know you're no stranger to pain and I know I'm the one who usually coaxes you back to the land of the living. Maybe this is my way of still helping you do that. Because the world misses you, Ada Mae, don't make it be without you too long. You're too bright a presence to stay locked away.

On the other sheet enclosed with this letter is the first set of instructions. You'll always receive them in plenty of time to prepare for the next task and any money needed to prep for things on your end. As I said, everything is planned.

If I could've spent the rest of forever loving you, I would have. Thank you for being the best woman I could've ever shared my life with. And even though I can't love you for the rest of your life, I'm glad I got to love you for the rest of mine.

It's okay if you're sad. It's okay if you're angry. It's okay if you're annoyed by what I'm asking you to do. You still have to do it because it's what you need.

I loved you until my last breath. Please know that.
- Cole

Even through my tears and the tightness in my chest, I flip to the second sheet and continue to read. I know if I stop, I won't be able to pick it back up again for a while and I need to do this one thing at least.

The first task doesn't require much prep on your end. Just pack clothes for camping.

. . .

I sniffle and wipe my eyes and nose on the collar of my tee-shirt. "Camping, Cole, really?" I roll my eyes and look back down at the paper.

Yeah, babe, that's right. I said camping. That's all you need to know. That, and it'll probably be warm and you'll be gone for three days. Everything else is taken care of.

Camping, huh? Why the hell not, I guess.

CHAPTER TWO

SILAS

Like every night for the past month, I sit in my office with a bottle of liquor. After the first couple of days following Cole's death, I blew through my personal stash of shine. And knowing Pap would kick my ass if I raided the stillhouse just to numb my pain, I'd resorted to cheap vodka from the liquor store on the highway to dull this unending ache. Unfortunately, all the liquor did was make it so I was hungover for a month straight. Even so, it wasn't enough to stop me from trying not to feel the loss of my twin, my best friend. I don't know how to do life without him. Even if I always knew there was a chance I'd have to.

Cole's letter taunts me from its position on my desk. I've read it so many times since it was delivered earlier in the week, I've probably got it memorized. And even though, with my visit to Ada today, I've set things in motion to complete the list of tasks he'd set up, I'm still unsure how I'm supposed to do this. How does he expect this to work? I mean, does he truly expect her to be okay with all this? Does he expect her to simply get over him with all these letters and tasks and fall into things with me? For such an intelligent man, he's a dumbass if he thinks there's any chance of success with this.

I pick up the bottle and twist off the cap and bring it to my lips before thinking better of it and rising to go to the kitchen and dumping it in the sink. Cole's voice has gotten more insistent over the past few days. Always saying the same thing: *It won't fix anything. I'll still be gone; you'll just be hungover. I need you to pull it together for Ada. She needs you, Si.*

If he were here, I'd slug him. Not only for asking me to do this but for giving me his blessing. For telling me he no longer has dibs on her. For telling me to take care of her. How am I supposed to take care of her—help her through her grief—when mine is still so raw?

Seeing Ada today and how much she's still reeling did nothing but make me feel even more guilty. I feel guilty for the way I feel about her. Guilty for still wanting her. Guilty for thinking she's still the most beautiful woman I've ever seen. I guess not even the loss of my favorite person on the planet can kill the feelings I've had for her since I was a kid. And God knows, I've tried to stop them myself.

As I took her in today when she opened the door, it nearly broke me to see how much her grief has consumed her. Her shiny, nearly black mane of hair was lank, greasy, and tangled. Her steel gray eyes were dull and wouldn't meet mine. Her face was pale and gaunt, her cheekbones sharper than I've ever seen them. Her full lips were cracked and split as if she's chewed them repeatedly. Her nails were bitten to the quick.

But those are things I shouldn't notice. Those are things the twin brother of the man you love shouldn't be able to see. Too bad I love her, too. I'd give anything to make it stop. I'd give anything not to have to do these tasks. To not put myself in a position where I'm forced to be near her so much. It's much easier not to think about her when I'm not with her. It'd be easier to pretend I could ever be content with someone who's not her. However, when I'm in her proximity, all I can see is her smile and how strong she's had to be her whole life. I can only see her quick wit and biting tongue, which have never ceased to amaze me.

I suppose all I can hope for by the end of this thing is for a possible friendship. I don't dare hope for more. Even if Cole did, the sadistic fucker. It's bad enough I had to watch him love her, be with her. It's bad enough that I was so jealous of him and what he had with her that I couldn't even be civil to her most of the time. Now, I'm expected to drag us both around creation in the infinitesimal chance that she could ever develop anything more than a tolerance for me. Fat chance, if I'm being honest.

Fuck. Why did I dump the vodka? I don't think I can do this sober. Not yet. A glance at my watch tells me it's still early enough that I can make a run to the liquor store before they close. The picture of Cole and me sitting next to my keys on the end table stops me. Hot, angry, bitter tears fill my eyes and I fall onto the couch. I want to rail and scream and break something. I want to kick Cole's ass for leaving me. For thirty-one years, he's been my constant. And as different as we were, he was my other half. I never thought I'd have to contemplate an existence that didn't include him. But sober, this hurts too fucking much. How am I expected to be strong for Ada if I can't even come out of this myself?

For who knows how long, I simply weep. Until I'm not sure there are tears left on the planet, let alone any left in my body. I cry until my throat is raw and my chest aches from heaving. I cry until I can't see straight. My phone rings from where I left it on my desk and I ignore it, knowing I won't sound like myself if I answer it. Once I calm down, though, I reluctantly stand and return to my office. The missed call is from Josie, which I should have predicted since I sent her to check on Ada after I left earlier. I grab a tissue from the box on my desk and blow my nose and clear my throat before returning my sister's call. She answers on the second ring.

"How was she?"

"I've never seen her like this. She was nearly catatonic, Si. She didn't even react when I helped her shower or anything. It's like she was shut down. I'm worried about her."

I consider Josie's words and fight the urge to climb into my car and bust into Ada's apartment to ensure she's alive. But I can't do that, so I take some deep breaths. "Okay, but did you at least get her to eat?"

"Yeah, she ate. She didn't protest when I washed her sheets or the clothes she was wearing and you were right; she's not talking. I hate I haven't been able to go see her before now."

"I know. It's not your fault. We've all been dealing with things. But hopefully, with what Cole planned, she'll start coming around. You know, if she and I don't murder each other."

Josie lets out a small laugh. "Yeah, I hope you've upped your life insurance policy if you're going to be spending much time with Ada. There's no telling how well she's going to to be able to put up with you."

"I don't guess it'll be that bad if she's not talking. You're going back over tomorrow, right?"

"Day after. I've got a meeting tomorrow. But Mom's going to take her some more food and make sure she eats. You know her; she'll get food into her." She's quiet for a beat before changing the subject. "How are you feeling about all this?"

Let's see, my dead twin brother called dibs on our sister's best friend when we were fifteen. Now, I find out he planned lots of couple-y type things as a way for her to grieve and process. He tasked me—a person she barely tolerates—with ensuring their completion. All the while, I've been in love with her for as long as I can remember. Because there's nothing fucked up about that, right? "I'm fucking aces, Jos. Cool as a cucumber."

She snorts a laugh down the phone line. "I'm sure. You know why he asked you to do this, don't you?"

Besides the fact he's always known I was in love with her? And now he's determined to play some fucked up version of matchmaker? "Because I've never been able to say no where Cole is concerned. I don't get why he didn't tell her about his heart. She could've at least been prepared."

Josie sighs. "I know. I'm so mad at him for that. All I know is, if she ever finds out, it's all our asses. But he was our brother; how could we go against his wishes, even for Ada?"

"I know. That's my thinking. I don't understand how he reconciled it to himself to let her be ignorant. I couldn't have done it."

"Me, neither. I guess, good luck?"

It's my turn to sigh. "Yeah."

My phone blares from the nightstand, jarring me out of a deep sleep. I hit the screen, thinking it's an alarm, but it's ringing. I pick it up and squint and see it's after five AM, but my eyes widen when I see who's calling. I swipe the screen to answer.

"Wednesday?"

"Fucking camping, Ass?" Ada asks. And judging by how slurred her words are, she's drunk.

"I see you read the letter. You been hitting the shine? Little early in the morning for drunk dialing, isn't it?"

"Cut the shit. What the hell is this? Cole hated camping."

I sit up and lean against the headboard, willing the pain in my chest to subside at hearing the sadness in her voice. "I don't know what to tell you. Like I said, I'm only following orders. I'll be there Friday morning to pick you up. Be ready by ten." I know if I continue talking to her, with her voice sounding the way it does, I'm not sure I'll be able to keep myself from going to check on her. So before I can stop myself, I disconnect the call and switch my phone to silent. Regardless of how much I'd prefer to keep hearing her voice.

Can I really do this? Not for the first time, I want to punch my brother in the balls. How can he expect me to do this? How can he expect her to get over fifteen years with him and fall into things with me? And how do I not come out looking like some sleazy asshole if his plan does work? I swoop in and begin pursuing what's essentially my brother's widow? What in the fucking twisted hell was he thinking?

At the ass crack of dawn, I'm up and packing the Winnebago with all the supplies Cole's instructions detailed. I swear, the things I do for my brother. Cole's voice screams in my head, *Yeah, because getting a weekend of uninterrupted time with Ada is such a hardship, right, bro?* "Shut it," I mutter under my breath. Even if he's right, it doesn't mean I'm exactly looking forward to this.

And still, right at ten, I pull the trusty, rusty Winnie in at Ada and Cole's apartment. I half expect her to still be holed up and not answer the door, but when I knock, it opens after only a few seconds. I stick my hands in my pockets and hope I look bored, even though, in reality, I'm nervous. Her hair is clean and pulled back into a sleek ponytail. Her face is free of makeup and those dark circles she had last week seem to be a bit less prominent. So, it would appear she's showered and gotten some rest at least.

Her clothes hang off her, making me believe she's lost weight. A lot of it. Weight she can't afford to lose. And yet, she still looks as beautiful as ever. Even in simple jogging shorts and a tee-shirt and hiking sandals. "You ready?" I ask casually.

She nods. *Oh, I see. We're back to not talking.* I look down next to the door. "Just this one duffle?" She nods again and I sigh. "Okay, let's go." She grabs a grocery bag from the kitchen and I shake my head. "You don't need to bring anything. I have it all. Your instructions were for you only to pack clothes, right?"

She pauses, her eyes darting to a bottle of wine, and I roll my eyes. "I have wine, too, Wednesday. Cole was very thorough in his notes. I can follow basic instructions, you know."

It's Ada's turn to roll her eyes, but she sets the bag on the counter. She turns off the lights and grabs her purse from the coffee table and I pick up the duffle bag and we head out the door. She takes a moment to lock up and we walk in silence down to the RV.

She stops short when she sees the Winnebago and turns to me, an incredulous expression on her face. "Oh, come on. I fumigated and cleaned it, tuned it up, ensured the A/C worked, and even installed new mattresses in the bunks. It's fine. I'm an asshole, but I'm not about to sleep with bugs, either, so it's all good. I had Dad look at it to make sure it was up to snuff before I left and it drove here perfectly. Winnie will get us where we need to go. Trust me." She levels me with a gaze and puts her hand on her hip and I deliver the final blow. "It was what Cole specifically requested. I followed his instructions to the letter."

Her jaw clenches and she looks like she wants to cry and I'm not sure I can handle that just yet. I have no assumptions that before all these tasks are complete, one or both of us won't be in tears. But so soon? I can't do it. I open the door and step in ahead of her. "Let's go, Peep. We're burning daylight."

I start the engine and she reluctantly climbs inside. She goes to sit in the back and I tug her up into the front and deposit her into the passenger seat. "Buckle up." She sighs and pulls the seatbelt over her shoulder. I do a mental rundown of my list of things to remember. "Wait. Did you bring his ashes?"

Her brow furrows and she shakes her head. "Cole wants a little of his ashes scattered everywhere we go." Her mouth falls open and I shrug. "It's what he wanted," I say matter-of-factly. "Do you want to get them or do you want me to?"

She swallows and releases the belt and stands and again, I think she might cry. I'm hoping against hope she doesn't since I won't know how not to comfort her and she won't know what to do if I do that. She won't know how to accept comfort from me since I've never offered it to her in the past, as it wasn't my place. Regardless of how happy I would've been to do it.

Ada steps down from the RV, treks back upstairs to her apartment, and returns a few minutes later with Cole's urn. She seems at a loss for what to do with it as she begins to sit. I take it from her, open the compartment below the stereo, and stick it inside. She lets out a noise that sounds nearly like a scoff and I shrug. "What, you got a better idea?"

She doesn't say anything and simply yanks her seatbelt over her shoulder and buckles it. She pulls her knees up and turns her head to look out the window. I fight the urge to sigh as I release the parking brake and shift into drive.

I don't know what I expected during this trip. I'm shocked she doesn't even ask where we're going. She doesn't fiddle with the stereo, request to pee, or do anything that's classic road-trip Ada. Even when I turn on music I know for a fact she hates— simply to try and garner some sort of reaction from her—I still get nothing.

She falls asleep about an hour into the drive. I have no expectations that she'll drive anywhere unless I force her and I don't think I'm up for being that much of an asshole this go-round. I simply leave her be until we have to stop for gas after another couple of hours.

I gently shake her shoulder and she stirs. "Go pee. Hopefully, this is the last stop before we get there." I dig in my pocket and bring out some cash. "Get some snacks." She looks down at my extended hand as though it might bite her and I nearly groan in frustration. I grab her hand and shove the money into it. "Get me a Coke. Get you a Dr. Pepper. Get us both a bag of chips."

She narrows her eyes but closes her fingers around the money and snatches her hand away. She practically jumps out of her seat to exit the RV. I watch her walk into the gas station, her arms folded and eyes focused on the ground. I finish filling up the tank and climb back behind the wheel.

Fifteen minutes later, when Ada still isn't back, I begin to worry. I grab the keys, head into the store, and glance around, my eyes catching on the top of a familiar dark head down one aisle. I approach her slowly and she doesn't acknowledge me, her eyes fixed on one particular spot on a shelf. I follow her gaze and slump. Fucking Milky Way candy bars. Cole's all-time favorite food.

I sigh and nudge her. "Come on, Wednesday." She blinks slowly, as if coming to, and flicks her eyes up to mine, but they don't stay. "Did you pee?" She nods. "Okay. Let's take care of these snacks," I say, gesturing to the sodas and bags of chips in her arms. She glances down at them as if just remembering she has them and my heart squeezes. All this is too much for her. Too soon. But I have no other recourse except to press on.

"You think you can pay for those so I can go to the bathroom?" She nods. "All right. I'll be out in a minute." I hustle to the restroom as she meanders toward the register. She's still in line by the time I'm coming out, so I join her in waiting. When we finally reach the cashier, Ada drops our items on the counter and pulls the cash I gave her out of her pocket, not making eye contact with the clerk.

I offer him a tight smile and I'm sure this scene looks like something out of some sort of kidnapping movie. Ada, despondent. Me, closely watching her. *That's all I need, to get arrested because people think I'm holding Ada hostage.* Would she even speak up to say she's here of her own free will or would she let them drag me off? I want to say she would speak then, but who knows, since she probably only talks when she's drunk anymore.

I grab the bag and the change from the cashier and usher her out of the store, not wanting to draw any more attention to us. I unlock the passenger door and open it to let Ada climb in. I set the bag in her lap and jog around to unlock my own door and slide behind the wheel. As I buckle up and start the engine, I reach into the bag and pull out my Coke. Noticing she's gotten two bags of chips, I ask, "Which chips do you want?"

She shrugs and shakes her head as if to say, *I don't care.* I sigh and go for the Cheetos since they're my favorite. I know I won't eat them all since they're her favorite, too. After twisting off the top for my drink and downing several good gulps, I stash it in the cupholder and pop a few chips into my mouth before taking off.

Despite Ada getting snacks for herself, she doesn't eat or drink anything. She doesn't do more than shift the bag to the floorboard, pull her knees back up, and return to looking out the window. Twenty minutes later, she's asleep again and I wish I had downloaded an audiobook to listen to so I could kill time.

I pull into the campground at Edisto Beach State Park in South Carolina a little before six. I know from the way the sites are positioned, I'm not going to be able to back in without a spotter, so I poke Ada in the shoulder to rouse her. She stretches and looks around, her brow furrowing as if trying to figure out where we are. "South Carolina. You're going to have to either be the spotter so I can back in or you back in and I'll spot."

She thinks for a minute and shrugs. I wish she'd fucking talk to me. It's one thing for her to be silent when it doesn't matter, but I actually need her voice in this instance. "Ada, which do you want? Answer me."

I so rarely call her by her actual name, I can tell it's caught her off guard. "I'll spot," she says, her voice barely above a whisper and gravelly from disuse.

"Okay. This is us. Campsite forty. Don't let me hit anything."

Her jaw clenches and she unbuckles and opens the door to step down, her posture tired, as if she hasn't slept for almost seven hours. *She is tired, bro. This is how she gets when she's depressed. Cut her some slack.* "You cut her some slack," I mutter. "This is all your doing." Okay, it's official; I've cracked. I'm having imaginary arguments with my dead brother and answering him. "Get it together, Silas."

I look from one mirror to the other and Ada motions for me to back up. Having helped Cole back into tight spaces with his landscaping trailer over the years, she knows what she's doing and even without words, we get parked in only a few minutes. I chock the wheels after putting Winnie into park and shut off the engine.

I point to a squat building a little ways off. "Bathhouse. We have enough water in the RV for cooking, but that's it. I'll get us plugged up and we'll have power in a minute."

The only indication she's acknowledged anything I say is her eyes flitting over to the direction of the restrooms. She steps past me and back into the vehicle. *So, I guess she's also not going to help set up. Figures.* Not that I expected her to, but still. I let out a frustrated sigh when I'm sure she's out of earshot and pull the hookup cord from an exterior compartment and take a couple of minutes to connect it. I roll out the awning for some shade and drag out a couple of chairs to set up next to the fire ring.

I know from Cole's instructions about this trip, that he'd paid to have someone deliver a couple of cords of wood before our arrival. All I had to do was call and give them the dates. Sure enough, there's plenty of wood for the three nights we'll be here.

Climbing back inside to turn on the A/C, I take a moment to ensure nothing is malfunctioning from the switch-on. I don't see Ada in the front, on the couch, or at the table. I step past the dining table and don't see her in the bed. I turn and look up and she's curled up with her back to me in the overhead bunk.

I debate prodding her but decide to leave her for now and step outside to take a walk. At least, if I'm alone, I can cry without her seeing me. I can pretend I'm okay. I can pretend I'm strong for her. Even if the reality is the fucking opposite. Even if going on a road trip reminds me of all the trips Cole and I went on in college and as kids. But I can't let Ada see how much it hurts. So, I'm thankful when I see a trail leading into the woods. And for the next hour, I cry silent tears of frustration and pain.

CHAPTER THREE

ADA

I feel like I'm drowning. When Cole's letter said camping, I thought he meant actual camping—tent, sleeping bag, hotdogs, marshmallows, roughing it. I wasn't expecting Winnie. Not that we ever camped in this thing, but we did a lot of other stuff in the RV. I even lived in it for over a year and simply being back in here is almost overwhelming. The memories of Cole and me. This was the first place we ever fooled around and, later, where we lost our virginity.

Surely Silas doesn't know that, right? Although, they were twins, so maybe he shared that kind of stuff with him. All I know is, I couldn't even look at the back bed. Sometime around dark, Silas says something about coming to eat, but I ignore him. I don't move or sleep or make a sound. I don't even get up to go to the bathroom.

"Wednesday, get your ass down here." I have no frame of reference for what time it is other than dark. "I know you're not asleep. You snore. You haven't been sleeping this whole time. Get down here and eat before I drag your bony ass off the bunk. And you know I will."

Having been subjected to Silas's torture as a young girl, I know he's not above dragging someone bodily out of bed. I sigh and climb down and sit at the table. A plate of grilled chicken chunks and roasted potatoes are already at my place, along with a glass of white wine.

I nibble a few pieces of meat but don't really taste them as I keep my eyes on the table and sip my wine. "Did you shower this morning?" I glance up at him, my brow furrowing, not understanding his question. "Did you shower before we left this morning, or do you need to take one tonight?" He looks like he's trying to be patient, but I can tell he's frustrated. Good thing I don't give a shit.

I shake my head and he releases a slow breath. "No to which question? Do you need a shower tonight?" I shake my head and his jaw clenches. "Jesus, Wednesday. You had no problem calling me at five in the morning to talk the other day. You can't say more than two words to me? Are you on a speaking budget I'm unaware of these days?"

I don't want to talk to him, whose voice is so like Cole's, it makes me ache and I look away, unable to continue to gaze at him. Not with those same warm brown eyes and messy, light brown hair—even if Cole's was much shorter. Not to mention that same long, straight nose, strong jaw line, and perfect lips.

Why did I ever think I could do this? Why did it have to be Silas? I know what Cole said, but this is too much. Too soon. I'm not ready to look into the face of the man I love and it not be him. It's almost cruel. My chest grows tight, and my throat hurts, and I know I'm about to cry. I don't want to cry. Especially not in front of Silas, who wouldn't know how to do anything but ridicule me for it; even if the tears are for his brother. I down my wine, push my plate away, slide out of the booth, and return to my bed. I roll onto my side, pull my knees up to my chest, and cry silent tears for I'm not sure how long, but at some point, I fall asleep.

When I wake up, it's still dark, and I have the overwhelming urge to pee. There aren't any lights on in the RV, so I assume Silas has gone to bed. *Good, I didn't want to face him anyway.* I glance outside and see the landscape is washed in the light from the large, full moon, so I don't even bother grabbing my phone to use as a flashlight.

I slip on my sandals, silently open the door, step down, and quickly make my way to the bathhouse and do my business. As I'm returning, I see Silas isn't in bed but sitting next to the fire. His back is to me, but there's no mistaking it's him and he's sipping from a jar. A jar I know contains some of Pap's shine. I don't know why I'm even surprised since it's Pap's Winnebago.

I make my way over, and Silas startles when I lean down to pick up the jar before taking the other seat at the fire. "Christ, make a noise or something, Wednesday. Damn." I ignore him and take a few healthy swigs from the jar. Apple pie. He watches me keep drinking. "You only had three bites of supper; I'm not holding your hair back if you puke, just so you know. And if you puke in Winnie, you're cleaning it up. I don't care how drunk you are." I roll my eyes and take a couple more sips before setting the jar on the ground. I pull my knees up to my chest and stare into the fire.

"I have a letter for you." I snap my eyes in his direction. "But I can't give it to you until our last night and you can't open it until sunrise the next morning. I'm supposed to walk you over to the beach and after you read the letter, we're supposed to sprinkle some of his ashes. Those are my instructions." I look down at my hands and nod. "Seriously, Peep, have you pretty much stopped talking altogether?" I shrug. "Do you talk to Cole?" I swallow and nod. "Figured. Does he talk back?"

I level him with a gaze and roll my eyes. I sit for a few more minutes before rising and heading back inside. I find my duffle on the sofa, pull out my pajamas, and step into the tiny bathroom to change. I deposit my dirty clothes into my bag and climb up the ladder to my bunk.

Sometime later, Silas opens the door and quietly steps into the RV. Obviously, he's trying not to make much noise, but since I'm not asleep, I hear everything he does. He takes off his shoes, opens his backpack, and unbuckles his belt and the button and zipper of his jeans. He shuffles around and something hits the sofa with a thud and a jingle. His jeans and keys, if I were to guess. The RV shifts as he must be tugging on his pajamas and getting into bed.

And even with the liquor I drank, I'm buzzed but can't seem to find sleep. I toss and turn, and soon, Silas starts snoring. I sigh, roll onto my back, and thread my fingers through my hair. I'm still lying in the same position when the sun comes up and birds start singing outside.

I'm still in the same position whenever Silas rises from his bed later. He starts a pot of coffee before slipping on his shoes and stepping outside. When he returns a few minutes later, he pours a cup of coffee and comes over to my bed. "Come on, Wednesday. There's coffee. Get up. You're not lying in bed all day." Not waiting for a response, he simply opens the door and goes outside.

I sigh, climb down from my bunk, and walk over to the small counter where the coffeemaker is set up. I pull a cup from a cabinet and open the fridge, hoping to find some milk to put in my coffee. I'm surprised to see my favorite creamer. *I guess*

Cole did give him instructions for everything. I pour some into my cup, followed by coffee, and step outside.

Silas, bent over the fire, is coaxing it back to life. I walk over and take my seat and look out toward the direction of the beach. I can't see it from our campsite, but I can hear the waves crashing against the shore behind a line of thick trees.

"Coffee strong enough?" he asks, glancing up from where he's stoking the fire. He's dressed in basketball shorts, a tee-shirt, and a pair of flip-flops. His hair is flat on one side and sticking up on the other, his jaw coated in a day's worth of beard growth. I nod. "Good. Pancakes or biscuits and gravy for breakfast?"

I shrug and he stops working the fire. "Come on, use a couple more words today. Pancakes or biscuits?"

I roll my eyes. "Pancakes." My voice sounds rough, even to me, and I wonder if your voice is one of those things that if you don't use it, you lose it. Would I care if I couldn't speak anymore? The only person I ever want to talk to again, I can't, so why does it matter? I don't have a job that requires me to speak to people, so what do I care if it fades away?

Silas gives me a slow smile, obviously pleased with himself. "Thank you. Bacon okay?" I nod. "All right." He returns to trying to get the fire to stay lit and asks, "Did you bring your bathing suit?" I shake my head. "Why not?"

I shrug and shake my head again and he lets out an exasperated sigh. "Didn't your instructions say to pack stuff for warm weather?" I nod. "Does that not include a swimsuit?" I shrug again and he clenches his jaw. "Can you have a fucking conversation with me, Ada? Damn. You know you're not the only one struggling with this, right?"

He tosses the stick he's been using into the fire, grips the back of his neck, and shuts his eyes in obvious frustration. I throw the contents of my coffee cup into the fire and drop my mug onto the ground. I rise from my chair and anger flashes in Silas's eyes. "What the fuck did you do that for? I've been trying to build the fire back up and you got the wood all wet."

I step closer to him, poke him in the chest, and scowl at him. "I didn't ask for any of this. I didn't ask to be stuck with you all weekend."

He narrows his eyes. "That makes two of us. At least I'm trying. You can't even do that."

"Fuck you, Ass." I stalk past him toward the bathrooms and hear him go into the RV and slam the door. I don't know enough about this campground to know if there are rules about quiet hours. I get the feeling that if there are, we broke them.

I stay in the bathroom long enough to blink away the tears that had begun to well in my eyes. I refuse to let Silas see me cry like he's hurt my feelings when he's a prick. God, I just want to go home and crawl into my bed. *Ada Mae, come on, babe. You're better than this.* "Not without you, I'm not," I say with a shuddery breath and now I couldn't stop the tears if I tried. I know if I weren't trying to hold back, they'd become racking sobs. But people are coming in and out of the bathroom and I don't want to have to tell someone I'm okay. Because I'm not okay. Not in the fucking least.

When I feel as though I'm in control, I wipe my eyes and nose with the collar of my tee-shirt and head back to our campsite. Because where the fuck else am I going to go? I sit in my chair and pull my knees up and sniffle. Silas comes out of the Winnebago a few minutes later and slowly makes his way over to me. He holds something out and I look but don't turn toward him. "Peace offering." It's my coffee cup and he's refilled it. "I put the creamer shit you like in it. You know that stuff's terrible for you, right?"

I sigh and take the offered mug. "Thanks." He nods and takes his seat and begins to stoke the fire again. I take a sip of my coffee and it's perfect. Not like I'm going to tell him that. "Talking wears me out," I admit a moment later. "I get really tired."

He works his jaw and his throat bobs with a swallow. "So, take a nap."

I have no clue why I expected him to be sympathetic or understanding. It's not like he's ever been that way before. I ignore him in favor of sipping my coffee and watching some seagulls fight over what looks like the remains of a lizard.

I must zone out because the next thing I know, Silas is nudging my chair with his foot. "Come eat, Peep." I glance over my shoulder. The picnic table at our campsite is set and he's piled a couple of pancakes and bacon on my plate. I sit across from him and look down at my plate. I know I need to eat. I know I only ate those few bites of chicken last night and nothing else all day and I'm currently swimming in my clothes. I simply can't bring myself to feel any kind of hunger for anything besides sleep. "And you're not getting up from this table until you eat every bit of food on your plate. I don't care if it takes you six hours. I'll sit here with you until it's clean. Two pancakes, two pieces of bacon. You usually put away twice that." I level him with a gaze and he digs into his own food. "You can give me that stink eye all you want; you're going to eat your food."

Ass. I narrow my eyes and try to muster the same energy to eat as I've devoted to my annoyance with Silas. I sigh, cut the stack of pancakes with the side of my fork, and notice l don't have any syrup. Sensing my dilemma, he wordlessly plunks a bottle down in front of me. I pick it up and drizzle some over my plate. I take a bite and chew and a thought occurs to me I didn't have the mental faculties to consider last night. "When did you learn to cook?" The words come out a bit more sarcastic than I intend, but I can't bring myself to care enough to feel sorry about it.

He blinks slowly, in obvious shock that I've spoken, and sips his coffee after he swallows the bite he's been working on. His right brow tics up for a beat before his expression neutralizes to one of indifference. "I've always known how, but I'll never turn down letting someone else offer to do it for me."

I nod, absorbing his words. "It's good."

His grin is smug. "I know."

And just like that, I'm annoyed again. I drop my gaze to my plate and focus on shoveling the food in my mouth simply to be able to get up from this table.

Arrogant ass.

Thankfully, he doesn't prod me to talk for the rest of the day. He simply tells me when food is ready and reminds me to go shower. I could be indignant that he's bossing me around, but I'm not. In all honesty, I'm not sure I'd remember anymore without the encouragement.

A little before dark, Silas pokes me in the back where I've been lying down. I glance over my shoulder at him. "Let's go. Supper time." I wordlessly climb down from my bunk and follow him outside after I slip on my shoes. Tonight, it's burgers and chips and an insulated tumbler of beer.

He's dressed my burger exactly how I like it: cheese, lettuce, tomato, mustard. Usually, I'd be grateful—and maybe a bit skeptical he's gone to so much trouble. Even so, I don't feel anything but numb. I nibble my food and don't see or taste anything.

He sweeps my paper plate away when I'm done eating and tosses it into the fire. I rise from the table and begin to go back inside and he grabs my arm and shoves me into my chair next to the fire. Okay, maybe *shove* is a bit harsh. *Redirected* might be a better term. It still doesn't stop me from giving him a death glare. He rolls his eyes and takes his seat.

He pulls a jar from somewhere. Hell, did he raid Pap's entire stash? Lord knows what he'll do when he finds out Silas depleted his stores. He'll likely make him work the still for a whole weekend. He removes the lid and takes a swig before holding it out to me. I reluctantly take it and bring it to my lips.

"Did Cole ever tell you about us getting drunk on shine for the first time?" I try to remember and shake my head and he smiles. "I think we were about fourteen and we'd seen Pap sneaking sips of something out of a jar. We didn't know about the still then. You know, we weren't to be trusted because we were shits and Pap and Mom and Dad probably thought we'd blab.

"But anyway, we didn't know what it was, but it sure seemed to put Pap in a better mood, so we thought it must be some pretty good stuff, right?" He doesn't wait for me to respond, he just holds his hand out for the jar and after I take another sip, I pass it back to him. He drinks and wipes his mouth with the back of his hand before continuing. "So, when Pap had gone into the woods one day, I grabbed the jar and opened it. The smell alone about knocked me down. Especially because it wasn't diluted like some of his other stuff; the stuff he sells or makes into apple pie or other flavors, you know?

"I dared Cole to drink some. But you know him; he was too cautious. I asked him if I drank some, if he would, too. And I guess he didn't want to feel left out because he said he would. So I squared my shoulders and took a huge gulp. And because I didn't want to look like a pussy, I swallowed it. And then I thought I was going to die.

"But since Cole hadn't drunk any, I wasn't about to let on

how bad it was, so I just handed the jar over to him and he took a drink. I don't think his was as big as mine, but whatever. And Jesus, that one drink was enough to make me so buzzed, I couldn't walk a straight line. But Cole acted like he was going to throw up. He said, 'this shit's nasty; how can Pap not be in a terrible mood after he drinks it?'

"And I thought it was the funniest thing I'd ever heard. And then, it didn't taste so bad by the second or third drink anymore. But we were skunked when Pap got back up to the house. He found us with his half-empty jar and we were so drunk we couldn't even run away. That expression, 'falling-down drunk'? Totally a real thing.

"We were so hungover the next day, Pap brought the cowbell into our room and rang it right next to our ears. He said, 'that'll teach you to drink a man's shine when you've not been invited, now get out here and help with the garden.' And God, it was like ninety in the shade that day, and he made us pick beans. Cole and I were so sick that we kept taking turns throwing up in the field. We never touched Pap's shine again until we were way over the legal age."

I haven't ever heard this story before, which is surprising. Since I've known Cole, Silas, and Josie for so long, I've always felt like I was part of their family. I thought I would've heard it all, but it's still lovely to hear stories about the antics of their youth.

Silas extends the jar back to me and I take it and down a healthy gulp, not even noticing the burn. "So, that's why he would only ever have, like, one sip."

He grins. "Yeah, I think he was traumatized."

The next day passes without event, with the same song and dance of me hardly talking and Silas prodding and cooking. I know I should probably thank him for going to all this trouble, but I can't bring myself to do it. As the hours stretch on, my stomach begins to knot up knowing he's going to give me another letter. And by supper time, I'm practically buzzing with anticipation.

I don't know if he doesn't notice or simply chooses to ignore how antsy I am. Probably the latter, if I had to guess. But finally, he puts me out of my misery after supper. He exits the RV with a bag in hand. "We've got an early morning with us having to be at the beach before sunrise. Can you wait to open this stuff, or do I need to hold on to it until then?"

I narrow my eyes and sigh and he holds it out. I snatch it from his hand like a starving person and clutch it to my chest. He huffs a laugh. "All right, then. We'll have to pack everything up tonight since we'll have to leave right after we get back from the beach. So put that in your bunk and help me prep." I could ignore him and he probably wouldn't give me too much shit about it, but I rise from my chair and do as he requests. We move around the campsite and put things away and get the RV ready to drive home again tomorrow.

I'm already awake way before Silas nudges me in my bunk. It's barely after five, and I practically run to the bathroom to change clothes, pee and brush my teeth. When I return, he's already stripped the bunks and piled the linens onto the back bed. He hands me a travel mug full of coffee. "I'm going to run to the bathroom, and then we'll walk over." I nod and fidget, bag and mug in hand, and wait.

When he returns, he grabs a quilt from one of the exterior

compartments and retrieves Cole's urn from where it's been stashed all weekend. My heart lurches when I see it because it's then I remember we're also supposed to scatter some of his ashes.

"Ready?" I shrug because, no, I'm not ready. And even if I'm so beyond thrilled I'll get to read another letter from Cole, the idea of me finishing reading it makes me never want to open it. "Okay, let's go." He nudges me toward the beach access and we walk in silence.

Once we get to the shoreline, he spreads out the blanket and plops down. He sets the urn down next to him and I take the opposite corner, wanting to try to have as much privacy as possible as I read. I glance at him because I don't know if I'm supposed to wait until a specific time or if I can go ahead, and I don't want to mess it up.

He senses me looking at him and nods. "Go ahead. The instructions only said sunrise. It's a few minutes before, but I think you're good."

I swallow thickly and reach into the bag. There's a box wrapped in brown paper and I pull it out. The letter is taped to the front and I set it down on my lap and tug the envelope off the box.

I shut my eyes briefly and blow out a steadying breath before turning it over and sliding my finger under the flap. I pull out the folded sheets of paper and steel myself, same as last time, and open it.

My Ada Mae,

I know you were probably a little pissed about the choice of accommodations. If I know you, you were thinking about the first time we kissed. And the first time you let me put my hand up your shirt. And the first time we got naked and I lasted about twenty-three seconds. Best twenty-three seconds of my life, let me tell you.

I huff a small laugh, even as tears burn behind my eyes.

I also know you love the beach. It was our first vacation, remember? It was the summer after you graduated high school. We went to Myrtle Beach and you ended up getting sun poisoning and we had to stay inside those last couple of days. But I'd like to think we still managed to have a good time. We played cards, had lots of sex, and watched that terrible movie about the clowns from outer space. Seriously, it was so bad, I think I broke out in hives.

If I also know you—which we both know I do—you will have also blown up at Silas at least once and maybe he deserved it. But then again, maybe he didn't.

I glance over at the man in question. His knees are drawn up and his wrists are draped over them as he looks out toward the ocean. Does he have letters, too, or only instructions? I return my attention to my letter.

Y'all have always butted heads; I know that. But he's doing this thing for me when I can't, so I hope you'll stop giving him the silent treatment. Even if it's not intentional. Even if it hurts to talk to him because he sounds like me. He's not me, babe. We're in no way the same person, regardless of how much we look alike. I'm sorry if looking at him hurts. Don't tell him I said so, but he's got a pretty nice face.

And Si can be a good friend to you, even if you don't want one. He's not gonna go away; it's not in his nature. He'll be a pain in your ass, but he's a loyal pain in the ass. He'll have your back.

All right, I'll get off my soap box about Si. Anyway, I wanted you to come out on the beach at sunrise to remind you that no matter what, a new day always comes. Even after the shittiest day you can imagine, the sun always comes up the next day. And it's a chance to start over and try to make the next day a good one.

I know right now it doesn't feel like there are any good days. I know right now, they all feel shitty. They won't always be. I don't expect this one trip will have magically mended your broken heart. But hey, maybe I am that good, who knows?

There should also be a box with this letter. Open it now and then read the rest of this.

I fold the letter, stick it under my leg to keep it from blowing away in the breeze and rip the paper on the box. My mouth falls open when I see what it is: a new digital art tablet. The exact one I've been saving up for over the last year. My throat aches and tears burn my eyes. I run my fingers over the front of the box, pull the letter back out, and pick up where I left off.

Yeah, I know, it's awesome. I know you've been working toward this. Now you have it. And I know you've probably taken the last month off and it's fine, but now it's time for you to get back to work. Re-open your store and sell your art. Make those people who read all that fantasy smut buy your fan art. I swear, those things you draw of those fairies and stuff are almost not safe for work. And I'm not sure why it makes me horny, but it does. So, I guess it does what it's supposed to do.

I snort a laugh. God, I miss his sense of humor.

Your hiatus is over. Get your fine ass back to work. Get your feelings out on your digital canvas. It's okay if it's only for you. You'll find your way back to your art, too.

I'll leave you with this until next time: the sun comes up every single day. Even on the days you don't think it should. Even on days when it hurts too much to look outside. The world keeps spinning and time marches on. And time is something you still have; use it wisely.

I know it would be easy for you to simply hunker down and wait for the next time Si shows up to drag you off to parts unknown. Don't do that. Don't retreat. Don't stay hidden away. Don't let only these glimpses of what's left of me be all you look forward to. Because soon, those glimpses will be gone, too.

I can't keep the tears from rolling down my face at the thought of having no more letters from him. Rationally, I know I can't receive them for the rest of forever, but even him telling me there are a finite amount makes my heart ache.

So, in addition to getting back to work, you're also gonna start going to family dinner again. And Silas has instructions to drag you out of bed un-showered and disheveled to deposit you in your chair at Mom and Dad's if needed. Don't make him have to do that. It wouldn't be pleasant for either of you.

Look out at the water, babe. Go ahead, do it.

I raise my eyes to the waves, where the sun is just starting to peek over the horizon. Everything is washed in a golden-pink glow and warmth is already beginning to creep in, burning off the slight chill of the morning.

Those waves are like the grief you feel right now. If you were to lie in the water, those waves would crash over you. Depending on how big they were, it might feel overwhelming. I know right now, that's how it feels. You feel as though you'll never get a break to breathe. But the thing about the ocean tides is, they recede and eventually, they pull back.

The tides are predictable. Your grief might not be. There may even be moments when you forget I'm gone. It's okay. It's okay to let the loss wash over you again. It'll pass. It's also okay if you laugh. Please, for the love of all things holy, laugh, babe. Your laugh is magical. Don't stop smiling or laughing simply because I'm not there to smile and laugh with you.

The first time you laugh—hell, I hope you've already had it by the time you read this. But it's okay if you haven't. Whenever you do, I want you to cherish it. Don't you dare tell yourself that you can't believe you laughed. I want you to laugh. I want you to laugh so hard you cry and throw up.

Laugh with someone. Hell, laugh at some dumbass thing Si does. He'll get over it. We both know he's got pretty thick skin.

Now, you should have also brought my ashes with you. As you scatter them, think about the first time we kissed. How nervous we both were. How your breath smelled like cinnamon from the stick of Big Red we'd split. Think about how I cradled your face. Think about how, when I gripped your hips and pulled you closer, you let out that little gasp of surprise. God, if you only knew how hard I got after I heard that gasp.

I knew the first time I kissed you; you were it for me. It was as if all the pieces of my life had fallen into place. You were my life, right up till I had no life left. I love you, Ada Mae. Forever.

- Cole.

CHAPTER FOUR

SILAS

Her quick snort of laughter makes me snap my head in her direction. She's enthralled in the letter. And for the first time since Cole died, she actually looks as though she has some life in her. I watch her for a while, even though I shouldn't, but she's not paying attention to me.

God, she's beautiful. Even in her grief. Even with her hair uncombed and her clothes rumpled from where she's pulled them out of her duffle. Even with her legs unshaved and her eyes puffy from where she's cried on and off all weekend. I'm not sure she's aware I know she's cried. She makes no noise, but I watched her shoulders shake in her bunk when she thought I wasn't looking.

And then, the silent, fat teardrops roll down her face again and I have to look away. It hurts like a visceral ache to see her cry. I know if I keep watching her, she might see the anguish on my own face and not the mask of indifference I fight so hard to keep in place when I'm around her.

She blows out a breath and I hear the papers rustling. I glance over at her, and she's putting the graphic tablet, the letter, and all the paper back into the bag. "Okay," is all she says and her eyes dart to the urn.

"Okay," I repeat, and we stand. I pick up Cole's remains, pop the latch, and extend the urn to her. Tears well in her eyes and my own burn and I blink, trying to hold mine back.

Ada dips her hand into the vessel and pulls it back out a beat later. I do the same and when we have our allotted amount, she looks at me. "What now?"

I shrug. "I don't have instructions for this part. Do you want to say anything?"

She shakes her head and I nod. "All right, I guess we let the wind take them? Seems kinda hokey for Cole, though. If he were here, he'd probably say something about the native vegetation or the waves or something science-y."

She looks down toward her bag of things and nods. "You're right. He would." I want to get my hopes up about her talking, but I don't dare, so I push the hope way down deep. "Do you know any facts about the native vegetation?"

I can't help but laugh. "No, Wednesday, I don't. I know stuff about fitness and nutrition. Plants are not in my wheelhouse."

She nods. "Okay. So we just do this, then?" she asks, unsure.

"I guess. Preferably with whatever direction the wind would be blowing away from us," I suggest.

"Probably best," she agrees. We both look back at the trees to determine which way the wind is blowing and turn our bodies so our backs are to the breeze. I step up behind her, leaving plenty of space between us, and bring my hand level with her extended one.

Ada lets out a ragged breath, and as soon as she opens her hand, I do, too. I watch as the wind carries my brother's ashes back toward the trees. It's only as my lungs burn that I know

I've been holding my breath. I release it slowly and drop my hand. I take a quick step back from her lest I get the urge to smell her hair or put my hand on her shoulder or do something equally dangerous for me.

I latch the lid on the urn, she gathers her bag, and I pull up the quilt. "Ready to go home?"

She nods. "Breakfast?"

"We'll stop on the road. I'll have to get gas soon, so we'll figure it out."

"Okay."

Ada stares out the window the whole way home, her knees drawn up to her chest. She doesn't sleep and seems to simply be contemplative. So, I take it as a good sign, even though she doesn't speak to me. I park and cut the engine when I pull up at the apartment. She grabs her bags and I get out. "I'm good," she says. "You don't have to come up."

"We both know even if you don't let me carry your bag up, I'm not leaving till I make sure you're safely inside," I reply matter-of-factly.

She heaves a heavy sigh, swings her duffle up, and nails me in the chest. I grunt when the bag nearly knocks the wind out of my lungs. She simply rolls her eyes. "Fine. Then make yourself useful."

I could be angry, but honestly, the fact that she's being sassy is a vast improvement over how she was only a few days ago. So, in all reality, I'm thrilled. Even if I'd never tell her that. I trail her up the stairs, and when we reach the door, she pulls out her keys and blows out a breath as she unlocks it. I watch as a visible shroud of sadness falls down around her. Does it have something to do with her coming home to the place she shared with Cole? Is the presence of his belongings—their memories—too much?

I open my mouth and close it again because what am I going to do, offer to take her home with me? She has nowhere else to go. She steps inside and turns and takes the bag from my hands. "I'm here safe. You can go now." She doesn't wait for me to respond and shuts the door and a weight drops into my stomach. And as much as I want to offer her comfort, she's not ready to receive it. I wait for the sound of the lock turning over before I rake my fingers through my hair and head back down the steps to climb behind the wheel of the Winnebago.

I drive the hour up the mountain it takes to reach Pap's farm and park the RV next to the barn. I make sure I've gathered up all the leftover food and the linens and shove the items in the back of my Bronco. I head toward the house and when I climb the steps, the front door flies open, Pap toting his shotgun.

I immediately raise my arms. "Pap, Jesus, it's only me, you paranoid old coot."

He steps closer and squints. "Oh, Silas. Right. These cataracts are getting worse. I couldn't make you out from the yard."

"Then why don't you go to the doctor?" I ask as I follow him into the house.

"Because they only want my money."

I sigh and pinch the bridge of my nose. "If it's about money, I'll take care of it. You have to be able to see, old man."

He props the gun against a wall in the kitchen and sits at the small table. "Listen here, you piss ant; I've forgotten more in this life than you'll ever learn, so watch it."

"Yeah, yeah. You got any coffee made?"

"On the stove." I roll my shoulders as I pour myself and Pap a cup of coffee and bring them to the table. "So, how was the trip? Winnie do all right?"

"Winnie was fine. The trip went about as good as could be expected."

"How's she doing?"

I sigh. "Not good. It's more than simple sadness. She's depressed. Like, legitimately. But I can't suggest she talk to someone because then it looks like I care, and she won't know what to do with that."

"Well, maybe have Josie or your momma bring it up. You don't think she'd try to hurt herself or anything, do you?"

I shake my head. "No. She just wants to sleep all the time and I had to force her to eat and she was barely speaking until today. And I'm not holding my breath she'll keep talking. It was weird, Pap. When I dropped her off, she seemed like maybe she was coming up for air a little. And then as soon as we got to her apartment door, it was like a switch flipped and the lights went back out."

He nods and sips his coffee. "She's in that place all alone. It's only been a month. Grief is different for everyone. You think Cole's plan is working, though?"

I shrug. "Too soon to tell. But if he were here, I'd knock his teeth in. It's too soon for her for all this. She needs time. I need time. Pretty sure she still hates me. I'm guessing she's not going to want to keep spending all this time with me."

"Who knows? I guess you'll have to see how it all plays out." He eyes me and even with his slightly clouded eyes, I know he can *see* me plain as day. "And what about you? How are you feeling after this weekend? You think you can keep all this up?"

I let out a heavy sigh. "I don't have a choice, Pap."

"You always have a choice, Si."

"Not when it comes to this. I'll follow through on this if it kills me. I watched her read some of his letter this morning; she looked a bit like herself again. I'll give this to her if it helps bring her back. How can I not?"

"What about you, though, son?"

"What about me?"

"What happens at the end of this thing when you're still in love with her and she's mostly put back together? Will you tell her?"

I swallow the lump in my throat and look down into my mug. "I just want her to be happy. Even if she can't ever love me. I know it's twisted to think she could. But it still doesn't stop me from wanting her. But even if it doesn't end up being me, I only want her to be happy. "

"So, you'll just fall on your sword and watch her walk off into the sunset with some other guy?"

"I've done it once before. If it was what she wanted, yeah."

He shakes his head. "You're a better man than me."

"It's Ada, Pap. I'll be in her life, however I can. Even if it's only as a friend, I'll take what I can get. I've loved her since I was ten years old."

"And what's it gotten you?"

"I've gotten to see her be happy. And it would be different if I knew Cole hadn't been good to her, but that's the thing; he was. He was perfect to her. It's been enough."

After I finally get home and unpack, I kick my shoes off into my closet. I sit behind my desk in my office and pull the accordion file folder toward me and flip to the tab marked "camping". I pull out the sealed envelope with my name on it, push the folder to the other side of the desk, and open the jar of shine I'd brought back from Pap's. I take a long drink, letting the burn comfort me, put the jar in the drawer, and blow out a breath. Telling myself it's just like a bandaid I need to rip off quickly to get the pain over with, I tear open the envelope and pull out the letter.

Si,

I would imagine the weekend was a bit surreal. She was Ada, but also not. She's still angry and sullen and withdrawn. And if I was gonna guess, she barely spoke to you. And maybe y'all even got into a fight. Wouldn't surprise me, knowing the two of you.

You don't say, Cole.

I know none of this is easy for you. I mean, I don't KNOW since I don't know what it's like not to be able to have the woman I love. To watch someone else love her. And maybe, if I'd been a better brother, I would've been able to sacrifice my happiness for yours. But I was selfish where Ada's concerned. And had I known how all this was gonna play out, I'd want to say I would've stepped aside from day one. But I can't say that. You know, since I'm dead and all.

Jesus Christ, he's so fucking nonchalant I want to scream.

I told Ada she had to start coming back to family dinner. Make her go. I told her you had my blessing to drag her unshowered and disheveled to Mom and Dad's. Hold her to it. Don't let her miss. Let her get pissed. Let her scream. I understand that makes you her punching bag. Sorry. I would be if I could.

I don't know if she'll heed my advice and lean on you. I want to say she will because I told her to. But you know her; she's stubborn and stoic and doesn't ask for help. Be a pain in her ass.

We've never talked about how things were between Ada and me—physically.

My mouth falls open and my eyes widen in shock. I swear to all the saints, if he talks about sex with her, I will lose my ever-loving shit.

And I'm not about to start now. I'm not gonna talk about any of that with you, so calm your tits. I know you're probably about to have a coronary. Sorry, bad joke.

I breathe a sigh of relief and my heart descends from where it's lodged itself in my throat.

I will say this, though, her love language is physical touch. And not only the sexual kind. Ada is an inherently affectionate person. It could have something to do with how little affection she got as a girl—you know, with her parents and shit. Or, hell, it might have something to do with how we used to yank on her braids, I don't know.

So, I would imagine, she's starved for simple affection. Little touches, shoulder squeezes. If I know you, you nudged, poked, and prodded her all weekend, but Ada is a physical creature. It's like it brings her to life. Like I said, I don't only mean sexually. Just thought that would be some helpful insight for you.

Hopefully, next month will be easier. Maybe the camping trip was too ambitious to start with, but I guess it doesn't matter now.

I get that all of this is a lot. You'll never know how much I appreciate your willingness to do this. You are my best friend and she's my girl. There's no one else I trust more with her happiness. I love you, bro.

-Cole

I do my best to breathe through the tightness in my chest and the ache in my throat. How am I supposed to do this? I'm so emotionally exhausted after keeping how I want to care for her pushed down; I want to crash. It's not that Ada and I haven't spent time together before, but Cole was always a buffer. His love for her kept mine at bay. But now, it's as if a gaping wound has opened up in my chest. I not only have to grieve my brother but figure out how to be what Ada needs in the moment. To not come on too strong or try to be more than what she can handle right then.

Ideally, she and I will be in an established place once all these tasks are done. I'll finally be able to tell her how I feel and have her hear me. To have her see me as something other than the lesser Campbell brother. To have her love me the same way I've always loved her. To have her share the rest of my life. But I know life is anything but ideal, and maybe the best I can hope for is being her friend. At this point, though, even that seems like a tall order.

On Sunday morning, I send Ada a text to let her know I'll be by to get her at four to go to dinner at my parents' house. When she doesn't respond, and it only shows as "delivered," I grow more concerned about having not heard from her.

By one, I'm crawling out of my skin and finally break down and swing by Josie's to get the spare key to the apartment. "Are you sure this is a good idea, Si?" she asks before handing it over.

I shake my head. "Not in the least. But she knows she has to be ready to go or I will drag her out exactly the way she is. Cole said so. So, no, it's probably not a good idea, but it's gotta be done."

"Do you want me to go with you?"

I consider. "Yeah, in case she needs a bath. Don't think she'll appreciate me getting all up in her crevices."

Josie snorts a laugh. "I'm sure you'd hate it, right?"

"I'm not thinking about that right now. She needs to be able to function. It's clear she's not. You and Mom might need to talk to her about going to see someone. It's been over a month. She's not getting better."

My sister sobers. "Yeah. I know. Let's go." Josie grabs her purse off the kitchen counter and trails me out to my car. "Actually, I'll drive separately. I don't really feel like crawling into that thing you call a backseat."

I shrug. "Whatever." When we get to Ada's, I knock on the door, and Josie stands with her arms folded. I knock twice more and we both try to call her. I hear her phone ringing through the door, but she doesn't answer. "I'm using the key." I try to tamp down my rising panic, but I can't say my heart isn't pounding when we get the door open.

"I'll check her room and bathroom."

I nod and head toward the kitchen as Josie walks down the hallway. I round the corner into the kitchen and stop short. Ada is sitting on the kitchen floor, her eyes open but unseeing. My heart and breathing stop when I see the red on her hands.

I rush over and fall to my knees in front of her. I examine to see where the blood is coming from so I can stop it, but then I see it's not blood, and I want to cry with relief. It's only strawberries. I gently shake her shoulders and try to keep my tone calm. "Wednesday? What you got going on here?" When she doesn't answer me, I examine her further.

She's clean and has on a pair of jeans and a nice shirt. Her hair is shiny and pulled back in a clip off her face and she looks to even be wearing some makeup. "I forgot."

It takes me a minute to realize she's spoken; her voice is so low. I scoot closer to her and reach for the towel hanging from the oven door handle. I swipe at her hands, trying to get her cleaned up. "What, Peep?"

"I forgot he was gone. He said I might. I thought there was no way. I was making those peanut butter and jelly cupcakes your mom likes. He always tastes the frosting. I turned around with the spoon to have him test it."

My chest tightens, and I have to take some deep breaths to keep my emotions in check. And because I don't trust myself to speak, I simply keep trying to clean the jam off her hands. Josie comes into the room and kneels in front of me. "What happened?"

"You go on to dinner. I'll stay here."

She frowns. "What? Why?"

I glance at Ada, who is still leaning against the lower cabinet, clearly unwell. I rise and pull Josie into the other room. "Because she can't be alone. She forgot Cole was gone and turned around to have him taste something and it hit her all over again. I'm not leaving her. I'll put her to bed and when I know she's okay, I'll head home. Tell Mom and Dad; they'll understand."

"Are you sure it should be you?" she asks, one brow raised.

"He left her in my care, so yeah. Go."

She looks unsure but finally nods. "Call me if you need me."

"Okay."

CHAPTER FIVE

ADA

When I wake up, I have no memory of how I got to bed or anything after I started making the cupcakes to take to Ingrid and Miles's. I'm still in the jeans and tee-shirt I'd put on, but my shoes aren't on my feet. I rise from the bed and walk toward the kitchen after making a quick pitstop at the bathroom.

As I get closer to the kitchen, I smell coffee. Did I make coffee yesterday and leave the machine on? Surely not. When I round the corner, my heart stops when I see who's in the kitchen, and then my brain catches up. Not Cole. Silas. Clothes rumpled, hair mussed, and barefoot, I realize he must've slept here. I have no memory of him even being here yesterday.

I must make some kind of noise because he pivots. "Hey, Wednesday. Sleep okay?"

"What are you doing here?"

Instead of answering, he asks me a question of his own. "What do you remember?"

I shrug and think. "I started making cupcakes."

He nods, his expression neutral. "What else?"

I shrug again. "Nothing."

His jaw clenches and he turns back to the coffee maker and pours a mug. He walks to the fridge, pulls out the creamer, and pours some into the coffee before putting it away. Bringing the mug over to me, he gestures to one of the kitchen chairs. "Sit," he commands. I do and lift the cup to my mouth. "You have to talk to someone."

"What?"

"You need help. This is more than just sadness. You're depressed. You have no memory of Josie and me coming in here yesterday?" I shake my head and his jaw clenches again. "Well, we did. It wasn't pretty."

I frown. "What happened?"

"I found you on the floor, your hands covered in strawberry jam. I thought it was blood, Ada. You almost gave me a heart attack."

I blanch. "Don't joke like that."

Color rises in his cheeks. "I'm not fucking joking. I texted, and Josie and I tried to call you and we beat on the door and then found you on the floor. I thought you might be dead." His tone is angry and I'm still trying to understand.

I shake my head. "I don't remember any of this."

"I know. You told me you were making the cupcakes to take to Mom and Dad's. You turned around with the spoon to have Cole taste something because you'd forgotten he was gone. Then you remembered again. You were nearly unresponsive when I found you. You weren't even blinking. This stops now. You're going to talk to someone. You're going to get help. I'm not going to let you keep doing this to yourself."

"I'm not doing anything to myself," I protest.

"I know. You're barely eating. You're barely showering."

"You don't know that."

His nostrils flare. "For fuck's sake, Ada. I went to do your laundry because you got shit all over my shirt when I carried you to bed. Your hamper only had the clothes you took with you when we went to the beach last weekend. Don't lie to me."

I rise from my chair. "I'm not your responsibility, Silas. Go home. I can take care of myself."

"Like hell, you can. And you are my responsibility. Cole made sure of it."

"I never asked to be your burden. Just leave me alone." I turn to go back to my room and he grabs my arm. I try to yank away from him, but he's a lot stronger than me. "Let me go."

"No. Sit your ass down." He shoves me—yes, this time it is a shove—back into my chair and braces his arms on the table and the back of the chair, caging me in. "Here's what's going to happen. You can make the appointment, or I will. You will go. You will talk or get medicated or whatever they think you need to do. You are not allowed to stop living simply because Cole is gone.

"You are not allowed to let my family lose another person who is special to them. You will get help. If I have to drag you kicking and screaming to every fucking appointment, you know I will. You can hate me, cuss me, bite, scratch, punch, whatever you need to do. I don't give a fuck. I have no problem being the bad guy. Right this second, though, you're going to pack a bag."

Indignant, I spit out, "The fuck I am. You're not shipping me off on some grippy sock vacation simply because I'm depressed, Silas. I'll call the doctor. Shit."

He's caught off guard. "*Grippy sock vacation?* What the fuck is that?"

I roll my eyes. "The psych ward, Ass."

Understanding dawns. "Oh. No, I'm not carting you off anywhere. Not yet. But you're going to pack a bag. You can stay with me or you can stay with Pap. It's up to you."

"Neither of those options work for me."

"Too bad, Wednesday. I'm not having you fall apart or go into shock or whatever the fuck happened last night and you actually try to hurt yourself because you don't know what's going on."

"I'm not going anywhere. This is my home."

He lets out a slow breath. "Okay. I'm not an unreasonable man."

I snort in disbelief. "I beg to differ."

"Shut up and listen to me. You want to stay here, fine. I expect you to text me in the morning when you get up. I want proof you're showering and putting on clean clothes. I want a text before you go to bed. When I text you, you will answer."

"You realize you're not my father, right? You're not my husband. You're not my family. You're nothing to me now except a pain in my ass."

His jaw clenches and I watch as his fingers roll into a fist. "I'm going to let the family thing slide because you're in a lot of pain. And I'll happily be a pain in your ass as long as your ass is around for me to be a pain in it. You're not the only one who lost him, Ada. He was my brother, my best friend. I've never lived a day without him in my entire life before now. So, don't, for one second, think your grief is any bigger than mine simply because you were fucking him."

Before I even realize I've done it, my hand strikes his cheek. The slap lands with a crack, and I shove him back and stand. "Fuck you, Silas. God, I wish it had been you. Get the hell out of my house."

Hurt flashes in Silas's eyes and I don't even care. His chest heaves. "Ada—."

I shove his chest again hard enough to make him grunt. "Get out. Now." I step past him and go into my room and slam the door. I hear the front door open and close a moment later and I try to breathe. I'm so angry I can't see straight and I want to hit someone. I want to break something. I want to cause someone great physical pain.

But then, it feels like my chest cracks open and the only thing I feel is agony. Huge, racking sobs well up from deep in my guts and I can't stop as I collapse on the floor next to the bed.

I'm still crying when Josie comes into my room sometime later. She sits next to me on the floor, puts her arm around me, and pulls me to her side. A moment later, her own tears are falling onto the top of my head. I wrap my arms around her and bury my face in her neck. "I miss him so much, Josie. It hurts so bad."

She rubs my back in soothing circles, her voice thick with emotion. "I know, honey. I know."

RAGE

APRIL: TWO MONTHS AFTER

CHAPTER SIX

ADA

Following my most recent fight with Silas, I'm currently only speaking to him to answer direct questions at family dinner. I'm still not ready to forgive him for what he said. Even if some of the things he said have merit. Even if I said some equally hurtful things. Even if I've started seeing a grief counselor.

On Easter Sunday, after dinner, I'm helping Ingrid wash the dishes when he comes into the room. "Mom, can I talk to Ada for a minute? Alone."

She glances at me and considers it for a moment, then extends the dish rag to Silas. "If you're going to be here, you're help her wash these dishes."

He rolls up the sleeves of his button-down shirt and takes the rag from her. "Okay."

Ingrid kisses me on the cheek and dries her hands on a towel before stepping out of the room, leaving me alone with the last person I want to see right now. He sidles up to me, plunges his hands into the soapy water, and picks up where his mother left off.

I refuse to look at him, but he starts talking as he places

scrubbed dishes into the rinse water for me to pull out and dry. "I know you don't want to talk to me and I'm not real keen on you right now, either, Wednesday. But it's time for another task." I stand up straighter, but still don't turn toward him. "There aren't written instructions for you for this one. Be ready on Saturday morning by nine. Wear comfortable clothes and sneakers."

"That's it?" I ask, my voice barely above a whisper.

"That's it," he confirms. I nod and we finish washing the dishes in silence before I leave to head home.

On Saturday morning, a little before nine, I'm sitting on my couch dressed and ready to go. I have on a pair of jeans and a tee-shirt and sneakers. My hair is in a braid down my back and I sip my coffee. I half expect Silas to simply text me when he arrives and not bother coming to the door, further expanding the glacial gulf between us.

But then, when his distinct three-rap knock sounds, I realize I should've known better. I set down my mug and rise and go to open the door, surprise flickering in his gaze for a split second before he shutters it. I lock the door and wordlessly follow him down the stairs. He unlocks the passenger door of his prized powder blue 1967 Ford Bronco before letting me enter.

As he walks around to slide behind the wheel, I try to remember if I've ever ridden in this vehicle alone with Silas. I can't say that I have. He's had it since he and Cole were fifteen when they began restoring it with the help of their dad, Miles, and Pap. They shared it until college, when Cole broke down and bought a truck to use for his business.

So, riding in the Bronco brings back visceral memories of

Cole and me. But having never ridden with only Silas, it's a bit unnerving. So unnerving, I can't look at him as he drives. And until he starts the engine and pulls away from the curb, I debate telling him I'll drive simply to have something to do.

But once he takes off, I don't have a chance to say anything because he cranks the radio. To disco. Fucking *disco*. Silas knows I abhor disco and he's blasting it simply to get a rise out of me. I reach over to switch the station since he refuses to install a stereo system from this century, and he smacks my hand away. "Driver picks the music; passenger shuts their cake hole."

"Fine. I'll drive. Pull over."

He snorts a laugh. "You think I'd let you behind the wheel of Blue? You can't even drive a stick, Wednesday. You'd ruin her clutch and transmission before we even made it out of the parking lot. Not happening."

"Then change the station. You know I hate disco."

He gives me a smug grin. "I know." I dart my eyes to the radio and he shakes his head. "You touch it and you'll come back with a nub, Peep."

I make a mental note to bring earbuds on our next excursion so I can listen to my own music. I fold my arms and grind my molars so hard my jaw aches.

"You eat breakfast?" Silas asks once we pull onto the highway.

"I had coffee. I'm fine."

"You sure? You're going to need your energy."

I sigh. "Why? What are we doing?"

"You'll see. I'm just saying; you're going to need energy."

"I'm fine."

"If you say so."

I'm not about to get into one of those circular conversations with him so I simply clamp my mouth shut. I resume looking out the window, all the while, disco continues to assault my ears.

Twenty minutes later, he pulls up at a squat, nondescript brick building and parks. "What's here?"

"You'll see. Let's go." He doesn't wait for a response and climbs out of the Bronco and I guess I have no recourse but to follow. I hop out of the cab and he lets me catch up with him before opening the door. He nudges me along, his hand on the small of my back, toward a reception desk. Behind it, there's a silhouette of broken glass with the word "Rage" in a large, angry font on the wall.

A teenage boy greets us and Silas tells him we have an appointment. The boy slides two clipboards forward and requests to see our IDs. We hand them over and he tells us to sign the forms. I glance down at mine and see it's a liability waiver. "What is this place?"

Silas scribbles his name without reading the form. "Sign the form, Wednesday. We're going to a rage room."

I blink slowly, trying to understand. "A what?"

He sighs. "You'll see. Embrace the chaos, Peep."

The teenager hands our IDs back and after I sign my name and we give him the clipboards, he gestures for us to follow him. Silas tugs me along and we stop at a set of cubbies. The staffer hands us helmets with thick face shields with something nestled inside. He leads us to a door and opens it. "You have one hour. A buzzer will go off when you're time's up. Have either of you done this before?"

Silas nods. "I have."

"So I don't need to go over the basics?"

He shakes his head. "I've got it. I'll make sure she understands."

The kid shrugs. "Works for me. Have fun."

Silas ushers me inside and the door closes behind us. I'm

still so confused, but he doesn't seem deterred. He takes my helmet and pulls out the items situated inside. "Put your purse in the cabinet over there." He points to a small, wall-mounted cabinet next to the door and I obey as he unrolls and shakes out what I now see are a set of disposable coveralls. "Here, put these on, we're losing time. Coveralls, gloves, helmet."

I hustle to pull on the items and after Silas is ready, he checks the strap on my helmet to ensure it's tight enough. He gestures around the room. Scattered all around us are old-school TVs, computer monitors, shelves of ceramic dishes, glass bottles and drinking glasses, globes from light fixtures, clay pigeons, phones, and other electronics. "This is a rage room. We have one hour to throw down on all this shit. The disco was intentional. It was to work you up."

He fishes his phone out of his pocket and connects it to a bluetooth speaker on a nearby shelf. He starts some music, but thankfully, it's not disco. It's heavy metal. I can do heavy metal.

Silas walks over to a bin, pulls out a metal bat, and hands it over. "*This* is what we're doing?" I ask in confirmation.

He nods. "Pretty timely, too, if you ask me." He picks up a clay pigeon. "Eye on the birdie, Peep. Square up."

What the hell, right? I turn my body and ready myself to swing the bat. He tosses the clay disc, underhanded, and it smashes into hundreds of pieces with a satisfying crunching sound when the bat makes contact.

"Get the picture?" he asks.

"Yeah. We just jack shit up, right?"

"You've got it. Have at it."

And then, I do. I pick up plates and toss them on the ground. I smash a TV screen to smithereens. I pull an *Office Space* and go apeshit on a printer-copier. I throw empty wine bottles against the wall, thoroughly enjoying the sound of the glass shattering.

At some point, I think my brain leaves my body because I don't stop moving until the loud buzzer sounds overhead. Silas comes over, grips my shoulders, and bends until we're at eye level. "How did that feel?"

"Badass," I say with a laugh of surprise, my chest heaving, and heart racing. It hits us both that I've laughed and I don't know how to feel about it. He squeezes my shoulders and nods.

"Hell yeah, it was." He takes my helmet off and sets it on a nearby table. "Did you bring the ashes?"

I swallow. "I didn't bring the whole urn, but I put some into a bag."

"All right, get 'em." I pull the small bag out of my purse and come back to stand beside him. He takes the bag and opens it and puts a bit in both our hands. "If Cole were here, he'd probably say something about how we should examine all of this as some kind of metaphor about the pitfalls of capitalism even though he owned his own business. But in this case, he wouldn't necessarily be wrong. If you look around, most of these things are those that have been replaced with newer, better versions of the same shit."

And I want to laugh because it sounds exactly like something Cole would say. "We don't have any wind this time."

"No, we don't. We'll just have to toss, I guess." And so, we do. We toss our handfuls of ashes onto the pile of rubble before shucking our coveralls and gloves and placing them in their required receptacles.

"All right," he says with finality, tugging at my arm. "Let's go get Mexican and margs." I nod and follow him out of the room.

Fifteen minutes later, we're pulling up at my favorite Mexican restaurant in town. All the adrenaline seems to have left my body and I'm exhausted. "Come on; you'll perk up once you get some queso." Once seated, we each order a jumbo margarita, and when they arrive, I take a massive gulp of mine. "You were kinda scary in there."

I nod. "I don't remember half of it," I admit.

He shrugs. "Sometimes, you need to turn your brain off and access that primal anger we all have." He looks down into his drink. "About what I said the last time I was at your place."

I shake my head. "Can we not?"

"No, we need to. I shouldn't have said that. I'm sorry. Cole would've kicked my ass if he heard me say something like that to you. I'd kick anyone else's ass if they spoke to you that way. It was uncalled for. It won't happen again."

I chew on the inside of my bottom lip and nod. "I'm sorry for what I said, too. It was hateful. The grief counselor says that even though there are five stages of grief, they don't necessarily happen in order and they can come back around. Apparently, the anger stage for me is more like bitter, seething bitch."

He opens his mouth to say something, but the server returns and we order our food. Once we're alone again, he sighs. "So, can we call a truce?"

I nod. "Okay." As the meal stretches on, I want to ask Silas if Cole left me a letter, but I don't want to have my hopes dashed if that's not the case.

"So, how's work going?" Silas asks when my second margarita arrives.

I shrug. "It's slow."

"Is that because you put your shop on hold and have to rebuild or because you're not producing?"

I sip my drink. "Probably both."

"So, you're not drawing or painting or whatever it is you do with that tablet thing?"

I roll my eyes. "It's digital. I can do almost anything. I sketch and then paint—exactly like I would on canvas. This medium is just a little more forgiving at times."

"But you're not?"

I sigh. "Not much inspiration happening these days." I'm not about to tell him most of my inspiration for my art comes—came—from Cole's and my sex life. Either because I was horny or because I was very, very, satiated.

"You'll get it back." He lifts a grilled shrimp to his mouth and chews. After he swallows, he examines my face. "But you're okay for money?"

I nod. "I'm fine. I don't foresee the need to peddle pictures of my feet on the internet anytime soon."

He huffs a laugh. "That's good. I'm sure right now, your feet look butt ugly."

I scoff, my mouth falling open in indignation. "My feet are not butt ugly. I have nice feet. I need a pedicure, but I have objectively nice feet."

"If you say so, Peep." He pours the remaining queso over his taco salad.

"Do your clients know you eat like a frat boy a lot of the time?"

"It's all about moderation. I don't tell them to restrict the intake of their favorite foods. There's no such thing as a 'bad food.' It's called balance. It's a normal workout day for me anyway, so this is just... me filling my energy stores."

"What, an hour in a rage room not enough exertion for you today?"

He chuckles. "I'm sure it would've been if I had done anything in there."

I frown. "What do you mean?"

"That was all for you. I was only there for support. You were the only one going Hulk on all that shit."

"You didn't do anything? Really?"

He shakes his head. "No. Like I said, all for you."

"So, you don't have any rage you need to work out?"

He laughs and nods as he takes a sip of his drink. "Fuck, yeah, I do. I usually run mine off, lift heavy, or torture my clients in their sessions."

"But you didn't want to smash anything today?"

He shrugs. "Watching you, with that wild look in your eyes, was plenty enough for me. Like I said, I was only there for support. If you had some kind of breakdown, and I was caught up in breaking shit, I wouldn't have seen it. The point of me being there during these tasks is as your wingman or safety net or whatever. None of this is for me."

He looks away and before I can stop myself, I ask, "Did he leave letters for you, too?" Silas turns his face back toward me and nods after several seconds. "Do you read the letters he wrote me?"

His brow furrows. "Of course not. Those are his private letters to you. I don't need to know what's in them. I'm just the messenger, Wednesday; the body to carry out the tasks. Kinda like in *Supernatural* when the angels and demons possess a body. I'm just a vessel right now."

I want to ask him if this is hard for him, but I don't know if I want to know the answer, so I don't ask. I nod. "Okay."

He points his finger at me. "And don't even think about asking how many tasks there are or what the next one is. You know I can't tell you anything."

I hold my hands up, defensive. "I wasn't going to. Damn."

"Good. So long as we're on the same page."

An hour later, after Silas has walked me to my door, he pulls an envelope from his back pocket and hands it over. He makes sure I get inside all right and I greedily rip the envelope before thinking better of it. Do I really want to read it while I'm covered in sweat and grime from the rage room? Do I want to rush into it when who knows how long it will be before I get another one? No, that's not how I want to take in Cole's words.

I walk back to my room and lay the letter on my bed before going to take a shower. And for longer than I can remember—before the funeral, surely—I notice how long my leg hair has gotten. I grab a fresh razor from under the sink and step under the hot spray of the shower. I let the warm water wash away the strain in my muscles, along with the sweat and grunge from working out my rage. Soon, the exhaustion from the lack of adrenaline left in my system sets in and I can barely stand upright.

But once I'm squeaky clean and newly hairless in places, I put on one of Cole's tee-shirts and a pair of panties and pour myself a glass of wine. I crawl under the covers, my hair up in a towel, and lean against the headboard. I finish opening the envelope and pull out the letter.

My Ada Mae,

Hopefully, after all is said and done, the rage room will have been cathartic. Sometimes you need to bust some shit up, right? Make sure you take some Advil, because tomorrow, you'll probably feel like you were hit by a truck. I know I did after Si and I went for the first time.

I frown and sip my wine. I never knew he and Silas went to a rage room. They went out for drinks at least a few times a month, but I guess that sometimes included the need to break things?

. . .

Yeah, we went. At least a few times a year. Stupid brother stuff, you know?

I can't imagine all the things that have gone through your mind over the last couple of months. How hard the nights have been. I would imagine those might be the worst. Since I'm not there for you to wrap yourself around.

I can't help but laugh since it's entirely true. I'm a stage-five clinger in bed and not having Cole to cuddle with has made it difficult to sleep.

But, like everything else, it should get better. Hopefully, the day-to-day is beginning to become bearable again. My hope is, you're painting again. I hope you're still going to family dinner and Mom and Dad are fussing over you. Please tell me you've gone back to giving Si shit about how he eats.

Not for the first time since I started receiving these letters, I marvel at how well Cole knows me. It shouldn't surprise me, that even from beyond the grave, he seems to know what I'm thinking at this moment.

Depending on the time of year it is when you read this, it might be getting to the warmer months, I don't know. But if that's the case, do not sit inside. Go to the lake and the pool and accept the invites to all the cookouts we always attend. Even if you only go for five minutes and then have to leave, you still have to go. I demand it. Drag Si or Josie along if need be.

Actually, take Si and make him play corn hole with you and dust him. You know how much you love to show him up. It might be your favorite thing to do. You know, aside from me...

I know this is only month two. It probably seems as though the time since you last saw me is this endless stretch of seconds, minutes, and hours. I'm sorry about that. At least, in your memory, I'll always be hot and fit and able to get it up. I'll never be old and frail. Although you know I would've loved you way past that point, too, right?

You are still young, babe. You are vivacious and beautiful and spirited. Act like it. You are not a Mary Bennet or a Beth March. If anything, you are Lydia—except, you know, not reckless. Or, Amy—except, not spoiled or self-centered. But much like both of them, you are a really good time.

Be a good time again. I demand it, respectfully.

I'd never want to be a Wickham, but I would've happily been the Laurie to your Amy. Except there never would've been a Jo, because there would've only ever been you. There only ever has been you, Ada Mae.

-Cole

If Cole were here, I'd argue with him about the fact that Amy wasn't self-centered, more like self-aware. But I'd also tell him I appreciate the sentiment. Especially as the tears roll down my face.

CHAPTER SEVEN

SILAS

Watching Ada go apeshit at the rage room was both the scariest and sexiest thing I've ever seen her do. She had this feral look in her eyes and I know at some point, she stopped even processing what she was doing and began moving with some sort of primal instinct to destroy.

I lie in bed after my workout and a shower, neither of these things helping to uncoil the tension that has taken up permanent residence in my shoulders whenever I have to be around Ada. Most of the tension seems to originate from having to hold myself back from touching her. Ever since I read in Cole's last letter about Ada possibly being touch starved, I want to provide that kind of comfort to her. Trouble is, I don't know how without making it seem forced. I've never been a touchy-feely person or a big hugger or anything, so casual intimacy is hard for me.

Hell, if I'm being honest, actual intimacy is hard for me. And yeah, I've slept with women, but as none of them was the woman I wanted, it made it easy to keep things surface level.

And it's not as if I haven't tried to have relationships. Especially as we got older and I knew for sure Cole and Ada were end game, I dated and tried to develop attachments.

But I also know, regardless of what happens with all this shit Cole's planned out, Ada's it for me. I hate this is a fact of my life. I hate that I'll never feel for someone else what I do for her. I wish with every fiber of my being I could fall in love with someone—anyone—else.

Mainly because I want marriage. I want kids. I want a family. But the only person I could ever see it happening with for me is Ada. It's so far beyond fucked up, I recognize it's absurd. But I guess the heart wants what the heart wants and all that shit.

I pull my phone off the nightstand and flip through the photos I took of Ada in the rage room. There's an excellent one of her with this look of indignation she got after a wine bottle didn't smash the first time she threw it. I crop it to only her face and arm where she's throwing it for a second time.

I send it off to her along with a quick message.

> Silas: Rage looks good on you, Wednesday.

I don't expect her to respond, even though we have called a truce and apologized for what we both said. But when the three dots bounce on her end, I can't deny the jolt of pleasant surprise that hits me in the middle of my chest.

> Ada: If you ever see that look on my face outside of the context of the rage room, it's best to run.

> Silas: Definitely. Rabid Peep is downright terrifying.

Ada: [eye roll emoji]

A slow smile pulls at the corners of my mouth. Hopefully, all this means she's beginning to come out of her depression. Especially after her saying she's been going to a grief counselor. Which, I knew from Josie, who's been keeping up with Ada after our fight. I hope this means she'll smile again and laugh. Really laugh. Her small chuckle at the rage room caught us both by surprise. Is that the first time she's laughed since Cole died? Judging by her expression, it would seem so.

My phone dings and I examine the screen.

Ada: Cole's letter said y'all went to the rage room several times. I never knew that.

I'm not about to get into that with her. About why we went. I didn't know he didn't tell her, though. It shouldn't be surprising that since he didn't tell her about his heart, he wouldn't tell her other stuff either. But because I refuse to outright lie to Ada, I don't respond to her text.

———

A few weeks later, I'm finishing a personal training session with one of my regulars. As I'm walking up to check my schedule at the front desk, I'm surprised to see Ada. "Hey, Wednesday, you here to finally let me torture you?" Judging by how she's dressed, I know this isn't the case. She's wearing a pair of cutoff denim shorts, a tank top, and pair of flip-flops. Her hair is up into a ponytail threaded through the back of one of Cole's ball caps.

She rolls her eyes. "Yeah, not likely. I came to ask a favor."

Secretly, I'm thrilled she'd come to me for something, that

she'd actually ask for help, whatever it is. I keep my features neutral so as not to let on about my delight in this turn of events. A small voice in my head says it could be something terrible. Like, snaking the drain in her bathtub or something equally disgusting. But even that would be all right since it's a favor for Ada.

"Okay, what's up?"

"Are you busy in the next few hours?"

I shake my head. "No, I just finished my last session for the day. Why?"

She chews the inside of her lip and I simply wait as she gets out the words. "Hensley's birthday party is tonight and Josie was supposed to go, but she bailed. Well, actually, she came down with a migraine, so she's forgiven, but still. Cole demanded I go to all the normal parties we usually attend and I don't have a good excuse not to. But I can't go by myself. I don't think I'm up for that yet."

I try to picture her at Hen's party. Hensley Scott is not one of my favorite people. Never has been, despite the fact I slept with her in high school. But knowing how these parties go, Hen will try to draw Ada out and make her talk. Or, worse, get her drunk and one of the scummy guys she runs with will want to try to get in her pants. The thought alone makes my blood boil. I feign indifference and hope it appears genuine and nod. "Sure. Is it tonight?"

"Yeah. I was on my way to pick up Josie when she texted and since the gym was on my way home, I thought I'd stop in. I figured if you couldn't, I'd go on home."

"All right. You have a few minutes to let me grab a quick shower and change?"

"Sure."

"Okay. You can wait in my office if you want." I gesture over my shoulder and she shrugs. "Follow me."

She comes around the counter and I lead her down the short hallway to my office. Once I open the door and turn on the light, she immediately plops down on the small sofa and pulls out her e-reader. I retrieve my street clothes out of the small closet, along with my toiletry bag. "What are you reading these days?"

She looks down at the device. "I'm rereading *Little Women*. Cole's last letter said something about how I was an Amy and I want to make sure he's right."

"Oh. Don't think I've ever read that before. I think I saw the movie a long time ago. Mom and Josie loved it, so I probably absorbed a lot of the plot in passing, but I don't remember anything specific."

"Yeah, it's been a while for me, too. Thus the reread."

I nod. "Well, I'm going to get ready and we can go."

"Sure."

When I emerge from the locker room twenty minutes later, Ada is still curled up on my sofa, her eyes glued to the screen of her reader. If it were up to me, I'd simply order pizza and let her tell me exactly why she is or isn't an Amy. But it's not up to me and apparently, she needs backup for a party I'd never, in a million years, go to for anyone else. But at this point, for Ada, I'll do a shit ton.

"Ready, Peep?"

She glances up at me and rises, slipping her reader into her purse and draping it over her shoulder. "Okay. I'm driving. And there will be no comment about my taste in music. Because at least you know I won't torture you with disco."

I shrug. "I don't mind disco, so bring it on. Bring on whatever terrible music you're likely to pick. Disco is timeless, by the way. Some of those songs are sampled in popular music today."

She rolls her eyes. "Whatever. I hope there's food at this party. I'm starving."

"It's Hen. There will be food. Maybe not good food, but there will be food."

As we slide into her Honda Civic and she starts the engine, she says, "I've never understood what you have against Hensley. Didn't y'all hang out back in the day? Weren't you a thing in high school?"

"Please don't remind me. I still have nightmares."

She snorts a laugh and my heart twists and I want to file the laugh away to examine later. At a time when I can give it proper consideration. Because that laugh was one she gave to me and it had nothing to do with Cole. I shouldn't feel almost giddy about it, but I do. And immediately following the giddiness is the guilt for feeling said giddiness. Realizing she's still speaking, I focus on her words.

"So, what, was it bad?"

I sigh. "You're friends or whatever with her. I don't want to bad-mouth her. Not when all that shit was over ten years ago."

"For starters, Hensley and I aren't really *friends*. She and Josie are better friends than she and I are. But she's always invited me to her party every year and I'd already agreed to go, so I hate to back out last minute. Especially since Josie couldn't go. And Cole wants—wanted—me to get out, so here I am."

"Got it. So if I get over here and have a terrible time, I don't have to spare your feelings on the way home?"

She rolls her eyes. "You wouldn't do that even if Hensley and I were best friends. You've never spared my feelings. Not sure you'd know how."

"You're one to talk. You don't spare my feelings, either."

She considers. "Nope, you're right. I don't. I'm not sure I'd know what to do with myself if you ever did. That's the thing about you, Ass. You're blunt and honest, almost to a fault.

Someday, some lucky girl is going to love that about you. You just have to find one who can give it right back to you."

I keep my mouth shut and simply look out the window. The only woman who's ever been able to return my attitude blow for blow is currently seated in the driver's seat next to me.

We pull up at Hen's house, or rather, Hen's parents' house a short time later. Her family has stupid money and her parents are probably off on some yacht in the south of France while Hen is here living it up on their dime. She's lazy and entitled and wouldn't know actual work if it bit her in the ass. It's a shame she has to be so hot. Her beauty's wasted on an empty head. Too bad I didn't figure that out before I got her naked at seventeen.

The party looks to be some sort of street fair theme. Several food trucks are set up in the large, empty field next to the house. String lights are strung from tree to tree, and loud music blares from a DJ booth set up at the far end of the designated party area. "I guess you only turn thirty once, right?" Ada asks as we climb out of the car.

"I guess," I mutter.

We make our way through the field and Ada's hands curl and uncurl into fists and I know she's anxious. I've seen her do that since we were kids. Pretty much any time she's had to do any kind of public speaking or when she was doing her SATs and most recently, when we were at the hospital with Cole at the end.

I nudge her elbow with my own. "If you decide you're ready to go after five minutes, I promise I won't complain. Even if it looks like one of the trucks is dedicated to chicken and waffles. I'll try to keep my disappointment to a minimum," I say, my tone more sarcastic than is genuine. For Ada, I'd stay all night if she wanted.

She nudges me back. "Thank you for coming with me."

"No problem. I didn't have anything else going anyway."

"Do you normally have stuff on Friday nights? Dates and stuff?"

I shrug. *Almost never.* "Sometimes."

"Well, still, thanks."

"It's fine, Wednesday. Let's not hire a banner plane or anything."

She rolls her eyes. "Yes, because they probably wouldn't be allowed to show what I'd put on the banner in public, since there may be children present. Not sure you can print things like 'Ass' on banners."

I can't help but laugh. "Probably not."

A shrill voice saying Ada's name grates on my nerves. "Ada! You made it."

Hensley comes running over and practically tackles Ada. She does a double-take when she sees me after they separate. Her eyes dart from me to Ada and back. "Well, Silas Campbell. Never, in a million years, would I have ever thought I'd see you at one of my parties."

That makes two of us. "Just here for moral support."

Ada elbows me and offers Hen a smile that doesn't reach her eyes. "Josie came down with a migraine, I roped Silas into coming with me. I hope that's okay."

Hen shrugs and gives me a dismissive eye roll. "You're not as cute as Josie, but I guess you'll do." She loops her arm through Ada's and I trail a few feet behind them. Hensley tucks a hair behind Ada's ear and peers at her with something that looks an awful lot like pity. I catch snippets of their conversation; mainly Hen asking Ada how she's holding up and how sorry she was to hear about Cole.

I'm already tired of being here. The last thing Ada needs is for everyone to handle her with kid gloves. She doesn't need tough love, but she's not fragile—or, as fragile, I guess. She's come a long way in only the last month. Part of me wonders if this entire party will be an excuse for people to pump her for how she's doing. To gauge her readiness to date or some other equally stupid and fucked up suggestion. The irony of that train of thought isn't lost on me.

Cole's voice sounds in my mind. *What do you call these "tasks" I send y'all on? If people knew y'all went away for a weekend, they'd probably see it as some sort of date, don't you think?*

Also in my head—because I'm not entirely cracked yet—I want to shout back at him, *Those are all things YOU set up. You and your fucked up logic. I am not interchangeable with you, Cole. Ada is probably never going to understand what your goal is in all of this.*

I shake away the thoughts and return my attention to Ada a few steps ahead. As we get to the party proper, Hensley notices someone across the field and gives Ada a quick squeeze before jogging away. I come up beside her and she's glancing from truck to truck, taking in the scene. "Drink first? Because I'm not sure I can do this without one. I wish I'd brought my flask. None of what I'm sure are going to be expensive and yet, entirely watered down drinks, would do nearly as well as Pap's brew."

I huff a laugh. "You're not wrong." I look around. "Let's see. Looks like we have a taco truck, so probably margaritas. There are burgers, so probably some beer." My eyes catch on a final option and I nudge her and gesture. "Or, we cut out the middle man and head straight to the bar."

She nods. "A bar on wheels? Yes, please." We make our way over and I order a beer. Ada orders a glass of wine and once we receive our drinks, we meander along the perimeter of the party. There's quite the crowd; a lot of folks we went to high school with, along with locals who are probably acquainted with Hen's family through society functions and things.

"So, what do you and Josie usually do at this thing?"

Ada sips her wine and looks around. "Not much. We people watch and speculate on who might be having affairs or who's started to have work done. If there's corn hole, I'm down for that, but I don't see any this year."

"Okay, so who do you think has had work done?"

"No, that's the game I play with Josie. We'd have to play something else."

"Why?"

"Because you're not your sister."

I huff a laugh. "Yeah, pretty sure that's an understatement." I want to add that I'm also not Cole, but I'm not sure how she'd take it. "Okay, so what game can we play?"

She thinks for a minute. "Let's play the game where Silas tells Ada why there's drama between him and Hensley."

I shake my head. Not getting into *that* in the least. Not for a million dollars. Not for ten million dollars. "Nope."

"Oh, come on. I'm dying for some juicy stories. I only have Josie for fun shenanigans anymore. I'm an old woman; I need vicarious fun."

"Peep, you and Josie are the same age. You're younger than me. You're not old and you know it."

She sighs. "I feel old. Come on, humor me. What happened?"

"No. It was, like, fifteen years ago. I'm not even sure I remember."

"Bullshit. You're a terrible liar. You forget I know you, Silas. I know when you're lying. And you are. What happened?"

And because I know Ada, I know she's not going to let this go. She's going to keep digging until she hits pay dirt. And honestly, seeing the almost normal look in her eyes is nearly enough reason for me to spill... a little. I heave a sigh and look around, even though I know it's just Ada and me in this area. "I called her another girl's name during sex."

And yes, it's exactly what one might assume, given my nearly two-decades-long crush on Ada. I was really buzzed at a party after the homecoming football game our senior year of high school. Cole, Ada, Josie, and I were celebrating. Cole and Ada were making out and I kept drinking to hide how miserable I was. Hensley happened to be there and we started making out. As these things usually go, one thing led to another and I lost my virginity and called her Ada. She threatened to tell Ada and Cole—not that Cole didn't already know how I felt about her, but still—if I didn't keep seeing her until she found someone she liked better. Worst six months of my life. Worst sex of my life. But when we split, she swore never to tell, so I guess there's that.

Ada's mouth falls open in shock. "Well, well, that is something."

I shrug. "I was drunk."

"But y'all were together what, like, six months?"

I nod. "Yeah."

"So you liked someone else while y'all were together? Or was it, like, the name of an actress or character or something?"

I shrug, not wanting to discuss this at all. "Like I said, doesn't matter. I don't like Hen; she doesn't like me. We were kids, Peep. Let it go."

"So, you did like someone else, then," she says knowingly. "Wow. Okay. Did you ever get a chance with said other girl?"

"No."

She frowns. "Really, not even after you and Hensley broke up? Why not?"

I sigh. Even knowing this is a dangerous conversation, I

know Ada will know if I'm not honest. So I try to be as truthful as possible. "She had a boyfriend."

"Gotcha. But you must have liked her an awful lot."

I nod. "Yeah." Wanting to change the subject, I point over at the makeshift dance floor. "Look, it's group dances. Your favorite."

She shrugs. "It's fine."

"Oh, come on, you love stuff like that. Go. I'll take pictures of you being goofy."

She shakes her head. "Nah."

"Ada, go. It'll be fun."

"Silas, stop. I don't want to."

"Are you sure?"

She nods and pivots and begins walking. It only takes me about half a second to figure out she's headed back to the bar truck. This time, she orders a tray of shots and alarm bells clang in my mind. Nothing good has ever come from Ada doing shots. But I'm not her keeper. I'm not her brother. I'm not her husband. As she said, right now, I'm nothing but a pain in the ass to her. Even if that knowledge makes my stomach feel like it's full of gravel. She doesn't look at me as she takes the tray to a nearby table and plunks it down. I follow and sit with her, attempting to appear aloof and indifferent, same as I've always been. "Whatcha doin', Wednesday?"

"I'm getting drunk. Surely you're familiar with the concept? Feel free to join in."

"I think I'm good."

"Suit yourself," she says, lifting the first shot to her mouth. Tequila, if I was guessing. Except she's going full bore, without even the aid of salt and lime to act as a buffer between shots. She turns the glass over and picks up another and downs it in quick succession.

"Do you want to talk about your sudden need to give yourself alcohol poisoning?"

"Nope."

"Okay. Like I told you at the beach, though, I'm not holding your hair back if all this decides to make an encore appearance."

Her jaw clenches as she holds my gaze and takes the third one. "I never asked you to, Ass."

I have to take several steadying breaths to not push the entire tray off the table. "Seriously, Ada, what's the deal? We were talking. You seemed fine."

She doesn't answer, just double fists the next two shots. She coughs and drops the glasses back onto the table. Her eyes are already starting to look glassy and she weaves in her chair. Ada's no lightweight—not by a long shot. But I'm guessing she hasn't eaten anything in a while and all this liquor is settling into an empty stomach.

I don't know whether to be horrified or impressed by the fact that she's still conscious after the seventh shot. But I can't just let her poison herself and I'd rather not spend the night in the hospital, so I down the two remaining shots simply so she doesn't have the opportunity. "Okay, they're gone. Let's go."

She gives me a jerky shake of her head. "No. I'm not done." Her words come out slurred and I know for a fact she's not going to be able to walk unassisted.

"Yes, you are." I rise from my chair and pull her out of hers. "Let's go."

"I don't want to go. I'm having a good time. This is what Cole wanted. That's what I'm doing. Living my life." She flings her arms out to her sides dramatically before dropping them again. Her raised voice begins to draw curious glances from other partygoers.

"Ada, stop. Come on, let's get you home." She pushes me

away, but can't stand on her own, so I pull her tighter against me.

"Silas, let me go. I'm just doing what Cole wanted."

I start dragging her away, despite her protests. "I'm pretty sure that didn't extend to you ending up in the drunk tank, Wednesday." When she continues to struggle against me, I finally stop and pull her over my shoulder and pray she doesn't puke on me.

She beats her fists against my ass. "Put me the fuck down."

"Sorry, Peep. Not happening."

"I'm supposed to be having fun."

"Yeah, well, I think you've had plenty of *fun* for one night." When we get to her car, I set her down and dig through her purse until I find her keys. She's nearly falling down and I have to put my hands on her waist to steady her as I unlock the car. Her head falls forward onto my chest and she hiccups.

"Do not puke on me."

Her shoulders shake and for a moment, I think she's laughing, but then I hear her crying. I sigh as the sound makes something twist in my chest. I lift her chin and she looks at me, her expression forlorn. Her gray eyes are wet and heavy from booze. "I was having fun."

I nod. "I know."

"I don't want to have fun."

"I know," I repeat, my voice sad, even to my own ears.

Her tears turn into full-blown sobs and I let her face drop and she slumps into me. And because, what choice do I have, I simply hold her. I rub gentle circles into her back and lean my cheek on the side of her head. Her hot tears soak through my shirt and I try to breathe through the ache in my chest. I realize the hat she was wearing must have fallen off while I was carting her over my shoulder.

And because apparently, my night actually can get worse,

Hen walks up with Ada's hat in her hand. "I saw her drop this." Her words come out softer and gentler than I've ever heard Hensley be in all the years I've known her.

"Thanks. She'll be glad to have it back."

She gives me a sad smile and again, I'm struck by the expression on her face. Maybe the emotion she exhibited earlier toward Ada was genuine. Her sobs seem to have turned into sniffles, so I open the car door, deposit her into the passenger seat, and buckle her up. I close the door and start to walk around to the driver's side and Hen grabs my arm. I turn to look at her and she holds out the hat and I take it.

"I've still never told anyone, just so you know."

I nod. "I know."

"I wouldn't."

"I appreciate that."

She glances at the passenger door, where Ada is currently leaning against the window. "Does she know?"

I snort. "No."

"You're playing a dangerous game, Si," she says, her tone serious.

"There is no game, Hen."

She leans in, her voice barely above a whisper. "Oh, so you're not still in love with her?"

"It doesn't matter."

"You realize you could both end up hurt, right? You're not Cole."

I pinch the bridge of my nose. "For fuck's sake. I know that."

"Do you?"

"Stay out of this, Hensley. None of it has anything to do with you."

"I just can't believe she's never seen it. All these years. I know Cole did, but I can't believe she didn't."

"Goodnight, Hen."

She sighs. "Just be careful, Silas. That's all I'm saying. I know you think I'm an idiot, but I'm not. I've never claimed to have a head for books or politics or anything remotely intellectual, but I'm not stupid. And I know you're playing with fire."

"What am I supposed to do, nothing? Let her self-destruct and withdraw and slowly kill herself when it was the last thing he'd ever want? He asked me to take care of her. That's all I'm doing."

She folds her arms. "Pretty fucked up for him to do that considering he knew how you felt about her. It's kinda cruel if you think about it."

I shrug. "I'm just trying to follow his wishes. Make sure she's okay."

She nods. "And who's supposed to make sure *you're* okay? He might have been with her, but he was your brother. Is anyone checking on you?"

"I'm fine."

"Well, I'm around if you need someone to talk to."

Although I'd never take her up on her offer, I still nod. "Thanks." I gesture to the car. "I'm going to get her home."

Except, I don't go to her home. The idea of trying to get her up two flights of stairs into her apartment isn't something I'm up for tonight. I drive her to my house and by the time I'm parked in my driveway, she's passed out. She doesn't even rouse when I scoop her into my arms to carry her inside.

I ferry her limp form back through the house and into my bedroom. I drop her onto the bed and roll her on her side before pulling off her flip-flops and lining them up next to the nightstand. I work the covers down and drape them over top of her.

If you had ever told me Ada Andrews would be in my bed, I'd be ecstatic. But I sure as hell don't want it like this. I hate seeing her in pain. I wish I never loved her. That I could simply be a supportive friend and brother of her late partner. That I haven't pined and yearned for her all these years.

A thick strand of her dark ponytail falls over her face as she shifts in the bed and I can't resist sweeping it off her cheek. I leave her in the bed, keeping the door ajar so I can hear her if she starts throwing up, and head across the hall to the guest room to fall into bed.

CHAPTER EIGHT

ADA

I'm pretty sure I'm regretting every one of my life choices when I come to. And when I wake up, I'm in an unfamiliar bed and I immediately panic. But as I squint and take in the space, the room comes into focus. Why am I in Silas's bed? I'm still wearing my shorts and tank top, but my flip-flops are on the floor beside the bed. I'm also alone. I rise on unsteady legs, feeling as though something died in my mouth. I walk into the bathroom, pee, wash my hands, and rinse my mouth before heading out of the bedroom. I smell bacon and almost want to puke.

Silas turns and gives me a wide grin. "Well, it looks like she lives. I tell you, Peep, you must have a hollow leg or something."

I fall onto one of the stools at the bar and put my head in my hands. "How bad was it? Do you have any Advil? And why am I here?"

He slides a glass and a bottle of pills across the counter. When I struggle to get the cap off, he opens it and dumps a few tablets into my palm. "I dropped a couple of Alka-Seltzer in the water. It'll help your stomach. I'm guessing you're not up for bacon and eggs?" I grimace and shake my head. "I figured." He leans on the counter across from me and sips his coffee as I down the pills and drink. "I wasn't up for carrying your ass up two flights of stairs. I'm not unfit, but dead weight is dead weight and I'd already had a full day at work. Wanna tell me why it was like you needed to consume all the tequila in existence last night?"

"I wasn't in the mood for vodka," I deadpan.

He levels me with a serious gaze. "Ada, come on; for real."

Shrugging, I look down into the dregs in my glass. "I tried having fun. I didn't like it."

"Was it me suggesting you dance?"

I sigh. "Partly. I already didn't want to go out, but I felt like if I didn't, Cole would be disappointed because it's what he wanted me to do. I don't know how to have fun without him, Silas. It feels like some kind of betrayal." My throat aches and I clear it and blink quickly as I try to hold back my tears.

"Wednesday, he'd never want you to be sad forever. You know that. Why do you think he went to all the trouble to plan everything he has for you? He wants you to heal. He wants you to be yourself again. Figure out who you are without him. I know that's scary for you. I've never had to know who I was without him, either. I'm trying to navigate it, too. No one tells you how you're supposed to get through grief. It's such a subjective thing. No one's experiences are the same. Yours is different from mine. Mine is different from Josie's and Mom's and Dad's."

"Yeah, but you all seem to be okay, at least. I don't understand it. I'd never say y'all act like you're fine or that you don't miss him, but y'all seem to have already moved on to the acceptance part of things. I don't get it."

He opens his mouth to say something, but then closes it and blows out a breath through his nose. "Everyone handles grief differently. You don't know what it's like for us behind closed doors. Just because some of us are better at putting on a façade doesn't mean we're all not falling apart inside. Least of all, me."

The look in his brown eyes is so much like Cole's when he was somber and dealing with shit, I can't hold his gaze. I chew my bottom lip. "I'm sorry I lost my shit and you had to take care of me last night."

He shrugs. "Probably won't be the last time."

"I don't want to be a burden. At this point, that's what I feel like I am. Relying on you and Josie and your parents, it's not fair to y'all."

Silas's expression softens. "Ada, you're not a burden. You're our family. Even if there was never a paper that said so. Even if you're not our blood, you're stuck with us. I know you probably still struggle with knowing what a family should look like. I can't say I know what that's like. I wish I could empathize with you; I'm sorry I can't. But from the time you showed up at our house when you were ten years old with your Wednesday Addams braids and your need to always have the last word, you've been our family. I think my parents would've adopted you if they could. Of course, it might've made things a little awkward later, but you're stuck with us. Forever."

"I feel like Wednesday Addams right now."

"Well, the cool thing about the Addams family was, they didn't expect Wednesday to snap out of her depression. They met her where she was. That's all I'm trying to do with you."

He sighs and thinks for a minute. "I think the reason Cole left me 'in charge' of you, so to speak, is because you and I are a lot alike. We're both smart asses with tempers, but we also feel things deeply. Maybe he thought me getting you to do all those tasks was a way to help us both. We were his favorite people. I like to fix things, people. I think it's one of the reasons I like being a personal trainer. People show up, they tell me what problem areas they have with their bodies, and I develop a plan to fix them. I wish I could magically fix your grief for you.

"But it's not a quick trip. Not for any of us. It's like one of those long-ass road trips in one of those wood-paneled station wagons with the way-back seat. The A/C's gone out and we've still got ten hours left. We're all hungry and hot and pissy and Josie's elbow keeps finding its way into my thigh but anytime Mom turns around, she's a perfect angel."

In spite of myself, I laugh. "Nice analogy. So what you're saying is, eventually we'll get there and hope never to get in that car again?"

He smiles. "Exactly. And hopefully, none of us ever have to get in that car again, not until we're a hundred years old." He walks over to the stove, pulls a pan of bacon out of the oven, and fishes the strips out of the pan to drain onto some paper towels. He lowers some bread into the toaster and makes quick work of scrambling some eggs.

He works methodically and with purpose. He butters the toast as it pops and dumps the eggs onto two plates, along with a couple of pieces of bacon. He carries them over to the bar and slides one in front of me. "I know you said you weren't up for it, but I thought you might try. If nothing else, eat the toast. It'll soak up some of the booze still in your system."

I nod and nibble the food. "Thanks."

"Anytime." We eat in silence and as I push my plate away, he drops an envelope in its place, making my heart lurch. "You've got a week. Once I get the dishes cleaned up, you can drive me back to the gym so I can get my car. I know you'll want to get home and read it."

"Okay," I agree.

An hour later, when I get home, I brush my teeth, take a shower, and down a whole bottle of Gatorade. I glance at my purse on the counter where the envelope sticks out of it and debate whether to open it now or later. I have a week, right? I can put it off. Delayed gratification and all that. But then, what if I need to prepare? What if I have to buy things? He wouldn't have given me a week without *needing* that kind of lead time, right?

My curiosity wins out, of course, and I snatch the envelope out of my bag, plop down on the sofa, and take my time opening it. I wish I'd had the right frame of mind to open the previous ones. I was so ravenous, I simply shredded them trying to get at the information inside.

Almost three months out, I can appreciate this moment and am thankful for how time seems to smooth those sharp edges. I open the envelope as carefully as I can, as this one feels thicker than the others. I pull it apart and look inside and see a folded sheet of paper, same as always, along with something else. I take the items out and examine what comes with the letter. It's a gift card to an athletic store. I'm not sure how to feel about that, since I'm not athletic in the least. I consider the trek up and down the stairs of our apartment complex to be my cardio, so a sense of foreboding fills me looking at the gift card.

Figuring I can only hope there's some kind of explanation in the letter, I unfold it to read.

My Ada Mae,

Don't start freaking out because the gift card is to a sporting goods store. We all know how much you hate working out. Your loathing of physical exertion is quite public knowledge. Well, unless the exertion is due to me taking you to bed. I think we both know you have quite the appetite for that kind of physical activity.

I'm glad we're clear on this, mister.

And while you need athletic wear, you won't be working out. Not really. But you will need a yoga mat and whatever you think you'll need to be able to move in comfortably. You will be outside —unless it rains. And make sure you pack your allergy meds.

Have some fun. I wish I could see your face once you find out what you're gonna be doing. I'm sure it will be priceless.

I'm sure you still miss the hell out of me, but I hope it's getting easier. I know this isn't a linear process. I know it's probably like two steps forward, twenty steps back. Make those two steps count for something.

I promise the world will not end if you have a good time. You will not be forgetting me simply because you cut loose a little.

-Cole

Athletic ware? What the hell does that consist of? And because there's only one person who'll know what'll work in this instance, I call Silas.

"Hey, Wednesday."

"What does 'athletic wear' mean?" I ask in the way of a greeting.

"What?"

I sigh. "You already know what we're doing next weekend. What kind of athletic wear do I need? He gave me a gift card, but I don't want to get the wrong thing."

He's quiet for a minute. "Are you asking me for opinions about clothes?"

"Ass, I just need you to tell me what to buy. Or help me pick it out or something because you know I don't work out."

He snorts a laugh. "Yeah, I know. Okay, I'm kinda booked up for a couple of days, but I can do Wednesday morning. Why don't we meet for breakfast and I'll follow you over to the sporting goods store and help you pick out some things."

"Okay. And a yoga mat?"

"Don't worry about it. I'll bring a couple from the gym. No sense in buying a new one if you're only going to use it once."

"And yet, I'm expected to buy new clothes?"

"Hey, maybe Cole wanted you to look good doing what he's got planned."

"Maybe. So, the stuff he has you do to prep, is it pretty extensive?"

"Some of it. Some of it is already taken care of and all I have to do is call to confirm dates."

"Is it hard for you, doing this stuff?" I can't help but ask since this is probably a lot of work for him.

"Nah. It's good, actually. I get letters like you do, so it feels like Cole's with me while I prep. Sometimes, when I read the letters, I want to scream because of how nonchalant and matter-of-fact he is."

I huff a laugh. "Yeah. Do you ever feel like you have conversations with him?"

"Yeah. All the time." I hear a smile in his voice and somehow, knowing he talks to Cole like I do makes me feel some sense of camaraderie with my love's surly twin.

"Okay. Well, I'll let you get back to whatever you were doing. Sorry to bother you."

"You're not a bother, Peep. You can call me anytime. I can't promise I won't bitch. You know, if it's five in the morning or I have to come and bail you out of jail or something. Don't make me come bail you out of jail."

"Eh, I'm pretty sure my days of criminal mischief are over."

"Good to know. I'll see you in a few days."

"All right. Bye."

I meet Silas on Wednesday morning at a diner a few minutes from the sports store. He's already seated and sipping a cup of coffee. "They have French toast on special today," he says as he pours me a cup of coffee from the carafe at the table.

I smile. "I love French toast."

Silas nods, a broad grin on his face. "I know. You and Josie got on that kick where it's all y'all wanted for months at your sleepovers. Y'all were, what, twelve? I got so burnt out, I told Mom if she made another batch of French toast, I was going to burn every slice of bread in the house the next time you came over."

I chuckle. "That's quite the mature solution."

He rolls his eyes. "What, like I could have asked y'all to pick something else? You would have picked French toast out of simple spite. Probably until the end of time."

I laugh. "Probably." I glance around, my eyes catching on something and all the color drains from my face.

Silas frowns. "What's the matter, Wednesday?"

"My dad is here."

He quickly looks around and sees him at the counter. His jaw clenches. "Do you want to go somewhere else?"

"No. It's fine. Maybe he won't see us. And even if he does, I can't imagine he'll come and talk to me."

He touches my arm. "Ada, it's fine. We can go somewhere else."

Giving him my full attention, I shake my head. "No. Why should I have to leave?"

He holds his hands up in surrender. "Okay. If you change your mind, let me know."

I nod. "I will."

"How long since you last saw him?"

Thinking for a beat, I blow out a breath. "Cole and I ran into him about three years ago. He was so high, he probably doesn't remember. Before that, I hadn't seen him since he got out of jail."

"Wow."

I shrug. "It is what it is." The server comes to take our order and I get the French toast, because of course, I was going to. Silas orders a veggie egg white omelet. "You might as well eat cardboard, you know," I say with a roll of my eyes.

Silas chuckles and sips his coffee. "It'll be tasty cardboard, to be sure."

"Ada?" My heart lurches and my breath catches as I hear my father's voice a few feet away. Even so, I can't stop myself from turning in his direction. He's standing about five feet away. "Well, well. It is you."

He begins to step closer and Silas stands. "I think where you are is fine." His voice has an edge to it and his posture is immediately tense.

"I just want to talk to my daughter."

Silas doesn't move. "So talk. You're not going anywhere near her."

"Listen, Cole—."

"I'm not Cole and I don't think I will listen."

Uncertainty flashes in my father's eyes but then he gives Silas a malicious grin. "What, she finally make the jump from Cole to you? Damn, I always knew things were twisted in your family, but I didn't expect Ada to play whore to both of you.

Guess I shouldn't be surprised, though. She's a lot like her momma that way."

I gasp in shock and Silas takes a step toward my father and I hurriedly stand, knowing where this will lead if I don't at least try to do something. I put my hands on Silas's chest and his eyes immediately snap to mine as he looks down at me and I shake my head. "He's not worth it. He's never been worth it. It's not worth you getting arrested over." His jaw clenches and he searches my eyes, but after a beat, he backs off and gives me a quick nod.

Pivoting, I step toward my father. "And you. You can go to hell. My life is none of your business. I don't give a single shit what you have to say. You no longer matter to me." I fold my arms and hold my chin high since I'm not about to cower to him. Not anymore. His eyes dart from me to Silas standing behind me and he huffs a disgusted laugh and turns to leave.

Once he's gone, Silas squeezes my shoulder and I turn. "Are you okay?"

Nodding, I retake my seat. "Yeah. I'm sorry about what he said."

He shakes his head. "You think I'm worried about that? I just hate he disrespected you that way."

I shrug. "I'm used to it where he's concerned."

He blows out a breath and rolls his shoulders as our food is being delivered. He glances from his omelet to my French toast. "I should've gotten that."

I give him a smug smile, slice off a chunk, and lift it to my mouth. "Sucker." He grabs my hand, brings my bite to his lips, and has it in his mouth before I can even react. My mouth falls open in indignation. "You ass. The first bite is always the best. It's got the perfect ratio of butter and syrup and bread."

He nods and drops my hand as he chews. "You're totally right. It's amazing," he says around the mouthful of food.

Giving him a death glare, I slide my plate farther away lest he gets any ideas about nabbing another bite. "You will pay for that, just so you know. When you least expect it, I will get you back."

He feigns terror. "I'm shaking in my boots, Peep. Bring it on. You're not exactly terrifying, you know. Pretty sure I can take you."

"Well, just for that, you can buy breakfast."

He laughs. "Fair enough."

CHAPTER NINE

SILAS

It would have cost me nothing to let Ada's father think I was Cole, but it's so second nature for me to correct people; it's a habit at this point. What will it be like when I never have to correct people anymore? What a depressing thought.

I wanted to punch the awful man as soon as Ada saw him. After everything her dad has put her through, I know seeing him on top of everything she's dealing with had to be a lot.

Hopefully, my stealing her food and redirecting her attention helped. It seemed to, anyway. And to say we had a nice breakfast would be an understatement. It was great, even considering the altercation with her dad. After we finish eating, I drop some cash onto the table to cover our breakfast. I nudge her as we stand. "Wanna ride over with me to the store? I can drop you back off after."

"Okay. It's not out of the way for you?"

"It's like a half-mile."

She narrows her eyes. "You promise no disco?"

I huff a laugh. "Nope."

She scoffs. "Fine. If you're driving this weekend, I'm

bringing headphones because I refuse to listen to whatever you call music for however long the drive is."

"All right, no disco. You have my word," I promise, holding my hands up in surrender.

"Thank you."

We climb into the Bronco and drive the half-mile to the sporting goods store. When we walk in, I tug Ada toward the women's clothing section. I point to the compression wear, tank tops, and sports bras. "You won't need anything with a ton of support. We're not doing an Ironman or anything."

"Yeah, because I can totally see that being something your brother would plan for me. My idea of a marathon is Netflix, Cheetos, and a glass of wine"

Nodding, I try not to stare at the sports bras as she flips through them, or think about her wearing one. "I'm aware. Probably some CW or BBC show. You still watch those reruns of *The Vampire Diaries*?"

She frowns. "How do you know I watched that?"

I snort a laugh. "Because you made Cole watch and then he'd bitch about it to me."

She gives me a soft smile. "Yeah, he hated it. He was a good sport, though. Honestly, I haven't watched anything in a while; haven't felt much like it these days. Everything I would consider watching is something I watched with Cole, so it's hard to want to watch anything."

"I get it. We watched a lot of stuff together, too. Maybe we each need a new show," I suggest.

She shrugs. "Is there anything you haven't seen?" she asks as she pulls a pair of compression capris off a rack. "Would these be okay?"

"Yeah, those are fine." I think about her TV question. "I haven't seen any of *Grey's Anatomy*. Is it any good?"

She considers. "Never watched it. It's got a ton of seasons, so there must be something good about it, right?" She pulls out a sports bra and tank top to go with her pants and again, I have to make myself not think about her wearing those clothes. This was a terrible idea.

Trying to get my brain back on track, I focus on our conversation. "Must be. You also need a swimsuit."

Her eyes snap to mine, curiosity furrowing her brow. "I do?"

I shrug. "I mean unless you have one already." She opens her mouth. "One you've not had for ten years." She closes it again. "That's what I thought. You've got enough on the gift card to get all that and a new swimsuit. Do it. We're going to be on the water." Her brow tics up. "The activity is not on the water, but where we're staying is," I clarify.

She looks around until she locates the swimsuits and goes through the rack. "We could buddy watch *Grey's Anatomy*."

I don't dare get my hopes up about what that might mean. It could mean she's bored and doesn't want to watch the same stuff she watched with Cole. Most likely, it doesn't have anything to do with her wanting to see me or talk to me or spend time with me—even as just a friend. "What's a buddy watch?"

"Where we watch the show at the same speed. Either separately or together and discuss. Josie and I buddy read books all the time. But we have vastly different interests in television and movies, so we've never tackled a show."

I consider. "Would you care if we watched together? I mean, wouldn't it just be easier? If we watched, we could pause and discuss if needed instead of trying to do it over text or whatever?"

She chews the inside of her bottom lip. "Okay. There are at least a couple of hundred episodes. We could do two a week. Make it a thing?"

Shrugging, I hope to conceal how overjoyed I am at the prospect of getting one-on-one time with Ada. Time that doesn't have anything to do with the tasks Cole set up. Fuck me, there's the guilt again. I tamp down the gnawing feeling in my gut to answer her. "Sure. Mondays? I don't have any sessions on Mondays. We could do take out or one of us cook, whatever's easier. And if we have a task involving a Monday, it gets pushed to the next week."

"All right. So, Monday, then? Since we'll be back from wherever we're going?"

"Sounds good to me."

She pulls a black one-piece bathing suit off the rack. "Okay. Chinese?"

"All right. Your place or mine?"

"My couch is more comfortable and my TV's bigger. What do you think?"

"Fine."

"Will the sneakers or sandals I already have be okay for this weekend?"

I nod. "Yeah."

"Okay, then I think we're done here." We make our way up to the register and she places her items on the counter. I give the clerk my loyalty membership number so I can get the reward points and Ada scoffs. "How do you know I didn't want to sign up for a membership so I could get those points, Ass. Those were my points and you stole them."

I try not to smile. "Okay, I'll make you a deal. Next time I come in, I'll bring you with me and you can sign up and I'll let you have the points."

She puts her hand on her hip. "I'll hold you to that. They have some cute tank tops and stuff."

As we're climbing into the Bronco, she extends the gift card out to me and I look down at it but don't take it. "What?" I ask, confused.

She rolls her eyes and shoves it into my hand. "We both know you'll be back here before I am and there's money still on it. Use it to buy some socks or a new jock strap or whatever you gym rats use."

"A jock strap?" I can barely hold back my amusement.

"Jesus, Ass. Whatever. Buy a pretty pink pair of panties for all I care."

"You know, I think I'd look pretty good in a pair of pink panties, so it's not the insult you think it is."

She shakes her head, but she's trying not to laugh. As I start the car, I'm about to change the radio and she smacks my hand away. "Ouch! My radio, my rules."

"Pot, meet kettle. You smacked me first. Besides, this is The Civil Wars. *This* is real music. It's sacrilege to change the station when they're on."

I could argue, but she cranks up the volume, closes her eyes, and sways to the folksy rhythm. She mouths the words, and watching her out of the corner of my eye is better than trying to have the last word over the radio. Lost as she is in the music, I'm tempted to take the long way around to prolong our drive by a few minutes. But all too quickly, we're back at the cafe. She hops down from the cab, bag in hand, and gives me a small smile. "What time?"

I frown, confused. "What time for what?"

"For the task. What time do I need to be ready?"

"Oh, right. Saturday at eleven. We'll be back Sunday."

"Okay. See you then. Be safe going to work."

"Drive safe on the way home."

She nods. "All right. Bye, Silas."

"See ya, Peep."

I wait until she's safely in her vehicle and pulled away from the curb before I leave. I pull in at the gym a few minutes later, and after greeting Mandy, the receptionist, I come around the counter to head back to my office. I change out of my street clothes into a pair of athletic shorts and a tee-shirt with the gym's logo over the left breast. I trade my Converse low tops for a more acceptable pair of running shoes and swipe on a bit more deodorant. After tucking my belongings away in my small office closet, I head back out front, my phone tucked in my pocket.

When I return to the front desk, I look over my schedule for the day, noting I've got two individual sessions with a couple of regulars and a group abs class. I see Mandy coming toward me out of the corner of my eye and look up as she gets closer. "Hey, how're things today?"

"About normal. Was that Ada in here the other day? I was doing a tour, so I was on the other side of the gym, but I thought I saw her come in."

Nodding, I stash the clipboard under the counter. "Yeah, why?"

"How's she doing?"

"I think things are getting easier."

"So, are y'all spending time together or something? Y'all left together that day."

I fold my arms and tilt my head in question, unsure I like her tone. It's almost accusatory and a bit judgmental. "Not that it's any of your business, but Ada and I have known each other for years. She's pretty much my family."

"Yeah, but don't you think it's a little tasteless for y'all to be running around together so soon after Cole's death? Or was that not y'all having breakfast over at the cafe this morning, too? Looked like you were having a pretty good laugh."

I take a deep breath and when I speak, my tone is harsher than necessary and may invite further scrutiny, but I don't really care. There's nothing wrong with Ada and me hanging out together. We are currently just friends. Or, sorta friends, maybe. Either way, there's nothing wrong us spending time together. Even if half the time I'm with her feels like some sort of betrayal to Cole. Mandy doesn't need to know that, though. "Again, not that it's any of your business since it doesn't involve you, but Ada and I are friends. She was Cole's girlfriend. He was my brother. We spend time together. We have since we were kids."

"You sure don't look at her like she was *his* girlfriend, Silas. You look at her like she's yours. It's twisted if you ask me, thinking you can just be a replacement for Cole or something."

"Good thing nobody asked you, Mandy. I'd appreciate you keeping your opinions to yourself. Don't you have an actual job to do?" The bell over the door chimes and I spot my first appointment coming in, so I happily leave the desk to greet them.

I'm hanging out in my office before my last appointment when my phone vibrates in my pocket. When I see it's Pap, I swipe the screen to answer the call. "Hey, old man."

"Hey, son. Got something to ask you."

"Okay. What's up?"

"Well, I think someone's been in my stillhouse. I'm missing several jars of apple pie. You wouldn't know anything about that, would you?" His tone tells me he already knows I took the jars in question.

"Yeah, I might," I admit.

"Were they put to good use at least?"

"If by good use, you mean as a balm to soothe the ache of a lost brother and partner."

"I figured as much. You owe me five jars, Si."

"Yes, sir. I can't come this weekend to work but I can next. Or, are you that hard up? I might be able to move some things around."

"How about this, you come next weekend and bring Ada with you. Y'all can work on it together. I'm assuming she's the one who drank most of it, right?"

"Despite her size, she does seem to know how to put it away."

Pap chuckles down the line. "Yeah, she might not be a Campbell by blood, but she sure can hold her liquor like one."

I can't help but smile. "You're not wrong about that. I'll check with her, make sure she's free."

"Sounds good. The garden could use plowed, too. I'm a little late getting started this year, but I think there's still enough time to get some corn and tomatoes out."

"All right. I'll let you know. Either way, I'll be there next weekend, okay?"

"Sounds good."

Pap disconnects the call without so much as a goodbye, and I open up my text thread with Ada.

> Silas: Pap busted me about the apple pie.

I don't expect a text back immediately, so I drop my phone onto my desk and return to assessing my booking projections for the next quarter. But it vibrates only a few seconds later, making me grin.

> Ada: Yikes. How pissed was he? How much groveling do I need to do?

Silas: Almost none, actually. He just requested your assistance in replenishing. Next weekend. You game?

Ada: I don't know anything about making moonshine. I'd be more a hindrance than a help.

Silas: Shine is already made. We're just flavoring. Pap also needs the garden plowed, so I'll be doing that, too. I figure, make a weekend of it. I'm sure your and Josie's room is still exactly as y'all left it.

The dots bounce and stop, bounce and stop, bounce and stop before her reply comes in.

Ada: Okay. I can do that. Leaving Friday, I assume?

Silas: Most likely. I'll let you know if anything changes.

She sends me a thumbs-up emoji, and I can't help but feel as though Pap is also trying to push Ada and me together. Not that I mind, since spending my weekends with her has become the bright spot of the ache I still feel with the loss of Cole.

GOATS

MAY: THREE MONTHS AFTER

CHAPTER TEN

ADA

I try to imagine a scenario that would require athletic wear, a yoga mat, and my allergy meds as I pack for the weekend. I toss in my new swimsuit, a few pairs of jogging shorts and tank tops, panties and sports bras, and my pajamas. On a whim, I toss in my sketchbook and pencils. I'm not sure what it means if I'm getting the urge to sketch again, but I'm not about to be without some of my supplies if inspiration strikes.

Tossing in my toiletry bag, I zip my duffle shut and carry it to the living room. I walk into the kitchen and grab a zip-top baggie and return to the bedroom to put some of Cole's ashes into the bag. I try to be conservative since I don't know how many tasks we have left to complete. What will I do when they're all gone? How will I feel? I latch the urn and sit on the edge of the bed and examine the bag of ashes in my hand. Will he feel even more gone once I don't even have this physical part of him? Even now, it's as if I can still feel him with me. Will that go away once they're all gone?

As my chest tightens and tears threaten, I try to breathe. I try to remember the last thing he said to me. He was walking out the door to go to work. I came over to give him one last kiss. His breath smelled like coffee and he gave me a sweet smile, his eyes roving over my entire face, seeming to memorize it for the millionth time. *I love you, Ada Mae. Don't forget, I'm going out with Si tonight.* I'd nodded and gone up on my toes to press a final kiss to his lips before he turned to go. He'd made it five feet and collapsed.

I could take solace in knowing the last thing he said was that he loved me, but I just feel cheated. Cheated of the life we could've had. Cheated of all the years we should've gotten to share. I knew it would never include marriage or kids; I was okay with that because I had Cole. None of that mattered as long as I had him. Now what? *Now, you come up with new plans for your life. New dreams. A new future. A new love, Ada Mae.* I want to shout at Cole's imagined face. I want to scream and wail and tell him he's full of shit if he thinks I can ever have any new dreams that don't include him. I don't know how. *So learn, babe. You cannot stop living simply because I did. I forbid it.*

"Well, you're not here to forbid anything, are you?" I ask angrily.

"What?"

I snap my head up to see Silas standing in the bedroom doorway. I wipe my eyes and nose. "How'd you get in here?"

"I still have Josie's spare from that day I came to get you for family dinner. I got worried when you didn't answer the door or your phone." He looks down at the ashes in my hand. "You and Cole get in a fight?"

I snort a sad laugh. "How'd you know?"

He shrugs. "Just a hunch. His voice is really loud sometimes."

I nod. "Yeah. It is." I clear my throat. "Sorry. I'm ready, I was trying to get his ashes and I had a...moment."

"I get it. Sometimes I want to punch him."

Standing, I follow Silas back toward the front door and I stick the ashes in an outside pocket of my duffle. "People would probably think we're unhinged if they knew Cole talked to us."

He huffs a laugh. "Not as unhinged as they'd think we are for talking back to him."

"True. Best keep that part to ourselves."

"Yep. What was it you called it, a grippy sock vacation?"

"Yeah, you think they'd let us have adjoining padded rooms if they shipped us off?"

Silas picks up my bag, I grab my purse, and we walk out the door. "We'd demand it." He loads my bag into the Bronco and as we climb inside, he nudges me as he starts the car. "Is it a bad day?"

I shrug. "Undetermined as of yet."

He nods and shifts into drive. "What were you thinking about before you got in the fight with ghost Cole?"

I snort in disbelief. "*Ghost* Cole? That's awful."

"What, you have something better to call him?"

"No, but still. I'm not sure I like it."

"Okay, well, come up with something better, then. In the meantime, what were you thinking about before the imaginary argument?"

I sigh. "The last thing he said to me."

"Oh, yeah? What was that?"

"That he loved me and to remember that he was going out with you."

He gives me a smug smile. "Oh, so really, the last thing he said was about me."

I narrow my eyes. "No, Ass. He said he loved me."

He nods, his expression morphing into one a bit more serious. "I know he did. What else?"

Swallowing past the lump forming in my throat, I shake my head. "After that, I just got mad and then the argument happened."

"Want to talk about it?"

"I've never talked with you before about arguments with your brother. I don't see why him no longer physically being with us changes that."

He considers. "Touché. Okay, how about this, what was the stupidest fight y'all ever had?"

"The stupidest fight? Let's see," I say, chewing the inside of my bottom lip in thought. "Probably the time I sent him to the store to get me chocolate because I was on my period and I was cranky and really, really wanted a Butterfinger. He said he couldn't find a Butterfinger, so he got me a Milky Way instead. Even though he knew I hated nougat. So I threw it at his head and told him until he showed up with a Butterfinger, he'd never get to see my boobs again." I can't help but laugh at the memory. "He came back a half-hour later with a whole bag full of Butterfingers and marshmallow Peeps to hedge his bets."

Silas rolls his eyes and grins. "You and your peeps, I swear. So I guess he got to see your boobs again?"

"Safe assumption considering it was ten years ago. What about you? Stupidest fight with Cole?"

He considers for a long moment. "I guess the one I had with him after the messenger delivered the package about the tasks. I was so pissed. But now, I'm glad, since I still get these snippets of him, even months later, so definitely a stupid fight."

"So, you're telling me the most stupid fight you and Cole had in over thirty years was one you had *after* he died? All right, you win."

He chuckles. "Well, duh. I'm a winner."

"You're an arrogant ass is what you are."

"It's not arrogance if you can back it up, Wednesday, it's confidence."

"Okay then, you're just an ass."

He shrugs. "Sometimes. And sometimes, you're a stubborn mule."

I scoff. "Did you just compare me to livestock? I resent that. If anything, I am one of those adorable dogs who looks harmless but will bite your face off if provoked."

"And sometimes even when you're not provoked," he mutters.

"I heard that," I say with narrowed eyes.

He pokes me in the arm, his tone teasing. "I meant for you to."

***

As we get onto the interstate, I notice we start heading south and although I have no clue where we're going, I'm not anxious. If the last two outings have taught me anything, it's that Cole knew what I needed at the time. I'm content to simply sit back and see where this adventure takes us. And as we cross the state line from Tennessee to Georgia, I assume that's where this adventure is taking us today. Considering the time of day we left and how long we plan to be gone, I can't see us traveling much farther.

Two hours later, Silas turns off a highway into a wooded area and I get the feeling we're close to wherever we're going. We begin passing what looks like several rental cabins and soon, he turns onto a gravel drive that dead-ends about a mile later. A small cabin sits a few hundred feet from a river. It's secluded and I can already tell it's a peaceful place.

When he parks, I look around and stretch. "How did you

get us here without some kind of GPS? This is, like, way out in the middle of nowhere and you came right to it."

"I've been here before."

I nod as we climb out of the car. "Is this a rental cabin? It's different from some of the others we passed."

Silas shakes his head as he unlocks the door using a set of keys he pulls from his pocket. "One of Pap's old buddies. It's a fishing cabin. So it's pretty basic, but it does have electric, water, and A/C. So, you know, we'll survive."

"Good to know."

Once he gets the door open, we schlep everything in and put away the couple of days' worth of food he'd packed. "You know, you don't have to get all the groceries and stuff beforehand every time. I don't mind shopping."

He shrugs. "Part of the planning on my end. If the instructions say, 'pack groceries', I pack groceries."

I look around as we finish stowing everything in the kitchen. It is a fairly rustic space and the cabin itself isn't overly large. It has two small bedrooms and one bathroom. A small living room with a single sofa and one ancient wingback chair take up two-thirds of the open space. A small, eat-in kitchen is to the right of the front door. The focal point of the entire cabin seems to be a giant stone fireplace in the living room.

"Too bad it's too warm to use the fireplace. It's beautiful."

Silas nods. "Yeah, but the outside is great. Go put your swimsuit on. I want to show you something."

"Oh, God. You're not going to push me in the water or something, are you?"

He rolls his eyes. "No promises, but not likely. Go."

I sigh and go into the bedroom on the right where he'd set my bag after we came in. I pick it up as I close the door and set it on the small double bed. I unzip my bag and fish out the new suit I picked out when we went to the sporting goods store. I change into it, pull on a pair of shorts, and trade my sneakers for flip-flops. I also grab the sunscreen and towel I brought, shove my sunglasses on top of my head, and walk back out.

When I return to the living room, Silas has also changed into swim trunks but has left his original tee-shirt on. He's pulled a ball cap on top of his messy light brown hair and also traded his sneakers for flip-flops. "Ready?"

"I'm not sure, am I? I don't know what we're doing."

"Yeah, you're ready." He spots the sunscreen in my hands. "Want me to put some of that on your back? Might be easier to just do it here in the house so we don't have to take it with us."

I shrug and extend the tube out to him. "Okay." I drop my towel onto the sofa and turn away from him.

"Hold your ponytail up so I don't get lotion in it." I take my hair down and rework it into a messy bun so it's off my back. "That works, too." He squeezes some sunscreen in his hand and rubs the lotion on my neck, shoulders, and back. When he gets to the middle of my back, he asks, his voice soft, "You covered them up?"

I don't have to ask about the *them* he's referring to. "Yeah. Tattoos are easier to look at than scars."

"Does it wrap around your ribs?"

"Yeah. I've always liked stars, so now, instead of ugly reminders of what my father did, I can make pretty constellations."

"When did you do it? I don't ever remember you or Cole talking about it."

"You remember when he got the compass tattoo on his forearm a couple of years ago?"

"All done." I turn and he nods. "Yeah, I remember."

"I got mine at the same time. He said whether we needed

the stars or a compass to help us figure out where we were going, we'd never get lost as long as we were together."

Something softens in Silas's expression and he gives me a sad smile. "I never knew that. I just assumed it was one of those nerdy things he liked; like when he got the one of the tree and its Latin name. That's pretty significant."

I nod. "Yeah. And now, I feel like, a lot of the time, it's too cloudy to see the stars and I have no compass. I keep walking in circles and I'll never find my way back home," I admit.

He hands the sunscreen back to me and squeezes my shoulders. "The clouds eventually all part, Peep. It won't always seem like you're wandering aimlessly."

"When did you get so philosophical?"

He rolls his eyes. "Who's to say I haven't always been? I'm not *just* a pretty face, you know. Even though you have to admit, I do have a pretty face."

I can't help but laugh as I squeeze some sunscreen into my palm to slather on my arms and chest and face. "Oh, and so modest, too. It's a wonder you can even get through doors with a head that big."

He snorts in amusement. "I know, right? Hurry up now. Let's go."

Extending the tube of sunscreen to him, I say, "You need some of this, too. Otherwise, your pretty face ain't gonna be so pretty anymore."

He sighs and takes it and begrudgingly swipes some onto his nose. "There, happy?"

"Ecstatic. All right, now what are you so gung ho to show me?"

"You'll see." Following him out the back door of the cabin, I'm surprised to see that the porch runs the full length of the house with a porch swing and rocking chairs.

"Wow, this is nice."

"This isn't what I wanted you to see." He tugs me down the few stairs and toward the river. "So, Pap's buddy comes here a lot over the warmer months and sometimes Pap comes with him. I've been here several times over the years to help do some maintenance since they're both old. A few years ago, I brought a small boat because I thought it was absurd to be on the water and not get out on it. Pap and Snowy, his buddy, are content to simply fish off the bank. I don't fish but I like to row in the mornings."

"Sounds like you've been here more than a few times."

He shrugs. "About once a year since high school. It's quiet. There's no wifi or TV. Sometimes it's nice to unplug for a weekend."

"Okay, so, a boat? That's what you want to show me?"

"No," he says, his tone one of forced patience, as if I'm a small child he's explaining something very simple to who doesn't understand. "Can't you just let it be a surprise? Jeez, Wednesday, you love surprises. Let me have this one thing, okay?"

I hold my hands up in mock surrender. "Okay. Fine. I'll try to be patient. And for the record, I like good surprises. Bad ones can suck it."

He huffs a laugh. "I know." He leads me to a shed I hadn't noticed from the house and flips the latch on the door and then pauses. "Step back; sometimes there are snakes and birds and stuff that like to hide in here." I quickly take about ten steps back since I want no part of snakes or other creepy crawlies. He opens the door and steps inside and after a minute, he hollers for me. "Come help me with this." I take a few tentative steps forward and he motions for me to hurry. "Here, carry the oars so I won't have to make another trip."

He brings the wooden oars out of the shed and hands them over to me. They're long and awkward, but not too heavy. The boat, on the other hand, looks cumbersome. "You sure you wouldn't rather have help with the boat? That thing looks like it weighs a ton."

"Weighs less than you, Peep, so not heavy at all," he says with a lopsided grin.

I scoff. "Are you calling me fat?"

He rolls his eyes. "No. Jesus. I was simply pointing out that the boat weighs less than you do. I carry you around no problem, so this boat is even less of an issue. You are not fat. You are too skinny if you ask me. Not as skinny as you were a couple of months ago, but you could still use some meat on your bones."

"I eat."

"Yeah, now you do." He doesn't say anything else and lifts the boat easily and holds it above his head as he comes out of the shed. I follow behind with the oars and when we get to the water's edge, he gently sets the boat down on the shore. "Come put the oars in." I bring them over and he shows me how to install them into the oarlocks. Once done, he nudges the back of the boat into the water. "All right, you're in."

When I give him a skeptical look, he sighs. "You have to get in first so I can push off. I'm not going to tip it and let you fall in because I don't want to hear you bitch. Get in. Sit on the wooden platform in the back."

I gingerly step over the side of the boat and walk the few feet to where he'd instructed. Once I'm settled, he seems to remember something. "Be right back." He runs back to the shed and returns a moment later with two ancient-looking life jackets. "Just in case."

"Oh, that's reassuring," I quip.

"I thought so," he says with a grin as he deftly pushes off the shore and hops into the boat, not even getting his feet wet.

He takes the middle bench facing me, extends the oars, and

begins to row. His movements are fluid and controlled and practiced. "Do you row a lot at work?"

He shakes his head. "Not really. Only when I come here."

"You make it look easy."

"That's because it is. It's all about rhythm and timing. You get into a good rhythm and pace and you can make some good time. But I don't care about that. I don't do this to set any records. This is just for fun."

I lounge back and rest my arms on the sides of the boat. "This is a nice little boat."

He nods. "Yeah, after my first trip here, I knew I needed some kind of kayak or canoe or something and I found this one on Craigslist. It's a little bigger than only one person needs, but I figured if Pap wanted to go out on the water, I'd be able to take him."

"You and Pap are really close, aren't you? Even closer than he is with Josie or how he was with Cole."

He shrugs, considering. "I guess. Dad says we're a lot alike. We both like our solitude and we can both be ornery. Neither of us minds hard work and, I don't know, I've always been able to talk to Pap. Aside from Cole, he's always been who I've gone to when I needed to get something off my chest."

"How's he doing these days?"

"His eyes are getting worse and he's being stubborn. It's only cataracts, which would be an easy fix, but he hates doctors. Probably has to do with Meemaw and her cancer. He's never trusted a doctor since then. I don't know if he's been the same since she passed."

"Well, Meemaw was a special lady." I look out toward the tree line on the opposite side of the river. "She was the first person who ever noticed things weren't right with me. Even more than your mom, who always made sure I had clean clothes and a bath before I went home. It's like she could tell without even having to see the bruises that my dad was mean to me."

"Well, her own dad was abusive, so it's not surprising. Takes one to know one, I guess."

"I miss her. No one makes biscuits like hers." I glance back at him and give him a sad smile. "Yours aren't too bad, though."

CHAPTER ELEVEN

SILAS

I watch Ada as I continue to row us to our destination. She has that faraway look she gets when she talks about her dad. It doesn't happen often, at least not with me. I only know a lot of the things I do because my parents helped her become emancipated at sixteen. Her dad went to jail for the scars she now has covered by tattoos and she didn't want to go into foster care.

This little boat trip wasn't part of Cole's plan; in reality, neither was the cabin. We could've done the activity tomorrow without having to stay overnight. I couldn't resist, though, and Snowy wasn't planning on coming in for a few more weeks, so it was a no-brainer for me. I'd called him and he readily agreed to let me use it and I couldn't be happier.

Seeing Ada in my little row boat—my peaceful place—does something for my heart and I push away the guilt I feel about enjoying getting to spend this time with her. Seeing her look more relaxed and less troubled than she did this morning when I picked her up definitely helps assuage said guilt. And many people would probably say our dark humor about talking to my dead brother is in poor taste. I say you do what you have to cope. Apparently, that comes in the form of jokes about our mental health in the wake of our loss.

The river begins to narrow as we get closer to what I want to show her. She leans over the side of the boat and drags her fingers through the water, a loud squawking sound a moment later making her perk up. "What kind of bird was that? Are there geese here?"

I shake my head. "Nope. You'll see."

A few minutes later, we come to a small inlet surrounded by scrubby cedar trees. The squawking sounds grow more prominent the closer we get and Ada begins to examine the trees. "What are those?"

Catching some movement in a tree to my right, I nudge her knee with my own. "Look," I whisper, gesturing to where a juvenile blue heron looks as though it's about to take flight. It perches on the edge of the nest, flaps its large wings, and hovers a few feet above the tree before falling back.

We watch in attentive silence as the bird tries over and over to take off. After about ten minutes, it leaves the nest as if it's always been able to fly, landing in a tree on the other side of the river, about fifty feet away. Ada turns back to me. "Wow. You think that's the first time it's flown?"

I nod. "Yeah, I'm pretty sure all these are fledglings. They're all about the right age. They leave the nest around sixty days old. Most of these probably hatched sometime in March so it's pretty close to that time."

She examines me with more interest than I've seen in a long time. "How do you know all this? It sounds more like something Cole would know."

I huff a laugh. "I was curious and did some research after I found this nesting ground. I counted once and there was something like a hundred nests. They rebuild the same ones every year. Obviously, I don't know if they're the same birds exactly, but it's still cool." I lift a brow and give her a lopsided grin. "Like I said, I'm more than just a pretty face, Wednesday. I know how to Google and everything."

She nods. "I know you're smart. I've always known that. Your intelligence just isn't as in-your-face as Cole's was."

"Oh, you mean because I don't spout facts about every single thing in existence? I swear, he was like this bottomless pit of knowledge."

She laughs. "Yeah, it used to drive me nuts. I'd bring home some new seasoning or spice to try and it seemed like he knew the history of its entire species and felt the need to make sure I did, too."

I nod. "He liked to do that with different types of bugs and birds when we'd be up at the farm with Pap. Meemaw encouraged his incessant spewing of knowledge. I blame it on her crush on Alex Trebeck. She was obsessed with *Jeopardy*. Pretty sure, she was convinced he'd eventually get to be on the show."

"He would've loved that. What do you think would've been his fun fact when Alex went to do the introductions?"

I think for a minute. "That he could solve a Rubik's cube in less than a minute. And then he'd want to prove it."

She grins. "Yeah. Or, that he could name all the presidents in chronological order, along with their spouses, children, and pets."

"What about his ability to differentiate between different types of grass by blade alone?"

Warming to the topic, she adds, "Or, his irrational fear of paper cuts."

"Or, how he felt like the perfect shower was eight minutes long."

"Lord, he was something," she says with a sad sigh.

I nod. "Yeah, he was." I put the oars back into the water and begin rowing back toward the cabin, suddenly feeling as though there are three people in this boat. Chest aching with something akin to shame for feeling any joy for this time spent with Ada, I try to keep my gaze from landing on her. It's not until a short time later, when she nudges me, do I realize she's speaking again and I finally give her my full attention.

"Thank you for bringing me to see the heron. It was amazing." Her smile is soft and I try to push down the happiness I feel seeing it. Maybe if I don't feel the happiness, I won't feel the guilt.

"It was," I agree. "I like watching them take off." When we get back into open water, I hold the oars up. "Switch seats with me. Take us back to the house." Maybe if she's the one rowing, I can try to focus my attention elsewhere.

She snorts. "Yeah, right."

"For real. It's not that hard. Come on. It'll be good for you. What if I fell in and hit my head and couldn't get us back, you'd need to know."

She eyes me with suspicion. "I think you're just looking for an excuse to put me to work."

"Maybe. But you still need to know. Switch seats with me and take us home."

She slowly stands and as she makes her way to my seat, I stand in an attempt to counterbalance and she wobbles and lets out a small squeak when she sways. I grab her hips and shove her down onto the bench to keep her from falling in. Unfortunately, the swift movement rocks the boat more than I can overcome. Losing my balance, Ada screams as I tumble into the water. I hear her alarmed tone calling my name, even under the water and I gasp for air as I reach the surface of the cold water. "Oh, God. Are you okay?"

Laughing, I tread water. "Yeah, I'm fine. Wet, but fine. Help pull me up." She extends her hand to me, disbelief flashing in her eyes a second before I pull her into the river with me.

As her head comes above water she sputters and shoves me. "You ass. You did that purpose."

I can't help but laugh even harder. "Yep, totally. Not the falling in part on my end, but as soon as I was in the water, I knew you were coming in, too. Your face was just too trusting. It was too perfect."

She splashes me and I splash her back, making her squeal. "I was trying to be nice. See if that ever happens again. You can drown for all I care."

"Oh, come on now, you know you'd miss me if I wasn't around to give you shit."

She shrugs, even as she treads water. "Yeah, I guess. It's about the only fun I have anymore. And this isn't bad. Not as cold as I thought it'd be. Especially for April"

I swim a few feet away. "Nope. Not bad at all."

"Do you swim a lot when you come here?"

"Some. It's not safe to swim alone, and even though I'm a good swimmer, I still don't like to do it by myself."

"So, do you ever bring girls here? Take them out on your boat? Go skinny dipping in the dark?" she asks, amused.

I shake my head. "No. I've never brought anyone here. I'm not sure Cole ever even came here. Obviously, he knew about this place, but it was a little too unplugged for him."

She thinks for a minute and asks, "But he wanted you to bring me here?"

Alarm bells sound in my head. I know I can't tell her the overnight part of the trip wasn't in his instructions since I'm not sure how she'd take it. So, I skirt the truth, even as I taste the bitterness of the half-truth. "He had the plans for the activity and left the accommodations up to me. Pap mentioned Snowy wasn't using the cabin, so I thought it'd be nice. I called him since the cabin is only about a half-hour from where we're going tomorrow. I'm never going to turn my nose up at free. Just because Cole left money to stay at a nice hotel or something doesn't mean I'm going to try to use up every bit of it."

Ada examines my face and I can only hope she's bought my explanation. She finally nods. "Makes sense. One of these days, you'll have to tell me how all this worked out." She begins swimming back toward the boat.

"How all what worked out?" I ask, following suit.

She turns in the water when I'm only a few feet away. "How all these tasks and stuff he planned worked out. How long was he planning all this stuff? How did he even know to plan?"

Some of this, I can actually tell her without feeling like I'm betraying Cole's trust, so I do. "He told me when y'all had been together about a year knew he wanted to grow old with you. But you know he's always been a realist. You know he's always believed in being prepared for whatever. He mentioned something when we were about seventeen. He made me promise if something ever happened to him, I'd look out for you; make sure you were okay."

"*Seventeen?*" she asks, shocked.

I nod. "First off, I told him to stop being so damn morbid, but you know him, he's pragmatic. Second, I asked him how he intended for me to make sure you were 'okay'. He said he had it all planned out. He'd tapped his temple like it was all locked away. The way I figure, he started formulating a plan as soon as he was old enough to sign up for life insurance and added things as time went on."

She swallows and blows out a breath. And even through the wetness from the river water, I can see the tears as they start streaming down her face. She reaches over the side of the boat and attempts to pull herself up but can't manage it.

"Here, let me get in first and I'll pull you in." She stops struggling and I haul myself over the edge of the boat. Once I'm in, I extend my hand to her and grab the back of her shorts to pull her in. I can't help but notice how the fabric clings to her ass and wedges itself into her ass crack. I'm not successful in the least in not looking, in spite of my best efforts to the contrary.

She tumbles to the floor of the boat and winces. "Talk about the wedgie from hell. Damn, Ass, trying to give me a rectal exam as you pull me out of the water? I'm all for buy one get ones, but that's a bit excessive, if you ask me." She digs her shorts and suit from where they've lodged themselves and I chuckle.

I shrug. "Just trying to do my part to check for leeches. They like to latch on to ass cheeks and the backs of legs."

All the color drains from her face. "Leeches? Stop it. That's not funny."

I shrug again, keeping my tone nonchalant. Truth is, I've never seen any leeches here. But knowing how Ada reacted to the scene in *Stand By Me* where the boys get covered in leeches and her subsequent freakout, I can't resist egging this on. "What? This is a river. Rivers have leeches."

Thankfully, her mind seems to be off her sadness for a moment in favor of having some kind of conniption. She yanks off her shorts and examines her thighs. Unable to hold my laughter back any longer, she looks at me, a murderous expression on her face. "You're an asshole, you know that?" She throws her shorts at me and they nail me in the face with a wet *thwap*.

"Do that again and you'll go back in the water and I'll let you swim back to the cabin."

She rolls her eyes. "No, you wouldn't. You're an asshole, but you'd never let me drown. You'd miss me too much."

She's definitely not wrong about that. "You're all right, I guess," I say with feigned annoyance. I row us back to the cabin and it seems to take less time to get back than it did to go out. All too quickly for my taste, I'm pulling the boat back onto the shore. Ada hops out and after I pull the oars from the locks, she carries them and the lifejackets up to the shed as I haul the boat back over.

Once we have everything put away, we head back into the cabin. "How do steaks sound?"

"Fine."

"Good, because that's all I brought for supper."

She shakes her head and huffs a laugh. "Then why did you even ask?"

"'Cause I can?"

"Want some help? What did you plan for sides?"

I'm surprised she'd offer to help but pleased nonetheless. The idea of cooking alongside Ada makes my chest tighten with something akin to contentment, sparking guilt just as quickly. Fucking emotional whiplash. I'm going to end up with an ulcer before it's all said and done. "Potatoes and salad stuff," I reply in answer to her question.

"All right. Do I have time to take a shower before we need to start cooking?"

"We're not on any kind of timetable, Peep. We can wait until midnight to eat if we wanted."

"The hell we can. I'm starving."

"Okay, then make your shower quick. Make sure to leave me some hot water?"

"Sure." She heads off to her room and is in the bathroom a moment later. I try not to imagine her taking off her swimsuit or climbing under the shower spray. I do my best not to picture the soapy water cascading down over her naked body.

"Fuck," I mutter under my breath, frustrated and feeling

shameful for my wanting of her. My dick reminds me of its nagging presence and strains painfully against the fabric of my swim trunks. *Saggy old man balls. That time Anderson Silva broke his leg during the UFC fight with Chris Weidman. Nails on a chalkboard. Mom walking in on me watching porn when I was fourteen.* Yep, all good now. Sweet Jesus, I need a drink.

Knowing the potatoes will take the longest to cook, I wash my hands and scrub the skin of the spuds to ready them for baking. I dry them off and prick them all over with a fork and coat the outside with oil and salt and pepper and wrap them in foil. I toss them in the oven and turn it to four-fifty.

I open a bottle of wine and pour half of it into a glass and down it, hoping to dull my senses and the ache in my chest. Bringing her here was a terrible fucking idea because from now on, I'm only going to be able to associate this place with Ada and taking her to see the herons. Why didn't I think this through? I down the wine and refill the glass, tossing the bottle into the trash.

Ada exits the bathroom ten minutes later in a pair of what look like Cole's boxers and one of his work shirts. *Guess it's safe to say she hasn't gotten rid of any of his stuff yet.* And even swimming in his clothes as she is, she still looks adorable. Not that I notice, except I do, and down the remainder of my glass of wine. "Shower's free," she calls.

"Okay," I answer, heading off to take my own.

Seemingly unaware of the internal battle I'm waging against myself, Ada asks, "Want me to fix the salad?"

"Sure," I toss over my shoulder without looking at her. No way I can look at her right before I go into the bathroom and get in the shower. Not when she'd be the only thing I can think of while I'm in there. I can't stop from berating myself as I shut the door. *Fucking pull it together, Si.* Shit. The bathroom smells

like Ada and the vanilla citrus body wash she uses. Mother-
fucker. Cold shower it is.

After supper, we sit on the porch, each with a beer. I've
taken up residence in one of the rocking chairs and Ada
stretches out on the swing next to me with a book. But it
doesn't look like she's reading. It appears to be a journal of
some kind and she's staring down at it intently. I down the
last of my beer, ready to rise and get another. "Don't move,"
she commands.

"What? Why?"

"Because I'm sketching. Don't move. I can't draw real life
from memory and if you move, I won't be able to finish."

My heart lurches. Ada's sketching? *Sketching me?* "Oh," is
all I can say. "What are you sketching?"

"Well, you. Duh. But the light is great right now. It's
making some really cool shadows."

"I take it you're working again if you're drawing?"

"Not much. Had the urge to pack my sketchbook, though,
so I figured I might as well. I was going to draw the river from
the porch, but I looked over at you and the light was hitting you
just right."

I'm not sure what to think about what she's telling me. I
don't want to read anything into it, but it's hard for me to not
take some sort of pleasure in her words, try as I might to tamp it
down. I've looked at some of the art Ada makes. It's mostly sexy
fan art based on several fantasy romance book series. From
what Cole always said, she does pretty well. Or, she did before
she shuttered her store when he died.

"Are you going to start working again?"

She sighs. "I'm sure I will at some point. I just haven't felt like it. This is actually the first time I've even picked up a pencil or stylus since Cole died."

I glance at her out of the corner of my eye, but I'm not sure if I can move, so I don't move my whole head. "And how does it feel?"

"Rusty," she says with a chuckle. "My hand's already cramping." As if to prove her point, she shakes out her hand and flexes her fingers. "It's good, though."

"Well, I'm glad you're getting back at it. Even if it is to draw me. Surely there are other subjects you'd prefer."

"You're all right. Like I said, the light is making some great shadows."

"Did you sketch Cole a lot?"

She snorts a laugh. "Yeah, but only when he slept. He couldn't sit still long enough to let me finish one. I have a ton of started sketches where he'd be lounging on the couch reading, his reading glasses perched on the end of his nose like some professor. But it was like some kind of radar his body had. It was as if, as soon as he sensed I had my sketchbook, he had to get up and do something. I don't think he liked the attention. Pretty sure it made him feel vulnerable.

"He was so open and honest and matter-of-fact about what he was feeling but he never liked to be stared at. I think letting me sketch him made him feel like he was under a microscope, so I didn't want to make him uncomfortable. I'd sketch him when he'd fall asleep on the couch, usually, with a book tented over his chest. Or, sometimes, asleep in bed, his face all smooshed into the pillow."

I can't think of anything nicer than having Ada look at me and see me and want to capture it. Knowing Cole, though, I get what she's saying, and not for the first time—or the thousandth, for that matter—jealousy stabs through me at the life Cole had with Ada. And as his brother, I could never be anything but overjoyed for that life and the fact he was happy. As a man, the envy is this near physical thing I carry with me, even now, knowing I'll probably never get to have with her what he did. The shame is there for the same reason, simply because I want to have it.

"All done," she says a few minutes later, knocking me out of my thoughts, and rolls her shoulders.

"Can I see?" I ask, unable to hide the hope in my voice. God, I'm such a pathetic simp.

She slides over on the swing and extends the book out to me. I take it, more than a bit nervous to see how she's captured me on paper. I examine the drawing and my stomach drops. God, she's good. It's a small sketch, about five-by-seven inches, but the detail is stunning.

I'm in profile looking out toward the river, sitting in a rocking chair. The lines of the log cabin are in the shade with the shadows stretching out behind me. My hair is mussed from my shower and she's even drawn the wrinkles in my shirt where it's been stuffed in my backpack. Somehow, she was able to capture the stubble on my jaw and the faint hairs on my forearms.

I'm forced to remind myself to breathe and I swallow thickly. "God, Ada, this is beautiful."

She snorts a laugh. "Think a lot of yourself there, do you?"

I look over at her, hoping she sees the sincerity in my expression. "I'm serious, this is incredible. Even if it wasn't of me. You're so talented."

Her expression softens. "Thank you, Silas," she replies quietly.

I hand the book back to her and she closes it. "You need to be working. I'm sure your fans miss your art."

She nods. "I miss it, too."

The next morning, following coffee and a breakfast of cinnamon rolls and sausage, we get ready for the day. I have to remind myself to breathe when I see Ada in the outfit she'd purchased at the sporting goods store. Sweet Jesus, I'm going to hell. The tight capris leave almost nothing to the imagination. And even more than in only a bathing suit yesterday, this somehow seems even sexier.

She's paired them with the sports bra and tank top she bought the same day. The top cuts low under her arms, allowing me to see even more of her star tattoos under the band of her sports bra. I know I'm not going to be able to look at her without creating an awkward situation in my athletic shorts. Her hair is in French braided pigtails, making me think of when we were kids.

I can't resist tugging on one of her braids as she passes me to drop her duffle bag by the door. "Ouch, Ass," she says through gritted teeth, punching me in the arm. "You know, hair pulling isn't really my kind of kink."

The idea of anything close to *kink* and Ada in the same thought makes my pulse tic up. Note to self: make a doctor's appointment for ulcer meds. Fucking hell. Luckily, I'm able to recover quickly enough that she doesn't notice my increased respiration. "Just nostalgic, Wednesday. Damn," I reply, rubbing my arm as if she's bruised me.

She rolls her eyes and scoffs. "Oh, don't be a baby. I barely tapped you. We both know I've hit you harder than that in the past. Don't tug my braids. I swear, between you and Cole, it's a wonder I wasn't yanked baldheaded as a little girl."

"Probably a good thing. Not sure you can pull off bald."

She narrows her eyes, reaching up to ruffle my hair. "You're one to talk. You wouldn't know what to do with yourself if you got an actual haircut instead of letting some student at the cosmetology school cut it. I don't know if I've ever seen you without crooked hair since we were kids and your parents quit paying for your cuts."

I finger my shaggy locks. "Hey, I'm a baller on a budget. I'd rather put my money toward more important things."

She grins, amused. "Like what, a new pair of sneakers? I know how you love your shoes."

I shake my head, sobering. "No, actually. I'm building a house."

Her brow furrows. "What? Since when?"

I shrug. "About a year. I'm building it as I get the money. My rent is pretty cheap, so I'm able to put back quite a bit. You know, with what I don't spend on haircuts."

She still seems as though she's processing the information I've just told her. "A house?"

I nod. Although I hadn't planned on her knowing about the house until I was ready to show it to her, it's not detrimental to any plans if she knows, I guess. "Yeah, the one I have isn't big enough for the long-term and I don't want to move a ton. Once it's built, it's my forever home, so if it takes a little while to finish, I'm all right with it." I glance down at my watch. "We're going to have to get on the road or we're going to be late."

She's thoughtful as we load up the Bronco and I turn the car toward the road. "Does anyone else know you're building a house? How did I not know about this? A *year*?" she asks, incredulous.

I shrug, not liking how her tone sounds as though she's been somehow slighted by my omission of this information. "What? It's not like you and I were close before now. I didn't think you would've cared. It's not like you told me about your tattoo."

"No, I guess not," she admits. "Still, when do you have time to build a house? Are you doing it all by yourself? For real, who are you?"

I huff a laugh at her flurry of questions. "Well, up until we started doing these little tasks, I had quite a bit of time on my hands. Weekends, vacations, holidays. Cole helped me pour the foundation and do a lot of the framing, but yeah, mostly by myself."

"Okay, so this house, is it in town? Or is it somewhere else?"

"No, it's local. When it gets closer to finished, I'll take you to see it. It's still pretty rough right now."

She nods, considering. "Okay."

CHAPTER TWELVE

ADA

I'm unsure how to feel about learning that Silas is building a house. I always thought Cole and I would've eventually built a home for us to share. We wouldn't have needed much space, not with just the two of us, but I thought we would've started planning soon if he hadn't died. What does Silas mean when he says his current home isn't big enough for the long-term? He's never mentioned wanting to get married or have kids, so I assumed he'd always live the bachelor life. I always assumed he was like Cole, content to simply *be*. But does this—this bigger home, a forever home, as he said—mean he does want a family?

I've known for almost as long as Cole and I had been together he never wanted to get married or have children. And with my complicated feelings about family, having kids wasn't something I felt was necessary for my happiness. Even if, in the past couple of years, I'd started to consider the possibility of it being something I wanted. Although, at twenty-five, Cole had a vasectomy so I wouldn't have to stay on birth control until menopause and it became a moot point. At twenty-four, it wasn't a big deal to me. Now, though, at thirty, I'm not entirely sure it's *not* something I want.

Like I said, new dreams, babe. Cole's voice breaks into my thoughts and I sigh and look out the window.

"What, you're going to clam up on me now that you found out something you didn't know about me? Lord, Peep. I'm sure there's a lot you don't know about me. Just like I'm sure there's a lot I still don't know about you."

I'm annoyed by the annoyance I hear in his tone. As if he thinks I wouldn't have wanted to know things. *That's because up until Cole died, you didn't care to know anything about Silas. He was simply Cole's brother, a constant thorn in your side.* What does it mean if he's not now and I'm offended I don't know things about him? Does it mean we're actually friends? That I want him to tell me things?

"No," I counter. "I'm not going to clam up. Just surprised, is all. I figured something like that would've come up in passing if you'd been doing it for a year."

He shrugs. "Like I said, we haven't talked much until recently. Not unless Cole was there or it was about something for him. If you're honest, you probably tolerated me, at best, only because Cole and I were so close. I've never been your favorite person."

"Oh, don't act like you tried to make an effort with me, either," I say and fold my arms.

His jaw clenches. "You were Cole's, Ada. I couldn't make an effort with you."

My brow furrows in confusion. "What's that supposed to mean? Because Cole and I were together, you felt it was your mission in life to torment me? Antagonize me? That we couldn't be friends?"

"You act like you were always sweet to me. You've always

given my attitude right back to me. So don't pretend you were 'friendly' to me because you'd be lying, Wednesday."

"God, you're so infuriating," I respond, my tone frustrated and louder than is warranted in the confines of this vehicle. "I just said I was surprised you didn't tell me about your house and you're acting like it's my fault I didn't already know."

He throws his hands up, his own frustration showing before bringing them back to the steering wheel. "Well, have you ever asked me about my life? Ever?"

"That goes both ways, Silas."

"We're here." The words leave his mouth with finality as if the subject is closed. I'm fuming and angry and maybe a little hurt, even though I don't know why.

I look around, but all I see are pastures with a small sign denoting some sort of farm, but he's driven past it before I can make out what it says. I take some deep breaths, not wanting to bring any negative energy into the activity Cole planned for me, regardless of how upset I am with Silas.

When he parks and cuts the engine, I begin to exit the vehicle and he puts his hand on my arm, stopping me. "Wait." I turn and look at him, my expression expectant. He sighs and drags his fingers through his hair. "I didn't mean for you to find out about the house like that. I'd always planned on telling you when the construction was further along. But let's be honest, Ada. Before Cole died, you and I hadn't really even been in the same room alone together for more than five minutes. That's just the way it is. We're both to blame for that. And I'm learning you're a pretty okay person and someone I would've liked to be friends with. So, I'm sorry if I haven't always been so warm and fuzzy toward you."

I nod. "Yeah, you're a 'pretty okay' person, too. I never thought you liked me, so I never tried to be friends with you. I felt like you put up with me because I was your sister's best friend and your brother's girlfriend. I didn't think you wanted to be my friend. I always felt like I was a nuisance to you."

He winces as if I've wounded him. "I'm sorry. That was never my intention. Can we start this day over, be friends?"

"You really want to be my friend?"

He nods. "Yeah, I do. I mean, I hang out with you more than pretty much anyone else these days. That's kinda friendly, wouldn't you say?"

He's not wrong. Silas is pretty much the only person I talk to anymore aside from Josie and Ingrid and Miles. "Yeah. Okay. Friends."

He gives me a lopsided grin and grabs the yoga mats from the backseat. "Good, now, get your ass out of this car so you can see what Cole planned for you."

Following the last few minutes of conversation with Silas, I actually feel lighter and more excited. I hop down and we walk up a dirt path toward a large, white farmhouse. There are people milling around and I hear the sound of some kind of bleating animal and I stop and grab his arm. "Are those goats I hear?"

He laughs when he sees the hopeful expression on my face. "Yeah, Wednesday, those are goats."

My mouth falls open in shocked glee. "Can I pet them?" I ask, excited. I adore goats. Especially small breeds, like Nigerian dwarfs.

He grins. "Yeah. But even better than that, you get to do yoga with them."

My eyes go wide. "Goat yoga? Holy shit. You're kidding."

His laugh is full and deep and I can't remember the last time I heard him laugh like that. His laugh is different from Cole's, richer somehow, and it's nice to hear. "No, not kidding. And these are those little goats, the kind you like."

If possible, my heart is in my throat and I want to cry happy tears for the first time in longer than I care to remember. "Nigerian dwarfs?"

He nods. "Yeah. There're places closer to home that do goat yoga, but this is the only place close he found that does it with the small ones."

I'm practically levitating with joy. "Oh, my God. You have no idea how much I love goats."

He gestures toward the farmhouse. "Then we better hurry." I tug him along, much like an excited child. He lets me, not even complaining when I take us to the wrong gate and we have to walk to the other side of the yard to enter the outdoor yoga studio. A table is set up with a greeter who verifies our appointment. She tells us to set up anywhere and we make our way to the far side of the grassy area. No goats are roaming around yet but anticipatory butterflies swarm in my belly as we roll out our yoga mats and wait.

"Have you done yoga before?" I ask Silas.

He nods. "Yeah, I try to take at least one class a week at work. It's good for your joints and decompression."

"You like it?"

He shrugs. "I usually feel relaxed after, so that's probably a good thing. And there are plenty of documented benefits of a practice. I'm no full-blown yogi or anything, though. I think you'll like it."

"Well, with goats, how can I not?"

He laughs and says in a whisper, "Yeah, and if you get bored doing yoga, you can always just play with the goats. Says so right on their website. But you should at least try the yoga. You might like it."

I narrow my eyes. "Are you trying to recruit me for your gym? You got a quota you're trying to meet for the month?"

He chuckles. "No, Wednesday. I know better than that."

A tall, willowy woman enters wearing some outfit made of

what I'm sure is un-dyed hemp or bamboo. Her dark green hair is styled in a messy bun, her face free from makeup. She has large gauges in her ears and both her nostrils are pierced, along with her septum. She might be the coolest person I've ever seen in my life.

Her energy is immediately relaxing, even in this expansive space, and I can't help but smile. When she speaks, her voice is soft, but still manages to carry the twenty feet or so to where Silas and I are situated. She has an accent I associate with Pap, as if she comes from the mountains. "My name is Sherri and I'll be your instructor today. In a moment, the goats will be released. They'll freely roam the paddock and nibble at the grass. Don't be alarmed if they happen to jump onto your back as you're in tabletop or a similar pose. If you need a break during the practice, feel free to rest in child's pose or simply sit and visit with any wandering and curious goats.

"Feel free to pet and cuddle the goats, making sure to be mindful that these are still animals and you are inhabiting their natural habitat. We hope you enjoy your practice and will join us again in the future. This is not a stringent practice by any means. Feel free to make modifications to make a pose more comfortable for you to complete."

She looks to her right and nods and about fifteen Nigerian dwarf goats are released into the area and I have to bite back my squeal of delight. Almost immediately, one comes right over to me and I can't resist rubbing its soft ears. It glances at Silas and runs at him, its head down as if to charge, and hits him in the thigh and I laugh. He lets out a surprised chuckle and picks up the goat and scratches it under its chin. Sherri looks on. "All right, if everyone is ready, we'll begin in a cross-legged position."

An hour later, I am both somehow relaxed and keyed up. I actually did more yoga than I would've thought with the goats wandering around. And as they're all drawn away with what I'm sure are very yummy treats, we roll up our mats to prepare to leave. "Well, Wednesday, what did you think about your first yoga practice?"

I shake my head and smile. "I might not mind working out if there were always adorable goats around. They nearly made the exercise worth it."

We begin walking back toward the car and he sighs. "When I called to make the appointment, I asked if there was a place we'd be able to scatter ashes." He points over to a field of cornflowers a few hundred yards off. "They said we could do it over there."

I nod. "Okay," I agree, sobering. It was almost as if for the hour we were with the goats, it was a normal day, a fun day. But with the mention of Cole's ashes, it's come to an abrupt halt.

When we reach the Bronco, he unlocks it and takes the yoga mats and sticks them in the backseat as I pull the bag of ashes from my duffle in the cargo area. We lock up and walk over to the field of flowers. "This is kinda perfect," I say with a smile. "He would have loved this."

Silas nods. "Yeah, I think he would've, too." I dump some of the ashes into his palm and then my own.

I close my eyes, letting the day wash over me. *Thanks for the goats, babe. Best day in a long time. I still miss you so much, but you were right, you would have loved to see my face. I hope you did.* I open my hand and drop the ashes into the flowers, the wind carrying some away on the breeze.

I let out a deep breath and look at Cole's twin, who gives me a small nod. "Ready?"

"Yeah."

We're both quiet on the drive home and I'm thankful. It gives me time to reflect on the weekend and the conversations Silas and I had. Friends. Silas and I are friends. Lord knows if we'll survive it, the way we argue, but he's not terrible company all the time, so maybe it won't be so bad.

He drops me off at home and as usual, carries my duffle to the door. "We still on for tomorrow?" I ask as I unlock the door.

He nods. "Yeah. Want to say, seven? I'll bring food. You still like orange chicken?"

"Yeah, and fried rice."

He grins. "I know. And spring rolls."

"Perfect. I'll get some beer."

"Sounds good." He sets my bag down inside the door and gives me one last nod. "See you later, Peep."

"Bye, Silas." I start to close the door and he pivots.

"Oh, yeah. Almost forgot." He pulls an envelope out of his back pocket and hands it over. "Can't forget your letter. Cole would be pissed."

"Right," I say, taking it. "Thanks. See you tomorrow." I close the door and lock it and carry my bag to the bedroom. I lay the letter on the nightstand and lift the duffle onto the bed. I make quick work of unpacking and dumping things into the dirty clothes. I stow my toiletry bag and duffle back into the closet and take a shower. Currently, I smell like a mix of sweat and goat, so I hurriedly get clean and shave my legs and underarms and hum some song Silas had playing on the radio.

Once I no longer smell like a barnyard, I dress in a pair of comfy shorts and a tee-shirt and head to the kitchen to make a quick supper of grilled cheese. I stand eating it over the stove so I won't have to dirty a plate. After I wash the butter off my hands, I head to my room and pick my sketchbook up off the bed where I'd pulled it out of my bag.

Flipping to the sketch I did of Silas, I can't help but be pleased. I don't do a whole lot of live work, as most of my art is based in fantasy, but Silas was a good subject. He seemed to be content to sit and let me draw him for as long as I wanted. Struck by an idea, I take the book across the hall to my office and sit at my desk. Using an exacta-knife, I cut the page from the book, and for the first time since Cole died, I turn on my computer.

CHAPTER THIRTEEN

ADA

The iMac comes to life with a familiar *bing*, as if it's not been more than three months since I last powered it on. Once it's fully booted, I go through the steps to install my new graphics tablet and adjust the setting to my preferred specifications. I scan the sketch of Silas into my photos and import it into Corel Painter.

I enlarge it so that when I sketch it digitally, I'll be able to print it larger if needed. I make one swipe of the stylus after the other until I have it outlined in more detail than the original. I add in wood grain and other features I left out of the smaller sketch. Satisfied with my starting point, I roll my shoulders and glance at the clock in the corner of the screen, shocked to see it's nearly midnight. It's been so long since I lost myself in work like that, I almost want to cry.

I flex my hands, growing achy with fatigue, and save my progress. I rise from the chair and stretch, my back and hips stiff from prolonged sitting before shutting down the Mac and heading to my room. I turn on the lamp and my eyes snag on Cole's letter, my heart lurching with the knowledge I haven't opened it yet. What the hell is wrong with me? I climb under the covers and after plugging my phone up, I carefully open the envelope and pull out the letter.

My Ada Mae,

What I would've given to see your face when you found out about the goats. Hopefully, you enjoyed yourself and have sweet goat dreams tonight when you go to sleep.

It's been three months, babe. I hope that means you're mostly back to your day-to-day life without much difficulty. I hope, if things are still unbearable, you've reached out for help. Don't stay that way. Of course, if I know Si, and you are still in that sort of state, he will have already browbeat you into talking to someone. He's good like that.

How's he doing, you think? Are y'all okay, or have you come close to killing one another? He's quiet in his pain sometimes, Ada Mae. As I'm sure you've discovered, he can be pretty good in a crisis and I hope you've leaned on him when you needed to.

But sometimes, the thing about Silas is, he pushes all his pain to the back to help others. And maybe me asking him to help you complete these tasks is cruel on my part. Maybe he hasn't had time to grieve properly and him helping you is bad for him, I honestly don't know.

Something I want you to know, though, Si is a good man. He's decent and kind and I hope y'all can be good for each other. I hope, in spite of your own pain, you'll check on him, too. He doesn't have anyone now, babe. I don't know if you know this, but he doesn't make friends easily. I know, shocker. And believe it or not, the guy is shy. I know it might not seem that way, but he is.

I hope you can be his friend. I hope over the past few months as y'all have completed the tasks thus far, you'll have learned some things about one another and found some common ground. I hope you don't let any of the perceived animosity between the two of you linger.

Between you and Si, you both hold all my secrets, my fears, my wants, my dreams. Unfortunately, I don't have any of those things anymore. I hope you know you can trust Silas to keep your secrets and anything else you'd want to give him. Like I said, he's a good man. He was the best friend I could ever ask for. He can be that for you, too. If you'll let him.

I hope the cornflowers were in bloom at the goat farm. And I hope, if they were, that's where y'all scattered my ashes. I mean, I'm not gonna know if you dumped them out the window on the way home, but I like the idea of part of me being laid to rest in a field of pretty flowers.

I'll leave you with this thought, my beautiful Ada Mae; homework, if you will. Laugh at least once a day, even if it's at yourself. Try to only cry happy tears this month. Make Mom some PB&J cupcakes and sweet talk Pap out of some of his apple pie shine—provided Silas hasn't bribed you with all he currently has in stock.

It's okay if there are hours or even whole days that are good for you now. I'd love it if that's the case. I want you to be so wrapped up in a moment you forget I'm gone. But it's okay if it's sad when you remember again. Remember the waves? They go out. They come back. Feel the pain, but don't let it stay. Life is too sweet to let the bitter be where you live all the time.

I love you more than you can ever know. And I don't know if it seems possible for you right now, but someday, I hope you can open yourself up to look for a new love. I'm not saying today or tomorrow or anything like that, but for you to feel like you can never love again means I didn't do an adequate job showing you how good love can be.

I know we'd never planned to marry or have children, but I know deep down, those are things you want. I was selfish to not let you have them. And for that, I don't know if I'll ever forgive myself. You are still young enough to have those things and I want them for you. If I'd been a better man, you would have. Even if it couldn't be with me.

You still have several tasks to complete. Don't ask how many, I'll never tell. But after, I hope you can move on and have the full life you deserve. You are worth so much more than I could give you. I love you to the moon and back, Ada Mae.

-Cole

The tears roll down my face and a weight settles into the pit of my stomach with his last few paragraphs. The thought of moving on, of loving someone—anyone—else makes me want to physically die. But more than that, how did he know I'd begun to think about kids? How could he have known? I never said anything, I never hinted. I never stared forlornly at a small baby in a stroller or baby carrier and wished for that to be my life. How could he have known?

Picking up my phone, tears still streaming, I call Silas. Surely, he would know if Cole had mentioned anything.

"Wednesday? What's wrong?" His voice sounds both sleepy and alarmed. Belatedly, I remember it was after midnight when I even sat down to read the letter.

"Oh, I'm sorry. I didn't think about what time it is. Go back to sleep, Silas."

I start to hang up and he yells, "Hey. What's wrong? Are you crying? Do I need to come over, are you safe?"

"I'm okay," I assure him, even if I can't stop crying.

"Are you sure?"

"Yeah. No. I don't know."

"Ada, what is it?"

I wipe my nose and eyes on the collar of my tee-shirt and sniffle. "Did Cole say anything to you about knowing I might have changed my mind about wanting kids?" He clears his throat and it's clear I've made him uncomfortable. Probably too soon in our fledgling friendship to discuss such heavy topics. "You know what, forget it. I'm tired, I should go to bed. You should go to bed. I'll see you tomorrow."

"Ada, stop. Talk to me. Why are you asking?"

"His letter." My words come out broken and I try to clear my throat.

"What about it?"

"Did you know Cole had a vasectomy?"

"No," he replies, genuine surprise lacing his tone. "When was this?"

"When he was twenty-five. I've always known he didn't want to get married or have kids. He told me when I was about twenty. And back then, after everything with my parents, kids were the last thing I ever thought I'd want. And I had Cole, so what did I care about hypothetical kids?

"But now, his letter says he knows deep down I wanted them. How could he have known? I never said anything to him or anyone else. Even if I did want them, I'd locked it away because I knew it wasn't even an option anymore. And now, he's saying he knows I want them and he was selfish for keeping it from me. How could he have known, Silas?"

He breathes a heavy sigh. "I don't know, Ada. The only thing I can think is, he knew you better than anyone else. He was perceptive and saw even what you didn't want him to." He's quiet for a moment. "Do you want kids?"

I shrug even though he can't see. "I don't know. Maybe."

"Then he was selfish," he says and his voice has an edge to it. "If he knew that about you, even if you wouldn't admit it to him or yourself and he kept it from you for whatever reason he might have had, he was selfish. And if that's the case, you have the right to be pissed at him. I know you love him but it's okay to be angry at him in this instance. Especially if he's admitted this. He could've never said anything and he leaves that for you to read without any recourse to confront him about it? God, I'd want to punch him. That matter-of-fact, pragmatic fucker."

I can't help but laugh. "Yeah. I'm not sure how I feel. I am angry. I'm hurt and I'm sad."

"I think however you feel is valid. And I think if you've decided you want kids, you should have them. If you want to parachute off the Empire State Building, you should. I think you can do whatever you want to do."

"Just like that?"

He huffs a laugh. "Well, you might want to find a guy to help make those babies. Might be more fun than the alternative."

I snort a laugh. "Probably." After a beat, I ask, "This house you're building. You said it's going to be your forever home because the one you have now isn't big enough?" He makes a sound in the affirmative, but that's all he gives me, so I continue. "Do want kids and a family? Is that why you're building the house? I don't think I've ever heard you mention anything like that."

Silas is quiet for a long moment before he speaks. And when he does, he sounds almost wistful. "For the right woman, I'd want those things. If she'd be okay with a simple life. I'm not a complicated man. I don't need loud parties or a ton of friends. My circle is tiny and I like it that way. I like spending time with my family. I like my job. It's not glamorous or prestigious and I'm never going to have a ton of money and I'm okay with that. I like who I am as a person and I'd like to think I'm a good man. So, yeah, given that I had the right woman, I'd want it."

"Sounds like you know what you want."

"I've had a lot of time to think about it."

"Goodnight, Silas."

"Are you okay, Peep?" His tone is concerned and I find myself glad I called him.

"Not right now. Maybe someday," I answer honestly. "I'm sorry I called so late."

"Don't apologize. If you ever need to talk, you call me. We're friends now. It's allowed. I won't even bitch," he says and I hear the smile in his voice.

"Noted." I disconnect the call and look over at Cole's urn, the tears of sadness and disappointment starting anew.

CHAPTER FOURTEEN

SILAS

Cole had a vasectomy? That selfish, fucking bastard. I try to go back to sleep following Ada's call, but the sadness in her voice makes something twist painfully in my chest and I'm wide awake. How could he have known she'd possibly changed her mind and not let her have it?

I want so badly to scream and punch something and wish more than anything, the rage room was open at this time of night because I could use it right now. I know there's a letter for me in the "Goats" section of the folder but I was so exhausted after getting back, I thought I'd wait until tomorrow to read it. But now, I need something from Cole. I can't say what, but I'm hoping he'll say something in the most recent letter to soothe this ache in my guts.

Springing out of bed, I'm in my office in a matter of seconds and flipping through the folder and yanking out the appropriate envelope with my name on it. I have the wild notion to toss all the rest of the tasks, but I know I'd never do it. I'd never rob Ada of closure or Cole of his last words to her, no matter how angry I am at this moment.

"Cole, you've got some explaining to do," I say through gritted teeth as I tear open the envelope.

Si,

I hope the goats weren't too smelly. I hope she loved it. Was I exaggerating about how much she loves those tiny goats? She has a whole Pinterest board dedicated to Nigerian dwarf goats. If you're unfamiliar with Pinterest, do some research. Ada's on there constantly getting inspiration for her art. You'll need to know what that is.

I'm about to tell you something only Ada knows. I've kept it from you because you would have likely beat my ass, even if my reasons were good. I had a vasectomy a few years back. Ada was having some issues with the birth control she was on and knowing I never wanted kids, I decided to get the old "snip-snip". That way, she wouldn't have to keep taking the pill and the side effects cause her so many problems. We talked about it at the time and she was on board. I'm not sure she knows I suspect she's changed her mind about wanting kids. She's never come out and said it, but she gets this look when we're around kids. It's not sad or wistful exactly, but it's like her eyes light up. I'm not sure she even knows it happens.

If it weren't for my heart, I would have married her and given her all the babies she'd allowed me to. But I can't know-ingly risk passing this on to my kids. I'm not willing to play roulette like that.

I know after reading all this, you're probably furious. I'm a selfish prick for taking the option completely away from her before she was sure what she wanted. I know if I was there, I'd welcome the punch you'd want to throw because I'd deserve it. If she confides in you, I hope you'll comfort her and tell her I was selfish and it's all right if she's pissed.

. . .

I can't help but chuckle at this, even if I am furious with him in this moment.

You would've made a hell of an uncle to Ada's and my kids if we could've had them. But you'll make an even better dad. It kills me to know you might get to raise babies with the woman I love. But I'd rather it be you than someone else. At least if it is you, they'd likely be almost identical to any kids I had with her so you know, win-win in my book.

I roll my eyes at his pragmatism.

Yeah, go ahead, roll your eyes. I told Ada in my letter to her you could be a good friend to her. I hope she lets you. I hope y'all are somehow able to carve out time for each other that has nothing to do with me.

It's so surreal to think about me being gone and you stepping up to love her. Granted, I know you've always loved her but now, you might get to show it. And selfishly, I hate it. Because if that's true, then I'm not there to do it. But if she can't have the real thing, might as well have the knockoff, right?

Jokes aside, you're not a knockoff. I think, even when we were kids, I knew it would be you. And maybe I was quicker on dibs just so I'd get to have her for a little while. In truth, you've always been the better of the two of us. As we've established, I'm selfish and you've been nothing but selfless. I'm loud and a know-it-all and you're contemplative and reserved. I've never met a stranger and you're shy, even if no one would ever suspect it.

But the thing is, you and Ada are so much alike. You're both full of piss and vinegar and always have to have the last word. Your tempers run hot and your punishment of choice is the silent treatment. But you also both have the biggest hearts of anyone I've ever met. And I think, in time, you'll find your way to one another.

Even if it's not magically at the end of this road I've paved for you. Even if it's not five years from now, although, in all actuality, I hope it's not that long. I truly believe YOU are her soulmate, she just had to love and lose me to know it. And I have faith she will. Keep the faith, bro.

-Cole

As the tears flow down my face, falling onto my bare chest, I want to punch Cole, but I also want to hug him. How can I be so angry with him and miss him so damn much at the same time?

I've never been more thankful in my life for having a Monday off than I am today. I tossed and turned and didn't fall back asleep until almost six AM. And then, a banging on my front door wakes me around nine. I stumble out of bed, dragging on some shorts over my boxers. Who, in God's name, would be knocking on my door when I've only had three hours of sleep?

I look out the window and see my mother and I open the door and peer out at her. "Mom? Everything okay?"

"I tried to call and you didn't answer."

I shrug and motion her inside and shut the door. "Sorry. Shit night of sleep. What's up?"

"What's going on with you and Ada?"

I'm immediately on alert and scrub my hand down my face in an attempt to wake up. "What? What do you mean?"

"Silas, I'm not stupid. I know you've always had a soft spot for Ada, even if you acted like y'all were oil and vinegar. But she's in a sensitive place right now and you need to be mindful of that. I'd hate for you both to take solace in each other and it morph into something less than is healthy."

"Mom, what are you talking about?"

"The goat yoga, Silas. I follow that farm on social media and saw pictures of you two on their account. You and Ada went to do goat yoga? That was something Cole was going to do with her. I helped him find that farm. What is your plan, you just step in and do things Cole told you he was going to do with her? That's sick, son. You're not a replacement for him."

I heave a heavy sigh. "Mom, sit down. I need coffee. I can't have this conversation without some caffeine." She takes a seat on the sofa and I step into the kitchen and start a pot of coffee. I walk back to my room and grab a tee-shirt and the letters I've already opened from Cole. That should be enough, if needed, along with the telling. I make a quick pitstop in the bathroom and wash my hands before pouring myself a cup. I offer one to my mother and she declines and I return to the living room, pages in hand.

"Mom, you remember when Cole got his hypertrophic cardiomyopathy diagnosis and he made us promise not to tell Ada? That he would tell her?"

She nods. "Yes, but he never got a chance to tell her."

I shake my head. "He chose not to tell her. He knew he had it for fourteen years. He could've told her at any time and he didn't." I sigh and take a sip of my coffee in an attempt to stall and figure out how best to word things. "To understand this," I say, holding up the letters, "I have to go back further."

She frowns. "Okay."

"You remember how Cole and I use to torture Ada? We'd pull her hair and we were shits to her?"

Mom snorts. "That's putting it mildly. Y'all terrorized her."

I nod. "Yeah, well, turns out, we both loved her, even back then. But it wasn't until high school, after she'd gone to visit her mom that summer, you remember?" She nods. "She grew up that summer. Cole and I saw her come into the school at the same time. And we'd already been talking about her, wondering how her summer had gone. We'd been pumping Josie for information. We missed her. But damn, she was something else when she walked in the door at school.

"Cole saw her about a second before I did and he called dibs. And, as you know, dibs is sacred. And it would have been different if Cole had treated her less than she deserved, but he didn't. And she was happy, so I was willing to be happy for them. Even if I still loved her."

Mom's eyes widen slightly. "*Love* her? You love Ada?" Her tone is incredulous and I shrug.

"I've tried not to. Believe me. And Cole's always known. It was one of those things we didn't talk about. I told him if he ever hurt her I'd beat his ass. But we both know he loved her well; he was good to her.

"So, back to his diagnosis. After we learned all the risks and possible outcomes, he made me swear I'd look out for Ada if something ever happened to him. I didn't know what he meant at the time and none of us thought he'd die, so I wasn't all that concerned about it. But I still promised I'd take care of her.

"I didn't think anything else of it. And then, about a month after he died, a currier delivered a package to me from his lawyer. There were all these... 'tasks' he called them. It's a bucket list of sorts, except not, because they're not super special things. They're everyday things Ada had mentioned wanting to do over the years or things they'd discussed together or other things he thought would help her grieve. They're his way of giving her closure."

"Why you, though? Is that fair to you? To have you help her complete all these tasks if he knew how you felt about her?"

"That's the thing. He's hoping these tasks help her fall in love with me."

Her mouth falls open in shock. "Silas, you can't be serious. That's ridiculous."

I shrug. "Blame Cole and his fucked up sense of logic. I think it's a long shot. Even if I'm thrilled to get to spend time with Ada, I don't have a clue how all it's going to end. I might end up as only her friend, which would still be pretty great. Hell, I might end up with my heart broken while she's all healed and I might have to watch her fall in love with someone else. Again."

My mother's expression softens. "Oh, son, that's awful. How can you do this to yourself? Put yourself through this?"

Tears burn my eyes. "Mom, how can I say no to Cole's dying wish? And how can I abandon the woman I love? I know now, more than ever, I'm in love with her. God, how I wish I wasn't. It eats at me. But knowing I love her, how can I not be here for her? She needs me."

"And who's here for you, Silas? You're doing all this work to fix her, but who's going to pick up your broken pieces? She's not the only one who lost him. We all did. Is any of this helping you, or are you simply falling harder for her only to have her leave you when it's all said and done?"

I shrug. "I don't know," I answer honestly. "I can only hope Cole's plan works. And seeing her get better, seeing her smile and laugh again, it helps my heart, Mom."

"So, who else knows about all this?"

"Josie and Pap. Ada knows about the tasks, of course, but only about the fact that Cole planned everything out. She doesn't know his end goal. She doesn't know any of us knew about his heart before he died. She doesn't know his heart is the reason he never wanted marriage or kids. She just thinks he never wanted any of it. She said last night, with everything that happened with her parents, she didn't know she possibly wanted kids until just the last couple of years."

She's quiet for a long moment. "What can I do, to help with these *tasks*, I mean?"

I huff a laugh. "Nothing, Mom. You know Cole, he was a planner to the max. Almost every detail is handled. Most of the time, I simply have to call to confirm things. I give Ada the letters when I'm supposed to and take her to complete the tasks. We scatter his ashes when we go places and then we come home."

"But you think they're helping you and her become closer?"

"Honestly, yeah. It's so surreal, knowing I know all these things about her because we grew up together, but I always had to keep her at arm's length so I didn't let slip how I truly felt. And now, I can be friendly with her and give her support and console her and make her laugh and get to know her the way I've always wanted to.

"Don't get me wrong, we still have some big fights. And they're not arguments, they're ugly fights. We're hateful to each other and have said some really terrible things; things I would have kicked anyone else's ass for if they'd said them to her. But somehow, we've managed to always apologize and talk it out. I don't know if it means we'll be okay forever. There are times I want to strangle her and I'm sure she wants to knock my block off. But God help me, I love her."

When I look back at my mother, her eyes are shiny with

unshed tears and her hand is covering her mouth. She pulls it down and lets out a slow breath. "Well, I'll be damned. You know we've always loved Ada. Since the day she came home with Josie, I've always had a special place in my heart for her. She's our family. I don't know what spell she's apparently put on you boys, but it's something else.

"And I've always wondered why you never found anyone to be happy with and I guess now I know. Part of me is deeply saddened by all this, Silas, I'm not going to lie. To know you've held a candle for Ada all these years and there was a possibility you might have never gotten to have her. That you would've ended up alone. But if she's whom you want and you two can love each other, then I'll be a very happy mother. But if she can't love you the way you deserve, I'd hate for you to settle for some shell of true love.

"You're not a replacement for Cole, Silas. And if Ada starts to think of you that way, you need to cut it off. She needs to see you for you. Anything less than that would be unfair to you. I get the feeling you'd take what you can get with her and I'd be so disappointed in you if that's the case. Please don't settle, son. You're too good a man for that."

I nod. "Thanks." I'm struck with a thought. "You can't tell Dad. He won't be able to keep it to himself. He's the worst blabbermouth in the entire family. And you can't mention any of this to Ada. I don't want her getting the wrong idea. Because even though I am in love with her, I want her better first. I want her back to her old self—well, as much as that's possible. I'm a patient man. I'm not rushing anything."

Mom scoffs. "Patient? I'll say. You'll have likely earned sainthood by the end of this thing." She stands. "Well, I'll let you get back to your day. And you're sure there's nothing I can do to help?"

I rise from my seat and follow her to the door. "No, I've got it. We're starting a new thing tonight, watching a show together. I hope it turns out well. Then, this weekend, we're going to Pap's. I owe him some jars of shine, so Ada's going to come along to learn how to make apple pie and Pap needs some plowing done. We should be back for Sunday dinner."

She nods and gives me a hug. "Okay. I hope all this works out for you the way you want, son. I truly do."

"Me, too, Mom," I say and return her embrace.

CHAPTER FIFTEEN

ADA

"Oh, God. You know they work together. He's probably going to be her boss," Silas says with a mouthful of shrimp-fried rice and I can't help but laugh.

"Well, it's Patrick Dempsey. I'm pretty sure he's got a big role in the show."

He turns to me, his expression incredulous. "Spoilers. I thought you said you hadn't watched any of this?"

I pause the show so we don't miss anything and take a bite of a spring roll. "I haven't, but I also don't live under a rock, Ass. This show's been on forever. Some things, you can't help but pick up. But damn, look how young he is. He was hot."

Silas laughs. "Wow, Wednesday, been a while?" It seems to hit us both what he's said and we sober. I turn back to the TV and resume the show. A few minutes later, he snorts. "Could George be any more obvious?" Secretly, I'm thankful things seem to be back on track.

"What? I think he's cute. Like a puppy."

He scoffs. "Yeah, like a puppy you can't housebreak."

I sip my beer and roll my eyes. When Bailey is introduced, I can't help but smile. "Ooh, I like her."

"Yeah, because she's a ball buster. But she's probably really squishy once she warms up. What you wanna bet?"

"They called her 'the Nazi'. And don't even get me started on how that probably wouldn't fly by TV standards today. Yikes. You really think she's going to be an M&M?"

Frowning, he asks, "An M&M? What's that?"

I shrug. "An M&M. Hard shell, sweet center. Or, if you prefer, a Sour Patch Kid or War Head or any of those twofer-type candies."

He nods, considering. "Okay, then yeah. I think she's totally going to be an M&M. What do you think, ten bucks?"

"Okay, I'll take that action."

We watch as the interns flail helplessly and when Dr. Shepherd is introduced, Silas nudges me, a winning expression on his face. "Told ya. She hooked up with her boss. Oh, man. I like Meredith. She tells arguably the most handsome guy on the show he wasn't that good-looking? She's got balls. And look at him, he's already half in love with her. I bet this entire show consists of everyone sleeping with everyone else."

I sigh. "We'll never know if we have to keep pausing it every three seconds so you can monolog."

He feigns injury. "But my monologs are fun and quippy. I think they'll grow on you."

"Like a wart," I mutter.

He scoffs. "I heard that."

I grin at him. "I meant for you to."

Later, when George's heart patient dies, Silas snorts and shakes his head. "Oh, man, he never should've promised the wife her husband was going to live. Amateur."

But all I can see is how clinical Burke is about having to let the patient go, how unfeeling. Were Cole's doctors like that when they were trying to save him? Did they joke about stuff behind the scenes?

When I don't say anything in reply to Silas's comment, he turns to me. He must see something in my expression because he pauses the show and puts his hand on my arm. "Hey, what's wrong?"

I shake my head, my throat tight. "I don't think I can watch this show."

He turns off the TV. "Okay. Want to talk about it?"

I shrug. "Do you think Cole's doctors were like that?"

"Ada, Cole was already gone by the time he got to the hospital, remember?" His tone is gentle. "They couldn't bring him back in the ambulance. His heart gave out."

I nod as it comes back. "Yeah."

"We can find a different show if this is too much. Or no show. Whatever you want. We can sit here and do nothing. If you'd rather be alone, I can go. If you want to go for a drive or hit something, I'll take you to the gym and let you go buck wild on a speed bag."

I shake my head. "I think I'll be okay."

"All right. Let's find a different show."

"No, it's okay."

"Ada, I don't want you to watch something that's going to trigger you every time we see it. You know I'll be here for you, but why make things harder on yourself?"

"You don't seem to be having any trouble."

He shrugs. "We're not the same person, Wednesday. Dark humor is my jam, apparently. It's how I cope. But I get why it would be hard for you to see this. Because now they're going to have to go tell that guy's wife her husband didn't make it. You've listened to that conversation. You can empathize with that wife. You know what it's like to never have your partner come home again."

"Do you remember what they said? I don't remember. I think I was in shock."

He lets out a breath and takes my hand in his and I let him. It should feel strange because he's never held my hand before, but honestly, it's comforting. "Yeah. They said Cole had hypertrophic cardiomyopathy. It caused his heart muscle to become thickened and made it harder for his heart to pump blood. It caused his heart to go into arrhythmia and basically short circuit. There was nothing that could've been done in that moment. He was gone almost as soon as he hit the ground. You kept him alive until the ambulance got here by performing CPR. You did a really good job, Peep. No one else could've done better."

I nod. "Yeah." He gives my hand a squeeze and releases it and I immediately miss his warmth. I look at him. "All right. Let's finish this episode."

"Ada—."

I cut him off. "Turn it back on, Silas."

He acts as though he's going to protest, but after a moment, he turns the TV back on and presses play on the remote. I watch as Burke berates George for promising the patient's wife and makes him deliver the news solo. And although I know exactly how the wife feels in this situation, I also feel sympathy for this baby surgeon who, by all accounts, is having a shit first day at work.

I blow out a breath when it's over. "It's actually a really good show. Lots of drama and stuff going on. Medical mystery, romance, infighting, burgeoning friendship. Do you think Christina and Meredith will end up as best friends? Seems like they'll be super competitive, but make each other better."

Silas blinks slowly, taking in what I've just said. I think I've given him emotional whiplash with my semi-breakdown and then calm appraisal of the show. "Yeah, probably. That one intern who was snarky to the nurse is an asshole, though. You think he'll last?"

"Only time will tell. Guess we'll have to keep watching to find out."

He nods. "Guess so."

The following weekend, as we pull up at Pap's farm, I can't help but smile. As a girl, there were so many weekends I spent with Josie where we'd come visit Pap and Meemaw. They'd treat me exactly as they did Josie, Cole, and Silas. Meemaw will always be special to me and since she passed, it's been hard for me to come here and her not be here when I visit.

As normal, Pap is on the front porch in his rocker, a shotgun laid over the armrests as he rocks. Even in the almost ninety-degree heat, he has on a thick flannel work shirt under his denim overalls. He slowly stands as Silas and I make our way up the porch steps. "Hey, Pap," I say with a smile and a big hug.

"How's my girl?"

I step back and Silas claps his grandfather on the shoulder in greeting. "I'm making it. I hear I'm in for a moonshine lesson this weekend. You going to teach me everything you know?"

The old man grins. "Well, someone's gotta learn. Might as well be you." He motions for us to follow him into the house. "I've got a pitcher of tea made, y'all come fix you a glass. Actually, Si, you fix Ada and me a glass so I can look at her up close. I swear, girl, you get prettier every time I see you."

I huff a laugh and drop into one of the chairs at the kitchen table. "You need to get your eyes checked, old man. How are those cataracts doing?"

Pap side-eyes Silas. "He rat me out?"

I shrug. "Well, he just wants to make sure you're taking care of yourself. What do you say we give the doctor a call this afternoon and make an appointment? I can drive you if you want." I lean in and whisper conspiratorially. "I'll even let you tell them you're my sugar daddy." Silas snorts a laugh and Pap blushes.

"Well, now, that might be something. Might be fun to rile up those stuffy docs. Okay."

Silas sets a glass of tea in front of me and gives my shoulder a squeeze and winks at me. Pap's always had a sweet spot for me for some reason, so I thought I might be able to grease the wheels to try and get him to go to the doctor. I sip my tea and give Silas a smile and he looks out the kitchen window toward the barn. "You haven't hooked the plow up to the tractor, Pap?"

Pap sighs. "No. I thought I'd let you do it. Make sure you remembered how." More like he couldn't see to do it, but neither of us is going to point that out to him.

He nods. "Okay. I'll go ahead and take care of it. Once I get it hooked up, you want to come out and check it for me?"

"All right. It'll give me some time to sweet talk Ada into making some chicken and dumplings while y'all are here."

Huffing a laugh and as Silas heads out to the yard, I sip my tea and turn back to Pap. "How you really doing, old man?"

"Not sure. I'm tired, Ada Mae."

I pat his hand across the table. "You know, you and Cole were the only ones I'd ever let get away with calling me that."

"What, it's your name? It's a pretty name. It's better than what Silas calls you. What the hell kinda nicknames are Peep or Wednesday? Plum stupid, you ask me."

"Well, he's called me those since we were kids. Kinda grew on me, I guess. I call him 'Ass', so I think we're even."

Pap laughs. "Well, good to know you can give as good as you get. How are you really doing these days?"

I sigh. "Some days are better than others. Do you know about the tasks? The ones Cole setup?"

He nods and takes a long drink of his tea. "Yeah, Silas mentioned something about those. How are they? Do they help?"

"I think so. I know I'm a lot better than I was that first month. And some days are actually good. Silas has been a good friend to me."

He examines my face and I wonder how much he can see. "How's he doing, you think?"

"Hard to say. He said something about a lot of his grief being behind closed doors and we talk, but I get the feeling he's not as good as he lets on. What do you think? He talks to you about as much as he does me."

Pap considers. "I think having you to help shoulder his grief helps. It's nice y'all can turn to each other with this thing Cole did. How did you like the cabin?"

I smile. "It was beautiful. I started sketching again while we were up there. You want to see?"

"Is it one of those wacky dragon picture things? I don't know anything about those, you know that."

I laugh. "No, it's a picture of Silas. I'm finishing it out and I'm going to give it to him for his birthday."

His expression softens. "Oh, well yeah. Let me see."

I pull out my phone and access the work in progress in my cloud drive and hand it over to him. He holds it close to his face and smiles as he examines it. "Ada Mae, this is really something. Does he know?" He hands it back over and I stick it in my pocket.

"He knows I sketched it. I showed it to him while we were at the cabin, but I'm making it full color and I'm going to print it out and frame it. You think he'll like it?"

"If he doesn't, he doesn't have taste. You sure are

something."

"Well, thanks, Pap. You're not so bad yourself."

———————

A few hours later, I've made Pap's requested chicken and dumplings and Silas comes in from the field drenched in sweat as I'm setting the table. "Good lord, it's hot," he laments, pulling a rag from his back pocket and mopping his brow.

"Did you get done with the plowing?"

He nods as he fixes himself a glass of water at the sink. He takes several large gulps and starts to sit and I swat him. "Don't you sit your dirty self down in this chair. You go clean up for supper. You've got time."

He rolls his eyes. "You sound like Meemaw."

"Well, she was a wise woman. And you know she would have gotten after you with a broom if you sat down at this table in less than pristine condition."

He eyes me. "I bet Pap's sweaty, dressed in that flannel as he is. And I bet if I come and give you a big hug, you'll be just as sweaty as the rest of us. Then what's it matter?"

He starts to approach me and I point my finger at him. "Silas Campbell, you come near me and I will wack you with a wooden spoon."

He gives me a wicked grin. "Oh, come on, Wednesday, don't you want a hug?" He holds out his hands, making to grab me and I back toward the other room.

"Not like that," I say with a squeal as he advances. I turn to run away and he lunges and grabs me from behind, pinning my arms to my sides. He rubs his sweaty head all over the back of my neck before bringing his cheek to rub against mine. "Eww, Silas, you ass." I squirm in his arms and he holds me tighter.

He laughs into my hair and I dissolve into a fit of giggles, but then, he abruptly releases me. "Sorry, I shouldn't have done that," he says, his voice soft. "You're probably going to need a shower, too."

I roll my shoulders and grab the rag from his hand and wipe the back of my neck and down my arms and face. "I think I'm okay. You will pay for that, though."

He gives me a lopsided grin. "You keep saying you're going to get me back, but I think you're all talk, Peep."

"Nah, I'm just saving 'em all up for a rainy day."

He laughs. "If you say so."

"Seriously, though, go shower. You smell awful."

He raises his arm and sniffs his armpit and grimaces. "Yikes. So much for all-natural deodorant. Whoever developed that shit obviously has never worked a day on a farm. Do I have time to shower?"

I nod. "Sure. This'll keep."

———

After supper and Silas and I wash up the dishes, I sit on the front porch on the swing with my sketchbook. Pap and Silas walk out, the older man toting his ancient acoustic guitar and the younger cradling a jar of moonshine.

Pap takes the rocking chair and begins to tune the Gibson and Silas plops down next to me. "Drawing anything good?"

I shrug. "Just the farm." I glance past him to Pap. "You planning on doing some serenading tonight, Pap?"

"Eh, just feeling a little restless. Okay if I pluck some?"

"It's your house, you know I don't mind music." I cut my eyes to Silas. "Good music."

He opens the jar with a grin aimed in my direction and sips. Judging by the way he squints as he drinks, this is the "fully leaded" stuff Pap keeps back for himself. He offers it over to me and I shake my head. "Not on your life, buddy."

He chuckles and passes it to Pap, who takes a long swallow and sets the jar down beside his rocker. A moment later, Pap begins to play some soft rhythm. Silas pushes us gently in the swing and I pull my legs up to allow him control and he leans toward me, keeping his voice low. "You think he's pickled his liver yet, with all that heavy-duty shine?"

"A definite possibility," I say with a laugh. "We're still doing the flavoring tomorrow, right?"

He nods. "Yeah, I've got to get the corn and tomatoes in the ground first thing, but after that, it'll probably take most of the day to work on the apple pie."

"Okay." I return my attention to my sketching. Currently, it's only the horizon of trees across the field on the far end of the property, with the hay field in the foreground. After a few minutes, I feel Silas's eyes on me, so I turn to him. "What?" I ask.

He gives me a warm smile. "Nothing, you just look really relaxed when you sketch. Looks good on you."

I return his grin. "Thanks. It does relax me. But so does the farm. I've always loved it here."

He nods. "I know. I think if the farm had been close enough to town that you could've stayed in the same school district when you emancipated yourself, you'd have lived with Pap and Meemaw."

I consider, sticking my pencil in the middle of my sketchbook and closing it. "Yeah, probably. Aside from your parents, they were always the closest thing to a real mother and father I ever had." I glance over at Pap, who's still strumming softly, his attention somewhere else. "I think he's tired, Silas."

He huffs a laugh. "Well, he's eighty-four. He probably gets out of bed tired."

I shake my head, keeping my voice low. "I think it's more than that."

Silas looks over at his grandfather and I watch as his throat bobs with a swallow and he lets out a long, slow breath. "I think with losing Meemaw a couple of years ago and then Cole, it's taken a toll. His tired might be soul tired. Parents and grandparents aren't supposed to bury their kids and grandkids. It's the wrong order of things."

I chew the inside of my bottom lip. "One twin shouldn't have to bury the other before they have gray hair, either."

He nudges me. "Why do you think Cole wanted to be cremated? He didn't want me to have to look down at a casket and see myself and have some sort of existential crisis and lose my shit."

In spite of how dark the thought is, I can't help but laugh. "That's terrible."

He shrugs. "Yeah, but true."

CHAPTER SIXTEEN

SILAS

Me grabbing Ada in the kitchen is nothing new. I've snatched her up and rubbed my sweaty face and body all over her clean one for years. When we were kids, nothing brought me greater pleasure than to hear her squeal and fuss when she'd be all mussed and stinky from my perspiration administrations.

But I think the last time I did it was when I was about fifteen, before she and Cole became a couple. I don't know what came over me to think I should do it today, but it was fun, and to hear her giggle was nearly too much. Then I realized she was in my arms and I could smell her shampoo because my nose was buried in her hair and it was like I came to and snapped out of my trance. Thankfully, she didn't seem to notice how abruptly I turned her loose.

It's getting easier to casually touch her; to squeeze her shoulder or hold her hand as I comfort her as I did when she was triggered by the episode of *Grey's Anatomy*. I don't know what it means if she doesn't seem to be put out by this new physical part of our relationship. I know it's nothing in the grand scheme of things, but I pathetically live for these brushes of my skin against hers. Of course, then the guilt stampedes right through any sort of joy I might draw from these moments. And try as I might, it won't go away. What if it never does?

I know Pap probably thought bringing Ada with me for the weekend would be a good way for us to spend time together under the guise of doing some work on the farm. Well, not even a guise since I busted my ass getting the garden plot plowed and ready to plant. But I also know what a special place Ada holds in Pap's heart and he's not seen her since Cole's funeral and he's missed her. Stubborn as he is, though, he'd never admit he wants her here simply for the sake of spending time with her. I'm more than happy to be complicit in his shenanigans since I also don't feel like I see him enough.

And Ada's right, he does look tired. More than simply his years and hard living and all the alcohol. He looks weary and I'm reminded that time is both free and the most expensive commodity ever and some of us are more blessed than others. I make a mental note to take more initiative in spending what little time Pap has left to learn anything he wants to teach me. As the sun sets fully over the ridge, Ada puts her hand on my arm. "I'm going to turn in. I'll have breakfast ready when you come in from the garden in the morning."

I nod and give her a smile. "Sure, Peep. That'd be great."

She unfolds her legs and drops them to the ground before rising and walking over to give Pap a kiss on the top of his head and tell him goodnight. She heads into the house, letting the screen door bang shut behind her. Pap starts to say something and I shush him until I hear her go into her room and then the bathroom a moment later. I know she likes to shower at night on the farm and in the old house, I can hear the water turn on, even from my place on the porch.

"What'd you shush me for? I wasn't going to say anything that would've gotten you in hot water."

"I know. Just making sure."

Pap lays his guitar across the rocker much the same way the shotgun was earlier and a slow smile creases his face. "Sure was nice to hear her giggling earlier. Been a long time since that sound made its way through the house."

"Yeah, it was."

"She's worried about you."

My brow furrows. "What? Why?"

"She said she worries you're not grieving. That you keep yours behind closed doors or something. Do you show her you're hurting?"

I shake my head even though he most likely can't see me well. "Not really. We've gotten into a few fights and I've said stuff during those moments, but it's not like I want to break down in front of her. I'm supposed to be strong for her."

"Son, sometimes strength is shown in your vulnerability. When we lost your uncle Joseph, I wouldn't let Beatrice ever see me cry. I thought if I could be strong for her, it'd get us through. I didn't know she needed to be able to comfort me, too. That she felt like I didn't care because I wouldn't show that part of myself to her. We'd lost a child and I couldn't even let my wife hold me as I cried.

"My idea of 'coping' was to go to the stillhouse and drink myself into oblivion. Almost lost me my marriage and any chance of a good relationship with your daddy. Don't be like me, Si. If you want Ada to let you in, you have to let her in, too."

Guess I'm more like Pap than I thought with our similar coping mechanisms. I've not heard Dad or Pap talk about Dad's older brother Joseph before. I know Josie is named for him. But other than knowing he died during a farming accident when he was around ten years old, I don't know much. So to hear Pap talk about him now makes something twist in my gut, as if he's trying to impart lasting wisdom.

I also know he's probably not wrong about me not being vulnerable with Ada. I've tried to be strong for her while I've deflected my own feelings with dark humor and kept my grief to myself and the confines of my office with his letters and a jar of moonshine. Can I let her see that part of me and if I do, will it somehow wreck this tiny flicker of something I'm trying to get to catch? Or, will it be like Pap says and it would make her see me as strong in my moment of weakness?

Over the next few weeks, Ada and I fall into a routine of our Monday *Grey's* day and Chinese food. We text sporadically and she seems to be working again. Judging by the notification I received on the app where her store is housed, she's returned from her hiatus. I hope this is a good sign.

After a particularly juicy episode of the show where it's revealed Burke and Christina are sleeping together, I turn to Ada. "Told you this show was going to be about everyone sleeping with everyone else. Meredith and McDreamy, Christina and Burke, and don't even get me started on pining George." The irony that I am currently George is far from lost on me.

"Well, it's still a good show. I wonder how it'll all shake out?"

I shrug. "We'll just have to wait and see, I guess."

Once the episode ends and we clean up, I pull the next task letter from my back pocket and drop it onto the counter. Ada glances down at it and swallows. "That time already, huh?"

I nod. "Yep. Although, honestly, I'm not sure who's going to enjoy this one more, you or me."

Her brow furrows. "Why would you say that?"

I shrug but don't want to give too much away. "This one surprised me, is all. I wouldn't have expected it."

She considers. "Do we have to go out of town for it?"

I nod. "Yeah, we'll leave Friday, come back on Sunday."

"All right. Do I need to get anything?"

I tap the letter. "You'll have to read to find out, you know that."

Ada nods and examines my face. "You seem oddly excited for this one."

I grin. "I am. I can't wait."

Her eyes narrow in suspicion. "Oh, God. It's not something that's going to put me into a fear spiral, is it? You know I don't like bugs or snakes or anything creepy crawly."

I laugh. "I know. No, it's nothing like that. I'm not saying anything else. Be ready to go Friday morning at seven."

"Seven? Why so early?"

"Stop asking me questions, Wednesday. Read the letter."

She nods and is quiet for a moment. "Will you give me a heads up when we're getting close to the end?"

"I'm not sure if I'm allowed to do that."

Her smile is sad. "I figured. Okay, I'll be ready." She seems to think of something. "Oh, what do you want to do for your birthday next month?"

I shrug. "I hadn't planned on doing anything. It's not a big deal."

"Yes, it is, Silas. It is a big deal. Especially this year." The unspoken, *since this is your first birthday without Cole,* hangs heavy in the air.

I rake my fingers through my hair and tap the letter. "Let this be my birthday gift, Peep."

Confusion evident in her expression, she opens her mouth and closes it again. She huffs and folds her arms. "That's not fair."

I shrug. "It's what I want. And then, on my actual birthday, I want an extra *Grey's* day and a cake. I don't want a big dinner or to go out. Even though that's what Cole and I always did, public displays aren't really my thing. I'd rather just chill. Especially this year."

"*Grey's* and cake, huh?"

I nod and put my hand on the letter and grin. "And this. That's all I want."

She sighs. "Okay. If you're sure."

I nod again. "I am."

"Well, I guess this weekend is a twofer, then."

"Yep," I reply, pleased.

VEGAS

JUNE: FOUR MONTHS AFTER

CHAPTER SEVENTEEN

SILAS

As I pull up at Ada's apartment a few minutes before seven on Friday—when did I start thinking of it as *hers* instead of Cole and Ada's? Hmm. Something to ponder, I guess. I shut off the engine and lock up before jogging up the stairs. I knock on the door and a few seconds later, I hear footsteps and it opens. "Oh, thank God," she says, her tone panicked.

Alarmed, I frown. "Whoa, where's the fire?"

"I have no clue what to bring. The letter said something to wear out on the town, but I have no clue what that means. Help."

I huff a laugh as I step into the apartment and shut the door. "Okay, how about you take a breath, Peep? You look like you're about to spontaneously combust." She doesn't seem to hear me so I put my hand on her shoulder and turn her around to face me and bring my eyes level with hers. "Breathe, Ada. This is not dire. We'll figure it out. We've got a few minutes."

She inhales deeply, her gray eyes locked on mine. Jesus, why do they have to be gray? Gray is such a unique color for eyes. You hardly ever see them. Why can't they be blue or green or even a basic brown like mine? Why do they have to be so fucking memorable?

After a beat, she nods, her demeanor a lot more calm. "Okay. This is always the part I hate about these things. He only gives me enough information to intrigue me and never enough to know how to pack. Some planner he is."

I can't help but laugh, even as I turn her back around and guide her, my hands still on her shoulders, to her room. "Show me what you're thinking."

She gestures to two dresses on her bed. One is shorter and red and I know she'd look sexy as hell in it. I'm pretty sure it would kill me to see her in it. The other is a little longer and black and still sexy. Fuck me sideways, I'm a dead man walking. "Since I don't know what we're doing, I don't know which one works."

I blink slowly as I try to formulate words. "Either one would work. Although you could wear jeans and you'd still look amazing, you know that."

Color rises to her cheeks and my heart lurches. It's the first time she's ever blushed because of something I've said and I'm not sure how to take it. Fuck. I shouldn't have said that. I shouldn't have said anything about how good I think she'd look. Because now all I can see is that damn blush and I'm going to be with her for two nights. I have got to get it together. I'm not here to tell her how good she looks. It's not my place. Although, friends tell each other they look nice, right?

"What did you bring to wear?"

"For tomorrow? For the outing?" I ask in confirmation, trying to get my racing thoughts back on track.

She levels me with a glare. "No, for the queen's state dinner, Ass. Yes, for the outing tomorrow."

In spite of my own personal hell, Ada's sassiness makes me want to go toe-to-toe with her. "Damn, you're feisty today, Wednesday. Fine, figure it out on your own. How about that?"

Her eyes narrow. "Fine, I'll just bring them both and decide tomorrow. You've been absolutely zero help, thank you very much."

"Whatever," I reply, rolling my eyes in feigned annoyance. "We've gotta go. Get your shit together. Our flight leaves in less than two hours and security will probably be a bitch."

Her jaw clenches and she throws up her arms in frustration. "Ugh. Can you at least make yourself useful and get my toiletry bag from under the sink in the bathroom?"

"Sure. Want to tell me why are you so frazzled? You're normally completely ready to go. What's up with you?" I glance at her from where I'm squatting to retrieve her toiletry kit.

She rolls her shoulders as she folds the dresses and tucks them into her suitcase. "I've just been hyper-focused on work. Don't get me wrong, it's a good thing, but I got behind and I don't like rushing."

"Okay, well, pack it in and we won't be rushing. After we get through security, we'll grab some coffee and chill and stop freaking out."

She zips her bag after she tucks her toiletries into the suitcase. "I'm not freaking out. This is not a freakout. This is simple nerves. I hate flying."

I take her bag from her and give her shoulder a quick squeeze in support even though I really should stop touching her. It's becoming way too easy for me to justify putting my hands on her skin. Even if it's not hugging or anything more than simple friendly and affectionate split-second shoulder squeezes, pats on the hand, and the like. "You have nothing to be nervous about. Flying is actually safer than driving, you know," I offer, trying to be reassuring.

She nods. "I know that, in theory. But one of the first times I ever flew was when I came back from visiting my mom in Texas. And then everything happened with my dad and I've always associated flying with all that and I don't fly well now."

Hearing her relay why she's truly anxious about the flight makes it a lot easier to focus on being a supportive friend to her in this moment. For that, I'm thankful. Not about her being anxious, but about being able to have a reason to strengthen my resolve to not think about the way I feel about her this weekend. To simply be her friend. Because a friend is all she needs right now. A small voice says that a friend is all she might ever need from me. I remind myself that even if that's true, Ada is a great friend to have and I'd be lucky if that were the case. "Gotcha. Well, if we were flying first class, I'd tell you to have a mimosa, but alas, we're economy all the way. As soon as we get on the ground, we can find a bar and drink to a successful flight."

She snorts. "Won't it only be a couple of hours later when we get to Vegas with the time change? I don't readily foresee a bar being open at ten or eleven in the morning."

I scoff. "Oh, ye of little faith," I say tugging her toward the front door. "It's Vegas, there are probably bars open at eight AM. We'll just have to find one."

―――――

Thankfully, when we touch down in Vegas a little after eleven local time, we do, in fact, find a bar. We console ourselves that it's well after noon at home and therefore, plenty acceptable to have a beer. Which, Jesus, Ada needs it. She was a wreck the entire flight. I basically had to pin her legs to her seat to keep them from jumping all over the place.

"So, now that we're here, can you tell me what we're doing?"

My rules don't exactly prohibit me from telling her, so I shrug. "Okay. You sure you don't want to be surprised?"

She sips her beer and sighs. "Silas, I just survived the flight from hell and only have two days before I have to do it again. I'm not really feeling overly giddy about surprises at the moment. I know that goes against my nature, but humor me."

And because she's in such a foul mood, I can't resist completely freaking her out. "Oh, well, if you must know, we're getting married." I keep my tone entirely neutral as if I've just told her she has food in her teeth.

She chokes on her beer, sputtering liquid down the front of her shirt and when I don't laugh, the color drains from her face. "That's not funny, Silas."

I shrug. "Sorry, that's just what my letter said. Who am I to go against Cole's final wishes?"

She blinks slowly as if she's trying to comprehend my words. Her mouth opens and closes and she looks very much like a fish at this moment. And because I can't keep up this ruse out of my own fear that she says something about how she could never marry me or something equally devastating, I nudge her and laugh. "I'm fucking with you, Wednesday. We're going to a UFC fight."

She visibly relaxes. "You are such an ass," she spits out, slugging me in the arm.

I rub the soreness away and chuckle. "You should've seen your face."

She looks out the window toward the Vegas strip and sips her beer. "I mean, I hope I'd warrant more than Vegas if that really was the plan."

I nod. "Yeah, Peep, you'd definitely get better than a Vegas chapel." And even though my tone is light, I know I'm entirely genuine. Fuck. Can I not even go half a day without letting my thoughts wander to that place? To think about what she might look like as a bride and wife? Especially after everything I told myself as we were leaving her apartment, can I not keep it pushed down for two fucking days? I mentally count to ten and vow to do better. To be better. For her.

After another drink each, I pay the tab. "So, what should we do before we can check in? We could hit a casino or drive out to see Hoover Dam. Whatever you want," I suggest as we begin walking down the crowded sidewalk.

Ada looks around in thought, her eyes snagging on something. "Do you trust me?"

I snort. "I'm not sure. I just pranked you by telling you we were getting married. You've been vowing to get revenge on me for all my shit. I'm not entirely certain how to answer that question at this present moment."

She rolls her eyes. "For real, do you trust me? No pranks. No shenanigans. There's something I've always wanted to do but I've always been too chicken shit. But life's too short, right? We should do things that scare us?"

I frown in consideration. "Yeah, I trust you, Wednesday."

"Promise?"

I nod. "Yeah, you're pretty much my best friend. I trust you with my life," I answer honestly.

Her eyes snap to mine, her expression soft. "I'm your best friend?"

"Yeah."

She gives me a soft smile. "Well, all right. Let's go."

"Go where?"

She loops her arm through mine, turning me around, her eyes alight with glee. "Kid, today you get your first tattoo."

I stop in my tracks, panic instantly gripping me. "Like hell."

She snorts a laugh. "I'm going to get one, too. And guess what, you get to pick it out. And I'm going to pick yours. We're goin' in blind, buddy."

My mouth falls open as she tries to pull me along. "Ada, come on. If this is some kind of revenge plot and you're going to have them put 'Welcome Aboard' above my junk or something, I will drag you down to a chapel and force you to marry me."

She laughs and stops, turning to look at me, her expression sincere. "No, I promise. Nothing like that. This is something I've wanted to do for a long time. And if you want to pick mine out first and I'll go before you so you can make sure I'm not fucking with you, that's fine.

"This is the first impulsive thing I've wanted to do since Cole died and I don't want to do it alone. Like I said, I can go first and if you decide you don't want to do it, it's okay. I still want you to pick mine out. If I'm your best friend, you should know me well enough to pick out a tattoo for me."

"It's a lot of pressure, Ada."

She snorts a laugh. "No, it's not. I already know what I'd pick for you."

My brows lift in surprise. "You do?"

She nods. "Yeah. It's not huge, either. Probably wouldn't take an hour." She leans in. "I'll even let you pick the location for mine," she says and wiggles her eyebrows and then seems to think better of it. "Well, not on my face. Or my ass. Or, like, my vagina."

I nearly choke on my own spit. "Jesus, Wednesday."

She shrugs. "Just setting some ground rules. Come on, take me to get inked."

I shake my head and relent. "Fine. I can't believe I'm letting you talk me into this."

"Oh, don't sound so dire. This is a fun memory. This is for your birthday, remember?"

I shake my head again and still let her pull me down the sidewalk. "No, going to the fight is for my birthday. This is simply one of your harebrained schemes. I'm still not convinced you're not fucking with me."

She stops again and looks up at me. "Silas, I like fucking with you. It's really fun, but this is not something I would do to fuck with you. I'm pretty sure you're my best friend, too. I want to do this with you. Be reckless with me, huh?"

The sincerity of her words twists something in my chest and I find myself nodding. "Okay. Let's do it."

She beams up at me and that smile would probably be enough to have her convincing me to rob a bank or steal some crown jewels or do something equally daring and idiotic. That smile is the kind of smile men go to war for. And right this minute, that smile is only for me and I'd love nothing more than to kiss it off her face. But I can't do that. I might never get to do that. So instead, we walk into a tattoo studio.

I rack my brain as we wait, because of course they had an opening for two tattoos at noon on a Friday. Why wouldn't they, right? Jesus, my luck. "You said you already know what you'd pick for me?"

She nods. "Yeah. Why?"

"Because I'm not sure about yours yet. I think I want to go first and get it over with. You know, granted I don't puke or pass out."

She laughs. "You're not going to puke. Can't guarantee you won't pass out, but probably not if you don't get it on your ribs or something."

I frown. "You have one on your ribs."

She nods. "Yeah, but they're over scars, I don't really have any feeling on those."

"Oh, right. Okay, so where would you suggest I get mine?"

She leans her hip against the counter and her eyes scan my body. And even though I'm completely clothed, this seems like a very intimate appraisal and my cheeks begin to heat the longer she looks at me. *Stop it, Silas. She's not "looking". She's an artist, looking at a canvas. The fact that* you *are the canvas changes nothing. It's critical and analytical looking, nothing more,* I tell myself. She pulls my left arm away from my body and touches the inside of my left bicep with her index finger. "Here." She spreads her thumb and index finger across the skin as if to show me how big she'd have them do it.

I can only nod, my heart racing. A moment later, the artist, a guy named Brick, gestures for us to come into the room and he glances from Ada to me. "Who's first?"

I sigh. "I guess that would be me."

"And y'all are sure about this blind thing? You realize there are no refunds, right? And I'm not responsible if y'all break up over this."

Ada nods. "Yeah, we're good."

I blink rapidly because I didn't expect her to skate right past the "break up" part of his spiel. She simply pulls out her phone and swipes to something and shows it to the artist, not allowing me to see it.

"And where do you want it?" he asks me.

I point to where Ada indicated I should put it since this is always going to be her tattoo. Regardless of the fact it's on my body, this is hers. He considers. "Okay, yeah. We can do that." He glances at Ada. "Email it to me and I'll print out the stencil." Turning his gaze back to me, he says, "Pull your arm out of your shirt and you'll stretch it out horizontal."

I nod. "Okay."

Five minutes later, he returns and I pull my arm out of my shirt, letting it bunch around my neck and drape over my chest.

I stretch my arm out how he'd instructed and try to relax. Ada sits to my right and smiles. "Okay, Ass, you can't look. Not until he's done. So I guess you're stuck looking at me for the next hour."

Yeah, because that's a hardship. "If you say so, Peep."

CHAPTER EIGHTEEN

ADA

I knew as soon as I suggested the tattoos, Silas would freak out. He's terrified of needles. Always has been. But I'd hoped he'd cave for me and I'm glad to see he was willing to do it. I have no clue what he'll pick for me, but I truly hope he likes his. I'm not sure if I'll ever tell him I sketched it or if he'll even know simply by looking.

Even as the buzzing of the tattoo gun fills the room and he tries to breathe through the sting, he still doesn't look. He keeps his gaze focused on me. And honestly, his is a nice gaze. He has a small nick on his chin where he recently cut himself shaving and as he breathes, his abs move and somehow, I've never noticed how nice those abs are. Granted, I know he makes his living off making sure he stays in good shape, but damn.

"So," I say, in an attempt to distract him. "What's the deal with UFC?"

He frowns. "What do you mean?"

"Why do you think Cole would pick it? I don't watch UFC."

"What did his letter say?"

"Just that we'd be going out on the town for a wild night. I thought maybe the *Magic Mike* show or one of those magic shows or something. You know, something Vegas-y."

Silas snorts at my *Magic Mike* comment. "Yeah, I can totally see him sending you to something like that."

I shrug. "Well, why not? I can appreciate a good-looking male form. How's it any different than guys going to strip clubs or burlesque shows?"

"I guess it's not," he admits. "And if you really wanted to go see some shameless display of man candy, I'm sure we'd have time to do it."

I shake my head. "Nah, I'm good. Aren't those fighters usually pretty fit? I can just watch them roll around and get all sweaty. It'll be like that time you and Cole got into it when you were sixteen at the farm. I don't even remember what it was about, but you were both shirtless and sweaty and decided to slug it out. Not going to lie, it was pretty hot."

He chuckles, color coming to his cheeks. "Yeah, well, he took the good hoe."

I snort. "Nice. First time I've ever been called a hoe before."

His mouth falls open as if I've offended him. "Ada, I didn't—."

I roll my eyes. "Jesus, Ass. It was a joke. Having sex with one person hardly constitutes the 'hoe life' or whatever. I know that. You're probably a bigger hoe than me, not that I'm slut shaming," I say, holding my hands up defensively. "I say, you do you."

His cheeks turn pink and I can see I'm making him uncomfortable. I guess Cole was right and Silas really is shy. He clears his throat and gives me a sheepish smile. "I'm hardly the player you'd imagine, Wednesday."

"Well, I know about Hensley. But surely there were others, right?"

I know if he had his arm free, he'd probably shrug, simply judging by his expression. "A few," he admits, his voice low.

My brows rise in surprise. "A *few*? That's it?"

He swallows, his eyes darting to Brick. "Can we not talk about this right now?"

I roll my own. "Ass, this guy pierces dicks for a living. I'm sure hearing about people's sexual exploits is hardly salacious in the grand scheme of things to him."

Brick stops inking and glances up from his work. "Actually, Diesel is the one who does the dick piercings. I stick to ink."

I huff a laugh. "Okay, whatever. Come on, Silas, you're telling me that since you were, what, seventeen, you've only slept with a few women?"

"Yeah, so? You've only slept with one man."

"Cole and I were in a committed relationship for fifteen years, that's hardly surprising. All I'm saying is, you're a good-looking guy. What's the issue?"

"Yeah, I know you probably think I'm good-looking. You were with Cole, so I would assume you'd think I'm all right. Who's to say there is an issue? What's wrong with me wanting to be in a committed relationship before I'm physical with someone? Some people don't like no-strings sex, you know. Even some men. I'm one of them. There's nothing wrong with that."

"I'm not saying there is, I guess I'm just surprised is all."

"I'm not sure why. In all the time you've known me, have you ever seen me with anyone? You know, aside from Hen. Which, if we can forget that was ever a thing, I'd appreciate it."

"No, I guess I didn't. But to be fair, it wasn't like we were braiding each other's hair on the weekends. I was kinda focused on Cole when I was at your house."

"I know you were. We weren't really friends before this

year, Wednesday, so it's not like I'd spill all my secrets to you. I would now if I had any, but I don't."

"How long have y'all been together?"

Both our heads snap in Brick's direction, but Silas quickly turns his back toward me so he doesn't spoil the reveal of his tattoo. "We're not," we say at the same time.

Surprise and confusion spark in the artist's eyes. "Coulda fooled me."

I don't really feel like getting into the complicated history and dragging everything out for a complete stranger, only to see that look of pity in his eyes when he finds out I'm a quasi-widow. "We're just friends," Silas says with a small smile aimed at me. "Best friends, actually."

"So, who's the Cole guy?" Nosy Nelly, the artist, asks.

"My twin brother," he supplies and I'm surprised he'd offer up the information.

"And after the breakup, y'all are just hanging out? How does your brother feel about that?"

I look down at my hands, willing a hole to open up below my chair and swallow me. Silas brings his free hand up and gives mine a squeeze and I look at him. "Not a breakup," he says softly. The buzzing stops for a second while the artist glances from me to Silas before resuming his work. "I'm just taking care of his girl since he can't anymore." Unexpected tears burn my eyes and I blink them away. "Okay, Peep?"

I nod and blow out a slow breath. "Yeah."

Things are quiet after that, only the sound of the gun and the occasional sharp inhale from Silas when the needle hits a tender spot. About a half-hour later, the artist rinses the area and applies some ointment. "All done."

Silas looks at me. "Can I see? How is it?"

I stand from my seat and lean over to peer at the perfect

picture of the heron I sketched. I give him a wide grin. "It's awesome. Look at it."

He examines it, his mouth falling open in surprise. "Is that a heron? Ada, it's perfect." He looks at it more closely, an expression of awe filling his face and warming my heart. "This is one of your drawings, isn't it?" he asks, already knowing the answer.

Pleased he'd recognize my work, I nod. "Yeah. When we were at the farm last time, there was one down by the creek and I sketched it. I knew if you ever let me talk you into getting a tattoo, I wanted it to be that."

"I love it." He turns to Brick. "It's amazing. Thank you so much."

The artist nods in appreciation and turns to me. "So, your turn?"

I nod. "Yeah, as long as Ass here knows what I'm getting."

Silas grins. "Oh, I know exactly what you're getting."

Brick takes a moment to cover the fresh tattoo with a bandage and they step out of the room and I take a seat in the chair.

Ten minutes later, they return and he looks at me. "Where's it going?" I ask.

Silas examines my torso, his warm brown eyes making a slow sweep downward and for the first time in the twenty-plus years I've known him, something like appreciation flickers in his gaze. It's as if he likes what he sees when he looks at me. I recognize it because I've seen it before. In Cole. When I'd be across the room and I knew his eyes were on me, slowly taking in my form and the knowledge I was his. My brain glitches for a split second and I blink rapidly. When I focus my attention back on Silas's face, passive indifference and consideration are there instead. Surely I imagined that, right?

Still, my heart seems to have decided my body is in dire

need of more blood and pumps furiously. Silas points at my left hip. "So you can keep it covered if you want."

I nod and swallow, my mouth suddenly going dry. Brick taps my side. "You'll have to lose the shorts."

I shrug, knowing I'm not that modest a person and stand and unbutton my cutoffs. Silas's eyes go wide and he quickly turns around. I'm both amused by and curious about his expression and I can't help but laugh, in spite of how caught off guard I was by his earlier appraisal. "What, did you think he'd be able to ink me through my shorts, Ass? You're the one who picked the spot."

I step out of my shorts and hear him blow out a quick breath as I lie on my right side and try to get comfortable. "I guess I didn't think about it," he says, his voice a bit unsure. He still faces away from me and I roll my eyes.

"Sit down, Silas. You're supposed to keep me company, not abandon me in my time of need."

He faces me, his eyes only on my face and I want to laugh. "What, are you suddenly shy?"

He narrows his eyes. "I am shy, Peep."

I nod as Brick cleans the area and applies the stencil after yanking the side of my panties up my waist and out of the way, giving me a massive wedgie. But I keep that to myself, lest Silas has some sort of fainting spell.

"I know you are." I feel the stencil paper peel away and I shift my arm under my head. "So, why UFC, you never did say earlier."

He frowns. "What do you mean?"

"Why do you think Cole would plan for us to watch a fight? I've never seen one." The gun starts to buzz and a second later, the needle drags across my skin, the sting immediate and bringing back memories of my last tattoo. I breathe through the burn and focus my attention on Silas.

"Really?" He thinks for a minute. "Yeah, I guess anytime he and I have watched them, they've always been at my place. What else did the letter say?"

I think back. "Just that we were going out on the town and it might get kinda wild. He said you'd really enjoy this one, too, so it might be more for you. That he hoped it'd be okay if one of my tasks was more for you. That maybe I'd learn more about something you liked."

He scratches his chin absentmindedly. "Well, he wasn't wrong. I'm definitely going to enjoy this. I love to watch the fights. But, for real, you've never watched?"

I shake my head. "I guess his timing was good, too, huh? Since it's so close to your birthday?"

He shrugs. "Maybe. Does it bother you if this task might be more for me?"

I give him a genuine smile. "No. I think it's good. He's put all this work into making sure I have closure. But what about you? You're pretty much his proxy in all this. Something should be for you, right? I wish I had something like all this to give to you." And I realize my words are true. Silas is carrying out these grand schemes on Cole's behalf, hoping to help me through my grief. But what does he get in return?

Silas shakes his head. "Honestly, seeing you laugh and smile again when I wasn't even sure it would happen, that goes a long way for me, Wednesday. Those first few weeks were terrifying watching you not talk or function."

I nod, remembering. "They were pretty scary for me, too. I wasn't sure I wanted to be around anymore."

"I know. But I'm glad you are."

"Me, too."

He grins, glancing down at my hip and his smile grows even wider. "Damn, that looks good."

I huff a laugh. "What, the ink or my nearly bare ass hanging out for all the world to see?"

He chuckles. "Both."

I roll my eyes. "Nice."

Twenty minutes later, as I'm about to start dozing off, the gun stops buzzing and Brick cleanses the area and applies ointment. I glance up at Silas. "Well, how does it look?" And much like when I examined his, he leans over and assesses the art, an approving smile pulling at the corners of his mouth.

"It's great."

I twist my body to look at it and my intake of breath is quick. A giggle bubbles up in my throat and I shake my head. "You're right, it is." It's a pair of black braided pigtails with a defined center part above a Peter Pan collar. "Wednesday, huh?"

"I didn't want to go too overboard, just a nod to Wednesday Addams."

"I love it, Silas." And I do. It's not something I would've picked for myself, but knowing that's been Silas's nickname for me since I was ten years old, it's pretty fitting. Brick covers it with a bandage and I gingerly don my shorts before we head to the checkout. I knock Silas out of the way when he attempts to pay. "No, this is my birthday gift to you. You will let me do this."

He narrows his eyes but finally relents and I hand over my credit card. Shortly before we head out the door, the artist goes over the aftercare instructions with us and gives us each a second-skin bandage to apply after twenty-four hours.

"So, what now?" I ask. "We're free birds until we have to get ready to go watch the fights tomorrow night, right?"

Silas nods. "Yeah. I don't know about you, but I'm pretty hungry. Want to grab some food and then go check into the hotel?"

"Sounds good to me."

After burgers and shakes a couple of blocks down from the tattoo studio, we make our way to the Venetian hotel and once we figure out the parking situation at a nearby garage, we tote our bags toward the entrance of the hotel. Silas glances at me, suddenly seeming nervous. "I tried to get adjoining rooms, but all they had was a double. There are apparently a lot of concerts and shows going on right now, in addition to the fights."

I huff a laugh. "Well, it's Vegas, so I'm surprised you were able to get us somewhere this nice on what was probably pretty short notice. It's fine. We stayed in the RV just fine. Will it be two beds, you think, or only one?"

He blinks rapidly as if the thought hadn't occurred to him and he opens and closes his mouth. I'm not sure how to take his expression, so I resort to my default where Silas is concerned: giving him shit. "What's with your face? Afraid if we had to share a bed I couldn't keep my hands to myself?" He huffs a tense laugh and color rises to his cheeks and again, I'm not sure how I'm supposed to interpret the look on his face. "Seriously, Silas, are you about to have a fit? You don't look well."

He clears his throat and drags his fingers through his hair. "No, I'm fine. I'm sure it's two beds. It'd be unusual if it wasn't, right?"

"Yeah, I guess," I say, without much conviction. I'm not sure how I'd feel about it. I shouldn't care about stuff like that, right? I shouldn't even think about what it might be like to share a bed with Silas. It's absurd. He's Silas. Ass. My reluctant best friend. Cole's favorite person.

I think back on Cole's letter about this trip. *Don't let on, but this trip is all for Si. I hope that's okay with you, Ada Mae. He would never do something like this for himself. But he would for you. Maybe do something reckless while y'all are gone, too.*

Finally convince Silas to get a tattoo. Do a blind one. You know, the kind I was never carefree enough to allow us to get. If I know y'all, you'll pick out the perfect one for each other. I have a feeling you know him better than you think. He knows you better than you think, too. Remember that, babe.

Let him blow off some steam and be free. Watch him watch the fights. His eyes light up like a kid at Christmas. It's pretty cool.

I hope you and Si are becoming good friends. I told you he was a good friend to have. I hope y'all will be best friends. Because even though he's a great friend, he's an even better best friend. He's someone you can trust with your life. I hope you can see what a good man he is. Under the asshole. Under that crunchy coating.

Why does Cole keep telling me what a good man Silas is? I already know that. It's almost as if—. My thoughts are interrupted by Silas's hand on my arm. "Come on, Wednesday, we're next."

"Oh. Right," I respond, shaking the thoughts from my mind. The out-there, preposterous, impossible thoughts.

CHAPTER NINETEEN

SILAS

I'm more than a bit relieved to see that it's two beds. I don't know if I would've been able to stand having to share a bed with Ada. It could be the biggest bed in existence and with the knowledge I was in it with her—only me and her—I wouldn't have survived it. As we make our way up to the room, she's quiet and contemplative. "What's the matter, Peep? Regretting the tattoo already?"

She gives me a soft smile. "Never. I told you. I love it. Is yours all right?"

My eyes widen. "Are you kidding? It's fucking fantastic. And you drew it, how could I not love it?"

A pleasant blush creeps into her cheeks and she nods. "I hoped you would. I thought, what with the nests at the cabin and then that one being from the farm, it could have a double meaning."

"Like I said, it's perfect. I couldn't have picked anything better. Have you ever designed tattoos before?"

She shakes her head. "No, but for all I know, someone has

turned one of my pieces into inspiration. It'd be really cool to get some commissions for tattoos, though. I'd love that."

"So, what would you like to do tonight?"

"Up to you. This is your rodeo, remember?"

I consider. "Well, Cole left us some money to gamble. There's always that."

She nods. "Always an option. Are you any good at black-jack or craps or anything?"

I snort a laugh. "I was thinking more along the lines of nickel slots."

She grins. "Okay, we can do that." We make it to our door and I swipe the key to unlock it and turn the handle and push. "They have shopping and clubs and stuff, too, right?"

A club? Me? Not likely. And Ada must see it in my face because she laughs. "Yeah, I know, no clubs. Not your thing." She glances around. "Wow, this room is huge. Even with the two beds, it's got a sunken living area. This is awesome. And look at this view." She walks over to the window to take in the expansive view of the city with the desert and mountains in the distance. I'm sure it all looks beautiful at night with the lights of the strip but all I can see is her. Even if I shouldn't.

"We could hit one of the nice restaurants," I offer. "You brought both those great dresses. Shame to let them go to waste."

She peers over her shoulder at me. "That might be all right." She resumes looking out the window. "You think we'd have time before we leave on Sunday to spread Cole's ashes out in the desert?" Her eyes light up. "Or, maybe over Hoover Dam?"

"Now that, I think he could get behind. I like that idea. We could do it tonight if you want. Or tomorrow during the day. We've got time."

"All right. Tomorrow?"

"Sure, Peep. So, do you want to go to one of the restaurants tonight? I can make a reservation."

"Okay."

She's still looking out the window and her tone has turned wistful, so I walk over to her and touch her arm. "You okay?"

She looks at me, a sad smile on her face. "This is something you should be doing with Cole. I feel like I'm intruding on something that was only for y'all."

I stick my hands in my pockets and shrug. "That's how I've felt with a lot of these tasks. Like it's not my place. Not that I haven't enjoyed them, don't get me wrong."

She huffs a laugh and raises one brow skeptically. "Oh, really? You enjoyed the beach?"

I shake my head. "No. I didn't, you're right. Not sure it was much fun for you, either." She shakes her head as well. "But the other stuff; the rage room and the goats, those have been nice. I know it's this entirely bittersweet thing. To think he should be here, either with us or instead of one of us. But honestly, I'm happy to share this with you, Ada. I meant what I said, you've become my best friend and I like getting to make these memories with you." I look down at my tattoo. "I would've never gotten a tattoo for anyone else, just so you know."

She smiles and it's small and sweet and makes my heart ache. "I know. And I'm not sorry I get to do this stuff with you. I have fun with you and I like giving you shit. I wish we could have been friends before now. I'm just sorry it took Cole dying before we could get along."

I swallow and look down at my shoes and nod. "Me, too." Although, it couldn't have been that way. Simply because I couldn't stand it. As much as I loved them both, I couldn't watch them be all lovey-dovey without being at least buzzed. And that made me be snarky and sullen and it's no wonder she thought I was an asshole all those years.

She returns her gaze to the city, as if she needs to look at something other than me. "Why do you think Cole wanted it to be you who did all this stuff with me? You know, aside from you being his brother. He could've given the tasks to Josie. She's my best friend, too. She would've made sure I followed through. He told me it was because aside from him, you knew him better than anyone. And I get that. But Josie knew him, too. He also said it was because your schedule was flexible enough to allow this. But everything we've done has been on the weekends. Josie could've made that work.

"I'm, in no way, saying I wish she was here instead of you. Please don't think that. But it just seems as though he deliberately chose you. Even though you and I fought like cats and dogs. Still fight like cats and dogs sometimes. It seems like he keeps pushing us together. He said he hopes I get to know you; what a good man you are. I know you're a good man, Silas."

She opens her mouth and closes it and the entire time she's been speaking, my heart is beating triple time, nervous for her to ask questions I don't know how to answer without revealing everything. Because I don't think she's ready to hear it all. It's only been four months. There's no way she's ready to have me split my heart open for her after only four months.

She shakes her head as if she's saying no or is in disbelief about something and then sighs. "I'm just confused, I guess. I get him wanting us to be there for each other; lean on each other following his death. I truly get that. But it seems like there's more to it than that.

"And a lot of this doesn't add up. All this planning. All this thought was put into what should've never occurred to him. I understand wanting to take care of me. His life insurance has been helpful, no doubt about it. It's allowed me to focus on my grief and not *have* to work. But even for a planner like Cole, this is a lot. And I know we were together for a long time, but I just don't understand how he could've thrown all this together. It would probably take years."

I know this is the part where I could tell her about his HCM. I could tell her what Cole kept from her all those years. Selfishly, though, I don't want to ruin this weekend. Selfishly, I want to enjoy this time I have with her. And fuck, does wanting to enjoy it make my stomach ache with the guilt. But today, the selfishness wins out. So instead, I keep my mouth shut and simply let her verbalize.

She shrugs. "Maybe it was his final way of showing everyone how much of a know-it-all he was. All these amazing plans and ideas he'd put forth. Lord knows he'd be real proud of himself for pulling all this off. I just wish he'd thought to do any of this while he was alive. Why put it off?"

"I can't answer that," I say honestly.

"What's your best guess?" she asks, turning to me. Her gray eyes are searching and I know she'll see through a lie because I've never been able to lie to her. Not even when we were kids.

I swallow. "My best guess? As to why he'd do all this?" She nods, still not taking her eyes from mine. "We were his favorite people, Ada. He wanted us to take care of each other; find some common ground, maybe. It would seem we're more alike than either of us probably ever thought. Maybe he saw that and knew we'd actually be good friends. I'm not sorry, though. Whatever happens, I'll never say I regret anything that's happened since we started spending time together."

I blow out a breath, my chest tightening with emotion. "I miss Cole every single day. I miss his stupid trivia and the way he always wanted to correct my grammar and knew the Latin name for every plant every fucking time we went to the garden shop. I miss having him to bitch about work with. I miss having him to bounce ideas off of." The tears well in my eyes and I know she sees them and I don't even try to stop them. "I miss how he had Mom and Dad's Christmas gifts planned in January. I miss the way he'd talk about how much he loved you. I miss watching his eyes light up when you'd come into a room. God, he loved you so fucking much, Ada. You have no idea."

Tears fill her own eyes and I don't trust myself to close the distance between us because if I do that, I'll reach for her and I'm not sure I can do that and not crush her to me.

"I don't know why he's done things the way he did; what went through his mind. I only know I made a promise to look after you and make sure you were okay. And he was my brother and best friend and I would've promised him anything he ever wanted. Especially when it came to you because he loved you." The words I can't say sit bitterly in my mouth, even as Ada throws herself against me, her tears turning into sobs. I wrap my arms around her, not caring about the stinging pain as my tattoo presses against her upper arm.

I simply hold her and wish I could tell her how I feel; how I've always felt. But I can't do that. I might never get to do that. So I simply rub what I hope are soothing circles on her back as her tears soak through my tee-shirt. I sniff and wipe my eyes with my thumb. "I didn't mean to upset you, Wednesday. I'm sorry."

She shakes her head as she pulls away, wiping her own eyes. "No, I'm sorry. I didn't mean to get all analytical about everything. I just wish I had answers."

"I know you do." I rub her arms supportively and give her a soft smile and I'm struck with a thought. "Can I propose a new plan for tonight, instead of going to a fancy restaurant?"

She nods. "This is your weekend. We can do whatever you want."

"How about this, we put on our pajamas later, order ridiculous amounts of room service, and raid the mini bar. We find a cheesy movie we hate and relentlessly rag on it until we both feel better."

She chews on the inside of her bottom lip. "Sounds like a plan."

And so, that's exactly what we do. Even before the sun has set in Vegas, we're both in our comfy clothes lamenting the jet lag likely to set in tomorrow. We order room service pizza, burgers, and ice cream and a six-pack of beer, and a bottle of wine. And although we're unsuccessful in finding a terrible movie, there is a late-nineties rom-com marathon of sorts on one channel and we settle in to watch.

By nine local time, Ada is barely holding her eyes open. She's really buzzed from the bottle of wine and keeps leaning on my shoulder. And not that I mind, but I'm not sure this is something I can get used to, and don't want to even know what it's like if I don't get to keep it. "Why don't you go to bed, Peep?"

"Because we're still watching this. I'm good. I can rally."

I snort a laugh as I down the rest of my beer. "Yeah right, you're practically drooling on my arm in between snores." I stand and tug her up. "Come on, I'll tuck you in."

"Ooh, a tuck-in," she says with a sleepy smile, her words barely slurring.

I guide her up the few steps to where the beds are located and she stumbles a bit, possibly more drunk than I thought. I pull her covers down and she falls into the bed and I tug the blankets up around her shoulders and look at her face. Her eyes are closed, so I can examine her without worrying about her catching me.

Her hand comes up to my jaw and I nearly startle from the touch. "You're not Cole, Silas." I'm unsure of her meaning and I open my mouth to agree, but she's not done speaking. "Your laugh is different from his. Cole was careful. I don't think you'd be careful."

I sweep her hair off her face. "What do you mean, Wednesday?"

"You pulled me into the river. I liked it. Cole would've never pulled me into the river."

"He would have worried about hurting you if he pulled you in."

"Yeah. Sometimes, I think he kept things from me because he thought they might hurt me. Do you keep things from me, Silas?"

A weight falls into my stomach. "Not if I can help it."

"Okay. You have really nice abs."

I huff a laugh. "Thanks. You have a nice ass."

"I know."

"I'm sure you do. Go to sleep, okay?"

"All right."

And because I can't help myself, I turn my face and press a kiss to her palm before pulling it from my jaw and laying it next to her on the bed. I watch her sleep for a few minutes before heading back down to the living area and cleaning up our supper mess. I make sure the curtains are closed and go brush my teeth and fall into my own bed.

I roll onto my side and even in the near pitch dark, I can make out Ada's form in her bed. She's snoring softly and my heart aches to be able to curl up next to her. To wrap my body around hers and feel her own heavy with sleep. To smell her skin and plant a kiss under her ear.

It was easy to love her from afar when she belonged to Cole; when he was here. And in a lot of ways, she still very much belongs to Cole. And his presence, even if not physical, is still very much felt. But without his substantial physical presence keeping my own urges tamped down, it's becoming increasingly more difficult to not reach for her or hug her for more than simple comfort or friendship. To do it because I want to. To press a kiss to the top of her head as she rests her cheek on my chest, her arms wrapped around my waist. But lord knows I don't give myself permission to think past simple hugs or affectionate embraces. I don't dare. Not yet. Not until I'm sure it's something I'm allowed to want.

CHAPTER TWENTY

ADA

A large hand snakes under my shirt and up to cup my breast. I arch into the touch as a thumb grazes my nipple, making it tighten painfully, a soft moan falling from my lips. I roll to face the broad chest, pressing kisses down a solid wall of muscles. Still sleepy, I relish the feel of the hands skimming over my hip to possessively grip my ass and pull me into him.

"God, Ada. This ass. Fuck."

I let my own hands roam down the strong chest and abs, the narrow hips, and muscular ass. "You're one to talk. Damn."

A low, rumbly chuckle warms the skin on my ear and neck and an impressive hardness nudges against my inner thigh. I part my thighs, pulling him closer, and hook my leg around his waist. He thrusts into me, the aching fullness so far beyond sinful, I gasp.

He rolls us until I'm below him and claims my mouth as he continues to drive into me, my heart racing. I rock my hips, needing him deeper and his kiss is hungry and searching and contains so much longing, my heart aches. When I'm so short of breath I'm nearly lightheaded, I pull back.

"So fucking good," he says with a groan and I smile, my hands coming to rest on a chest. A chest with no tattoos.

Confused, I scan the face above me. Warm brown eyes, a cocky grin, and messy, light-brown hair. He presses his lips to mine and it's good. God, it's good. But something's different. I let my eyes trail down his arm and they catch on a tattoo. Not of a compass, but a heron.

I gasp and sit bolt upright and frantically try to think. The aching pulse between my thighs reminds me it was only a dream and I try to breathe, my nipples straining painfully against the fabric of my sports bra. My neck and chest are damp with perspiration and my heart pounds in my chest. What. The. Fuck. I hazard a glance at the other side of my bed, and sure enough, I'm alone.

A thin stream of light peeks around the curtains and it's just enough to make out the form in the other bed. Thankfully, Silas is still sleeping. As if my vagina senses I've looked at the man I've just dreamt about, warmth spreads low in my belly. Not that I needed the reminder that only moments ago, I had a very graphic, very realistic sex dream about him.

I fall back onto the bed, my head swimming with confusion, while my body buzzes with blatant need. It would only take about ten seconds to get myself off, wound up as I am. Probably less, if I'm honest. Can I do it with Silas in the other bed? Jesus, what's wrong with me?

Uh, how about it's been months since you got laid? You're only one woman. So you had a dream about Silas, it doesn't mean anything. Just do it. You'll feel better. If you don't, you're going to be all squirrelly and he's going to notice something's up with you.

I slide my hand under the covers and into my sleep shorts and panties. The moment my fingers press into my clit, I sigh. I glance over at Silas, simply to ensure he's still out and he hasn't moved. What if he wakes up before I get off? Or worse, while I'm coming? As if spurred only by some primal need, my fingers seem to move of their own accord, working my clit in steady circles. Within seconds, my breathing is shallow, but I manage to stay quiet.

I should probably be ashamed I still have my eyes on Silas, but fuck, I don't even care anymore. The only thing I care about is needing to get off in the next ten seconds. And when my orgasm explodes, I have to clamp my mouth shut to keep from crying out with the intense pleasure. My heart threatens to burst from my chest and I take several ragged breaths as I come down.

But then, the guilt immediately crashes into me and tears burn my eyes. What the hell was I thinking? I love Cole, why the hell would I dream about Silas? *Because, Ada Mae, Silas is there. I'm not.* I nearly choke with Cole's imagined words and a sob wells up in my throat and I clutch the pillow to me and cry.

"Ada?"

The sound of Silas's sleepy voice makes me cry that much harder and I jump from the bed and rush into the bathroom and lock the door. I lean back against it and slide down until my ass hits the floor.

"Ada? Are you okay?"

"I'm fine."

"No, you're not. What's wrong?"

"Go away, Silas. Please. I just need to be alone." My words come out between sobs.

"I can't do that." I hear his voice, close, even through the door. He must be leaning against the other side, possibly sitting on the floor, same as me. "Want to talk about it?"

Absolutely fucking not. "No."

"Did you have a bad dream?"

"No." Because in all honesty, it wasn't a bad dream.

Unnerving and jarring and confusing, maybe, but not *bad*. "I just miss Cole." And I do. Except that's not why I'm crying. I feel as though I cheated on him. Even if it's not possible, it still feels that way.

"Yeah, I know you do, Wednesday. I'm sure us talking about him last night made you miss him worse. I'm sorry if anything I said made it harder on you." It sounds like he thinks what he shared is what caused me to "miss Cole" and have a breakdown. I definitely don't want him to think he can't share his grief with me. I want him to talk to me.

"No, it wasn't that. I appreciated you sharing with me. I want you to be able to talk, to share when things are hard for you, too, Silas."

"Okay, I will. I appreciate you listening to me."

My tears have turned into sniffles and I wipe my eyes. "I'm sorry I woke you up."

"It's all right. It's almost ten at home, so we actually slept really late. Probably needed to get up anyway. Want me to order breakfast in a little while? Coffee?"

"Okay," I answer softly.

He gently taps on the door. "Take as long as you need. I'm out here if you want to talk."

I can rationalize in my mind all day long that nothing actually happened between Silas and me. But if I dreamed about it, does that mean I want it to, even subconsciously? I could argue not, since I've dreamt about riding a giant ant like in *Honey, I Shrunk the Kids* and the idea of that is fucking terrifying. So, it's probably simple lack of sex and his proximity, right? Right. That's all it is.

I blow out a breath and rise from the floor. I pee and wash my hands and splash water on my face. I look at myself in the mirror, wondering if it looks like I just had an orgasm. My face is flushed, but that can easily be explained away by the crying.

And I suppose, other than that, there are no outward physical signs I came so hard I nearly saw stars.

I can act cool, right? I can pretend I didn't dream about Silas's hands all over my body, his mouth on mine, his hard, thick—. *Stop it, Ada. Shit.* I nearly want to smack myself. I count to ten in my head and attempt to regulate my breathing. When I feel as though I'm more normal, I open the door and step out of the bathroom, only to be greeted by the sight of a shirtless Silas standing at the window. He looks out over the city, his phone held up to his ear.

I guess since his back is to me, it can't hurt to look, right? I can look at the defined muscles of his lats and traps. His ass— even in the pajama pants he wears—is like two perfect, round globes. What would it be like to run my hands—. *Fuck. Stop, Ada. Get it together.* I shake the thoughts from my head. Again, I mentally count to ten. I think of having gnarly food poisoning that traps you in the bathroom for days. Or the yeast infection I got in college that made me want to literally remove my vagina and destroy it. Or the time I had an ingrown hair in my bikini line that oozed so much puss and blood, I thought I'd throw up. *Yep. That'll do it.*

I can't hear Silas on the phone, but I can tell by the tension in his shoulders, something's wrong. I immediately walk over and put my hand on his arm and he snaps his eyes to mine, his brow furrowed. "Dad, I'll have to call you back, okay?" He listens for a second and drags his fingers through his hair. "Yeah, I know. Our flight is tomorrow. We'll be back around three. I'll go as soon as we get back." His eyes close in frustration at something Miles is saying. "There aren't any flights until tomorrow. Not without a shit ton of layovers and costing three times as much as I've already paid for this one... No, it's not about the money. He's stable. I talked to him. He's giving the doctors and nurses hell and he already told me not to come back until tomorrow. If I show up there, he's going to want to beat my ass. And frankly, Dad, I'm more scared of him than I am of you."

I know something's happened to Pap and my stomach knots up. Silas examines my face. "Dad, I'm sorry, but I have to go. I'll see you tomorrow." He doesn't wait for a response and disconnects the call.

"What's wrong with Pap?" I ask, my tone panicked.

He brings his hands up and squeezes my shoulders. "He fell. They think his hip is broken. He stumbled over a chair because of his damn cataracts and took a spill. He called Mom and Dad and they rushed him to the hospital. They berated him and treated him like a child and I'm so angry I can't see straight. It's not like he's stupid or incapable or lost his marbles. But I talked to him. I told him we'd come home, but he said I better not. And you heard what I told Dad, right?" I nod. "But he's going to be fine. Get that worried look off your face."

I try to give him a smile, but I'm unsuccessful. Silas bends down until we're at eye level. "He's going to be fine, Ada. I'll go see him tomorrow when we get home." All I can think is, *I just lost Cole, I can't lose Pap, too.* "Stop thinking that. He's going to be fine." Silas's tone is harsh and I snap my eyes to his, his dark brows pressed together in anger. Or, more likely, fear. "Don't you dare think what I know you were just thinking. I can read it on your face plain as day. This is not the same thing at all. He's fine."

I nod. "Okay. Yeah. He's Pap. He's too stubborn to let something like this keep him down, right?"

Silas gives me a tight smile. "That's right."

With his hands still on my shoulders, his arms are extended. And even though it's covered by a bandage, the vivid image of a heron tattoo flashes in my mind and my breath catches. Silas gives me a gentle shake. "What's with your face,

Wednesday? You look like you're having trouble breathing. I already told you, Pap's going to be fine."

I nod and back out of his grip. "I know. I'm just a bit out of sorts, I guess. Emotional morning and all that."

His expression softens. "I know. I'm sorry. I'll order breakfast, okay? And we get to change our bandages around noon, right? And I can shower?"

Thankful to have something else to think about, I answer, "You can shower now. It'll actually help remove the original bandage. Then once you get out, it needs to air dry and you can put on the other one."

"Oh, in that case, I'm going to grab a shower right after I order the food. When I get out, would you care to help me put on the other bandage, so I don't mess it up?"

I nod. "Sure."

"And if you want me to help you put yours on, I can. You know, so it doesn't get any air bubbles. Might be kinda hard for you to do it yourself."

The image of me with no pants on and Silas's hand on my hip, his face in close proximity, flashes in my mind. *Sweet Jesus, this has to stop.* I blink rapidly. Silas says my name and concern laces his expression. "Seriously, are you okay?"

I clear my throat. "Yeah. Fine."

He nods, still unconvinced and grabs his toiletry bag and some clothes and steps into the bathroom. Unsure what to do at this moment, I do the only thing I can: text Josie.

I know I can't give her all the details, or even that the dream was about Silas, but she can at least help me work through my thoughts about it.

> Ada: I need to talk through something.

Almost immediately, my phone vibrates with a response.

Josie: What's going on? You need me to call?
Where's Si? He can't help? Y'all are together,
right?

I roll my eyes at all her questions, although I shouldn't have
been surprised, with how little I gave her.

Ada: Can't talk about this with Silas. Can't
call since he's in the room. I had a dream last
night.

Josie: Okay... What kind of dream? One of
those where you're in front of class naked
and have to give a speech? I hate those.

Ada: Not that kind of naked dream, Jos.
Except, it wasn't Cole. It was someone else
and I felt like I cheated and I felt sick when I
woke up.

The three dots bounce for several seconds as she formulates
her response.

Josie: Okay, for the sake of this argument,
we're going to pretend Cole wasn't my
brother, because EWW. So, have you had
dreams like this before?

Ada: Well, yeah, but it's always Cole. Until
this one.

Josie: Since he died, you've had dreams
about him?

Ada: No. I haven't had any kind of libido or anything since he died. I was too depressed for the most part, I think. Last night/this morning—whenever, is the first one I've had since before he died. And this is the first time I've had any desire to… help myself.

Josie: Okay, well, first of all, this is probably a good thing. It means your system is returning to normal. You're not 80, Ada. You're a woman in the prime of her life. And simply because you lost the man you love doesn't mean all those needs you have are going to vanish for the rest of your life. It's been months since you've gotten any. I'm sure you're a bit… tense. And you didn't cheat. Jesus. Cole died. He's not off at war or working a job. He's not coming back. He wouldn't want you to be miserable forever and you know that. It's why he sent you and Si off on all these quests. Even if you did end up sleeping with someone, it wouldn't be cheating. Even if you fell in love, it wouldn't be cheating. I know he was my brother and he loved you until the day he died, but you cannot stop your life simply because he's not here to live it with you.

I sigh. Somehow I am both buoyed by her response and still sad.

My phone vibrates again.

Josie: How are things with Si? Are you wanting to toss him off the Hoover Dam yet?

Ada: It's all good. We got tattoos yesterday.

Josie: HOLD THE FUCKING PHONE. Silas got a tattoo? Needle-phobic Silas Fredrick Campbell got a fucking tattoo?

Ada: Yes and he was a total trooper. We
went in blind. I picked his and he picked
mine.

Josie: Shut the front door. I cannot
comprehend this. Pictures or it didn't happen.
I demand evidence, ASAP.

I can't help but laugh at how excited she is. A knock sounds at the front door and I rise to check the peephole before opening the door and rolling in the room service cart. I start to pick up my purse to fish out some cash for a tip and Silas comes over, money already in his hand. He puts his free hand on my back as he extends the tip. "I've got it, Peep."

Has he always been this *touchy*? And granted, I'm a hugger. I love snuggling and holding hands and casual intimacy. But I don't know what to do about touches from Silas. Even as he steps back and his hand drops, it's as if my body chases the touch because I subconsciously lean back as he pulls his hand away. What the fuck is wrong with me?

When I turn to look at Silas, he's still not wearing a shirt. Did he suddenly sign some sort of contract with some unknown force who told him he must be shirtless twenty-three hours a day? Why do his abs have to look like that?

"What?"

Fuck. Did I say something out loud? The color drains from my face and I swallow. "What?"

Silas huffs a confused laugh. "You said something about abs, but I didn't catch all of it."

I blink rapidly, trying to come up with some sort of explanation. "I had one of those old *8-Minute Abs* infomercials in my brain for some reason. I hated those things."

He nods, his expression skeptical. "Okay. So, do you think you can put my bandage on? And does this look normal, it's really red." He holds out the bandage to me and extends his arm, exposing that damn heron.

I glance at it, trying not to look anywhere but at his arm. "Did you wash it like the guy told us?"

"Yeah. And it itches really bad."

I nod. "That's normal. And it looks fine. Some redness is normal. Put your arm like this," I instruct, demonstrating to show him to position it as if his fingers are laced behind his head so I'll have the best angle to apply the bandage. When he does, I make quick work of putting on the bandage. "All done."

"Thanks. You going to take a shower now?" he asks as he tugs a tee-shirt over his head.

I nod. "Yeah. If I need help with the bandage, I'll let you know."

"Sure. I'll wait on you to eat."

"It's okay. Go ahead," I say, dismissing his offer.

"Ada, I'm not going to eat without you. Go shower. This'll keep. And if we're going to go to Hoover Dam, we'll need to get a move on."

"Okay."

My tone must come across as snarky or something because his brows press together in confusion. "Are you all right? Are you PMSing or something? You seem awful on edge."

"I'm fine," I say through gritted teeth.

His eyes narrow in suspicion. "Bullshit."

"I don't want to talk about it, okay?"

"You know you can talk to me, though, right? Didn't we say yesterday we were best friends? Best friends talk about stuff."

I huff a quick laugh. "Not about this."

Hurt and confusion flash in his eyes. "Seriously, Ada, what the hell? I thought we were past not talking to each other about stuff that matters. I thought we could tell each other things. Do you think I wanted to spill all that shit about Cole? Do you think I like being vulnerable like that? No. I fucking hate it. But I wanted to tell you that stuff because you're my best friend."

I throw my hands up in frustration. "For fuck's sake, Silas. I had a sex dream last night and it wasn't about Cole. And I don't know how I'm supposed to feel about it. Jesus." I walk into the bathroom and slam the door.

CHAPTER TWENTY-ONE

SILAS

I had a sex dream and it wasn't about Cole. My brain plays this sentence on a loop for a solid three minutes straight. First off, Ada had a sex dream. File that away to think about later. Much later. Preferably when I have an hour to think about it. Alone. Secondly, it wasn't about Cole? Then who was it about? *It could've been about you, dummy.* Yeah, not even considering that since it could lead to hope and I'm not giving anything like that a voice.

But part of me thinks she must have recognized whomever it was for it to affect her like this. And is she edgy because she's horny? I mean, that would definitely make sense. She got all worked up with the dream and then couldn't do anything about it. Well, I guess she *could* do something about it. I really shouldn't think about that, either.

I hear the shower start and then shut off and Ada lets out a frustrated groan and I quickly get as far away from the bathroom door as I can so I'm not in the path of whatever destruction she seems to have planned at this moment. I sit on the sofa and pretend to read the travel guide on the coffee table. The door flies open and she doesn't look at me as she storms out of the bathroom. She stomps over to her suitcase and pulls out her toiletry bag and some clothes. She quickly pivots and returns to the bathroom and slams the door once again.

I brainstorm how to make this less awkward. And I know it's only awkward because I pushed. I dug and needled and drug it out of her. It's my fault, so I really should figure out a way to fix it. The rational part of my brain says she and I are both adults and we can talk about shit like this. Not a problem, right? Wrong. I'm sure if I had no interest in Ada beyond the platonic, we could discuss it like adults. But knowing if she tells me anything about this dream she had, I'm going to get pretty worked up myself and she'll see how affected I am, I can't do that.

And part of me even understands why she's so upset by the whole thing. She had a dream that wasn't about Cole. That has to be difficult for her. The fact he's the only man she's ever been with or even kissed and she had a dream about another man? Or, maybe a woman? She didn't specify. I should probably stay out of it, but I already know I won't.

Twenty minutes later, Ada exits the bathroom, in a bathrobe, her dark hair still damp from the shower. She stalks over, the tattoo bandage in hand, and huffs, extending it to me. "I can't do this myself."

She doesn't look at me and even in her frustration and possible embarrassment from telling me about the dream, she's beautiful. Her face is scrubbed clean and she smells great, even from a few feet away and her skin is shiny from whatever lotion she uses. "Are you asking for my help, Wednesday?" I ask, amusement in my tone. My hope is, if I give her shit, things will feel normal for her—and me—again.

Her jaw clenches. "Yes, Ass. I just said I can't do it myself."

I fold my arms, still not taking the bandage. "I don't recall hearing you ask. You simply stated you couldn't do it yourself."

She blows out a slow breath through her nose, color rising to her cheeks and I have to press my lips together to keep from smiling. "Silas, will you help me? Please." The last word comes out through gritted teeth and her nostrils flare and fuck me if she's not sexy when she's perturbed.

"Sure. That's all you had to say." I take the bandage from her and lean forward. She turns her body so her hip is facing me and rucks up the hem of the robe. And now I'm thinking this was a terrible fucking idea because damn, I shouldn't be watching her do this. I struggle to keep my breathing controlled as more of her skin is exposed. But I can't take my eyes off her, regardless of how hard I try. And Jesus Christ, she's wearing a thong? Fuck me. I blink rapidly and make myself focus on the tattoo. "Does it itch?" I ask, looking up at her.

"Not really," she replies softly. "You know what to do with that?" She jerks her chin at the bandage.

I nod. "Yeah. Try to make sure there aren't air bubbles, right?"

"Pretty much."

I peel the backing off the bandage and position it over the middle of her tattoo. The tattoo I picked out for her. The tattoo representing the nickname I gave her when she was ten. The tattoo she loved when she saw it. I can't help but smile as I smooth the bandage over the supple flesh of her hip.

"What?" she asks, curiosity lacing her tone.

I look up at her as I finish pressing out a small air bubble. "Nothing. It's cute. You still like it?"

In spite of her obvious ire from this morning's events, she gives me a small smile and nods. "I love it."

I pull my hand away. "Good. Go get finish getting ready so we can eat."

She's quiet through breakfast and I simply let her be. As we make the drive over to the dam, I let her choose the music and she stares out the window. I'm struck by how similar this feels to the first trip we went on; this quiet, brooding silence. Except this time, I know she's okay, she's simply processing. And eventually, I will prod her about it, but for now, I'll let her stew and think to herself.

As we get through the security checkpoint before we cross the bridge, Ada perks up. She looks at the dam below with interest and makes a small sound of curiosity. "What is it, Peep?"

She shrugs, shaking her head. "It seems bigger on TV."

I huff a laugh. "Well, yeah, but we're pretty high up. I'm sure when we get down there, it will seem a lot bigger."

"Probably," she agrees.

Ten minutes later, we park, prepared to make the trek over to the dam. Before we exit the car, she pulls some sunscreen out of her purse and slathers some on her arms and face and then extends the tube toward me. "Put some of that on. There's no shade or clouds or anything. You'll roast."

I could be annoyed by her command, but secretly, I love that she cares enough to make sure I don't get sunburnt. "Aww, Wednesday, didn't know you cared so much," I say with a syrupy smile.

She rolls her eyes. "No, I just don't want to hear you bitch when you're blistered. Josie and your mom tan, but you take after the Campbells. You burn."

I love that she knows my family so well. I love that she knows which of us burn and tan and what our favorite foods and movies and books are. I love that she has this history with us; that she's one of us. I love that she's my family. And I know, regardless of what happens with all this shit Cole's done, she'll still be my family and she'll still be in my life. Even if she's not with me. The thought makes my chest ache, but I push it down.

I take the tube from her and obediently rub lotion on my face and arms and legs. I hand it back over and she tucks it into her purse. We grab the bottles of water we brought with us and exit the vehicle and fall in step next to one another and begin the long walk over to the dam.

It takes several minutes and by the time we actually make it, sweat pools under my arms and low on my back and I've almost drained my entire bottle of water. "Jesus, it's hot. You'd think we were in the desert or something," I say, mopping my forehead with the sleeve of my shirt. I nudge her and she shakes her head and huffs a laugh.

"Yeah, you'd think. But it's different than at home. This is dry. It's not suffocating like in Tennessee."

"Nope. But I still think I prefer our mountains to these," I comment, gesturing to the rocky expanse of the desert.

"Me, too. I love all the green at home. Have you ever thought about living anywhere else?"

I shake my head. "No. I love home. Pap and Mom and Dad and Josie are there. You're there. I don't want to live anywhere else. You?"

"No, I can't see going anywhere. I mean, obviously, I think it's cool to travel and stuff, but home is home. I like home. I can't imagine not being able to go to Sunday dinner or visit Pap or even hang out with your annoying ass on Mondays for our *Grey's* days."

"Yeah, none of those things would feel right without you, either." I glance at her out of the corner of my eye. "Have you talked to your mother lately?"

She swallows and looks down, stuffing her hands in the pockets of her shorts. "I called her after Cole died. I don't know what I thought would happen, that she'd drop everything and come be with me? I don't know. She said how sorry she was, but she 'just couldn't leave Fort Worth' and 'everything is so hectic'. I didn't call her again and she hasn't called me. I shouldn't have been surprised, and yet, I was. Thankfully, most of the wives and girlfriends of Cole's employees were in and out. They must've had some sort of schedule worked out. Of course, I don't remember them being there much. Even your mom and dad were in at least once a week, I think."

I can't hide my surprise. I didn't know Mom and Dad went to see her immediately after Cole's death. I focus my attention on her as I realize she's still speaking. "Your parents have always been so good to me. Even as stoic as your dad is, he still patted me on the shoulder the couple of times he came to check on me. He brought sandwiches from that deli he likes. He'd sit with me and make me eat and he'd have his glasses on and read the paper, nudging me to take bites.

"Your mom, of course, flitted around and made me cups of tea and tried to get me to shower, but she's so small, it's not as if she could physically drag me to the bath. And as much as your dad loves me, I don't think he was up for that. After you showed up, Josie came and made me strip down and I'm pretty sure she scrubbed off my top layer of skin."

She scratches her nose and blinks quickly and clears her throat. I can tell she's trying not to get emotional and my heart lurches. "I don't get it. Y'all were all dealing with things, too, and you still all came to check on me. Your parents lost their son and they still made sure I was alive. Y'all could've abandoned me and no one would've blamed you. I'm just me. Just the poor, little, white trash girl y'all included in all your family stuff.

"And yet, that's how y'all have always been. Your parents and grandparents loved me more than either of my own parents. Y'all overlooked how messed up my family was and how I never had on clean clothes or probably hadn't bathed in days. Y'all just loved me. I never understood what made y'all want to do that."

I have to clear my own throat to keep my emotions in check. I can't keep from putting my hand on her arm to stop her and turn her to look at me. Even with the sunglasses she has on, her eyes are sad. "You're our family, Ada. You have been since that first day. And I can't say what it was that originally made Josie pick you as her best friend. All the stars must have aligned because she came home the first day of fifth grade and wouldn't shut up about the little girl with the long black hair and pretty gray eyes who she shared her marshmallow peeps with at lunch. She's always been fascinated by your eyes.

"Ours are all muddy brown. But yours? They're like pewter. Except when you're pissed, and then they're this dark, stormy, gunmetal color. That color terrifies me." She huffs a laugh. "Whatever the reason you came to be a part of our lives, I know none of us would ever trade you for anything. You're ours. And just because your parents are dumb shits who never deserved to even breathe the same air as you, and *they* are trash, doesn't mean you are. You are not trash. You've never been trash, Ada. You are treasure. You are precious. You are gifted and funny and smart and a pain in my ass, but I'll take it every day of the week."

She brings her hands up to pull my sunglasses down and I nearly startle when her fingers brush my cheeks. "Your eyes aren't muddy brown. They're rich and warm and make me think of dark chocolate. They're expressive and honest and as much as yours are like Josie and Cole's, they're not, somehow. I can't put my finger on it, exactly."

She pushes my glasses back up and drops her hands and turns to start walking again. I'm glued to my spot for a beat as I will my heart to stop racing. The way she seems to stare directly into my soul with those amazing eyes of hers is nearly too much.

I hurry to catch up with her and about five minutes later, we're standing on the dam. It's windy as we stare down at Lake Mead and I'm struck by a thought and pull her along. "Come on. I have an idea."

She doesn't question me, simply follows behind me as we weave our way around other tourists. When we reach the dead center of the dam—or as best I can figure is the center, right on the state line, near a plaque—I stop. Ada looks around. "Okay, now what?"

"From what I can tell, we're pretty much in two places at once. We're on the state line. We're also in two different time zones."

She laughs. "Well, that kinda makes us time and space travelers then, doesn't it?"

I shrug. "Sounds about right to me. You bring the ashes?"

Nodding, she pulls a small shampoo bottle out of her purse. My eyes widen in surprise. "You packed Cole into a shampoo bottle?"

She shrugs. "I wasn't sure they'd let me take them through security at the airport. It was all I could think of. How about next time, you come up with the plan to cart him around the country, huh?"

I chuckle at her sass. "No, I'm sure he smells real nice now. Like," I glance at the outside of the bottle, "coconut. Ironic since he hated coconut."

She laughs and rolls her eyes. "Yeah, well, you do what you can with what you have. So sue me." She glances around. "You think this is legal?"

I shrug. "Hell if I know. Maybe we should hurry." I tug her over toward the concrete barrier.

She twists the top off the bottle and I step behind her and cover her hand with my own. "Just pretend we're looking over the side." I make it look as though my arm is around her and we lean over the side. I bring our hands to the edge of the concrete and drape them over the side, tipping the bottle. Immediately, the wind pulls the ashes away. When the bottle is empty, I pull our hands back and drop mine from hers after giving it a squeeze. She looks up at me as she replaces the lid and shoves the bottle back into her purse. "That's that, I suppose."

I nod and pull my phone out. I tap on the camera app and stop a passerby. "Excuse me, can you take our picture?" The tourist, a man in his early fifties, smiles and takes my phone. Ada looks at me questioningly and I shrug. "What? We're at the Hoover Dam, Wednesday, we need to document it. Not every day we'll be in two places at once." I lean in a little closer to her. "I'm pretty sure we won't break my phone if we're in the same picture. You never know, but I'm willing to risk it."

She rolls her eyes. "Ass," she says with a grin.

I put my arm around her shoulder and pull her against me and we smile into the lens. A moment later, the man hands my phone back over. "See, we survived it." I look at the photos he took and show her one. "This one's not bad."

She looks down at it. "Nope. Send that one to me? Also, Josie wants a picture of our tattoos. She doesn't believe you got one."

"Oh, you told her?" I ask as we start walking back toward the car.

She nods. "Yeah, I texted her this morning. She asked if I'd thrown you over the dam yet."

I can't help but chuckle. "Sounds about right. Y'all talk about anything else?"

I know I'm fishing. Most likely she told Josie about her

dream because she's the only other person Ada really hangs out with. Ada simply shrugs. "A little of this, little of that."

"Oh, so you told her about your dream?" I ask with a knowing smile.

Even in the heat, I can see the blush bloom on her cheeks. "I'm not talking about that with you."

"Okay, that's fine. But it's not a big deal. I mean, I'm sure it was an emotional thing for you, considering, but you're not the first person to have sex dreams, Peep. Even people in relationships have dreams that aren't about their significant others. Not that I speak from experience, of course, but I'm sure it's true."

She looks straight ahead. "Like I said, not discussing it with you, Silas."

"Okay, well, answer me this, was it a man or a woman?" I ask, my tone teasing.

"Not discussing."

"So, you're just going to let me work up this fantastical scenario in my head?"

"You can think whatever you want. I'm not discussing it with you."

"I mean, I know it's been a while, so that has to be what caused it. It's probably a good thing. Means you're getting better."

She stops abruptly and turns to me. "You talk to Josie or something?"

I shake my head. "No, why?"

She starts walking again. "That's what she said."

"Well, we Campbells are a smart bunch. But for real, I can understand why it would upset you. And I'm sure things are getting back to... normal, so to speak. It's been months, I'm sure that's all it is. You and Cole were together for fifteen years. That's like having unlimited access to an all-you-can-eat buffet and then it's taken away. You didn't even get to go on a diet. You just had to go cold turkey."

Ada sighs. "Yeah." After a minute, she opens her mouth and closes it again, shaking her head.

"What, Wednesday?"

"Nothing."

"No, I know that look. You want to say something or ask something. Out with it."

She sighs again and chews on the inside of her bottom lip and after a long moment, she speaks. Her tone is nervous and I find it utterly adorable. "So, you said you've only slept with a few women, right?"

"Yeah," I answer immediately. "Why?"

"And you said you don't like sex without an emotional connection?"

"Yeah."

"So, what does that mean? You slept with those women, but after, you didn't feel anything, so you didn't do it again? How's that work?"

I consider her question. I can't tell her the reason it never worked with anyone else was because she's the only woman I've ever wanted. That every time I tried to be with someone else, she was the one I pictured. And considering I'm not a user, it's just easier to not be with someone than feel guilty about the experience later. That being with other women only reminded me how fucked up I am for wanting what—who—I can't have. That if Cole would've lived, I would have eventually settled for someone simply so I could have the things I want in life— marriage, kids, a family. That the thought of settling makes the guilt and shame eat at me even more since it wouldn't have been fair to the woman I ended up with or even the children I would've had.

No way in hell can I say anything close to that so I try to be honest, but vague. "I went on dates with them and they seemed nice. You know, with the exception of Hen. She was simply convenient, I think. And she's hot, but not much going on up top. So, I went on dates. The women were nice and fun, I guess, but I couldn't see anything long-term with any of them. They didn't pass my vibe check, or whatever. And if I slept with them, it was simply to see if maybe I might feel more for them after. I never did, so I wasn't going to continue to see them and give them false hope I'd want anything more than what I could give them."

She thinks about my answer and pulls her mouth to the side as she works through things in her mind. "So, when was the last time you went out with anyone?"

"Are you asking when was the last date I had, or the last time I slept with someone?"

"Are the answers different?"

"Yeah. I don't sleep with every woman I take on dates, Ada. Like I said, I'm not the player you imagine me to be."

"Okay, so answer both questions, I guess."

I sigh. "The last date I went on was about a year ago. The last time I slept with someone was about five years ago."

She stops dead in her tracks, her mouth falling open in shock. "What?"

"What?"

"Five years?"

"Yeah, so?"

"Why?"

"What do you mean, why? I just haven't found anyone I wanted to sleep with." *And none of them are you.*

"I don't get it. I would think with your job, you'd have women throwing themselves at you."

I shrug. "Even if that were the case, I don't sleep with clients. I don't shit where I eat."

She huffs a laugh. "Well, yeah, I guess. But don't you miss it?"

I shrug again. "I'm sure if any of it was with a woman I truly wanted—a woman I loved—I probably would. But no, not really."

"That makes me sad for you, Silas."

"It is what it is. At least, this way, I don't have to worry about STDs, unplanned pregnancies, or drama. I can continue to live my quiet life."

"I guess there's an upside to everything, right?"

CHAPTER TWENTY-TWO

ADA

Cole was totally right. Silas's eyes light up like a kid on Christmas morning when he watches fights. It was a sight to see. And I must admit, the adrenaline rush you get from watching two people try to beat the hell out of one another was pretty good. The crash after the rush, on the other hand, was not so good. I fell asleep in the Uber on the way back to the hotel and Silas ushered my drowsy behind up to our room and tucked me in.

The next morning, amid the rush to pack and not miss our flight home, we barely had time to talk and I found myself reflecting on the conversation we'd had the day before at Hoover Dam. For some reason, our whole lives, I assumed Silas was this guy who never wanted to settle down and only dated casually. I assumed he never talked about the women he dated because there were too many to name and keep up with. I never would've imagined it was because there weren't many to begin with.

For the life of me, I can't figure out why. Silas is a catch. He's smart, grounded, undeniably good-looking, and funny.

Well, he's funny when he's not a massive pain in the ass. But in reality, he's not even a pain in the ass. And when he is, it's typically for your own good. I'd imagine it's why he makes such a good personal trainer. And so, I can't understand why, if he wants love, he hasn't been able to find it. He can't be that picky, right?

As our plane lands back home, we climb into the Bronco after loading our bags into the cargo area. Silas's phone rings and he answers it as he starts the car, but he doesn't drive off. "Hey, Dad...Yeah, we just landed...I was going to head that way in a bit...Oh, okay. That's really good news. What about the cataracts?" He listens and nods along with whatever Miles is saying before he speaks again. "All right. Sounds good. I'll go check on him. Thanks for the update. Talk to you later." He disconnects the call and turns to me. "Pap's hip isn't broken. So that's fantastic news. He's pretty bruised up and sore, but they were able to talk him into going through with the procedure to remove the cataracts. No family dinner tonight, unfortunately. Mom and Dad are too tired."

"Silas, that's wonderful. Not about dinner, of course, I'll miss that. But great news about Pap. I'm sure he's bitching to anyone who'll listen, though."

He grins. "I could hear him in the background fussing about how they kept letting his ass hang out when they helped him to the bathroom."

I can't help but laugh. "Sounds about right."

"Ready to go?"

I nod. "Yeah." He pulls out of the parking lot and onto the highway and I ask, "So, did you enjoy your weekend?"

He smiles. "It was great. Crossed some stuff off of my bucket list."

"Yeah?"

He nods. "Yeah. Got to see a UFC fight in Vegas. Got to

see one of our country's great industrial marvels. Got to be in two places at once. Got to see you in that red dress."

I snort a laugh and heat fills my cheeks. "It was just a dress."

Silas's eyes widen. "Just a dress? Jesus, Wednesday, I'm pretty sure you stopped traffic in that thing. You looked beautiful."

"Thank you. It was fun to get dressed up for a night on the town. You didn't look so bad yourself. I swear, do they give guys lessons about how to attract women by rolling up the sleeves of button-down shirts? Because I think it's one of those catnip type things for most women."

He laughs. "Lady catnip, huh? I'll have to remember that."

"What are some other things on your bucket list?" I ask, curious.

He thinks for a minute and smiles. "Normal stuff. Get married, have kids, grow old with someone."

"What about not normal stuff?"

His grin widens. "You sure you want to know? Might be too much for you."

I roll my eyes and chuckle. "Why? Am I too delicate to know those kinds of things? Too preposterous for my fragile, girlish mind to comprehend?"

He shrugs and gives me a slow smile as if to say, *you asked for it*. "Join the mile high club. Skinny dip in the middle of winter. Ring in New Years in Times Square. See a Broadway show."

"Wow, those are pretty good." I'm genuinely impressed with his list. None of them are undoable. Most of the items on his list would be ones he'd either want or need someone else to help him complete. Who's he got in mind for that, I wonder?

Twenty minutes later, we're pulling in at my apartment and Silas pulls an envelope out of the glove box and hands it over with a smile. I slide it into my purse and climb down from the cab as he fetches my suitcase from the cargo area.

We walk up the steps and as I unlock the door, I turn to him as I open it. "Do you want to come in for a bit? I can fix some lunch. I'm sure you're hungry."

He sets my bag down. "Actually, I'm going to go pick up something to take and eat with Pap. They're probably going to keep him for a couple more days to make sure he's out of the woods. I want to see if he needs me to do anything on the farm."

I nod. "Okay. I'm glad you had a good weekend. Take care of that tattoo."

"I will."

And I'm not sure why I do it, but I close the distance between us and wrap my arms around his waist to give him a hug. Maybe it's because, in spite of my awkwardness with that stupid dream, he truly has become my best friend. I'm thankful to have him in my life and I'm glad he opened up to me and let himself be vulnerable.

Silas seems surprised I've done this, and he's stiff for a second before wrapping his own arms around me and pulling me closer. I lay my head on his chest and breathe him in. He smells like clean laundry and something else. Eucalyptus, maybe. "Thank you for everything you've done for me these past few months."

He huffs a laugh into my hair. "I've been happy to do it, Peep. I hope you know that."

I step back and give him a smile. He sticks his hands in his pockets and his own smile is warm. "Do we need to cancel *Grey's* day tomorrow? You know, if you're going to the farm?"

He considers and shakes his head. "Nah. If I need to go, it'll be early. I'll be back way before supper time. But I'll let you know if anything changes."

"Sounds good. Give Pap my love?"

"Will do. See you tomorrow."

I step inside and after a final wave to him, I shut the door and lock it. I carry my bag to the bedroom and make quick work of unpacking. I pull out the tee-shirt I bought at the fight last night, and toss it in the hamper along with my other soiled clothes.

I stow my suitcase and put my toiletry bag away and once I come back into the bedroom, I strip out of my travel clothes and toss them in the hamper as well. My eyes catch on both my tattoos in the mirror and for some reason, I like the fact I have a tattoo and a coordinating memory to go along with them for each of my two favorite men. Although, I guess Silas isn't *mine*. Not really. *Isn't he, Ada Mae? Do you see him out chasing a bunch of other women? He spends all his free time with you. Kinda hard for him to be someone else's when you're his focus.*

I don't know how I keep getting into these imagined conversations with Cole. Especially over something like this. This is his brother. It's absurd. Isn't it? It's only been four months. Regardless of the possible return of my libido, it's too soon to even begin considering anything. Let alone with Silas. He's Cole's brother. *I'm not there anymore, Ada Mae. Why not Silas?* Needing to not think about this anymore, I walk into the bathroom and start the shower, wanting to wash the travel off.

Later, as I'm curled in bed, I finally pull Cole's letter out of my purse and open it. For some reason, I'm nervous to read it, but I'm at a loss as to why. And yet, I unfold it and begin reading.

My Ada Mae,

Was I right or was I right about the way Silas looks when he watches a fight? It's pretty great. I hope he enjoyed getting to experience it and y'all made a great memory. Did you go see Hoover Dam? Is it as big as it looks on TV? Did y'all win any money at the casinos?

Silas and I actually hadn't done any gambling, but I can't say that kind of thing ever appealed to me, so it wasn't any great loss to me.

I hope, going forward, you and Silas are able to create lots of new memories. Now that you know how much he loves fighting, I hope it might be something you do with him. Well, not the fighting part, I'm sure y'all are still good at that. But the watching fighting part. Watch the fights with him, babe.

Did you know, when he was fourteen, he wanted to be a UFC fighter? He thought he wanted to make a career of it. He was good, too. He trained relentlessly and loved it.

Unfortunately, he gave it up a few years later, in favor of becoming a personal trainer. But deep down, part of me thinks he wishes he'd still gone the route of the octagon. Maybe the fights y'all have are his new octagon. And you're not one to back down from a fight, either, Ada Mae. And if I know you, you love fighting with him. You love the smart-ass retorts y'all sling at each other and giving him shit. Pretty sure he likes giving you shit, too.

I'll never regret we hardly argued. We both know I'm not a confrontational person. I love peace and think all arguments can be solved logically. Sometimes though, I think you might have wished to fight. Sometimes, I think you needed it. If for nothing else than some spice, some excitement. Maybe I failed you on that front.

I only know, I never saw you so alive as when you and Silas were at each other's throats. It's one of the reasons I knew he was perfect for this job of making sure you complete all these tasks. He won't hesitate to push back on you when you balk at an idea or a scheme. He'll call you on your bullshit and make you follow through. But I feel like, y'all would also be good at working things out; clearing the air and apologizing to one another. Because while y'all both run hot, you also cool down just as quickly. Well, maybe not quickly, per se, but you both are good at apologizing when you know you've fucked up.

The next couple of tasks will be fun, but they'll come at a price. The ones after those will probably piss you off and push you out of your comfort zone. Embrace the discomfort, babe. It'll do you so much good. I love you.

-Cole

Unlike Cole's other letters, I don't feel the normal rush of sentimentality and heart-wrenching emotion in this one. This one seemed to be more about Silas than anything. Well, Silas and how well Cole thinks we like to fight and how alike we are.

Perplexed, I try to figure out why I'm out of sorts. It seems like the last few letters have focused more on Silas and how great he is. And now Cole is telling me about how Silas used to fight and loved it, but likes to fight with me? Jesus, it almost sounds like he's hyping him up. Or am I merely looking for things I want to see? What is wrong with me?

Even unsure as I am about what all this means, I can't help running my fingertips over the bandage covering my tattoo. Silas's tattoo. I also can't help but check in with Silas about how Pap is doing.

> Ada: How's Pap?

Silas: Giving the nurses hell. Giving me up the road for letting you pick out my tattoo.

> Ada: Hey. I like your tattoo.

Silas: I love my tattoo, Wednesday. Seriously. It's amazing. I will have a piece of Ada Andrews art with me forever. Well, at least until I'm too old and wrinkly to make out what it is anymore. Then people will speculate.

I can't help but smile at his text.

> Ada: I didn't know you used to train to be a fighter.

The dots bounce for several seconds and I wait, wondering what he'll say about that part of his life.

Silas: Yeah. For a few years. Cole tell you that?

> Ada: Yeah. Why did you stop? He said you were great.

Silas: I was. We couldn't afford training anymore. I found something I like pretty well, though.

> Ada: Do you ever do any sparring or anything? You know, for fun?

Silas: Only the verbal kind with you, Peep.

Warmth fills my chest with his answer, but I'm not sure why I like it so much.

Ada: Ooh, good answer, Ass.

Silas: I aim to please. Verbally sparring with
you might be one of my favorite things to do.

My heart seems to skip a beat with his words and I'm
suddenly nervous, but I answer honestly.

Ada: Me, too. Do me a favor?

Silas: Of course. Anything. You know that.

Ada: If you were to pick a song for me to
listen to right now, what would it be?

Silas: What genre?

Ada: NOT disco. But otherwise, anything is
fair game.

Silas: Will you pick one for me, too?

Ada: Sure. Are you stalling?

Silas: No, just curious if this was a quid pro
quo situation. Listen to "Duet" by Penny and
Sparrow. What about you? Song for me?

Ada: "Carried Me With You" by Brandi
Carlisle. Thank you for carrying me these last
few months until I could walk again.

Silas: Anytime, Peep. I've got you. Always.

CRASH

OCTOBER: EIGHT MONTHS AFTER

CHAPTER TWENTY-THREE

ADA

And again, Cole was right. The next few months' tasks are mostly fun. July consisted of a pie-eating contest at a county fair that I did not win. It was also when we celebrated Silas's birthday by having a *Grey's* marathon and me making him his favorite chocolate cake. He also loved the painting I gifted him from my sketch at the cabin. I thought he was going to pass out.

August was a paintball game. But not like the kind of paintball you shoot. More like the kind in the movie *10 Things I Hate About You*. Because why not, it's one of my favorite movies. September consisted of me finally learning how to drive a stick shift. Followed by Silas and me not speaking to each other for two days because we kept fighting during the lesson. Granted, Blue is old and I was literally grinding her gears. No one was happy with me, not even myself.

Somehow during all these months, Silas has become the person I rely on most in the world. We text and talk multiple times a day and have somewhat formed a bubble for ourselves. If you'd told me a year ago this would be my reality, I'd have said you were delusional. Honestly, though, I like this quiet existence. I like my routine of snuggling up on the couch with Chinese food for our Mondays *Grey's* nights, Sunday dinner at Ingrid and Miles's, occasional evenings out with Josie, visits to the farm, and working more than I have in years.

I still miss Cole every day, but it's become a bearable kind of pain; a dull ache I've learned to live with. Having Silas helps and he's become my favorite person in the world. He's kind and sometimes cranky. He's funny and intelligent and his taste in music has come a long way since we started hanging out.

But I know from Cole's letters, harder, more personally-challenging tasks are up ahead. I have no clue what it means, but I know Silas will be with me every step of the way. He truly has become my rock.

After a particularly heartbreaking episode of *Grey's Anatomy*, Silas pulls a familiar envelope from his back pocket. He lays it on the coffee table as we're cleaning up our supper mess and I sniffle and wipe away what remains of my tears from the episode and gape at him. "You're going to drop that on me right after my heart's been ripped out?"

He shrugs. "Sorry, Wednesday. Them's the breaks."

I glance at the envelope. "Is this one a hard one?"

"Depends on your definition of hard."

I sigh. "Is this one that will make me uncomfortable?"

"Maybe. You have a week."

"Do we have to go out of town?"

He shakes his head. "No, we're local for this one."

"Oh. Okay." He glances at his watch. It's not the first time he's done it tonight and it's unusual because he never checks his watch when we're together. Three times in one night? It's so out of character for him, it's a bit unsettling. "Got somewhere you have to be?"

"Why?"

Annoyed, I narrow my eyes. "Answering a question with a question. Okay. Whatever. You've checked your watch three times in the last hour. Like I said, you got somewhere you have to be?" He's fidgety and I'm at a total loss.

"Actually, yeah. I have to meet someone."

Something twists in my gut. "Oh. Okay." I hope my tone sounds nonchalant instead of flummoxed. He's never bailed on me when we watch *Grey's* before. And it's not as though we get together every day since he works a lot of evenings, but this is so unexpected, I'm not sure how I'm supposed to react. "Okay," I repeat. "Well, you go on. I'll get all this. Don't want you to be late."

"It's all right. I've got a few minutes."

I shake my head and give him a forced smile. "Really, it's no problem. I've got it," I say firmly. He rakes his fingers through his hair. It's something I've noticed he does when he's nervous or unsure about something. "Really, Silas. It's fine. I should probably read Cole's letter anyway." I intentionally soften my voice so he doesn't think I'm mad. And I'm not mad. I'm hurt and confused.

He gives me a tight smile and walks over to me and gives me a quick hug. "I'll talk to you later, okay?"

"Sure. Be safe."

He nods and practically runs out the door. What the hell was that about and why do I feel like I was just jilted? I mean, it's not like we're a couple or anything. I don't have the right to feel as though he's thrown me over to go hang out with the guys or whatever when we already had plans. But for almost five months, this has been what we do on Monday nights. We've only ever had to miss once when I had a stomach virus and had forbidden him from coming to take care of me since I had what felt like ten years' worth of food coming out both ends. And so this perceived abandonment hurts. If he needed to go do something, he could've told me and we could've gotten together earlier or pushed it a week. But for him to just jump ship without warning hurts.

Then the thought hits me: what if he had a date? Is that something he would talk to me about? I know he says he doesn't date women he meets at work, but there's also the grocery store, the bank, and Pap's doctor's office. Many different places to score a date. And what right do I have to feel slighted if he's met someone? I should want him to be happy, right? He's building a house for the wife and children he hopes to have someday.

If he's met someone, where does that leave me? He'll go on dates and fall in love and get married. And no woman would probably ever be okay with a man like Silas—a good, handsome, caring, genuine man—being close friends with a woman. Regardless of our shared history and the fact I'm practically family, resentment and jealousy would be a real issue. Would he agree to something like that? Would he agree to cut ties with me for the sake of a relationship? I suppose if he loved the woman, I should be willing to let him do that.

But why does the idea of that hurt so much I can't breathe? Why does the thought of never spending time with him again make me want to sob? What does it mean if I don't ever want to give him up? Can it mean anything? I think it's safe to say there are times when Silas and I are together things could possibly be construed as flirting. Especially if someone who didn't know us saw us interacting.

We snuggle on the couch, normally with my legs draped over his or my feet in his lap. Sometimes, when he's really sore from working out, I'll rub his shoulders. We hug a lot and kiss each other on the cheek sometimes and I'd be lying if I said I wasn't attracted to Silas. How could I not be, he's gorgeous. Some might argue that of course I'm attracted to him, he's Cole's twin. But I never felt that way growing up or after Cole and I got together. I never saw him as anything other than Cole's brother.

Now, though, I don't know. And he and Cole are not the same people, not by a long shot. Their mannerisms and the way they carry themselves are different. Cole would tug his ear when he was anxious or nervous. Silas drags his fingers through his hair. Cole used to sit ramrod straight on the couch, even when we were cuddled up together. It was like trying to snuggle a brick wall. Silas lounges and manspreads and curls up next to me. Cole was a back sleeper. Silas sleeps on his side or stomach, if the RV and Vegas are any indications. Cole was serious and methodical, but also a total social butterfly. Silas is playful and spontaneous, but shy.

They are not the same.

But what does all this mean? Would it be preposterous to have feelings for Silas? Surely that's not what this is. I can't be developing feelings for Silas, right? *Why not, Ada Mae? You think he's not good enough for you?* Cole's challenge in my mind brings me up short and makes me want to glower at his imagined face. Silas is a good man. Any woman would be lucky to have him. But there's no way he'd want me, right? Not his brother's long-term girlfriend. Would that be weird?

I need to stop thinking about this. I need to deal with the fact Silas left and I need to do the dishes and read Cole's letter. I need to do some laundry and focus on work. I need to do anything except think about Silas.

I hurriedly place the dishes in the dishwasher and toss the empty Chinese food boxes in the garbage. As I straighten up the living room and see Cole's letter, I pick it up. Feeling nervous and anxious and maybe a bit off-kilter from the way Silas up and left tonight, I pour myself a glass of wine and climb into bed to read the letter.

My Ada Mae,

This task shouldn't be too personally taxing or daunting, but it will probably make you a bit anxious. You should also find a prepaid debit card in the envelope.

Buy a pretty dress and get dolled up. Channel your inner Vince Vaughn. You're crashing a wedding. Si will let you know what time to be ready.

I knew a wedding was never gonna be in our future, regardless of whether I lived or died. But it isn't because I wouldn't have loved being married to you. You would've made an amazing wife. I also know you would've been a gorgeous bride.

You still can be. You can do the whole thing. Let Dad or Pap walk you down the aisle toward a wonderful man. Have the cake, dance the dance, drive into the sunset.

It was never gonna be me, Ada Mae. I've always known I was here for a good time, not a long time. I can only hope I lived while I was here. I'm sure you've questioned over the last several months why we didn't do all the things I'm having you do now. And I'll tell you, but it's damn cheesy, so I hope you'll overlook my need to be sentimental for a minute. I never felt the need to do all those things because I had the only adventure I ever needed in getting to love you. You are the greatest adventure I've ever had. Thank you for letting me have it.

This isn't goodbye, not yet. You still have work to do, babe. But I hope, by this point, you're starting to picture a life beyond me. A life beyond the one we had together. I hope you are opening yourself up to new, everyday things. I hope you open yourself up to love. I know it hasn't been very long and people might talk. I say, fuck 'em.

Don't you dare hold yourself back from someone because you think I'd disapprove. You deserve love, Ada. More than anyone I've ever met before. There is nothing in this world I want more than for you than to be happy. I know we were happy together, so you know what it should look like to be happy with someone else.

And I know, no man is ever gonna be me. I mean, come on, it's hard to beat perfect, am I right? But that doesn't mean I don't want you to look for it. Be happy, my beautiful Ada Mae. Please. Find someone to be happy with. Even if it's not for forever, although, I hope it is.

I will love you until the end of time but don't keep your heart shuttered. Open it up and let the light in.

-Cole

Tears roll down my face. Even with his words to bless the possibility of something with someone else, it's such a bitter-sweet thing. And in this moment, I'm sadder than I have been in months.

CHAPTER TWENTY-FOUR

SILAS

For the third time today, my phone rings and it's Josie. I've not been able to answer due to some meetings at work, but a third call is unusual for her, so I hurry to answer. "Hey, Jos. What's up?"

"Have you talked to Ada today?"

"No. I had to bail on her last night and I'm pretty sure she's pissed at me. She seemed weird when I left. I couldn't tell her why I had to leave and I think it upset her. Why?"

"She's down, Silas."

"What do you mean, *down*?"

"We had plans to meet for lunch and she canceled. And we were going to that great place with the lobster rolls she likes. We've been looking forward to it for weeks. She didn't say anything other than she didn't feel like it. Don't you have another task this weekend?"

"Yeah, I gave her the letter to go with it last night. You think it might have anything to do with that?"

She sighs. "I don't know. It's probably not a coincidence, though. Does she normally get introspective with these things?"

"Not with the setup letter. Sometimes with the letter she gets after, she's a bit teary, but even that's been a few months, I think. She's seemed good lately. Happy."

"And what about you, are you happy?"

I sigh. "Getting there. Just trying to take things a day at a time." *And not let the guilt and shame consume me.*

"Okay, so what's your plan?"

"What plan?"

"Are you ever going to try to, like, actually kiss her or anything? What if, all these years, you've built all this up in your head about what it would be like between you two? What if you kiss her and it's like kissing your sister? What if there's no chemistry?"

"I have no clue. Honestly, though, we're in a really good place right now. Or, at least I thought we were. But you think I should check on her?"

"Can't hurt. You're her person or whatever. Isn't that the *Grey's Anatomy* thing y'all say?"

"Yeah." After a beat, I sigh again. "All right, I'll check on her. Thanks for letting me know."

"Sure thing. Let me know if you need backup. Let's hope she hasn't gone into some kind of grief spiral. I know sometimes, it can hit you at the strangest time and take you out."

"Yeah, I hope not." As soon as Josie disconnects the call, I'm pulling up Ada's name in my contacts and calling her. She answers on the third ring and sounds like she's been sleeping.

"Hey, Peep. You okay? Did I wake you up?"

She clears her throat. "I'm fine. Did you need something?"

I'm struck by the flatness of her tone. "No, Josie said you canceled lunch with her, so I didn't know if something was wrong. I wanted to check on you."

She heaves a heavy sigh and I can hear her rolling her eyes even through the phone. "You know, you all don't have to discuss my wellbeing at every turn. I'm allowed to cancel lunch plans simply because I don't feel like going."

"No one is saying you can't, but she said y'all were looking forward to wherever it was you'd planned on going. I think she's disappointed is all."

"Like I said, I'm fine, Silas."

"You don't sound fine, Ada."

"Ugh," she says with a grunt of frustration. "I'm just having a bad day. I'm not going to go postal or forget to eat or shower. Stop overanalyzing me. And stop having discussions with your sister about me behind my back. I don't appreciate being put under a microscope."

"Why are you being like this? We're allowed to be concerned."

"Why? Because Cole left you in charge of me?"

I'm so far beyond confused by her tone and the stuff she's saying, I don't even know where to start. "You know that's not the only reason. You're my friend, Ada; my best friend. Stop acting like you don't matter to me."

"You bailed on me last night, Silas." *That's* what this is about?

"I know. I'm sorry."

"Why? If you had something else you needed to do, we could have rescheduled. Or, we could've skipped this week or gotten together earlier in the day."

"Like I said, I'm sorry."

"Where did you have to go?"

Knowing she won't like my answer, I still say the words. "I can't tell you that."

"Oh. Well, next time, just cancel. It's easier for me to deal with than being abandoned. I've had enough of that to last a lifetime, thanks."

A weight drops into the pit of my stomach. "Ada, I'm—."

She cuts me off. "Like I said, it's fine. I'm having a bad day is all. I'll reschedule with Josie. I'll see you on Saturday." And before I can even respond, she disconnects the call. I try to call her back and after a couple of rings, it goes straight to voicemail. Hoping she'll respond to a text, I send off a quick message.

Silas: Talk to me, Wednesday. Please.

I can tell she's opened it since she has her read receipts on, but when she doesn't respond, a while later, I try again.

Silas: You know I know where you live, right? If you don't talk to me, I can drive to your place.

That gets her attention.

Ada: You come over and I won't answer the door.

Good thing I don't need her to answer.

Silas: I still have Josie's spare, so I don't need you to answer the door.

Ada: You don't get to use that simply because you're pissed I hung up on you. You bailed. I'm allowed to be mad. Especially when you won't even tell me why.

Silas: I already apologized. I want to talk about why you feel like I "abandoned" you.

She leaves the last message on "delivered" and I rake my fingers through my hair in frustration. I'd love nothing more than to drive over to her place and let myself in and make her talk to me, but I know I won't. She wants to be alone, I guess I should honor her wishes; give her some space. Even if it's the last thing I want to do.

For three days, I'm stewing in my own misery. Ada hasn't responded to any of my texts, but I know she's reading them, so at least she's alive. I shouldn't crave talking with her the way I do. I should be able to go more than half a day without needing contact with her. And yet, by Thursday, after I get off work, I'm miserable and not wanting to simply go home and stare at the walls and stew even more, I stop by the bar Cole and I frequented most often to hopefully drown my sorrows.

I'm two beers in and the jagged edges are starting to dull when I feel a hand clamp down on my shoulder. When I turn my head, I'm surprised to see my dad. I give him a quick smile and nod. He looks around. "You by yourself?"

"Yeah."

"Can I join you? I stopped by to order some food for your mom and me and it's still going to be a few minutes."

I shrug. And even though I'd rather be alone, I'm not going to be a dick. "Sure."

"You okay, Si? Everything okay with you and Ada? Seems like we don't see one of you without the other these days, so I'm kinda surprised you're not with her tonight."

I stare down into my glass. "We don't spend that much time together." Even if we do, I don't want anyone to read anything into it.

Dad huffs a laugh. "Yes, you do. But I think it's good. You look the happiest I think I've ever seen you, Si." The knowledge that I am happy makes guilt and shame stab through me and I swallow the lump forming in my throat and try to breathe in spite of the tightness in my chest. I down my beer and signal the bartender for another beer. "Jesus, you've got it bad, don't you, son?"

I don't dare look at my father, for fear he'll see the truth in my eyes. "I don't know what you're talking about."

He snorts. "Yes, you do. Does Ada know you're in love with her? Or that the guilt of it is eating you up?" When my beer is set down, I take a long gulp but still can't look at Dad. He claps me on the shoulder. "I'm going to take that as a no. Why do you feel guilty? Cole wanted this, right? For y'all to be together?"

I do look at him then. He gives me a knowing smile. "I know y'all think I can't keep a secret, but for your mother, I can. Someday, you'll learn that from your spouse, there aren't secrets. Not ones like this. If all this stuff Cole planned out was intended for you and Ada to grow closer together, why are you letting all this guilt nag at you? You should be happy."

I blink rapidly, trying to fight back the tears. I'm in public for fuck's sake. "That's the thing, I am, Dad. I'm so fucking happy, it's eating me alive. I hate myself for it. I shouldn't get to be happy, not without Cole." My voice cracks at the end and I sweep my thumb across my lashes to swipe away the tear before it rolls down my cheek.

He gives me a sympathetic smile, his own eyes shiny. "I know. It's hard to think about being able to live when the people we love most aren't here to enjoy it with us. To feel like we're leaving them behind. But do you honestly feel like Cole would want you to carry all this shame with you? There is nothing wrong with falling in love and God knows it's sometimes the last person you should ever want to love. But I would think the fact that he's given you his blessing would soothe a lot of that guilt for you."

I shrug. "It just feels like I'm trying to take over his life. Part of me feels like, even if she ever developed feelings for me, she'd only see him. It's stupid and selfish, but I don't want her to see him when she looks at me. I'd rather not have her than for her to look at me like that."

"It's not stupid or selfish for you to want someone to love you for you and not who you resemble. But do you really think that's possible, Si? You and Cole are nothing alike. The way Ada is with you is nothing like she was with Cole. The way y'all are back and forth with each other is not the way it was with Cole. She's not stupid, son. And I truly don't think she'd ever consider getting involved with you unless it was *you* she wanted."

He blows out a breath and scratches his chin. "I don't know what's going to happen with you and Ada. Even if all y'all are meant to be is friends, it's evident she cares about you. And lord knows I don't understand how she can't see the way you look at her. But you don't have anything to feel guilty about. You were a good brother to Cole. You've followed through on everything he wanted. It's okay to have this for yourself, you know. You don't have to continue to martyr yourself. If Cole was here, he'd tell you the same thing."

And that's the crux of it. Cole's given me his blessing at every turn. And later, after Dad convinces me to go home without having another drink, I sit in my office chair hovering once again over that first letter. It's almost in tatters now, I've read and reread it so many times. I down a large gulp of moonshine and read it for probably the thousandth time.

Si,

If you're reading this, you know what time it is. We always knew this was a possibility, even if we never wanted to admit it. And even though we were kids when I made you make this promise, I'm calling it in. Ada needs you and you're the only person I trust to make this shit happen.

I trust you'll keep your word and never tell her I made you make this promise since she'd never forgive me.

Brother, if you only knew how many times I've come close to spilling that fucking secret and how it's killing me to keep it from her.

If I know her, she's not processing. She's not leaving her room. She's hunkered down and has probably shaved her head or done something equally drastic. And if she's gone that route, I hope you'll chop your mop in solidarity. Although, I really hope she hasn't shaved her head since that long mane of shiny, almost-black hair is one of my favorite things about her.

I think back on those first days after I went to her. How hollow she was. How scared I was for her and how many nights I worried she wouldn't come out of that black hole.

I know this won't be easy. Some of the shit on the list she won't want to do, but she needs to do it all. Some of them are stupid and some are awesome, but they're all valid. Don't let me down, yeah?

Leave a little bit of me everywhere you all go. Don't take no for an answer when she slams the door in your face because we both know she probably will. I know you've always had to be a certain way with her and I'm sorry about that. Although I had her, so I really can't be too sorry. Sorry to rub salt in that wound. But, I guess since dibs don't extend past death, she's yours. You know, if you can make her see you aren't really the asshole she's always thought you were.

If I'm honest, I don't think she views me as the asshole anymore. Hopefully, she sees how much I care, even if I've forced myself to hold back. Can I give myself permission to finally be the man I want to be with her? To put myself out there for her and hope she sees *me*. To hope she could want *me*.

You're both my favorite people on this earth. And I could hate the fact I'm not there to still love her, and God knows I do. But knowing I have you to watch over her gives me peace. Because if it can't be me, I'm glad it gets to be you.

Like I said, if she'll have you. All I can say is, good luck. You're gonna need it.

-Cole

If it can't be me, I'm glad it gets to be you. And like every time I read it, the pain comes. The pain of missing him like a limb. The ache of knowing something you've had your entire life that's no longer there. The knowledge that he should still be here to love her. The knowledge that I'd gladly sit back and watch them be happy for the rest of their lives if it meant he was still here. The guilt for being happy I've gotten to experience what it's like to spend any amount of time with her and feel like it's all mine. The shame for hoping she loves it just as much as I do.

There's a letter addressed to me in the folder with only the words *You'll know when it's time for this one...* written on the front. And I can't help but feel as though now is the time. I have no clue how I know, maybe it's one of those wacky twin things. But something in my gut tells me the letter was intended exactly for a moment like this. Once more, I take a gulp of the shine, feeling the pleasant buzz settle in as I rip open the envelope.

Si,

I don't know how long it'll be after I'm gone before you open this one. But something tells me, it'll be exactly when you need it most. If I were a betting man, I'm guessing all these months while you and Ada have spent time together have been somewhat unreal for you. Throughout our lives, you watched her and wanted her and now you get to spend time with her. You get to laugh with her and hopefully, you've been able to comfort her when she needed it. Hopefully, she's been able to comfort you, too.

God, how I've wished on so many occasions you'd been able to find happiness elsewhere. I'd be lying if I said it wasn't partly out of territorial jealousy. I'm only a man, after all. But another part of me has always wished for you to find someone simply because you're my brother and I want you to be happy. You have no idea how much I've hated that you haven't found someone you could allow yourself to freely love because it's the best feeling in the world.

But knowing what it's like to love Ada, I understand the kind of spell she weaves on a man. And for that, I can't fault you. So, I get why you've not been able to move on from the want of her. I'm sure, if you'd been the one to call dibs first, I'd be in the same boat as you.

And knowing the way you've sacrificed your happiness for mine our whole lives, you're still doing it, even now. You're letting yourself get bogged down in the guilt you've saddled yourself with—even if you have fuck all to feel guilty about, bro.

I am gone, Silas. I can't be any plainer than that. I've laid the groundwork. I've tried to hype you up to Ada as much as I possibly can without coming out and telling her my exact intentions for all of this. If you're still dealing with guilt or shame for wanting her, knock it the fuck off. If you want her and she'll have you, please don't waste this opportunity you finally have to love her.

It would be one thing if she didn't want you. If she turns you down; hey, we tried, right? And if that's the case, I hope you'll still be there for her. I hope you'll screen any guy who tries to get close to her; to ensure they're good people. I hope the friendship you're building or have built with her won't go away even if things don't turn romantic for the two of you.

But if she does want you, let her. Let her love you. Otherwise, what will it have all been for? Just so you can continue to be the better person you've always been? Stop it. For once in your life, you're allowed to have everything you've ever wanted. If you don't go after it, you're a fucking dumbass.

I love you, Si. I love Ada. And if the two people who I love most on the planet can find happiness again once I'm gone, I'll be able to go to my grave knowing my life won't have been a waste. Please don't let it have been for nothing.

-Cole

CHAPTER TWENTY-FIVE

SILAS

After Cole's letter and the conversation with my father, I toss and turn all night replaying their words over and over again. I don't know if Ada wants me. I don't know if we'll ever be more than what we are, but Cole's right, I can't waste this opportunity. Even with thoughts of doubt about her ever being able to want me for me and not as some replacement for my twin brother, I have to try, right?

And when I finally climb out of bed, I miss Ada so much I can't stand it. Hoping against hope she'll finally talk to me, I extend a last-ditch attempt at an olive branch.

> Silas: Can I cook for you tonight? We can have some makeup Grey's time.

I watch my phone screen as the message goes from "delivered" to "read". And when the dots start bouncing, I want to fist pump the air, but I try to keep calm.

> Ada: What are you offering?

> Silas: Meemaw's taco bean soup, cornbread, peach cobbler.

> Ada: With ice cream?

I smile to myself knowing I've got her.

> Silas: You know you can't have cobbler without vanilla ice cream. It's a crime. Be at my house by 7.

She sends a thumbs-up emoji and I finally feel as though I can breathe. Now, I just need to get her to talk to me.

By six-thirty, I start watching the door. By six-fifty, when there's a knock, I breathe a sigh of relief. I wipe my hands on the kitchen towel I've thrown over my shoulder and walk to the front door. Standing on the other side is Ada, cradling a bottle of red wine, a contrite expression on her face.

"Hi," she says, her voice quiet.

"Hey, Peep." I open the door wider to allow her entry and she hangs her purse and light jacket on the coat hook by the door. "Want me to take that wine and open it?"

She hands over the bottle and follows me to the kitchen, where I've set two place settings at the table. Her brows lift in curiosity when she sees it. "Oh, we're not going to watch while we eat?"

I shrug. "Eh, taco soup and cornbread can be kinda messy." I pull two wine glasses from the cabinet and the bottle opener from the drawer. I make quick work of pulling the cork and pour us each a glass. As I hand hers over, I take in what she's wearing. Nice jeans, a thin, long-sleeved henley, pair of Toms.

Her hair is braided over one shoulder and she has on a little makeup. "You look nice."

She looks down at herself. "Thanks. So do you." I have on a pair of faded jeans and a black v-neck tee-shirt and I'm barefoot. I had my hair cut yesterday in anticipation of us having to crash a wedding tomorrow. "Did you get a haircut?"

I scratch my scalp and nod. "Yeah. And you'll be proud of me, I went to an actual barber and everything."

She huffs a laugh and steps closer to tousle my hair. "Well, it's about time. It's nice. Not even gapped up. You need any help with supper?"

I shake my head. "No, it's pretty much done. Just waiting on the cornbread. About ten minutes." I lean back against the counter and cross my legs at the ankles and sip my wine. "Want to tell me what your freakout earlier this week was about? It's not like you to blow up and then not talk to me."

She looks down at her feet. "I was having a bad day. I'm sorry I took it out on you. You left so abruptly on Monday and it threw me off since you've never done it before. I felt like you'd abandoned me." I open my mouth to protest and she holds up a hand to stop me. "I know it's not rational. I know you didn't, but that's how it felt. With my parents, even though they were around—you know, until they weren't—it felt like they abandoned me. Then Cole died and I know that wasn't something any of us could control, but it was sudden and again, I felt abandoned.

"I've come to rely on those Monday nights. It's like my happy time. I know it's probably pathetic, but I look forward to it all day on Mondays. And then, you just left." She chews the inside of her bottom lip and curls and uncurls her fist anxiously. "And then Cole's letter had me in my feelings. I get the feeling, by his wording, things are coming to a close and I'm not sure how I feel about it.

"He said stuff about me moving on and it feels like he's saying goodbye. I don't know how to process it. I've known since the beginning there would only be so many letters and tasks, but it's hard." She blinks back tears and blows out a breath and my chest aches with the pain I see in her face. "Like I said, it was a bad day. I'm sorry I was a bitch."

I shake my head and step closer to her and pull her in for a hug. She comes willingly and my heart squeezes with love for her. I rest my chin on the top of her head and I can smell her shampoo. "I'm not going anywhere, Wednesday. You're stuck with me. I'm sorry I had to bail on Monday. I can't tell you why, but I will soon. I promise. And you're allowed to feel how you feel. Just don't shut me out, okay? You can be pissed at me. I'm used to it." She huffs a laugh against my chest. "But you don't get to deprive me of my best friend. That's not fair. Especially when you won't even talk to me." I pull back and look down at her. "Got it?"

She nods. "Yeah."

"Good. Now that we're all zeroed out, let's eat."

After supper, we decide to hold off on dessert. I refill our glasses and we head into the living room and queue up the show. Ada slips her shoes off and sits on the couch. I join her, thankful my sofa is a lot smaller than hers and she's automatically forced to sit closer.

Although, these days, it doesn't seem like much forcing is necessary. Most of the time, ten minutes into the show, she has her legs pulled up on the couch and she's snuggled against me. I'm sure as hell not going to complain about it.

"So, about this wedding," she says after a bit.

I pause the show and look at her. "What about it?"

"Are we legit crashing, or do you know the couple?"

I shake my head. "Nope. Cole had specific parameters for what the wedding could be like and I found one. Never even heard of the couple. How are your acting skills?"

She shrugs, considering. "I don't know, why?"

"We should probably get our story straight about how we know the bride and groom. The bride's father is some big wig over at an insurance firm, so this thing's likely to be a huge event. Let's hope it's so crowded no one pays attention to us." A thought hits me and I give her a playful smile. "Although, depending on the dress you wear, you might steal the show."

Ada rolls her eyes. "Not likely."

"So, not the red dress then?"

She grins, amused. "No, not the red dress."

"I'm sure whatever you wear, you'll look great. I'll pick you up at five-thirty on Saturday."

"All right."

On Saturday evening, right at five-thirty, I'm pulling up outside Ada's apartment. I climb from the car and jog up the stairs to knock on the door. I tug on the cuff of my dress shirt and adjust my cuff links one last time as I wait. A few seconds later, she opens the door and my heart seems to stop for a full five seconds, and my breath catches. Her dress is form-fitting and strapless with lace overlay in a dark, almost black, purple. It's knee-length, and she's paired it with some sort of thin wrap currently draped over her arm and black high heels. Her dark hair is pulled back off her face and curly. She's done her makeup a bit heavier than I've ever seen before and her gray eyes look almost silver, her full lips a dark red.

I give myself several seconds to take her in before speaking, and even then, I can only shake my head, a goofy grin on my face. "Damn, Wednesday. This one might be even more stunning than the red dress."

She blushes and looks down and then also appraises me. "Thank you, Silas. You look amazing as well. I'm not sure I've ever seen you in a full suit before. Very suave."

I straighten my tie. "Thanks. You ready?"

"Actually, I'm pretty sure my zipper is stuck." She gestures over her shoulder. "Can you see if you can get it? I'm hoping it's not busted. Clothing manufacturers really should get the memo that real women have asses."

I huff a laugh and step inside. "Sure." She shuts the door behind me and turns to allow me to assist her. And, damn, that's some ass Ada has. The zipper starts just above the small of her back and I squat down to see if the fabric is hung in the teeth of the zipper.

Upon examination, I can see a tiny bit of lace is snagged in the zipper. I gently work it back down, hoping it doesn't rip. Once it's free, I slowly run it up, fastening the hook-and-eye closure at the top. When my fingers brush her bare back, goosebumps scatter along her skin and her breath seems to falter for a split second—good God, what I'd do to hear that sound again.

I drag my knuckle up the remainder of her spine, marveling at how soft her skin is. Knowing I probably shouldn't be touching her like this, I drop my hand. I clear my throat, hoping my voice sounds normal when I speak. "All good. And it wasn't your ass; it was hung on some lace. There's absolutely nothing wrong with your ass in this dress."

She turns to me and laughs. "That's nice to hear. I guess we're ready now." She opens the door and I follow her out.

After she locks the deadbolt and nestles her keys into a small clutch purse, I offer her my arm. "Shall we?"

She hooks hers through mine and offers me a sweet smile.

"Let's do it." We make our way down the two flights of stairs and when we get to the parking lot, Ada looks around. "Where's your Bronco?"

I continue guiding her to the Town Car I've hired for the night. At her questioning glance, I shrug. "Blue's a little conspicuous, even for me. Plus, if we decide to take advantage of the open bar, neither of us has to DD."

She considers. "Well, it sounds like you've thought of everything."

CHAPTER TWENTY-SIX

ADA

Riding in a chauffeured car isn't an experience I'm used to. Even at Cole's and my prom, he drove the Bronco. I'm shocked Silas didn't see how taken aback I was by his appearance—because, damn, this is one fine ass man in a suit. And the fact he rented a car makes it feels like a legitimate night out on the town. And if I got butterflies when I saw Silas, no one has to know, right? It's not my fault he's so good-looking.

"So, before it's all over with tonight, you think we'll be found out?"

Silas shakes his head. "Nah. No one will be looking at us. Especially once the cocktail hour starts."

"And how do you know they're having a cocktail hour?"

"Research."

"How much research did you do?"

He gives me a mischievous grin. "A lot."

"What does 'a lot' mean?"

"Exactly what I said. I researched the bride and groom and the location. I found a copy of their wedding invitation. It's amazing what you can find out on social media."

"So, what were the parameters Cole set up for this thing? Isn't that what you said, he had specs he wanted met?"

Silas nods and looks up, remembering, and counts off on his fingers. "Cocktail attire or better." He grins at me. "He always loved you in formalwear." His eyes travel down my body, making me blush. "And for good reason, too. Damn, you look gorgeous, Wednesday."

"Thank you," I reply, my voice quiet. I'm thankful he can't see how much I blush in the dark. I try to make myself sound normal again by clearing my throat. "What else?"

"It had to be at a hotel or somewhere public."

I frown, confused. "That's a weird requirement."

He shakes his head. "Not if you think about it. If the wedding is at a hotel, and we were found out, we could simply say we're guests and were coming back from another event and got curious."

"But we're not guests."

He leans over to me and I get a whiff of his cologne. "Good thing it's not at a hotel then, isn't it? My recon says this place is huge, so if we need to hide for a little while, we can."

I let out a surprised bark of laughter. "You did *recon*?"

He gives me a lopsided grin. "I don't half-ass anything. I wasn't going to go into this thing blind."

"All right, so what about the dinner portion? Don't these kinds of things usually have, like, assigned tables or whatever?"

"I've considered that. From my research—believe it or not, there are tip guides for gate crashing. There are usually a couple of tables without labels for guests who don't RSVP. You know, just in case." After a beat, he adds, "We also need fake names. And a backstory."

"What, in all your *research* you didn't already give us one?" I ask with a chuckle.

"I can if you want. But I figured you'd want to pick your own name. Mine is Freddie White."

"Freddie? Why Freddie? You don't even look like a Freddie."

"Fredrick is my middle name. It's easy for me to remember. And I certainly don't look like a Fred or Fredrick, so Freddie it is."

I consider and smile. "Wednesday."

He nods. "Well, that'll be convenient. And what's our story?"

I think for a minute and look down at my hands. On my right hand, I have a costume ring with a large emerald. I transfer it to my left ring finger. "We're married. Did the couple go on any vacations in the last year that you know of?"

He closes his eyes, mentally cataloging information. After a moment, he snaps his fingers. "Italy."

"Perfect. We were on our honeymoon and met them while we were there. Americans in a foreign country and all that. We had a lovely dinner together and they invited us to their wedding."

He nods. "That could work. And the only people who would know it's not true are the bride and groom, right?"

"Exactly."

Ten minutes later, the car pulls in at an industrial-looking, brick building downtown. Silas jumps out and extends his hand to help me exit the vehicle. He places his hand on the small of my back as we walk toward the building. I look around as many other guests, dressed much the same way we are, file into the venue and I take in the expansive space as we enter. Silas was right, it's huge.

The room, complete with exposed metal beams in the ceiling, light hardwood floors, and exposed brick walls seems to be separated into a ceremony area and a reception area. We follow the crowd and find seats about halfway back from the makeshift altar set up at the front of the room under a suspended floral swag.

I adjust my wrap and fidget with the ring on my left hand. Silas drapes his arm around the back of my chair and leans closer to me. "You keep playing with that thing and people might think you're not a happy wife."

I give him a playful grin. "Or, maybe they'll think it's so big, I have to shift the weight of it every now and then so I don't sprain my finger."

He laughs and pulls me into him and presses a kiss against my temple. "You know I have more fun with you than anyone?"

Pleased, I turn my face toward him. "Well, you should. I'm a lot of fun."

He nods and gives me a genuine smile. I look into his eyes and I still can't figure out what's different about his eyes compared to Cole and Josie's. He must see the puzzlement in my gaze because his brows draw down. "What?"

I shake my head. "There's something different about your eyes than Josie and Cole's. I can't put my finger on it. It's bugged me since we went to Vegas. That was the first time I ever noticed it, but I can't figure out what it is. They shouldn't be different, since you and Cole were twins."

He nods. "Yeah, but we're not identical. His and Josie's eyes are wider set than mine. Mine are like Pap's. They took after Mom. We all have Dad's eye color, though."

Shocked, my mouth falls open. "Y'all weren't identical? How did I not know this? You look so much alike, though."

He nods. "Yeah, but look at Mary-Kate and Ashley Olsen. They're not identical, either. But they sure do look like it. Some fraternal twins do look almost identical. I'm also a half-inch taller than Cole was."

"Well, consider my mind blown. I would've never known."

"Always happy to blow your mind, Peep," he says with a wink. His tone makes my skin prickle and it's as though my heart skips a beat.

What is this, *flirting?* Am I only imagining this chemistry between us? I'd be lying if I said I wasn't having an increasing number of filthy dreams. Most of which include a man with a certain heron tattoo. Are all the dirty dreams I've had in recent days responsible for the way I'm feeling at present? But it's only because of our proximity, right? The tons of time we spend together? The way we give each other shit? It's not anything *real,* right?

What if it is, Ada Mae? You could do a whole lot worse than Si and you know it. Even if that's true, what would it look like for me to take up with Cole's brother? I mean, is that even something he's interested in? Would it even work between us? He's too important to me to risk ruining what we have. His family's too important. What if it went badly? I'd lose the only real family I've ever had.

"You okay, Wednesday?" Silas squeezes my shoulder and his expression is concerned.

I school my features and give him a small smile. "Yeah, of course."

He searches my eyes. He opens his mouth to say something, but music begins streaming from a DJ booth toward the back of the room. He closes it again and simply returns my smile with one of his own. We turn our attention to the front of the room where the officiant, groom, and groomsmen walk in from a side door.

Next, bridesmaids in dark green, floor-length gowns enter from the rear, followed by a small flower girl and ring bearer. Once they've cleared the aisle, the music changes and the officiant signals for everyone to stand. A sweeping instrumental ballad begins to play and a beautiful young woman in her mid-twenties starts up the aisle on the arm of a man who can only be her father.

The look of love on her face is evident and I glance back over toward the groom to see the same expression mirrored in his own. Something in my heart twists. I would've never had this with Cole. Even if he'd lived, we would've never married. Never once, since I was fifteen, have I ever doubted Cole loved me. And for all intents and purposes, we lived like we were married. It shouldn't bother me we never exchanged vows or rings. We were fully committed to one another. But I know now, I want it. Now that it's a possibility for me, I want it all; marriage, kids, the picket fence, the whole big American dream.

The knowledge hits me like a truck and my breath catches and I have to blink back tears. I'm thankful Silas is behind me and can't see my face while we wait for permission to sit again. By the time we do, I've composed myself and blow out a slow breath as I retake my seat.

I don't hear any of the words the officiant says or the vows or any part of the ceremony as I try to think about what all this means. Does it mean I would've eventually resented Cole for even taking the option away of dreams I didn't know for sure I had? Does it mean I'm ready to pursue those types of things now? I glance at Silas out of the corner of my eye, his gaze firmly fixed on the ceremony. Is Silas someone I could see having those things with? Am I someone he'd even want or would the thought of me having been with Cole be too much for him to overlook?

Silas is a good man. Cole's stated this in his letters over and over again; almost as if he's some sort of wingman. Are these continued praises for Silas's character simply to remind me of the fact he's a good man, or is it something more? Sometimes, it's almost as if he's pushing me toward him. Is it absurd for me to even be thinking this might be a possibility? Surely that's not something Cole would do, right? *What if is, Ada Mae? What then?* What indeed.

Everyone begins to clap sometime later and it brings me out of my thoughts and I join in. Silas leans in and whispers in my ear, "Those were pretty good vows." And because I have no idea what the vows were, I simply smile and nod. Soon, the congregation is standing as the officiant pronounces the new couple. A moment later, when the bridal party has made its way back down the aisle, it is announced the cocktail hour will begin immediately.

Guests begin milling toward the reception area so the staff can convert the ceremony space to a dance floor. Silas takes my hand in his and tugs me toward the bar. "Let's get a drink. You think they have any shine?" he asks with a goofy grin.

In spite of the tumultuous thoughts ricocheting around my brain, I huff a laugh. "I sincerely doubt it. Even if they did, it wouldn't be like Pap's, so would you even want it?"

He shakes his head. "Not a chance. What would you like?"

"Red wine. A pinot noir if they have it. Otherwise, a cab is fine." When we reach the bar, he orders my wine and his beer and we take our drinks and wander toward the outer edge of the room to a semi-secluded spot. Silas keeps his hand on the small of my back as we sip our drinks and I try not to enjoy the feel of his hand on me as much as I do.

"This is some venue. It's industrial, but with the flowers and string lights and stuff, it's pretty cozy and inviting."

I nod. "Yeah, it's great."

By some stroke of luck, there are no assigned tables and the food is served buffet style. We chow down on roasted pork loin, rosemary roasted potatoes, bacon-wrapped asparagus, and butternut squash ravioli in a brown butter sauce. And because the food is so good, I'm immediately in a much more positive mood and vow to push my previous thoughts away in favor of a fun evening with Silas. I point to the ravioli with my fork. "This is my favorite food ever. I want to marry this ravioli and have its little ravioli babies."

He laughs. "Yeah, it's pretty good. You should find out who the caterer is, so you can try to get the recipe. Meanwhile, I want to eat my weight in these potatoes. Seriously, how are they both super crispy and fluffy? It makes no sense."

I nod and touch his arm and lean over to him. He tilts his head in my direction so I can whisper in his ear. "You picked an excellent wedding for us to crash."

He grins. "Definitely." He glances around. "You know, we're really good at this. Maybe we should make it a thing. On weekends, we sneak into fancy nuptials and eat all the food, get sloshed on free booze, and talk shit about people we don't know."

"It certainly sounds like something Meredith and Christina would do."

He laughs. "Yeah, except they'd start doing tequila shots and get found out."

"Quite possibly," I agree.

The DJ announces the bride and groom for their first dance and they take the dance floor. The sounds of Ray Lamontagne stream from the DJ booth and they sway to the music and it appears they spend the entire song laughing and sharing sweet kisses. "You think they'll go the distance?" Silas asks after a moment.

"Look at them. They're laughing and if you were able to bottle the way they look at each other, no one would die miserable and alone. Yeah, I do."

"Me, too."

I look at him. "What do you know about them—their story?"

He thinks for a minute. "They've known each other since they were kids. Their families summer in the same place or something. Happened to go to the same college, but he was dating her roommate. Neither of them knew they were going to be at the same school until she walked into her dorm room one day and he was making out with her roommate."

I huff a laugh. "You're joking."

He shakes his head. "No, there was a whole thing about it on their wedding Facebook page. The roommate is the maid of honor."

"Wow. That's something," I say, surprised.

He nods. "Yep."

A few minutes later, after the bride and groom dance with their parents, the floor is opened up to the other guests. Silas drains his wine glass. "Come dance with me."

"Can you dance?" I ask, amused.

"I'd say about as well as you can, Peep. That's not going to stop me from dragging your ass out onto the floor, though. Let's go."

I grin and take off my wrap and drape it over the back of my chair. And knowing I don't have anything in my bag except my keys, phone, lipgloss, and Cole's ashes, I leave my purse as well. I take his hand and let him lead me out to the floor. He pulls me into his arms, wrapping his right arm around my waist and taking my right hand in his left. I rest my left hand on his shoulder.

I don't recognize the song, but it's easy to dance to and as it progresses, Silas pulls me closer and peers down into my eyes. Even in my heels, he's still a good four inches taller than me and I'm forced to tilt my head back to look at him. "You having fun yet?"

I nod. "Yeah, the food alone was worth it. And you're not a bad dancer."

He grins. "Probably those ballet classes my fighting coach made me take to help with my footwork."

A surprised laugh falls from my mouth. "Ballet? For real?"

"Yeah. I only did it for about six months, but it was plenty."

"Do you ever wish you were still fighting?"

He shakes his head. "Nah, life had other plans for me. I like the life I have, the people who are in my life. I'm exactly where I'm supposed to be."

I chew on the inside of my bottom lip. "I think I am, too." The smile he gives me is warm and genuine and makes my heart melt. God help me, I like Silas. As more than my friend or best friend. He's my person and I have feelings for him. I shift my hand to the back of his neck and my fingertips thread through the short hair at the nape of his neck. "What do your mom and dad think about all the time we spend together?"

His brows rise in surprise at my question. "What do you mean?"

I shrug. "Do they say anything to you? Or, do they not know we see each other so much? Do they think we only see each other at family dinner?"

He shakes his head. "No, they know. I would think they're happy about it. They see how much better you're doing and they're glad you're still part of our family. They love you, you know."

I nod. "I know. I love them, too. I'm so thankful to them." I look into his eyes. "And to you. For being my person. You're my favorite person."

His hand drops a bit lower, to the small of my back. He tugs me flush against him and my heart skips what seems like ten beats. "You're my favorite person, too." He presses a light kiss to my forehead and I let my eyes fall closed.

Thankfully, when the song ends, another slow one takes its place and we don't have to stop dancing. After a moment, I return my gaze to his. "In Vegas, if Cole's task had been for us to get married, would you have tried to get me to go through with it?"

He laughs. "No."

For some reason, his answer stings, and I have no clue why and I look down at his chest. But then he speaks again after giving my hand a squeeze to bring my eyes back to his. "It wouldn't be because I wouldn't marry you. But I'd never do it simply because Cole handed down the instructions like some kind of order. That would never be a reason for me to marry you. If I married you, it would be because you're my best friend and you're smart and funny and a monumental pain in my ass, but in the best way possible. I would marry you because you're the most beautiful woman in the world. If I married you, Ada, it would be because I loved you. No other reason." His words and the earnest expression on his face and the tone of his voice make my breath catch. He gives me a sweet smile. "That'd be why I'd marry you. Cole wouldn't have a thing to do with it."

I open my mouth to say something—anything—but no words come. Even though I'd love nothing more than to tell him how touched I am by what he's said, I'm literally unable to speak at this moment. Tears burn my eyes and although I attempt to blink them back, they still spill down my cheeks. Silas's expression morphs into one of concern and he swipes the tears away with the pad of his thumb. "Did I say the wrong thing? I'm sorry. I shouldn't have said any of that." He swallows, looking anxious. "I fucked up, didn't I? Shit, Peep, forget everything I just said. I didn't mean to upset you."

I shake my head. "You didn't. It was perfect, Silas."

The anxiety is replaced with relief and he grins. "Oh.

Okay. I wasn't sure. I thought maybe...Hell, I don't know what I thought. I was just trying to be honest with you."

"I appreciate your honesty." I look down for a moment before looking back up at him. "Can I tell you something?"

He nods. "Of course."

"I realized as the bride was walking down the aisle toward the groom, I want it. I want all of it. Maybe I always have, I don't know. But I always knew with Cole, it wasn't an option, so I never let myself want it. And so, I can't help but wonder, if Cole was still alive, would I have eventually begun to resent him because he couldn't or wouldn't give me the things I needed? Would that have been my life?"

Silas considers my question for a long moment. "No one can answer that but you. I think half the battle in life is realizing the things you want and don't want. You and Cole loved each other, there was never a doubt to anyone about that. But might your love have been able to satisfy you in the long-term if you'd figured out you wanted things he couldn't give you? Who knows?

"I think if you want those things, you can and should get to have them. And any man in his right mind would be lucky to have you. He'd be the luckiest son of a bitch on the planet. Truly."

CHAPTER TWENTY-SEVEN

ADA

An upbeat song starts to play so I step out of Silas's embrace to begin walking back to the table. He follows me off the dance floor and I pick up my wrap and purse. For some reason, I'm sad and confused and happy all at the same time and I don't know which emotion is more prominent at the moment. I turn to him as he reaches the table. "Would you care if we call it a night, I'm tired all of a sudden."

He brushes a stray hair off my forehead and nods, a small smile pulling at the corners of his mouth. "Of course. We just have one thing we need to do."

"Okay." I let him lead the way and as we reach the foyer, he glances around and takes my hand and tugs me around a corner and up a flight of stairs. I don't question him, since I know he wouldn't be going somewhere without a purpose, so I simply try to keep up. He opens a door and I realize we're on the roof. He sees a large rock next to the door and wedges it between the door and the frame so it won't close.

"You brought ashes?"

I nod and pull them out of my clutch. We walk over to the

edge of the roof and I take the lid off the shampoo bottle, the same one from Hoover Dam. It's a windy night and chilly since the sun's gone down. When I shiver, Silas immediately shucks his coat and drapes it over my shoulders. And now, all I smell is his delicious cologne. I have to make myself focus on the task at hand instead of letting my mind wander to what might happen if this was an actual date. Would Silas kiss me? What might that be like?

"Well, we crashed a wedding and didn't get caught," Silas says with a grin, bringing me out of my thoughts.

"Night's not over yet. We still have to successfully navigate our way down the steps and out the front door."

He dismisses my words with a wave. "Psh. Details. We got this. Cole would've loved the food, but not the music. A little too poppy for his taste, I think."

I nod. "Probably." I hold the bottle out to him. "I think you should do it this time."

He shakes his head. "We do it together, same as always. We'll do it just like we did in Vegas, over the rail." He turns me toward the roof railing and steps up behind me. He runs his fingers down my arm and covers my hand with his own. He rests his other hand on the railing beside my hip and his chest is flush against my back and his closeness makes my pulse tic up. He leans his cheek against the side of my head and I let myself lean back against him. Together, we tip the bottle and let the ashes float away on the wind.

For several seconds after, neither of us moves. Silas tilts his head down until his lips are right under my ear. His breath is warm on my skin and sends goosebumps scattering down my arms. My heart races and I'm struggling to breathe normally. He moves his hand from the railing to settle on my hip. "Is this okay?" he asks, his voice low and a bit husky.

"Yeah."

He brushes a kiss under my ear and heat floods my entire body. "And what about that?"

"Yeah." My voice sounds breathy and I struggle to remember why I shouldn't let Silas kiss me. You know, besides the fact I was pretty much married to his brother for the last fifteen years and Cole's been gone less than a year.

"Turn around, Ada."

I obey, my chest heaving, and when I do, his face is only inches from mine. Even with only the light from a nearby street lamp illuminating his features, I see his gaze travel down to my mouth. His grip tightens on my hip as he brings his other hand up to cradle my face. It's in that moment, I know he's going to kiss me. Alarm bells and joy buzzers sound in my mind as he closes the distance between us.

"Hey. Guests aren't allowed out here." Our heads snap to my left toward the door and a staff member stands with a blank expression on his face.

Silas nearly jumps back away from me, almost as if he's been electrocuted. He heads toward the door, me trailing behind him. As we walk down the stairs, he pulls out his phone and shoots off a text, presumably to our driver.

When we exit the building, I return Silas's jacket to him and he wordlessly takes it and pulls it on. Somehow, in the time it's taken us to get down from the roof and out the front door, things have chilled considerably between us and I'm not sure how I'm supposed to feel. I glance at him and wonder if he's as confused as I am in this moment or if he's downright regretting that he almost kissed me.

Only a couple of minutes pass before the Town Car pulls up at the curb and Silas opens the door to allow me to enter. I slide inside and he climbs in behind me and shuts the door. After a few suffocating moments of silence where we both seem to simply stare out opposite windows, I attempt to break the tension. "It was a great wedding," I say with a darted glance in his direction.

"Yeah. It was. And you looked really nice."

"So did you. Was that new cologne?"

"No, but I don't think I've worn it around you much."

"Oh. Well, it's great."

"Thanks."

It's as if we've gone back to how things were when Cole was alive. Only making small talk and not even looking at one another. A weight drops into my stomach at the thought of that being our reality. Have I somehow ruined things? He was the one who leaned in. He was the one who touched my hip and kissed my neck. He was the one who would've initiated the kiss. I haven't done anything wrong.

That's not to say Silas has done anything wrong, either, but he was the one moving things in that direction. I was just the one okay with it. Unless he thinks I wasn't. Did he somehow think I didn't want him to kiss me? I thought the signals I was sending him were pretty clear. And yet, here he is, freezing me out, reducing things to small talk. What the hell?

Twenty silent minutes later, we're back at my apartment. I don't wait for him to open the door and when I exit, I slam it harder than is necessary. And even though I know he follows me up the stairs, I don't even glance over my shoulder. I unlock the door and step inside and when I go to close it, he catches it before it latches. "What, I can't even tell you goodnight?" He steps inside and shuts the door behind him.

I wheel on him. "I don't know, can you? You hardly spoke to me on the way here, I figured you'd just wanna leave."

He frowns. "What's your problem?"

I raise my brows in a mix of frustration and surprise. "I don't have a problem, but it seems like you do. I thought..." I don't finish the sentence, even as heat fills my cheeks. I look away and busy myself taking off my shoes.

"You thought what?" he asks, shoving his hands in his pockets. His expression tells me he knows exactly *what* and he only wants to hear me say it.

I take a step closer and put my hands on my hips. "I thought we had a moment or something. I thought you were going to kiss me." The last sentence comes out rushed.

His jaw clenches and he looks down at his feet. "I was."

I'm alarmed by his seemingly defeated answer. "But you regret it." I hope it's a question, but I phrase it as a statement to conserve what's left of my dignity.

His head snaps up, his expression angry. "No, I don't regret it. Fuck, Ada, I wanted to kiss you more than anything. You have no fucking clue. But when that guy walked out, it hit me we'd just dumped some of *Cole's* ashes at an event *Cole* wanted me to take you to in an attempt to help you get over *Cole*. I don't want to kiss you at something *he* fucking set up. I want to kiss you when it's on *my* time, not his." He pounds his chest with his fist as if to drive the point home. His chest heaves and I blink slowly, trying to absorb his words. He reaches into the inside pocket of his jacket and pulls out an envelope and tosses it on the coffee table.

He doesn't wait for me to respond and pivots and walks out the door. I stand, unmoving, for five solid minutes while I let the realization sink in that Silas wanted to kiss me. I glance down at the letter and guilt slams into me as I drop onto the sofa. I'm not sure if it's guilt over the fact I almost kissed Silas or because I wanted him to. Regardless of Cole's imagined words in my head and even some of the ones he's written over the past several months, it's only been eight months. Not long enough to have completely processed my grief, right?

Can I truly begin something with Silas if I'm not over

losing Cole? A quiet voice in my head says I might never get over losing him. Can I live the rest of my life alone simply because I'm not over Cole?

Maybe it's good Silas left. It'll give us both time to think and process on our own. I'll give it a couple of days for everything to settle in and we can decide where we want to go from here.

Sighing, I begin to reach for the letter and a knock at the door stops me. My heart lurches. *Silas.* He's come back. To talk or finally kiss me, I don't much care which. In spite of my thoughts only seconds earlier about space being a good thing, elation floods my system and I launch myself off the couch and run to the door. Unable to keep the smile off my face, I open it, my stomach and grin immediately dropping.

It's not Silas, but my father. "What are you doing here? It's late."

"I just want to talk to you." I can tell by his tone he's not sober so there's no way I'm letting him in.

"I don't want to talk to you. You need to go." I attempt to shut the door and he shoves it, knocking me off balance and I fall on my butt with a pained grunt. He enters and slams the door. I start to scramble up and he pulls something out of his pocket and waves it at me and I instantly freeze. My mouth goes dry at the sight of the knife.

I try to focus my attention on my father's face and finally see his eyes. They're red-rimmed and wild, his pupils tiny pinpricks. He's high as shit and I try to stay calm so I don't provoke him. I've taken my safety for granted all these years and forgotten the sheer terror I've felt when he's like this.

"Whatever you want, take it. I won't even call the cops. Just take it and go."

He stands over me, the knife pointed at my face. He's

twitchy and he narrows his eyes to look at me. "You got money? I want money."

I shake my head. "I don't have any money."

"Bullshit. I know Cole died. He would've left you life insurance. I want it. You've been going on all these trips and shit. Look at you, all dressed up for some fancy party. I want money, Ada."

I try to keep my tone even. "I told you, I don't have money. Most of Cole's estate paid my rent for a year and made it so I didn't have to work. Most of it's gone. Like I said, you can take whatever you want, but I don't have any money."

He backs up, still keeping the knife pointed at me, and glances around the room. He's obviously assessing things for portability and profitability. I try to stand and he snaps his head in my direction. "Sit your ass down."

Trying to think fast, I throw out the only thing that comes to mind. "You want my credit and debit cards? You can have them."

He snorts. "So you can cancel them? I'm not stupid, girl."

I shake my head. "I won't cancel them. I'll give you two days' head start before I report the cards stolen." Somehow, I'm able to keep my voice steady, regardless of how terrified I am. My phone sits in my clutch purse on the coffee table ten feet away and I know I'll never be able to get to it while he's here.

My father considers my offer. "Two days?" His head and shoulders twitch and he rubs his nose.

"Yes."

"Get 'em. All of 'em." I scramble to my feet and over to my purse on the bar. I hurriedly fish out my wallet and my debit and two credit cards.

I hold them out to him and he snatches them and takes off out the door. I run and bolt the door and barely make it to the couch and collapse before I start hyperventilating.

CHAPTER TWENTY-EIGHT

SILAS

The whole way home, I kick myself for not grabbing Ada and kissing the hell out of her. The look on her face when I turned to leave nearly killed me. But I meant what I said. I don't want to kiss her with Cole looming over us. I know tonight was a turning point for us and I hope it's only the beginning of our future.

I'm just stepping out of the Town Car and tipping the driver when my phone rings. I'm surprised to see Ada calling me. I figured she'd read Cole's letter and need time to process everything and I wouldn't see or hear from her until at least family dinner tomorrow.

I swipe the screen to answer, all the while, I'm shedding my suit jacket as I start toward the front door of my house. "Hey, Wednesday, I didn't—."

"Silas." The fear in her voice stops me in my tracks.

"What's wrong?" I pivot and immediately head for the Bronco.

"I need you. Please." Her words come out between sobs. "My dad. He was here."

Terror grips me and I nearly drop the phone as I try to get the car started. "I'm coming. I'll be there in fifteen minutes. Stay on the phone with me, okay?" I break every traffic law known to man and make it to Ada's in half the time it normally takes me. I throw up a silent prayer of thanks to God and the saints and every deity I can think of I arrived unscathed. I don't bother knocking and use my key to unlock and crash through the door.

She's on the couch and it's only then, when I see she appears unharmed, I breathe and hang up my phone. I slam the door and lock it and drop to my knees in front of her. She throws her arms around me and sobs. Huge, racking sobs full of fear and probably a bit of relief that the ordeal is over. I simply hold her and rise to take a seat on the couch, not letting go of her.

I'm so thankful she's not hurt, all I can do is pull her closer to me and will my heart to stop pounding. I rub her back and press kisses into her hair until she begins to calm down. Tears of relief burn my eyes and I blink them back so I can focus on her.

"Can you tell me what happened? Do I need to call the police? Do we need to go to the hospital?"

She pulls back and shakes her head. She wipes her face with the back of her hand, mascara smearing across her cheek. She sniffles and when she speaks, her words come out between shuddery breaths. "He didn't hurt me. He was high and he had a knife. He only wanted money. He assumed because of all our trips and stuff, I had some. I gave him my debit and credit cards and told him I'd wait two days before I reported the cards stolen."

I take her face in my hands. "You're not hurt? You're sure?"

She huffs a small laugh and sniffles. "Only my ass, where he knocked me off my feet with the door."

I swallow and blow out a breath. "If I had stayed, this wouldn't have happened. Fuck, I shouldn't have left you here."

"If you'd been here, one or both of us would've gotten hurt. I thought I could talk him down and I did. I learned my lesson last time trying to fight him off."

In spite of my best efforts to the contrary, hot rage bubbles up in my chest. "I'm going to kill him, Ada. This is so far beyond fucked up, they never should have let him out of jail. You have to tell the police it was him who stole the cards."

She nods. "I will." She brings her hand up to my jaw. "I'm okay, though. I promise. I'm just a little shaken up." She bites the inside of her bottom lip. "I thought it was you. I thought you had come back and I was so glad, I didn't even look through the peephole. It was so stupid of me."

A jolt of something akin to joy shoots through me at the thought she'd be happy I'd come back. "You're not stupid, Ada. Your dad hasn't visited this place in, what, eight years? When he got out of jail and came to tell you he was sober and sorry."

She nods. "Yeah."

"Then there was no reason to suspect it wasn't me." I press a kiss to her forehead. "I'm sorry it wasn't me. I wish it had been."

"Me, too," she agrees, her voice soft.

Part of me wants nothing more in this moment than to give her a proper kiss. To show her how much I love her. But I already know I won't. Not after what I said earlier and everything that's happened since. She's not in a good emotional headspace right now and I'm probably not either. So I simply lean against the back of the couch and bring her with me and we stay cuddled up for a long time her head resting on my chest. For a while, neither of us says anything.

She's quiet for so long, I think she's nodded off, but she finally raises her head. "I should go wash my face and get ready for bed." She looks down at my shirt and winces. "Oh, God. I'm so sorry. I got makeup all over your shirt. I'll clean it for you. Take it off and I'll put some stain remover on it."

I huff a laugh. "Hey, if you want me to take my shirt off, all you have to do is ask. You don't have to pretend to want to do my laundry."

A surprised bark of laughter escapes her and she smiles and blushes and I'm so happy to see it, I nearly want to dance a jig. "Arrogant ass. I'm not asking you to take your shirt off. I'm serious, you have stuff all over it."

I shake my head. "I don't care, Wednesday. I can buy ten more shirts. I'm not worried about it."

She rises and starts to walk toward her bedroom and then stops and turns back to me. "Will you undo the hook-and-eye at the top of the zipper, I don't think I'll be able to get it. And then, can you unzip me, I don't want to snag the zipper on the lace." The thought of unzipping her dress makes my dick instantly swell and when I stand, I'm thankful her back is to me.

I sweep her hair over one shoulder and unlatch the hook. I hold the top of the dress between my thumb and index finger to keep tension as I start to lower the zipper. As her skin is revealed, an aching need settles itself in my balls. I'm going to have to get out of here soon or risk doing something Ada may not be ready for, even if she might be willing in the moment.

Once the zipper is all the way down, I quickly drop my hands lest I feel the urge to throw her over my shoulder and take her to bed. Especially since I'm not even sure if it's something she wants. "Thank you." She holds the front of her dress against her chest and bends to pick up her shoes from in front of the TV before heading down the hall.

"Anytime." I know I should go, but honestly, I'm not sure how to leave her. I'm not sure if she's okay to leave alone. What if her dad comes back? I know it's not my choice if I leave, but I can't stand the thought of not knowing she's okay. I decide in that moment, if she wants me to go, I'll sleep in my car, out in the parking lot to be able to keep an eye on her, even from afar.

I sit on the couch and scrub my hands down my face and roll my shoulders. My eyes snag on Cole's letter, exactly where I left it. Seeing it is like having a bucket of cold water dumped on my head. I want all these fucking tasks to be over so I can focus my attention on only Ada. I don't want to have to follow through with any more plans. I want Cole to not be hovering over us anymore. I feel like, until he's not, she and I will be in this state of limbo.

Then, I instantly feel guilty. Without these tasks, I would've never had the opportunity to build any type of relationship with Ada. I drag my hand down my face and hang my head. Fucking emotional whiplash. Jesus.

I'm broken out of my thoughts by the feel of Ada's hand on my shoulder and I snap my head in her direction. Her face is scrubbed clean and she's changed into her Vegas shirt and a pair of shorts, her hair in a thick braid over one shoulder. "You okay?" Her expression is concerned and another stab of guilt hits me in the chest. She shouldn't be concerned about me. I should be the one concerned about her right now.

"Yeah, I'm fine," I reply with a nod. "Are you?"

She gives me a small smile. "Yeah." The hand at her side opens and closes like she's anxious. "Can I ask you for a favor, though?"

"Of course. Anything."

Her throat bobs with a swallow and she looks away for a second as if she's working up the nerve to ask for what she needs. When she looks back at me, her eyes are pleading. "Will you stay with me tonight? I don't want to be alone. I'm still a little freaked out."

I stand and look down at her. "Of course, Peep. Whatever you need."

She lets out a slow breath. "Would you hold me? Just until I go to sleep. But if it's weird or whatever, we can forget it."

I run my fingers down her arm and take her hand in mine and give it a squeeze. "Ada, stop. Like I said, anything you need." I drop her hand and turn her around. "Let's go." I nudge her in the direction of her room, turning off lights as we go, and she shuffles down the hall.

As I enter the bedroom, I notice the closet door is open. The sight of Cole's shirts still hanging there makes me realize this is still very much *their* room. His room. And I know there's no way I'm ever going to be able to try to seduce Ada in this room. Not right now. Good thing that's not what we're doing tonight.

She climbs under the covers and I take a moment to toe off my shoes and pull off my socks. I unknot my tie and pull it off and lay it on the bench at the end of the bed. I untuck my shirt before working the buttons loose. I shrug it off and lay it on the bench as well. All the while, I feel Ada's eyes on me and that ache begins to settle into my balls again in spite of the knowledge I'm surrounded by my brother's belongings. I empty my pockets and take off my belt, but leave my pants on, along with the undershirt I'd worn under my dress shirt.

I crawl onto the bed but stay above the covers to help me resist temptation even more. To let her know this is only for comfort. As I lie down, she rolls over to switch off the lamp and the room is plunged into darkness. I turn onto my side and pull her into my arms and it's a bit awkward with her being under the covers and me being over them, but somehow, I manage. I curl my body around hers and breathe in the smell of her shampoo and clean skin.

Ada relaxes against me and lets out a sigh that sounds like

she's lost a thousand emotional pounds. "Thank you, Silas." Her voice is thick with emotion and after a moment, her shoulders shake as she begins to cry.

"Hey, hey," I say and squeeze her tighter. "What's all this?"

"I'm sorry." She sounds embarrassed and my heart squeezes.

"You don't have anything to apologize for. What is it?"

"I've just missed this. And it's been a weird night. I'm emotional. I'm sorry."

I press a kiss to the side of her head. "Like I said, nothing to apologize for. It's understandable you'd have a lot of feelings going on. I'm happy to hold you all night if it's what you need. I know that part of Cole being gone has probably been really difficult for you."

She sniffles. "Yeah. But he wasn't really a cuddler. It was more him lying flat on his back and me being like some sort of spider monkey clinging to him all night."

I can't help but laugh. "Well, feel free to climb me like a tree."

She snorts and leans back against me. After a few minutes, she asks, "Is this weird for you?"

"Not gonna lie. A little. But only because this is the bed you shared with him."

"Yeah."

I blow out a breath. "And part of me is nervous that if you wake up next to me in the morning, you'll be triggered or something and freak out. Not that I'm not willing to calm you down, but I don't want to be the reason you have some sort of emotional meltdown."

"You and Cole aren't the same person, I know that. I know just by the way you sleep, you're not Cole. Plus, you snore."

I huff a laugh. "Do not."

"Yeah, you do. It's not loud or annoying, but you do. Cole

didn't. He also didn't move when he slept. Whatever position he fell asleep in, that was the position he'd wake up in. You wallow in your sleep. You're not one of those people who could simply pull the covers back up and it'd look like you were never in the bed. How do you keep sheets on your bed with as much as you roll around?"

Pleased she's observed these things about me, I smile. "I have to literally remake the bed every morning. Fix the sheets and everything. It's a pain in the ass."

She rolls to face me and snuggles into my chest and I trail my hand down her back. She pushes the covers down around her hips and rests her hand on my waist. "This okay?" she asks.

I huff a laugh. "Yeah, Wednesday, it's fine."

Her hand slides lower and up under the hem of my shirt. Her fingertips brush my skin and my heart lurches. "And what about this?"

"Yeah."

She presses a kiss to my chest and I have to remind myself to breathe. "And was that okay?"

"Uh-huh," I reply, my voice husky. I clear my throat and will myself to not read more into this than simply her needing some sort of physical connection in light of how emotional this night has been. She shifts her body and I feel the tip of her nose run up the side of my neck just before her lips graze my skin. I nearly groan with the contact but bite it back. My dick certainly believes things are a go because I'm instantly hard. I move my hips away from her so she doesn't feel it.

"What about that?"

I take some deep breaths. "Ada, what are you doing?" My words come out sounding pained because honestly, I am. For almost twenty years, this moment is all I've ever wanted. Even when I didn't let myself want it, I always knew I'd never be able to want someone as badly as I've always wanted Ada.

Her hand moves up my shirt and she grips my waist, her thumb brushing over my ribs. "Nothing." But she's kissing my neck and I'm about to lose my ability to think straight.

"You sure about that?"

"Why, do you want it to be something?"

"Are you trying to kill me? Because that's what it feels like."

"Do you want me to stop?"

"I should."

She pulls her hand away and stops kissing me. "Okay." She sounds disappointed and I'll be damned if she thinks it's because I don't want her.

I reach over her and turn on the light because I'm not having this conversation in the dark. I shift my body to cage her in and bracket her hips with my knees and brace my hands on either side of her head. "Ada, look at me."

Her expression is questioning and open and vulnerable and I'm not sure my heart will ever survive this woman. "Don't, for a single second, think I wouldn't want you. I already told you earlier I wanted to kiss you. I wasn't lying. So I don't ever want you to feel like I wouldn't want you. Fuck, if you knew how bad I want you." I huff a breath and close my eyes, hanging my head.

"It's hard for me, Ada. I don't want to fuck this up. You are my best friend and I'll be damned if I ruin that part of things. Even if we both wanted more than that, I don't want you to end up resenting me because I tried to move too fast. I don't want you to get hurt. I'd never forgive myself. Regardless of how badly I want you or how deeply I feel things for you, I don't want you to have any regrets." I look into her eyes. "I'm not Cole." My words come out more harshly than I intend and anger flashes in her eyes.

She sits up and pushes me back. "You think I don't fucking know that? What, you think I just assume y'all are interchangeable? I'm not an idiot, Silas. And I shouldn't want you. It should feel twisted and weird and I should want to be ashamed. But you know what? I honestly think this is somehow what Cole wanted. That letter in the living room? I haven't even opened it and I can pretty much tell you exactly what it's going to say. It's going to say he hoped we had a great time at the wedding and how he hopes I realize I want to get married and have babies and I should find someone to give them to me. It's going to say how wonderful and kind and amazing you are. And then there will be some story about you; some memory of his to help me know you better.

"If I were to look back through all the letters he's written, I guarantee you over half of the content is going to be about you. Like he's some kind of fucked up wingman, pushing me toward you. He has been since the very beginning. I don't understand it, but I'm done feeling bad about wanting you.

"When my dad left, the only thought I had was that I needed you. And you came, no questions asked. You're my person, Silas; my best friend. And I know it would probably be weird for people to accept if we somehow got together, but I don't know if I care. Why should I? Haven't I suffered enough heartache in my life to not want to try to be happy however I can?" Tears well in her eyes and my chest tightens.

Ada brings her hands up to my face. "You are a good man, Silas. You have been here for me when I didn't want to do anything but let my grief overtake me. In spite of your own pain, you've made sure I was okay. You've made me follow through on the things Cole wanted because you knew it was what I needed. I can never thank you enough for everything you've done for me." Tears roll down her cheeks and I reach to wipe them away with the pads of my thumbs.

"You are my best friend and I don't deserve how good you've been to me." Her jaw clenches and her eyes turn flinty.

"And I know you're not Cole. I could tell you every way y'all are different. Simply because you look like him doesn't mean I would be confused. I'm not stupid."

I nod. "I know you're not. You're a lot of things, Ada. Stupid isn't one of them. And I don't give a shit what people think. If we started things, it would never enter my mind to give a fuck what anyone had to say. But it's not been that long. Like I said, I don't want you to have any regrets. Not when I can be patient and wait for you to be ready. Fuck, Wednesday, if you only knew how patient I am," I say with a heavy exhale.

Her brow furrows. "How patient?"

I shake my head. "It's not important. Just know that if we started this, it wouldn't be a fling. It wouldn't be casual. It would be because you're it for me, Ada. It would be because I wanted to spend the rest of my life with you." Her breath catches and I give her a small smile. "Like I said, I'm a patient man. And I refuse to fuck this up. So I can wait. For as long as I need to. Believe me."

Knowing I can't stay on this bed and keep my hands off her, I rise and walk out of the bedroom.

CHAPTER TWENTY-NINE

ADA

I let Silas's words sink in. *It wouldn't be casual... It would be because you're it for me... It would be because I wanted to spend the rest of my life with you.* And then, he's leaving the bedroom and I am instantly pissed. He says something like *that* and walks out of the room? What the hell? I scramble from under the covers and go after him, speaking to his back as I get closer to where he stands at the end of the hall, his hands on his hips and head hung. "So, you just get to say all that to me and walk out? What the hell, Silas?"

He pivots and stalks back in my direction. I expect him to blow up and we have some sort of big fight. It wouldn't surprise me since it's kind of our M.O. When emotions run high between us, we fight. So I steel myself for whatever he's about to say. But when he's within inches of me, he grabs my face and crashes his lips to mine. It's not a tender or sweet kiss. It's possessive and hungry and full of something that feels an awful lot like frustration.

I'm caught off guard for only long enough for him to slide his hand to the back of my neck and tilt my head back to deepen the kiss. And God, what a kiss. I grip the front of his shirt and pull him closer as my heart begins to race. Heat surges through my middle, and I can't help but moan into his mouth.

Silas drags one hand down my side and squeezes my hip, pushing me back. I grunt when I hit the wall of the hallway and he breaks our kiss. "Fuck, I'm sorry." His chest is heaving and his cheeks have gone pink.

I shake my head and huff a laugh. "I'm fine." I pull his mouth back to mine and tug him toward the bedroom. I slow our kiss, wanting to really taste him. To savor this moment. To truly feel his lips and the slide of his tongue against mine. But when we reach the bedroom door, he stops, pulling back. "I can't do this here, Ada." His expression is pained and I furrow my brow in frustration.

"What? Why?"

He huffs out a breath in resignation and shuts his eyes and hangs his head. "Look around your room."

I turn and do as he says, taking in the space. I see the open closet, with Cole's shirts and shoes visible. I see several photos of us on the tall chest of drawers that still houses his other clothes. His reading glasses on the nightstand on top of the book he was reading before he died. Realization hits me that this was a space Cole and I shared and is still very much *our* room. But I'm not sure I'm ready to give up those reminders of him, not yet. Tears spring to my eyes and a shuddery sob works its way up my throat.

Silas comes up behind me and turns me to face him, pulling me in for a hug. "I know, Wednesday. It's a lot." He leans back and looks down into my face. "Like I said, I don't want to fuck this up. I don't want to do anything before you're ready. I can be patient. Especially now that I know it works between us. Fuck, Peep," he says with a goofy grin and I can't help but laugh, in spite of my pain.

He brushes a kiss across my forehead. "Come on, let's go to bed. I promised to hold you all night. I'm still going to do that." I let him turn me back around and guide me to bed. I crawl under the covers and he pulls them up around me. He climbs in bed beside me, above the covers, and reaches over me to turn off the light, pulling me into his arms. He presses a kiss under my ear and a sense of peace washes over me.

I startle when the bed shifts next to me. It's then I remember Silas slept over and my heart returns to a normal rhythm. Opening my eyes, I assess the situation and smile when I feel his arm still draped around me, his hand splayed across the small if my back. And even though he stayed above the blankets all night, I somehow worked my way from under the covers and my leg is thrown over his hip. Currently fitting together like some sort of weird puzzle pieces, I can't help but look at his face as he sleeps. Even the expressions he wears in sleep are different from Cole's. How anyone could ever mistake these two men for one another is beyond me. They could have the same haircut and same outfit and I'd be able to pick them out from across the room.

For some reason, knowing this brings me immense satisfaction. Like it's some kind of secret only I'm privy to. I extricate myself from under his arm and the twisted covers and climb quietly from the bed. I leave him and as I pass the end of the bed, I see his soiled shirt. I pick it up and bring it with me to the kitchen, where the stackable washer and dryer are housed in a tiny closet.

I lay his shirt on the counter and pull out the stain stick from under the kitchen sink and dab the gel onto the stains left from my tears and smeared makeup. I let it soak for a few minutes before starting a pot of coffee and pulling a pack of bacon from the fridge.

After laying the strips of bacon onto a baking sheet, I pop it into the preheating oven and wash my hands. I tiptoe back into the bedroom and gather up some of my light-colored laundry to wash with Silas's shirt and head back to the kitchen to toss in the load. The coffee finishes brewing a moment later and I pour myself a cup and go sit on the couch, my eyes immediately falling on Cole's letter. Wanting to see if my prediction is correct about what's in it, I open the envelope and pull it out.

My Ada Mae,

I'm sure the wedding was beautiful. A loving couple declaring their love for the whole world to see always is. I will forever regret I couldn't give you that. As you watched the glances the bride and groom shared, the vows they made to one another, and the tender way they held one another when they shared their first dance, I hope you can see how much you want it.

Whether you know it or not, I've suspected for a while it would eventually be something you'd want. At least now, I won't have to worry about you resenting me when we're fifty and past the point of you being able to have all the things you're realizing you need.

I hope you'll let yourself have them. I hope you'll allow yourself to be happy. Sooner rather than later, babe. Truly. Life is too short to waste time worrying people will think it's too soon. I know you loved me, that was never in question. And simply because you find someone new to love, it doesn't mean our love is somehow invalid.

My thinking is, if you're able to move on soon, I will have done my job with these tasks and will have given you such good closure by the end of this thing. Which, I'm sorry to say, will come sooner than either of us would probably prefer. My hope is you will be able to love someone freely, without reservation or worry about what I would think about it.

And I believe you're still capable of great love, Ada Mae. Our love was just the warm-up for the big game. Your happy ending is still out there. You've always been my forever, even if I knew there was a good chance I couldn't be yours.

Did you know, when Si and I were working on the Bronco when we were fifteen, we'd talk about our hopes and dreams? Yeah, I know, teenage boys shouldn't wax poetic about stuff, but we did. I had no clue at that time what I wanted for my life. I didn't know I'd want to be a landscape architect or even that I wanted to love you.

But Si, let me tell you, he knew what he wanted. At that time, he still thought about being a fighter, but even more than that, he wanted a wife and kids and a home. At fifteen, Ada. He already knew exactly what he wanted.

It blew my mind and the idea of the things he wanted scared the shit out of me. As calculating and plan-focused as I am, I couldn't see past the next week, let alone into the next twenty years.

My point is, once Silas has set his sights on something or decided he's in, he's ALL in. As spontaneous and carefree as he can be, he's not a flake. He's steady and sure and if he makes a promise or commitment, he follows through. Whatever he tells you, you can take it to the bank. He's true and honest and the best man I know. Something tells me you already know this, Ada Mae.

It's okay to trust yourself.

-Cole

. . .

I sigh and close my eyes and let my chin fall to my chest.

"Well?"

My head snaps up to see Silas leaning against the wall next to the hallway. "Well, what?"

"Was his letter what you thought?"

I hold it out. "You want to read it?"

He shakes his head. "No."

I nod. "Pretty much," I admit, refolding it and sliding it back into the envelope. I walk past him into my office and lay it on the large stack containing all of Cole's letters before returning to the kitchen. "You want some coffee?"

He stands on the other side of the kitchen, hands stuffed in the pockets of his dress pants. "Sure." I pull a mug down and pour him a cup and walk it over to him. He closes his hand over mine when I extend the mug to him. "You okay?"

I nod. "Yeah."

"It's okay if you're not, you know. Last night was a lot. Between the wedding and your dad and... later."

I look up at him, into his warm and sincere eyes. I bring my free hand up to grip his jaw, now covered with a night's worth of stubble and rough against my palm. "I'm all right. I'm not freaked out and I don't have any regrets about you kissing me."

Color rises to his cheeks and he blinks slowly. He swallows and his Adam's apple bobs in his throat. "That's good because I'd very much enjoy doing it again. Soon."

I can't help but smile. "I'm glad."

On Monday morning, Silas went with me to report my debit and credit cards stolen. The police questioned why I waited to report the crime and I told them I was afraid to leave my home for fear he'd be lying in wait somewhere to accost me again.

Silas held my hand as I described my father's behavior and I didn't even have to fake the tears that poured from my eyes. I also filed a restraining order in the event he's found and somehow makes bail.

On Wednesday, the police notified me they'd found my father in a hospital. He'd overdosed on meth and a good samaritan happened to find him before he'd died. I couldn't even muster up any sort of compassion that he was still alive.

Silas hasn't kissed me again. I'm not sure if it's because he thinks I'm currently too fragile, what with all the upheaval with my father and the stress of trying to get my finances back under control. It's a nightmare, but hopefully, all my money will be returned soon.

The Friday afternoon nearly two weeks following the wedding we crashed, Silas sends me a cryptic text.

> Silas: Pack a bag. Don't ask questions. Be ready by five.

Unsure what to even make of his text, I shoot back a lot of questions, in spite of his request for me to ask none.

> Ada: What do I need to pack? How many days? What type of weather?

Not even thirty seconds later, his response bounces back.

> Silas: No questions, Wednesday. We'll be back on Sunday and there is no required dress code. That's all you get. See you at five.

Still confused, I pull out my duffle bag and toss in comfy clothes. Next, in goes my toiletry bag, cushy socks, and some cute pajamas I'd picked up yesterday when Josie and I had lunch. I pack my sketchbook and pencils and call it a day.

I shower and shave and dress in a pair of leggings and a tunic. I dry and curl my hair and put on a bit of makeup. Even if I have no clue what Silas is up to, I still want to look nice. I tug a warm cardigan on over the tunic and assess my appearance. Comfy but cute.

I know I could probably text Josie and she might know what Silas is up to. But I'd be lying if I said the idea of a spontaneous—hopefully romantic—weekend away didn't excite me. I can't help but hope he plans on kissing me again, otherwise, I might have to kiss him. And if that happens, I'm not sure I'll be able to be sedate about it. Not that I want him to be sedate about kissing me; not in the least. Since we've all but confessed our desire to be with one another, I'm hoping this weekend is the beginning of that.

Maybe this is a way to get us out of our normal environments since both our homes seem to be full of reminders of Cole. I tamp down the lingering pangs of guilt at the thought of being with anyone who's not Cole. I have nothing to feel guilty about, right? Isn't me moving on what he wanted? Even knowing that's what he's said, the thought still makes me anxious. Even if the person I will be sharing myself with is Silas, it's still someone other than Cole. And although I want him, it's still strange to know that possibly after this weekend, Cole won't be the only man I've ever slept with.

I never would've imagined at twenty or twenty-five I'd be considering—hoping—to be intimate with someone who wasn't Cole. Of course, I never thought I'd live in a world without him, either.

By four-thirty, I'm antsy and nervous and find myself pacing my apartment, arranging and rearranging the magazines on the coffee table. By four-forty-five, I walk into the kitchen and down a large swig of apple pie moonshine from the batch Silas and I flavored a few months back on the farm. I cough as the liquor burns all the way down. I take several deep breaths and feel the calm settle over me. And right at five, there's a knock at the door.

CHAPTER THIRTY

ADA

I open the door to see Silas dressed in jeans and a long-sleeved henley, the top two buttons undone. He gives me a warm grin. "Hey, Peep. You ready?"

I nod and he picks up my bag from the floor and I follow him out to the Bronco. He opens my door and after I climb in, he takes a moment to stow my bag in the cargo area before sliding behind the wheel. Before he starts the car, he brings his hand up to my face and runs the knuckle of his index finger along my jaw. "You look beautiful."

Pleasant heat rises to my cheeks. "Thank you. So, where are we off to?"

He shakes his head. "Nope. Don't even ask."

"Okay, but we're going for the whole weekend?"

He nods. "Yeah. We'll probably have to head straight to family dinner when we get back."

"Okay."

He starts the car and backs out of the parking spot and pulls away. He turns on the radio—thankfully, not disco—and I sing along to a James Taylor song. In the growing dark, I don't recognize anything except that we're headed south on the interstate.

About two hours later, it's pitch dark and I still don't see any discernible landmarks that would give away where we're going. Not even after Silas exits the interstate and starts down a two-lane road. I've given up trying to figure out the mystery once he makes the turn onto a curvy road in a wooded area. There are no street lights, but occasional lights from the windows of houses flicker in the distance.

Even when he pulls into what I know is probably our destination, I can't make out anything. There's no moon to assist me in seeing. Nothing except the headlights illuminating the porch of a cabin I now recognize as he drives closer to the house. "Snowy's cabin? How'd you manage this?" I ask, surprised.

He shrugs as he coasts to a stop and puts the Bronco into neutral and shuts off the engine and sets the parking brake. "He needed some work done. I offered. Figured it'd be nice for you to get away after everything with your dad and the banks and stuff. Win-win for me to get to keep you to myself, too."

I grab his face and plant a huge kiss on his lips and he laughs when I pull back a second later. "I take it you like the idea?"

"Love it." We hop out of the cab and take a few minutes to unload the groceries and our luggage. I also notice there's a chainsaw and large ax in the cargo area. "What kind of work do you have to do?" I ask, carrying a grocery bag up the stairs.

"There are a couple of trees that got knocked down during a bad storm a couple of months ago. He wanted to let them dry out a little more so they'd be easier to split into logs."

"Sounds like a lot of work for one person."

He starts putting away groceries and shakes his head. "Nah. They're not that big. Probably won't take me a few hours to get the trees cut up as long as I don't have any issues with the chainsaw. Splitting the logs will take longer, but it'll be a good workout." He gives me a wicked grin. "I'll even let you watch."

I chuckle. "Well, color me intrigued." I pull out a few bottles of wine from a grocery bag and set them toward the back of the counter. "Thank you for bringing me with you."

He turns to face me and closes the distance between us and takes my face in his hands. "Thank you for being up for it." He examines my eyes and gives me a warm smile and presses his forehead to mine and I let my eyes fall closed. I wrap my arms around his waist and tug him closer to me as he slides his hands to the back of my neck, threading his fingers into my hair.

We seem to share breaths and for several seconds, we simply stand like this, in this intimate embrace. It's comfortable and makes me feel like I'm home. "Ada?"

"Hmm?"

He pulls his face back and I open my eyes. "I meant what I said that night."

Although I'm pretty sure I know what he's referring to, I still want to hear him say it again. "Which part?"

"All of it. How I can't do casual with you. This would be a big deal for me. But I don't want to rush you, either. I can be patient. I didn't bring you here with any expectations in mind. Getting to spend time with you really is my only goal. I've waited a while for us to get to this point and I'm not about to fuck it up by being hasty."

I nod. "Okay." I chew the inside of my bottom lip. "And you really don't care what people might think if we're together?"

He shakes his head, his expression serious. "No, I don't. We can tell everyone or we can tell no one for now, if you want. Either way, if we do this, it's not going to be a fling for me. I'd want this to be a long-ass time, Wednesday. Hopefully, forever. And I'm sorry if what I'm saying scares you, but I'm not going to sugarcoat the way I feel about you. So, eventually, we'd have to tell everyone, and anyone who loves us will be happy for us. Everyone else can go to hell. Cole would be happy for us. I have to believe that. Because he loved us."

His confidence about all this buoys my own and I give him a smile. "I know he did." He lowers his mouth to within inches of mine just before his stomach growls loudly. I burst out laughing. "Hungry?"

He nods, a wide grin on his face. "Yeah. You?"

"Starving."

"Okay. Why don't I throw something together for supper and you can get settled."

"I can help."

"I know, but I'm only making grilled cheese. Tomorrow, you can help cook. I might not have the strength to lift my arms after I'm done working tomorrow and you may have to take care of me. So relax while you can. I brought a bluetooth speaker in that tote bag if you have any music downloaded on your phone. Service is pretty spotty here, so you probably can't stream anything. But if you don't have anything on yours, I do on mine."

I walk around the counter to where he's gestured to a canvas tote bag. Sure enough, there's a speaker, along with a few books and a deck of cards. Silas begins moving around the small kitchen making supper. "What's the first song on your playlist currently?" I ask.

He stops digging in the fridge and looks at me. "Right now? 'What Would It Take' by Anderson East. It was the most recent song I added. Why?"

"Just seeing who had a better song as the first one. Mine is 'Someone You Loved' by Lewis Capaldi. I think you win. Anderson East is good." I turn on the speaker and set it up on the counter. "I tell you what, your taste in music has greatly benefitted from you hanging out with me."

He scoff-laughs. "I'll have you know, I have excellent taste in music."

"Only because of my influence."

"I think we can agree to disagree." He pulls out his phone and starts the music and I sway to the rhythm as I watch him cook supper.

After supper is finished and cleaned up, we lounge on the sofa and simply talk. It's nice and homey and I can't deny how much I love it. It's nice to have been able to get away for the weekend, even if Silas's plan isn't to seduce me outright. Even if I wouldn't mind.

That's not to say I probably wouldn't be nervous knowing it's been a while and Cole was the last—and only—man I was with. Would Silas get in his head about that? I'd hope not. Because despite the fact Cole was Silas's brother, I have no hesitations about wanting to pursue a relationship with him.

Around ten, I let out a deep yawn and shake my head quickly and cover my mouth with the back of my hand in an attempt to stifle it. Silas chuckles and gives my knee a squeeze. "Bedtime?"

I stretch and shrug. "I think I'm okay." But then, not two seconds later, I yawn again.

He grins. "Uh-huh. Come on."

"What are the sleeping arrangements?"

His grin widens. "Whatever you want them to be, Peep."

I scoff. "You say it as if I should know. You're the one who said there weren't any expectations, I'm simply trying to respect that."

His expression softens and he takes my face in his hands. "If you wanted to sleep in my bed, I have no issues with it. Honestly, I'd love it. But I don't want you to think it's expected." He presses a soft kiss to my lips and drops his hands.

"Well, if it's an option, I'd like to sleep with you." I'm fully aware my tone conveys my double meaning and color rises to Silas's cheeks and I laugh. "I'm going to go get ready for bed."

"All right. I'm going to make sure everything's locked up. I'll be in soon."

I pick up my duffle from where I've left it by the door and take it into the room he stayed in the last time we were here. I pull out my pajamas and toiletry bag and step into the bathroom. I quickly wash my face and brush my teeth before pulling on my sleep shorts and matching camisole. I work my hair into a quick braid over my shoulder and assess my appearance. Not bad, if I do say so myself.

I return to the bedroom and drop my clothes into my bag. I turn on the bedside lamp and crawl under the quilt and sheet and pull them up to my chest. Five minutes later, Silas walks into the bedroom, his own bag in hand. He's already changed into a pair of pajama bottoms slung low on his hips and no shirt and my breath catches seeing him. Sweet baby Jesus, he's a fine ass specimen of the male form.

"You'll catch flies with your mouth open like that, Wednesday," he says with a smug grin as he drops his bag next to mine.

I clamp my mouth shut, even as heat floods my face. "Not my fault you look like that. Good lord."

He laughs as he climbs into bed next to me and gives me a cocky smile. "Oh, so you like what you see?"

"I think that's a given. Damn. And here I thought all that working out only gave you a big head," I say with a wink.

"No, all that working out gave me tons of stamina."

"I thought you said you didn't have any expectations? You

keep talking like that and I'm going to think you're trying to seduce me." In spite of the calmness in my voice, heat settles low in my abdomen.

"I never said I wasn't. I only wanted you to know that I don't consider it a given that you'll do anything more than spend time with me. And give me shit. And drive me to the brink of madness." He tugs the covers away from my body and examines my less-than-modest sleepwear. "Like wearing this. I think you're trying to kill me."

"Oh, so you like what you see?" I ask, mimicking his cocky tone from earlier.

"I've always liked what I saw, Wednesday." His tone and expression are sincere and he reaches over me to turn off the lamp and I lean forward and capture his mouth with mine. He tastes like mint and smells like the eucalyptus aftershave he uses. I reach up to grip the back of his neck to hold him in place and he kisses me back. It's deep and hungry and I feel his hand settles on my waist as he shifts his body, lowering me to the bed. He wedges his knee between my thighs and I hook my leg around his hip, pulling him closer.

My heart races and scorching heat shoots through every inch of me. And when he groans into our kiss, I nearly lose my mind. I run my hands down his chest and waist and over his hip to squeeze his muscled ass. It's my turn to moan when he grinds his hips into me and he's already hard and impressive and I'm seriously hoping he brought condoms because I'm going to need him inside me real soon.

Silas breaks our kiss and even though I can't see him in the dark, I can feel his chest heaving and he huffs a ragged breath against my skin. "Fuck, Ada." I chuckle and try to pull his mouth back to mine and he stops me. "We don't have to do anything. I'm fine just like this."

"I appreciate you trying to be noble, Ass, but I think we

both know where this is headed. I, for one, won't complain if that's the case. But if you want to take things slow, I respect it. If we get to a point and you feel like we should stop, I'm cool. But don't think I'm not willing, because I am."

His forehead drops to my chest. "Like I said, I just don't want you to do something you're not ready for."

I reach over to turn on the lamp so I can see nd I lift his face and look into his eyes. "Are you afraid I'd regret this?"

I see the split-second flash of confirmation in his eyes and he looks away before returning his gaze to mine. "I don't want you to."

Pressing a soft kiss to his lips, I smile. "You're such a sweet, good man. Jesus." I bite my lip. "You remember my freakout in Vegas?" I watch him search his memory, but I go ahead and supply the answer. "The dream."

He nods. "Yeah."

"It was about you." He blinks slowly, taking in my words. "But that wasn't why I was so upset. I got really turned on and knew it would only take me, like, a few seconds to get off. So I did. You were still in bed and I looked at you while I did it and then I felt guilty and confused about it because it was a *really* good dream."

His mouth falls open in shock. "You're telling me you got yourself off in the next bed and I slept through it?" I nod. "Your dream was about me?" he confirms. "You're sure?"

I drag my finger down the inside of his left bicep, where his heron tattoo is located, and nod. "All my dreams since Vegas have been about you."

"Fuck, Wednesday," he says on an exhale.

I shrug. "Just making sure you know I've thought about this. More than I wanted to at times. So you have nothing to worry about. I want this, Silas. I mean, if you do."

He lays his forehead against mine. "You have no idea exactly how bad I want this."

I tilt my chin so our lips touch, but I don't kiss him. "So prove it." And then, I do kiss him. I wrap my arms around his neck and run my fingers through his hair as I rock my hips against him. He lets out another groan as his hands skim under the hem of my shirt and when his thumbs brush my ribs, I huff a breath when he hits a ticklish spot.

He pulls back. "Okay?"

I grin up at him. "Just ticklish. I'm fine." I pull his mouth back to mine and kiss him how I've wanted to kiss him since the wedding. I relish the way his lips feel against mine, the slide of our tongues, the way he tastes. I run my hands down his back, loving the way his muscles feel beneath my fingers.

He breaks his lips from mine and kisses down my cheek and jaw. As he nips and licks his way down my neck, I let out a soft gasp. I tilt my head to allow him better access and he takes his time moving lower toward my chest. "God, you smell good," Silas says, brushing kisses over the exposed swell of my breast.

"You feel good," I reply, more than a bit breathless. He begins to pull the front of my shirt down, but I know it doesn't have any stretch, so I put my hand on his chest and push him back a bit so I can raise up and pull it over my head.

When my top clears my breasts, his intake of breath is sharp and I blush. I lie back down and his eyes drag down my body and he shakes his head, his expression full of awe. "Even fucking better than I imagined." He brings his left hand up to gently cup my right breast, almost with reverence. His thumb brushes over my already hard nipple and it tightens even more with his touch. I want to press my thighs together, but since his hips are between my legs, I can't. I arch up into him, grinding myself against him and he blows out a breath. "You're going to have to quit that or I'm going to embarrass myself."

I huff a laugh. "What happened to all that stamina."

"Five years, remember? I can't guarantee I'll last more than a few seconds this first time. I'll make it up to you later."

He bends his head and kisses his way down my chest and I let my eyes fall closed as his mouth moves lower. When his tongue swirls over my right nipple, I let out a soft moan and thread my fingers through his hair. After so many months without anyone touching me, my body is taut as piano wire. I probably won't last long, either, if I'm honest. As he continues to lick, suck, and kiss my breasts and nipples, I'm already feeling my pleasure starting to build and my breathing grows ragged. "God, Silas. Fuck, that's good."

I feel him smile against my skin and he looks up at me. "Do you have any idea what it does to me to hear you say my name like this?"

I bite my lip and give him a wicked grin as I try to breathe. "Why don't you see how many times you can get me to say it?"

His smile widens. "Fucking hell, you're something else." He trails his fingers over my star tattoos. "Can you feel that?"

I shake my head. "Not really."

His fingers skim lower and circle my belly button. "And this?"

I huff a laugh. "Yeah. No scars there."

He runs the tip of his index finger under the trim of my shorts. "What about that?"

"I most definitely feel that."

Silas bends to brush kisses down my stomach and I try to memorize the way his lips feel on my skin. How his stubble scratches and tickles. How his hair brushes my stomach. How his fingers, callused from years spent lifting weights, skim over my skin as if I'm delicate and precious. He hooks his fingers in the sides of my shorts and looks up at me, confirming I'm okay. I nod and he slowly drags my shorts and panties down my hips. He scoots down the bed to pull them off my legs and when I'm fully bared to him, it's as if he's seeing some priceless piece of art. His eyes sweep down my body hungrily and heat spreads through my middle seeing the way he looks at me. As if I'm sort of feast to be devoured and savored and damn if my heart doesn't skip a beat under his approving gaze.

He looks at my—his—tattoo and leans down with a small smile to press a kiss to it. "I wondered if I'd ever get to see it again."

"You can look at it any time you want."

"You're gorgeous, you know that?" He skims his fingertips down the outsides of my thighs before sliding his right hand back up the inside. He braces his left hand next to my head and raises above me to look into my eyes. My heart pounds as his fingers brush higher and higher on my inner thigh. "I've wanted this for so long, it doesn't even seem real, Ada."

I'm about to ask him how long is *so long* when the pad of his middle finger sweeps over my clit and I gasp. Silas smiles. "And fuck, hearing you make these noises is liable to kill me before it's over with." He works the bundle of nerves in sure, steady circles and I let my eyes fall closed. "No, Ada, look at me. I want your eyes on me when you come."

I reopen them and find his warm brown ones, hooded with lust. I run my hand down his chest and abs and along the waistband of his pajama pants. He snatches it away and I scoff. "Not fair," I object, my breathing labored.

"It is for me. You touch me and I'll go off. I'm not ready for that yet." He lowers his mouth to mine and as he kisses me, he continues to work my clit until my heart is racing and my breaths are coming in ragged huffs.

I grip his waist and he pulls his face away to look into my eyes. I grind myself against his hand until with a deep moan, my orgasm crashes into me. And even with my pleasure-addled brain, I'm able to say, "Please tell me you brought condoms."

He huffs a laugh and gives me a quick kiss as he pulls his hand away. "I said I didn't have any expectations, I didn't say I wasn't an optimist. Hell yeah, I did."

"Thank God," I reply with a wide grin. I prop myself on my elbows as he scrambles from the mattress to dig in his bag. He tears off a condom and brings it with him back to the bed. He pushes his pants past his hips and my mouth falls open at the sight of him. As Cole is all I have to compare him to and the fact they were brothers, I assumed they'd be similarly built. I was wrong. Very, very wrong. Apparently, height is not the only way Silas exceeds Cole. "Holy shit," I say under my breath and he blushes.

He rips the foil packet with his teeth, a cocky grin on his lips. He takes a moment to roll it down and I am transfixed. Silas climbs onto the bed and wraps his hands around the sides of my knees and tugs me down the mattress. He settles himself between my thighs and takes my face in his hands. "Don't worry, we'll make it fit," he says with a smug smile.

A surprised bark of laughter falls from my mouth as I run my hands down his sides. "You're such an ass."

He gives me a soft kiss. "Yeah, but I'm *your* ass."

I'm about to tell him I'm glad he's mine and I'm happy to be his, but then he claims my mouth with a deep kiss. His hips punch forward and I gasp with the sudden fullness. Silas takes some deep breaths and I tilt my hips, growing accustomed to him. "Fuck, Silas."

He huffs a laugh. "You're telling me. Shit." I bring my hands up to his face and look into his eyes and I let out a soft moan as we begin to move together.

For several moments, the only sounds I can hear are our mingled, labored breaths punctuated by low moans, the squeak of the ancient bed with our movements, and my own rapid heartbeat in my ears.

I lean up and lick and kiss the side of his neck up to his jaw. I taste the slight sheen of sweat that's dampened his skin before covering his mouth with my own for a hungry kiss and wrapping my arms around his neck. He trails his hands over every inch of my body as he fucks me, seemingly wanting to remember how I feel under his fingertips. He breaks our kiss, his breathing ragged. "Jesus, Ada. Fuck. You're perfect."

I let his words wash over me and I smile up at him. "You, too." I rock my hips, driving him deeper and he groans. His kisses turn frantic and we both seem to recognize the urgent need growing between us.

His thrusts turn brutal, nearly stealing my breath. And when he shifts to push my knee back, bracing it on his arm, I scream with the change of angle. "Fuck, Silas. Oh, God." He hits me so deliciously, it's only a few moments before I feel a powerful climax building.

Silas buries his face in my neck as he slams into me. If the tension in his muscles and the change in his breathing are any indications, he's close, too. "Ada. I can't. Fuck."

I give him a jerky nod. "So close." Sure enough, a few seconds later, I let go with a hoarse rasp, my nails digging into his shoulders.

With a few more hard bucks of his hips, Silas joins me, a guttural groan coming out through gritted teeth. He braces himself on his hands to keep from collapsing onto me and he takes some deep breaths, attempting to get his breathing to return to normal. As he pulls out, I know without a doubt, I'll be sore tomorrow, but damn if I'll complain about it. He gives me a quick kiss. "Be right back." He walks out of the bedroom and the bathroom door closes a beat later.

CHAPTER THIRTY-ONE

SILAS

As I shut the bathroom door, I replay the night's events in my mind while I dispose of the condom and pee and wash my hands. I just had sex with Ada. Ada and I had sex. And it was, hands down, the best sex of my life. Not that I had any doubt it would be, but still. To have confirmed what I'd always thought would be the case is the cherry on the sundae.

It was effortless and fun and sweet and everything I ever wanted with her. I can only hope she's not having second thoughts or guilt or anything like that. I open the door to see her holding her pajamas in her hand. Her eyes trail down my body with appreciation and any doubts I had are pushed further down. "I have to pee, move your ass," she says with a grin.

I huff a laugh. "I think you just want to watch me walk away." I press a quick kiss to her lips and as I walk past her, she gives my butt a playful slap.

"What's the saying, 'hate to see you go, but love to watch you leave'? You most definitely embody that," she replies as she shuts the door.

I walk back into the bedroom and pull on my pajama pants and climb back into bed, wiped out. I'm almost asleep a few minutes later when she comes back into the room and crawls under the covers with me. She turns off the light and rolls onto her side, facing me. I pull her into my arms and she rests her head on my chest.

She drags her fingertips down my chest and I trail my own down her bare arm. "How do you feel?" she asks a few minutes later as I'm about to nod off.

I yawn and plant a kiss on the top of her head. "I'm perfect, Peep. Better than perfect. How are you feeling?"

"I'm good. Honestly, I thought I'd have a moment—like a freakout or something—after, but I didn't. I just feel... good."

To say I'm relieved would be an understatement. But I still want to reassure her. "I'm glad. But it would be understandable if you did have some confusing feelings, even if they're delayed. And if you need time to process, I get it. Just don't shut me out, okay?"

Ada kisses my chest and I feel her smile against my skin. "I won't. Thank you for being so good to me, Silas."

I hug her closer to me. "I just want to take care of you. I want to make you happy. Whatever that looks like. Whatever you need, okay?"

"And what about what you need?"

"Ada, I've already got everything I need."

She's still asleep, her body wrapped around mine like some kind of octopus, her arms and legs tangled up with mine. *At least it wasn't all a dream.* I carefully extricate myself from her grasp, making sure not to rouse her fully. Within seconds, she resumes her soft snoring as she rolls over. I grab my work clothes from my open bag and step into the bathroom to grab a quick shower, pee, and get dressed.

Leaving the bathroom, I head to the kitchen to start a pot of coffee. I roll my shoulders and stretch as it brews, feeling more at peace than I have in months. It could simply be because I had sex after five years of celibacy. But in truth, I think it has more to do with the fact that Ada and I have reached this point. It's all I've ever wanted for so long. Even when I couldn't want it, I still did. And now I have everything I've ever wanted. Is it possible to die from happiness?

I'm probably the most despicable human on the planet. I'll never be thankful my brother is gone. I would happily still be on the sidelines, watching them live their idyllic existence. But I can't deny I'm happy and I refuse to feel guilty for it any longer. I refuse to let anyone tell me what Ada and I have is wrong. I meant what I told her, the people who love us will be happy for us. Because, in truth, everyone who needs to know already does. Josie's always known how I've felt about Ada, as has Pap. And after the conversations I've had with Mom and Dad in recent months, they know, too.

Coffee brewed, I pour myself a cup and sip it as I walk out the front door. I retrieve the chainsaw and maul from the Bronco, along with my work gloves, safety glasses, and protective earmuffs. I carry everything around to the back of the cabin where the downed trees rest in the yard next to the river. They fell precariously close to the storage shed and I'm thankful they didn't land any closer because my boat would've been left in pieces.

I set the maul and saw down and examine the trees as I sip my coffee, attempting to assess the best way to dismantle the two large cedars. I sigh and set my empty mug down a few feet away. "Like an elephant I guess. One bite at a time."

I slip on my glasses and earmuffs before donning my gloves.

I make sure the chain brake is engaged on the saw prior to flipping the power switch to "on" and opening the choke. I press the fuel primer button several times to ensure it's ready to go before I pull the start cord. Thankfully, it starts on the first try and I walk over to the larger of the two trees and make quick work of cutting off all the branches.

Although I do have to pay attention, I've done this kind of work enough on the farm to know I can let my mind wander. I think about the way Ada felt under me. The sounds she made, how well we fit together, and the way she looked at me the first time. God, I love her. I knew that already, but knowing we have this kind of chemistry solidifies my resolve to want to spend the rest of my life with her.

Moving to the other side of the tree, I glance up at the porch to see Ada on the swing sipping a cup of coffee with what looks like a book. She smiles when she sees me and I jerk my chin up in acknowledgment and return her grin.

Two hours later, I have both trees stripped of their branches and broken down into large chunks for me to bust up further with the maul. Deciding I've earned a break, I shut off the saw and set it on the ground. I shake out my arms, hoping to prevent muscle fatigue from setting in so quickly. I knock the sawdust off my clothes and shed my glasses, muffs, and gloves.

I grab my mug and jog up the stairs and step into the house to refill my coffee before heading back out onto the porch. I take the seat next to Ada on the swing and let out a deep breath. "Tired?" she asks, sipping her own coffee. Her hair is still damp from her own shower and piled into a messy bun on top of her head. She has on an oversized, long-sleeved tee-shirt and leggings, along with a pair of cushy socks. Comfy and utterly adorable.

I nod. "A little. Been a while since I did tree work. And

Cole was always there to help, so it wasn't bad. But it definitely could've been worse."

"Well, you looked real manly out there."

I mop my face with the hem of my shirt. "If you liked that, you'll love watching me use the maul."

"What's a maul?"

"The ax I brought. It's got a sledge side in case I needed to use a wedge, but I don't think I will."

"You think you'll get it all busted up today? It's a lot."

I consider. "Hopefully. We'll have to see." When I sat down, she'd pulled her knees up to allow me to sit with her. I pull her feet into my lap so she can be more comfortable and I squeeze her foot and run my thumb along the arch, massaging. "How did you sleep?"

She smiles as she continues to sketch. "Perfect. Best I've slept in months, actually."

"I'm glad. I'm going to start breakfast in a few minutes since I need to get back out there. Want to help?"

She sticks her pencil into the middle of her book and shuts it, securing it with the attached elastic. She looks over at me and nods. "Sure." We rise from the swing and head into the kitchen. I wash my hands and pull a pack of bacon and a container of rosemary from the fridge. From the cabinet, I retrieve an onion, two sweet potatoes, and two apples. Ada eyes the ingredients as I begin to lay the bacon in a large cast-iron skillet. "So, what's all this going to be?"

"Sweet potato hash with bacon," I say over my shoulder. "Want to wash those potatoes and peel the onion? And then we'll need to chop everything up and strip the rosemary from the stems. Once everything is ready, I'll finish it off with a couple of fried eggs."

"Sounds easy enough. I wouldn't have thought to put all these things together."

"It's really good and super filling, so it makes a great brunch."

"I'll trust you." She sets about helping with prep and as she's chopping the onion, she asks, "So, really, when did you learn to cook? I don't remember you ever cooking before we started hanging out."

I shrug and cube the sweet potatoes. "Exactly as I told you. I've always been able to cook, but pretty much the only time we were ever together, someone else always did the cooking. I've been on my own since college. I can follow a recipe or video fairly well, believe it or not. And cooking is relaxing. It's almost like a production. You source your ingredients, you prep, you cook, and you enjoy the fruits of your labors. It's kinda like working out. You have a starting point and a goal and it feels good when you reach it."

I turn back to the stove to flip the slices of bacon and Ada comes up behind me and wraps her arms around my waist. "I'm probably all sweaty," I warn

She huffs a laugh. "Definitely wouldn't be the first time you rubbed all over me when you were covered in sweat."

I turn in her arms and look down at her. "You're right about that. I had way too much fun doing that to you growing up."

She lays her forehead on my chest and I hear her inhale deeply. "You smell like cedar and grease and bacon and you. I think I like it."

I plant a kiss on the top of her head. "You smell like none of those things. I like it."

She looks back up at me and grins and rises on her toes to presses a kiss to my lips. I bring my hand up to grip the back of her neck to deepen and control the kiss. It only takes hearing her let out a soft moan before I'm hard as a fucking rock and needing to be inside her. I blindly grope behind me to shut off the stove eye, thankful when I feel the click.

I slide my hands down Ada's back and over her ass and grabbing two glorious handfuls, I lift her off the floor. She squeaks in surprise and wraps her arms around my neck and her legs around my waist as I carry her back to the bedroom. I squat down when we reach my bag and I dig around until I find the condoms, not letting her go and not breaking our kiss.

When I rise back up, I take the two steps to the bed and lay her down. Ada pushes me back and sits up, reaching for my belt and the button fly of my jeans, hurriedly loosening them. I pull her face back to mine and nip at her bottom lip before trailing my mouth down her jaw and neck.

I attempt to toe off my boots, but with the laces, I know I won't get them off. I back up and let out a frustrated sigh. "Fucking laces. Give me two seconds."

She laughs and proceeds to get naked in the time it takes me to rid myself of my troublesome boots. I finish shucking my jeans and tugging my shirt over my head. Ada pulls me to her and I brace myself on my arms and brush kisses across her forehead, cheeks, lips, and down her jaw. She huffs out a breath as my tongue grazes a sensitive spot on her neck and I relish the way her skin feels under my lips.

As I make my way down her chest, she threads her fingers through my hair, a soft moan falling from her mouth as my lips close around one tightened nipple and then the other. I could listen to her moans and gasps all day long and never get tired of hearing them.

I let my fingertips skim down her ribs and waist and around to her ass to give it a possessive squeeze, all the while, I continue kissing lower and lower down her stomach. When I reach her belly button, I nip at the skin right below it and she lets out a soft squeak.

I raise my eyes to hers. "Those sounds you make are going to be the death of me." I scoot farther down the bed and hook her knees over my shoulder and give her a wicked grin. "Let's see what other noises I can get you to make." I kiss my way up her inner thighs and Ada exhales raggedly, the sound going straight to my dick.

Taking in the sight of her, wet and pink and waiting for me to devour her, I nearly come just from thinking about what I'm about to do. "Fuck, that's a pretty pussy, Wednesday."

She gives me a slow smile. "I bet it tastes better than it looks."

I waste no time finding out. I lick a hard line up her slick center and groan when the taste of her hits my tongue. She gasps when I suck her clit into my mouth and when she begins to tilt her pelvis, I wrap my arms around her thighs, holding her in place. A little cruel? Maybe. But I've dreamt about this for too long to not enjoy every minute of it. I don't want her getting off too quickly, because I'll want to be inside her and I'm not ready to give this up yet.

Her grip on my hair turns nearly painful, but I ignore it and simply chuckle. "Shit," Ada says on a breathy exhale. I can't help but smile against her. She scoffs. "Are you smiling? You're torturing me and you're *smiling*. Fuck, you're sadistic." I raise my eyes to hers and suck her clit even harder and she whimpers, her own eyes falling closed. "Oh, God. Silas, please."

Hearing my name on her lips is almost too much and I know I can't go much longer without feeling her pussy wrapped around my cock. I release her legs and slide two fingers into her, crooking them as I slide them in and out. Ada gasps and begins to ride my face and hand in earnest, using me to find her own pleasure and fuck, how I welcome it. A moment later, she's clenching around my fingers, a raspy cry falling from her lips.

Once she's beginning to come down, I withdraw my hand and kiss my way back up her body. She jerks my face to hers and gives me a deep kiss. My dick is practically weeping and her pussy is so close, I could simply shift my hips and be enveloped in her warmth. But common sense won't let me do that and I reluctantly pull away.

Ada reaches for the condoms I dropped onto the nightstand and tears one off and rips it open, handing it to me. I take it and roll it down and settle back between her thighs and I slam myself inside her. She lets out a long moan. "Fuck, that's good," she says with a smile.

I already know I'm not going to last long. I need her coming around me and screaming my name and digging her nails into my back again. I set a brutal pace and lower my mouth to her nipple and suck it into my mouth, unable to bite back a groan when Ada rocks her hips, driving me deeper.

She threads her fingers through my hair and I brace on one forearm while I play with her other perfect tit with my free hand. I roll the nipple between my fingers and Ada gasps when I tug the other gently between my teeth. I look up at her, her face and neck flushed and her mouth open, her breaths shallow. "Shit, you look good when I fuck you, Wednesday."

She smiles and brings her eyes to mine. "You look good when you fuck me, too." She pulls my face to her and kisses me deeply and I get lost in her. She tastes like coffee and smells like smoky bacon and that scent that's just *her*. The way her pussy feels as I slide in and out of her and the sound of our ragged breaths. I can't get over the rightness of us together. I'm beyond thrilled to know all my years of longing and pining weren't in vain.

Ada reaches between us to work her clit. A moment later, she gasps my name, her pussy clenching so tight around me, it triggers my own climax. I come so hard I see spots and huff what sounds like a mix between a laugh and a grunt.

I let my forehead fall to hers as I brace myself on my arms. "Fucking hell, Ada."

She chuckles and lifts her chin until our lips meet. "That was nice."

I laugh. "Nice, huh? Shit," I say with a groan as I pull out. "I'm going to be so exhausted tonight." After giving myself a few minutes to recover, I climb out of bed and head to the bathroom.

When we finally keep our hands off each other long enough to actually cook breakfast, it's turned into lunch. I'm not looking forward to the next few hours I know it will take for me to split the wood into logs and stack them under the back porch. And yet, I drag myself outside to do it, because that's what I agreed to.

Ada offers to clean up the dishes while I get started on the wood and I give her a quick kiss and head outside. What feels like ten hours later, but is probably more like three, I take a break. As I turn to head into the house to grab a drink of water, I see Ada carrying the wood I've been splitting to stack. She must have been at it a while because a lot of the logs I'd done are gone.

As she comes back, she brings a glass of water with her and hands it to me. I down it in about two seconds. "Tired?" she asks knowingly.

"Yeah."

"So, there's no way you could finish tomorrow?"

I blow out a breath and wipe my brow with my sleeve. "I'd rather just get it done today so I don't have to worry about it tomorrow. I probably won't be able to move tomorrow and I'll need the two days to recover before I have to go to work on Tuesday."

She nods. "Want me to run to town and get some epsom salt and you can do a soak tonight so you're not so sore?"

I raise my brows in surprise. "You want to drive Blue to town?"

She shrugs. "I'm good with a stick now."

I give her a slow smile. "Yeah, you are."

She rolls her eyes. "Such a guy response." But she still grins. "You're the one who taught me to drive. You don't trust what you've taught me?"

"No, I do. But you've never driven her by yourself."

"I think I can manage. Do you think it will be cold enough for a fire tonight?" Her tone is hopeful and I can't help but chuckle. "I don't think so, sorry." I pull her to me and give her a kiss. "We'll have to plan a trip when there's a chance we get snowed in for a couple of days and have to rely on our combined body heat to keep us warm."

She considers. "Now, I think I like the sound of that." Bringing the subject back to the original topic, she says, "You never did answer me. Do you want me to go get some epsom salt so you can do a soak?"

"Sure. That'd be great. Think you can find your way out and back without a problem?"

"Will the GPS be pretty accurate if I punch in the address?"

"Should be." She pulls out her phone and I give her the address and she gives me a deep kiss before digging my keys out of my pocket and taking off.

CHAPTER THIRTY-TWO

ADA

I make it to the small town about twenty minutes after leaving the cabin, only grinding Blue's gears a couple of times. But no one has to know, right? I'm wandering the aisles of the local Walmart trying to kill time. I know if I go back to the cabin and Silas is still busting up those logs like some sexy, muscled lumberjack, I will spontaneously combust. Simply watching him swing that big ax was enough for me to want to get him naked in the yard and let him bend me over the chopping block.

Finding the epsom salt in the cosmetics section, I choose one that actually smells good, hoping he'll let me join him for his soak. I also toss in some massage oil with the intention of giving him a massage after his soak to further loosen his muscles.

I'm wandering through the books section, humming an old Ray Charles song when my phone rings. I don't recognize the number, but it's an area code from home, so I swipe to answer it. "Hello?"

"Is this Ada Mae Andrews?"

"May I ask who's calling?"

"Yes, this is Detective Justin Montgomery with the Loudon County Sheriff's Department. Are you Miss Andrews?"

I stopped walking as soon as he identified himself. "Yes, sir. How can I help you?"

"Your father is Arnold Andrews, is that correct?"

I heave a sigh. What's my father done now? "Yes, sir. But if you've read his file, I'm sure you're aware I have a restraining order against him."

"Yes, ma'am, we are. I take it you and your father weren't on the best terms?"

"No, sir. He accosted me in my home and threatened me with a knife. What's this about, if you don't mind me asking?"

"Would it be possible for you to come into the station so we can speak with you? We attempted to catch you at home, but weren't successful."

"No, I'm out of town. Whatever it is, you can tell me over the phone if it has to do with my father."

"Miss Andrews, there's no easy way to tell you this, but your father's body was found yesterday. He died of a drug over-dose. It appears, once he made bail, his first stop was to try to get a fix."

I sigh again, unable to even muster enough emotion to appear shocked. "Thank you for letting me know."

"Yes, ma'am. Again, I'm sorry to tell you over the phone. His body can be recovered at the Knox county medical examiner's office as soon as tomorrow if you'd like."

I can't stop myself from asking, "What would happen if I didn't claim the body?"

He's quiet for a moment, but after a beat, he says, "If the body is unclaimed, it will be cremated by the state. You also have the option to donate the body to the Forensic Anthropology Center up at UT."

"Wait, is that the Body Farm, or whatever it's called?"

"Yes, ma'am. If that's something you'd want to do, once we release the body to you, you'd only need to call the Center and they'd do the pickup. You wouldn't have to do anything after that."

I consider. Might as well make his death meaningful, right? "All right. So, I'd need to come and sign papers, or what?"

"Yes, ma'am."

"Okay. I'll be by on Monday. Can I ask for you?"

"Yes, ma'am, that's fine."

"Thank you, Detective. Have a good day." I disconnect the call and quietly make my way to the register and check out. I slide behind the wheel of Blue and make it back to the cabin without issue. Silas is standing at the kitchen counter drinking a glass of water when I come in the door.

"Finally got all the wood chopped. Still have to stack the rest, but—." He stops talking when he turns to look at me. Although I don't feel as though I look any different, he must see something in my face. He closes the distance between us in three long strides and takes the shopping bag from my hand. He drops it to the floor before cupping my face. "What's wrong? What's happened? You're white as a sheet."

"The police called. My father's dead."

Silas's inhale is sharp and he pulls me into his arms. "Ada, God, I'm sorry." He steps back and looks around. "Okay, well, give me ten minutes to shower and change clothes and pack up and we can hit the road."

I frown. "Why? There's no point. I'm not going anywhere."

His brow furrows. "Ada, your dad died, we need to go home."

Angry, I shake my head and push him away. "Bullshit. I say good riddance to bad rubbish. Do you know how long I've been expecting this call, Silas? Since I was ten years old. When I went home with Josie and realized houses aren't supposed to be crawling with cockroaches. When I learned cabinets are supposed to have food and clothes and bodies should be clean. I've been waiting for a visit from a man or woman in a uniform to tell me my father was dead since I was ten. So, no, I'm not going to make a hasty retreat home simply because he's finally gone."

He squeezes my shoulders. "I know your relationship with him was really complicated. I know I wanted to kill him myself after last week. But he was still your father."

"No, he was a sperm donor who got stuck with me and liked to use me as a punching bag when he was high. He was the man who regularly liked to spend any grocery money we had on meth and heroin. He was the man who was content to let me go to school with lice and dirty clothes. He was the man who got so high one night, he thought someone was out to get him. And when I tried to calm him down, he stabbed me seven times with a pocket knife and I almost died. So, no, I don't consider him my father. He wasn't even a man. He was scum and I'm glad he's dead.

"As far as I'm concerned, I never had a father. I had your dad and I had Pap. *They* are whom I consider my fathers. Arnold Andrews is simply the piece of shit who donated half of my DNA."

His expression morphs into one of great pain. "I never knew it was that bad for that long. I knew when you were around fourteen or fifteen you had some bruises. I really only knew anything for sure after you ended up in the hospital and he went to jail."

I shrug and drop into a chair at the kitchen table, exhausted. "I think only your parents and grandparents knew how bad it was. I honestly don't think I would've survived without them. I know your parents must have instilled it in y'all to be nice to kids who look like they need a friend. Josie took one look at me on the first day of fifth grade and decided she was my best friend.

"Her birthday party was the first one I'd ever been to. And I think she was so adamant about trying to get me to stay over so your mom could help me get cleaned up. The reason I had the Wednesday Addams braids was because of the lice treatment your mom put in my hair. And I was so skinny from not having a full meal in I couldn't tell you how long, I fit into a lot of the clothes Josie had outgrown. Your mom was the only real mom I've ever had.

"I'd beg my mom to let me come live with her. From the time she left, I'd call her and write her and plead, but all I got was that one summer. And in reality, she only wanted me there because her boyfriend had a little kid. They needed a babysitter while he was out of school for the summer and they didn't want to shell out the money for daycare.

"So, I think it's safe to say, I'm an orphan. I probably have been my whole life. And if it weren't for your family, I would probably be dead."

He blinks rapidly and tears well in his eyes and I shake my head, indignant. "Don't you dare cry for me, Silas. I'm fine. I've been fine. As far as I'm concerned, I'm free and will never have to worry about him ever again."

He drops to his knees in front of me and takes my hands in his and presses kisses to them. "I'm so sorry I never knew any of this. Fuck, I want to go and bring him back just to kill him all over again."

I slump in my chair. "I never wanted you and Cole to know any of this. It was embarrassing."

He frowns. "Cole didn't know?"

"Yeah, he knew. I used to have nightmares." Worry flashes

in his eyes and I shake my head. "I don't anymore. Not in a long, long time."

Silas nods. "So, what now?"

"On Monday, I sign to have the body released, and then I call the Forensic Anthropology Center to come and get it."

His eyes widen. "The Body Farm?"

I nod. "Yeah, at least he can do some good with his death, right?"

"Yeah, I guess. Damn."

I lean down and press a kiss to his lips. "I'm fine, Silas. Really. No need to stand watch to ensure I'm not going to shut down. I'm not going to lose my shit or stop eating."

He looks up at me and searches my eyes. "You promise to tell me if you're not fine?"

I nod. "I promise."

In spite of his protestations about my need to stay in and process, I refuse to mourn a man who doesn't deserve it. And when Silas heads out to stack the wood, I follow him out to help. I wear myself out carrying and stacking the logs he'd split. Once we're done, I'm breathing heavily. "I can't believe you did all this today."

He shrugs. "Just kept going until it's done. If I'd thought about how much I had left, I wouldn't have been able to finish it. I think it's like that with a lot of stuff. If you look too far ahead, you get bogged down with how much of it there is."

I look at him. "*It*? What is *it*?"

He shrugs again and rolls his shoulders. "Everything. Take grief for example, if you focus on how long you're going to be miserable instead of trying to have one good moment in the day you're in, it'll consume you. Sorta like focusing on the destination at the cost of the journey."

"There you go, getting all philosophical again," I say with a small, amused smile.

"Just the truth. Or, rather, the truth I try to embody." He turns to start back toward the house and I fall into step beside him.

"Is that how you processed your grief?"

He sighs. "Sometimes. During the month before I came to see you, I was drunk. A lot. But I knew Cole would've hated it. So, I tried to have one good moment a day; to remember some dumbass thing we did that made us both laugh. I tried to remember how good a life he lived. How a good a brother he was. I decided I wanted to come back and be the kind of person he'd be proud of. And then the package arrived with all the letters and tasks and I was pissed again and I got drunk again."

As he's been speaking, we'd climbed the stairs to the back porch and taken seats on the swing. I watch him as he looks out toward the river. "I'm sure it was hard for you, to have to put your grief on the back burner to follow through on what he wanted. Especially considering how terrible I was to you."

He takes my hand in his and strokes the back of it with his thumb. "It was hard, but focusing on you helped me. I hated how lost you looked. It broke my heart, Wednesday."

I bite my lip. "I thought you hated me."

He turns his face to mine and his expression is sincere. "I've never hated you. Not a day in our lives."

I draw my brows down in confusion. "You barely ever said two words to me from the time we were kids. And when you did, you always seemed so closed off and hateful."

He sighs and runs his free hand through his hair, dislodging some sawdust. "I'm sorry. I'm sorry I wasn't a friend to you. I wish I could've been." He gives my hand a squeeze. "But I'm really glad I get to be your friend now."

I nod. "Me, too. I'm thankful for you, Silas." I scoot closer to him and rest my forehead against his jaw and wrap my arms around his shoulders. I draw my leg up and my shin and knee lie against his thigh and hip. He smells like hard work and wood and sweat and I like the way it smells on him. "What do you think it will be like when we get home?"

He turns his face to press a kiss to my forehead and squeezes my calf. "Who knows? I know I don't want any of our normal routines to change. I still want us to go to family dinner and have our *Grey's* days and Chinese. I still want us to go visit Pap at the farm. I still want you and Josie to have your girls' nights. But I also want the added aspect of us as a couple."

He pulls back to look at me. "I don't know what the last tasks will be like for you or how you'll feel with still having letters from Cole. If you need space during those times, I get it. I could understand if you have confusing feelings. I'm a strong enough man that my ego will not be damaged by the love you still have for him, I want you to know that. I'm okay if part of you still loves him for the rest of our lives.

"If he was still here, I'd be content to watch the two of you be happy forever. So don't ever keep the way you feel about him pushed down because you think I can't handle it. I know you loved Cole. I only hope someday, there's room in your heart to love me, too."

Tears burn my eyes from the sincerity I hear in his words and the vulnerable expression I see on his face. I could very easily love Silas. "God, you're perfect, aren't you?"

He gives me a soft smile. "I don't want to be perfect. I would settle for being perfect for you, though."

When we pull onto Ingrid and Miles's street to make our appearance for family dinner, I'm antsy. Silas frowns and keeps giving me side glances the closer we get to his parents' house. "What's wrong with you?"

"Do you think we should tell them? I'd hate for them to find out from someone else or catch us making out somewhere and be upset. Will they be upset, you think? God, this is weird. It's easy when it's just you and me because we know what it took for us to get here, they don't." My words come out rushed and almost in a single breath. As he sets the emergency brake on the Bronco, Silas's eyes widen.

He takes my face in his hands. "Okay, first of all, you're going to have to breathe. Because, damn, that was a lot. If you want to tell them, we can, but I think they'll be happy. All they want is for their kids to be happy, whatever that looks like. *All* their kids—including you, Wednesday.

"I think they wouldn't be too surprised if they found out we've decided to give us being in a relationship together a try. We've spent the last eight months pretty much going on dates and spending a shit ton of time together."

I consider. "Hmm. I hadn't thought about it like that. I guess that's pretty true." I nod and inhale and exhale deeply. "Okay. Maybe we should tell them."

"Okay, if that's what you want. I told you, we don't have to. Not that I'm opposed. I'm happy to show you off as mine to whoever wants to know. And like I told you, anyone who loves us, will want us to be happy. And you make me so damn happy, Ada. Please know that."

I give him a warm smile. "I'm happy, too."

"Okay, so it's settled, we tell them? Tonight?"

I nod. "I think so."

His smile is radiant. "Well, fuck yeah."

I can't help but laugh.

DONATE

NOVEMBER: NINE MONTHS AFTER

CHAPTER THIRTY-THREE

SILAS

As predicted, my parents were as overjoyed for us as I hoped they'd be. Mom and Josie both gave me knowing smiles. Dad simply nodded and pretended to be shocked and said, "As long as you're happy, I'm happy." He went on to tell Ada, "You've been our girl for twenty years, that won't ever change." And then she teared up, per usual. Then Josie said something about things being a little too touchy-feely for her and that was that.

We've begun having our *Grey's* nights at my house since I still can't take Ada to bed at hers. Thankfully, she gets it; the same way I get she doesn't want to rid her life of Cole's belongings.

I miss her every moment I'm not with her and her random texts throughout the day are my highlights. We don't spend every night together, since there are some nights I work late and she does, too. No doubt, time she uses to process our new relationship in relation to Cole, same as me.

If I could, I'd thank him for his blessing. I still would've wanted her regardless, but knowing I have it makes all the years of longing I had for her worth it. Knowing he wanted us to end up together—fucked up as it might be—makes me happier than I have any right to be.

Today though, I'm bracing myself for backlash. I'm delivering a letter and she's going to hate it. I already know it. The upcoming task might be easier if it wasn't coming on the heels of us beginning things. I'm almost wishing I could hold off, but one task a month is my instructions and I have to follow through.

I'm showing up unannounced since I think it might be easier for me to deliver it if there's no time to psych myself up about it. And so, here I stand at her front door knocking. In spite of the fact I still have Josie's key and can't remember the last time I actually knocked.

She answers the door and her expression is amused confusion. She rises on her toes to give me a kiss. "Why'd you knock?"

I sigh and step into the apartment. "Because I'm not here as your boyfriend. I'm here as taskmaster."

Her smile falters, but then she nods. "Taskmaster? Took you nine whole months to come up with that title, huh?"

I huff a laugh and shrug. "Yeah, I guess." I pull the envelope out of my back pocket."

She takes it from me. "Let me guess, I have a week?"

I shake my head. "Not this time. You have two weeks."

Her brow furrows. "Oh. Wow. Must be pretty big."

I nod. "Kinda."

She looks down at the envelope and blinks slowly. "This is weird."

I nod again. "I know. I told you it's okay if it's confusing. It's okay if you need time to process. I get it." Changing the subject,

I give her a smile. "You're birthday's coming up. What do you wanna do?"

She considers and sighs. "Honestly, I don't have a clue."

"Okay. Want me to plan something?"

"You don't have to."

I take her face in my hands and look into her eyes. "I want to. Will you let me?"

She gives me a small smile. "Okay. It'll be after this, though, right?" She holds up the envelope.

"Yeah, your birthday's not until after Thanksgiving, so probably the first weekend in December. That all right?"

"Sure."

I give her a quick kiss. "I have to go. I have a session. I'll talk to you later, okay?"

"All right."

Around nine PM, as I'm finishing up my last session, my phone rings. It's Ada and she's in tears. I'm in my office and I know she's read the letter and I close my eyes and blow out a deep breath.

"This is a fucking joke, right?"

"I think we both know it's not, Peep."

"This is bullshit, Silas."

"I'm sorry." And I am. If there was any way I could fix this for her, I would. If I could take this pain away, I would.

"Five items? That's all he wants me to keep? How am I supposed to whittle down fifteen years to five fucking items? It's cruel."

"That's why he gave you two weeks."

"He could've given me a year and it still wouldn't be enough."

"I know. But I think that's why he only gave you two weeks. So you'd be forced to act."

"Can you help me choose?"

And as much as I would love to do exactly that, I can't. "No. I'm sorry. I can't."

"Why not?" Her words come out broken and my heart squeezes with sympathy for her.

"Because that's what he said."

She snorts. "Oh, because he said. Right. Because you do everything Cole says? He tell you to fuck me, too?"

I try to take into account the pain she's in with the task he's handed down, but her words still sting. "Ada, stop. Don't do that. You know the way I feel about you has nothing to do with Cole. I know you're in pain. Don't take it out on me."

She sobs. "I'm sorry. I don't know how to do this. This is impossible."

"I'm sure. You want me to come over? Or, do you want to come to my house? I don't think you need to be alone right now."

"I can't drive. I'm drunk."

"Okay. Want me to pick you up? I just finished my last session and was headed out the door in a few minutes anyway."

"All right."

"I'll be there in twenty minutes." She disconnects the call and I scrub my hand down my face. I don't even bother changing back into my street clothes and grab my wallet and keys and after locking up my office, I walk out of the gym.

I let out a deep breath as I park at Ada's and hope she's still sober enough to walk down the steps to come home with me. Using my key to let myself in, I scan the living room, my eyes going wide when I take in the scene. It appears the place was robbed. But if I was going to guess, Ada took her hurt and anger out on some of the things of Cole's she knew she wouldn't be keeping. Books and DVDs litter the floor, along with dirt and pottery from some of the plants that used to sit on the window sill.

I follow the path of destruction to the bedroom where it appears she's ripped out every article of clothing from the closet and the dressers. I find her sitting in the floor leaning against the far wall next to an overturned lamp, a jar of moonshine in her arms. She's wearing one of Cole's work shirts and she's still crying.

Saying nothing, I sit next to her and wrap my arm around her and pull her into my side. She lays her head on my chest and cries. I press a kiss to the top of her head and rub her back. "I love what you've done with the place," I say after a while.

She snorts a wet laugh. "This fucking sucks."

I sigh. "I know, Wednesday. You want to stay for a while longer or are you ready to go?"

"I need to get out of here."

"Okay. Let's go. Have you eaten supper yet?"

"No."

I nod and stand, pulling her with me. "All right. How about we stop by McDonald's and get some comfort food and go to my place and go to bed?"

She nods and we cut off lights as we head back toward the front door. While she's a bit unsteady on her feet, she still manages to walk unassisted down the stairs. She doesn't bother bringing anything with her, save her purse. As I help her into the front seat of the Bronco, she drops it on the floor and a pill bottle rolls out.

Confused, I pick it up and examine it, since I know Ada doesn't take any prescriptions. But then I see the label and know it's one of Cole's heart medications that Ada knew nothing about. I tuck it back into her purse with a sigh.

There's no sense in trying to hide it or pretend it fell out of the car or something equally ridiculous. I don't know what she'll find when she researches the medication, but I'm not going to stop her. I'm also not going to lie to her if she asks me questions. I've long felt she deserved to know the truth and Cole keeping his HCM from her was cruel, even if his reasoning was understandable.

I slide behind the wheel and ten minutes later, I'm pulling away from the drive-thru and headed home. Ada is leaning against the window, her knees drawn up to her chest.

As I'm turning onto my street, she finally looks at me. "I'm sorry for what I said. It was hateful. I know you're only trying to follow through on what Cole wanted. I shouldn't take it out on you. I'm sure it's not easy for you, either."

I take her hand in mine and give it a squeeze. "You're allowed to be angry. It's a lot."

"It is, but it's not your fault and you don't deserve my ugly attitude. Forgive me?"

I pull into my driveway and set the brake. "There's nothing to forgive. Let's go in and eat and go to bed, okay?"

She nods and climbs out of the vehicle and I pull her into my side as we walk up the stairs. I unlock the door and tug her inside and we fall onto the couch. I dig out our food and hand hers over and we eat in silence. Ada sips her soda and sighs. "You know what he said?"

I turn to her. "What, in his letter?"

She nods. "Yeah. He said, 'It's time to let go a little. It's time to make room in your home for your things.'" She looks at me. "He called it, 'your' home. Not ours. Yours. Like he doesn't want any part of it anymore. Like he just expects me to get rid of all his stuff and fully make the apartment mine."

I nod. "He was nothing if not practical."

"Well, I hate how casual he's being. Just a bunch of shit about making a fresh start and not having his stuff holding me back." She bites her bottom lip as a tear rolls down her face. "And I knew I'd eventually have to pack up a lot of things because it's not fair to you to keep seeing all his stuff anytime you come over. I—."

I put my hand on her arm to cut her off. "No. I never would've expected or demanded you get rid of Cole's stuff. Especially not so soon."

She lifts a brow. "No, but you can't *be* with me there. So you can't act like this doesn't help you, too. I'm sure you'll love not having his stuff around anymore."

I take a deep breath and try to give myself a moment to not explode in anger. Because this is simply Ada lashing out in pain. I know she's not angry with me, she's only angry and hurt because of the situation and I can understand why she'd be in pain. "Ada, I'm not going to lie to you and say the idea of having sex with you in the bed you shared with my brother doesn't bother me. Or, that seeing photos of the two of you together messes with my ability to want to be intimate with you in that space. I have fifteen years of memories to remind me of that fact. I don't need physical reminders, too."

"Silas, I can't help the fact I was with Cole."

"Neither can I. But even if it weren't Cole, I would still have issues. I still wouldn't expect you to toss his stuff, though. So don't get it twisted. I'm not happy he's asking you to get rid of his things. I can't imagine how hard this is going to be for you. I hate seeing you in pain."

"What were his instruction to you?"

"That I can't help you narrow down, but if, once you've done that, you need help finding somewhere to donate everything, I can organize that part of things. Or, if you need to be distracted the day things are being taken away, I can do that, too."

"He gave you permission to 'distract' me?" She puts the

word in air quotes and raises a skeptical brow. "What did he have in mind for that?"

I huff a laugh. "He didn't specify. I'm sure he figured I could come up with something."

She nods, considering. "Okay."

"Okay to what?" I ask, unsure what she's agreed to.

"Okay to you organizing the donation and distracting me."

"All right."

Once we finally go to bed, Ada sleeps fitfully and seems to cry on and off all night and I simply hold her. By morning, we're both still exhausted and bleary-eyed and I'm struggling to hold my eyes open as I pour us each a cup of coffee to take back to bed. She sits up and leans against the headboard as I crawl back under the covers with her. "You don't think he's going to expect me to move, is he? Is that the last task or whatever?"

"No. That's not on the task list."

She nods and looks down into her mug. "It's not even going to feel like the same place when his things are gone."

I sigh. "I know. It'll take some getting used to, I'm sure."

"What if I can't stay there? What if it's too hard?"

"I think you can do whatever you think you need to do. If you end up wanting to move, I can help you find a place. Your lease is up next year, right?" Secretly, I hope when she sees the house, she wants to move in with me, but I'm not an idiot. An optimist, yes. Idiot, no.

"Yeah, in March."

"Okay, so after his things are gone, that gives you a few months to live with only your things. You can decide what you want to do at that point."

She rubs her thumb over the rim of her mug. "These were

not things I thought I'd ever have to think about. You know, not for a long, long time. I assumed this year, we'd start looking for a house or talk about building one. We were in a good place financially to do that. I would have preferred to build because I had a dream house."

I feign surprise, even though I'm intimate with the idea of her dream house. "Oh?"

She nods, not looking at me. "Yeah, I sketched it when I was about twenty, I guess. It's what I imagined the perfect house to be."

"And is that dream house still perfect in your mind?"

"Yeah. It's a lot like the farmhouse. Probably because so many of my favorite memories are from there. But the porch wraps all the way around the house, with swings on every side. That way, no matter where the sun is, you can always either be in it or out of it if you prefer.

"It has an art studio with north-facing light. It has a drafting table and a setup for my computer and an easel. You know, since I never know what medium my art needs to be put down on. It has dark floors and light walls and plenty of room to entertain.

"It has one of those wash stations in the laundry room for a big dog, because I always wanted a dog, but bending over a bathtub to bathe one sucks. It has a huge bathtub for two people, because honestly, taking a bath with someone is sexy, and conserving water is the responsible thing to do. It has a big kitchen where everyone wants to hang out. That's one of the things I've always loved about your parents' house. Even though it'd probably be more comfortable if we all hung out in the living room, somehow, we always just end up at the island or kitchen table.

"It has big windows to let in a ton of natural light and ideally, it would be surrounded by mature trees that would provide shade. It would be white with these large wooden columns on the porch so I could wrap them in lights at Christmas. And if I were to design it today, it would have to have room for kids. When I first drew it, it didn't since I knew it wasn't something Cole wanted. It was only two or three bedrooms originally. But it would have more, now."

"Because you want kids?"

She nods and looks at me. "I do."

"Okay."

"What does your house look like?"

Knowing I can't get into too much detail without giving things away, I shrug. "Still a long way to go yet. It'll have four bedrooms by the time it's finished, with two-and-a-half baths. Big kitchen. Big fireplace in the living room. It sits on top of a hill. Big, level yard so it can be fenced in for a swing set or something for kids."

"Sounds nice. You said I can see it, right?"

I huff a laugh. "Yeah. Soon, hopefully."

She sets her coffee down on the nightstand and snuggles against my side. "How long do you think it will be before I don't have these kinds of breakdowns anymore?"

I press a kiss to her forehead. "Honestly, probably years. There might be weeks or months or even years without them, but grief isn't something you take off like a hat and never put back on. It's probably something we'll deal with for the rest of our lives. I think it'll get to a point where the good days outnumber the bad and that's what we have to appreciate. We'll be able to look back on Cole's life and be glad we were part of it. We can be thankful he loved us until the day he died. We can be thankful we were his favorite people." Tears burn my eyes and I set my mug down and wipe them away and clear my throat.

Ada raises up and takes my face in her hands. "Don't hide

from me. Please, Silas? You don't have to be the strong one all the time. We can have hard days together. Someday, I hope I can be strong for you. I'm sorry you've had to push all your shit down for me." Tears roll down her face and I drag the pad of my thumb over her cheek.

"Helping you has helped me. Watching you come back to yourself has helped. Watching you smile and laugh and have good days has helped. Finally being allowed to love you has helped, Ada."

Her brow furrows. "What does that mean? *Allowed* to love me."

I search her eyes and hope she sees the truth in my words. "Ada, I've loved you for as long as I can remember. Since we were kids."

She sits up straighter. "What?"

I shrug. "It wasn't something I planned. And God knows I tried not to, but I've always loved you."

"You never said anything."

A bark of laughter leaves me. "Oh? What was I going to say, 'hey, I know you're with Cole, but I'm in love with you'? No, I wasn't going to do that. You were happy. Cole was happy. I told him if he ever hurt you, I'd beat his ass. He didn't. He was good to you. Watching *my* two favorite people love each other was enough for me."

"Cole knew?" she asks, her tone incredulous.

I nod. "Yeah. He'd always known." I shrug. "He called dibs."

Her mouth falls open, her eyes turning flinty. "*Dibs?* Fucking dibs? I'm a person, Silas, not the last slice of birthday cake."

"Yeah, I know that. And had it not worked out between you and Cole it would be one thing, but it did. You were happy."

"Still, I deserved to know."

"Why? So it could be awkward? So you might question what you and Cole had and then it damage my relationship with him? No, it was better this way."

Her eyes narrow and she scrambles off the bed, angry. "So, what, when he died, he pretty much said, 'she's yours now, here's the stuff she likes in bed. I put a lot of miles on her, but overall, she's still in good shape'?"

I scrub my hands down my face, frustrated. "Fuck, Ada, you know it wasn't like that." None of this is how I ever planned to tell her, but it's too late to take it back.

"So what was it like then, Silas? All these years, I thought you hated me and it was all an act? And then the way you treated me after Cole died? How ugly we were to each other. *That* was you loving me?"

"Ada, if I had swooped in that day I showed up with a letter and his urn and held you and comforted you, you wouldn't have known what to do with that. It would have freaked you out. And we've always fought. Even when we were kids. Before Cole or I ever developed feelings for you, it's always been our M.O."

CHAPTER THIRTY-FOUR

ADA

I pace the room of the man who supposedly has always loved me. For several moments, I don't say anything and simply walk a path back and forth in front of his bed. "Wednesday, please sit down and talk to me."

I stop and look at him. "This is just a lot, okay? How do you expect me to react to this? You expect me to say, 'oh, well, I guess it's okay Cole's dead, because at least you always loved me.'?"

His eyes flash with hurt and anger and he stands and closes the distance between us. His expression is hard and he keeps his voice low. "Don't you dare insinuate I'm happy Cole's dead. That's fucking low, even for you. I would have happily watched you and him live out the rest of your lives together. I would've never said anything and as long as the two of you were happy, I would have been content to watch it.

"Would it have meant I never got to love you in the open? Yeah. Would I have carried that with me for the rest of my life? Yeah. Would it have meant I would've eventually settled for a woman who wasn't you and lived out the rest of my days with that knowledge? Yeah. Would it have meant I never got to see you have *my* babies? Yeah. Would I rather have Cole still be here knowing all that? Yeah. Because it meant the two of you were happy together. All I ever wanted was for the two of you to be happy."

He sits on the edge of the bed and hangs his head, all the fight gone out of him. And knowing him, none of what he's told me has probably worked out like he planned. And knowing if everything he's told me is true—and I have no doubt it is—how vulnerable he had to be able to tell me, I'm struck even more by what a good man he is. To know he would've stood by and watched me love Cole for the rest of his life reminds me how selfless he is. And I shouldn't be allowed to love him. It's too soon and I'm probably too damaged to be able to love him as much as he deserves, but God help me, I do love him. I fall to my knees in front of him, tears in my eyes, and take his face in my hands. "I'm sorry. God, I don't deserve you."

He looks at me, his own eyes wet. "You deserve love, Ada. You, more than anyone I've ever met. No one tells you how to do this. Especially in a situation like ours. It's fucked up and I wish it wasn't something we had to deal with. I will forever hate that Cole's not here to still love you, but I'll never be sorry for loving you. And I'm not sorry I get to love you now."

I shake my head. "I'm not sorry, either." I press my lips to his and he wraps his arms around me and pulls me into his lap. He deepens our kiss and it's desperate and frenzied and after only a few seconds, I'm yanking his shirt over his head, followed by mine. Our mouths collide again, almost painfully, and he grips me tightly and flips our positions until he's above me.

I frantically shove his shorts and boxers down using my hands and then my feet to push them the rest of the way. Silas yanks open the drawer of his nightstand, almost pulling it out entirely as he fishes out a condom. Seconds later, he's rolling it down and doesn't bother to slide my thong down, he simply shoves it to the side and pushes inside me and we both let out moans.

I pull his mouth back to mine as we begin to move together. It's frantic and needy and our breaths grow short in only minutes and my heart thunders against my ribcage. He breaks our kiss and grips my face, forcing me to look at him. "I fucking love you, Ada." His words come out between labored breaths and I give him a jerky nod as I run my hands down his sides to grip his waist.

"I love you, too," I say with a moan.

His movements falter for a moment and his chest heaves. "You do?"

I nod, lifting my face to his. "I do, Silas. I love you." I press soft kisses to his lips and he slows his thrusts and deepens our kiss and I can't for the life of me figure out how I got this lucky. To have the love of not one good man, but two.

He presses my knee back and I gasp into his mouth at the change in angle. "Fuck, Silas."

"God, Ada, you feel so good. Shit." He reaches between us to work my clit and I can't bite back a sharp moan. "Come for me. Please. Fuck."

And sweet baby Jesus, how I come. My orgasm explodes within me, radiating out, making my legs shake, the edges of my vision turning black as I struggle to breathe. When I clench down, Silas's own release finds him only a few final, brutal pumps later. He lets out a loud groan, his head falling forward onto my chest.

As we begin to come down, he brushes my chest and neck with gentle pecks, moving up toward my lips. I run my fingers through his hair and let him simply kiss me. When he pulls away to look at me, I smile. "So, you really weren't joking when you said you were a patient man."

He laughs. "No, I wasn't." His expression grows more serious. "I meant everything I said, though. All I wanted was for y'all to be happy."

I nod. "I know. You're a good man, Silas. You are a good brother. You are a good friend. You're also mine."

He lets out a slow breath. "I've always been yours, Ada. Even when you weren't mine."

When Silas drops me off at home on his way to work, I sigh as I assess the carnage I caused after reading Cole's latest letter. I grab a garbage bag from the kitchen and sweep up all the potting soil and fragments of pottery and the plants and toss them in the bag. I return all the books and movies to their original locations and bring the garbage bag along with me to the bedroom, picking up any trash I find along the way.

Knowing I can't do all this in complete silence, I turn on some music. I take some time to rehang all my clothes while laying Cole's out on the bed so I can determine what, if any, of his clothes I'd like to keep.

I decide photos don't count toward my five items. Even if I won't display them after it's all said and done, I will keep them. I leave the one of Cole and Silas taken a few years ago at the farm, as well as one of Cole, Silas, and Josie from last Christmas when they all had on ugly sweaters. The rest, I pack into a plastic tub. I also set a couple aside for Ingrid and Miles and Pap.

Going through everything is much like taking a walk down memory lane. I can remember an instance where he wore everything in his closet; each shirt, every pair of shoes, all the different pairs of jeans.

I come across his hoodie from college and know for a fact it goes in the keep pile. I also choose one of the hats that advertise his business that he'd had made after the first year he turned a profit. I toss in one of the tee-shirts, too, because damn, they're just that comfy. I decide I'll let Silas and Miles go through any of Cole's clothes to see if there are any they want. I already know I won't be keeping anything other than what I've picked.

I mentally catalog all the books and movies and know they can all go, too. I glance at his nightstand. I haven't opened it since he died. I'm still not sure now is the time. But then again, I'm on a roll and if I stop, I might not start again, right? Right. Walking around the bed, I kneel in front of the nightstand. I open the top drawer, knowing some of the things I'll find. Lube. Bowl of spare change. Flashlight. Chapstick. Spare phone chargers and cables. Earbuds. I toss the chapstick and allow the rest to stay.

I close that drawer and open the second and find a few landscaping books, along with a sketchbook where he'd brainstorm ideas. I decide it goes into the keep pile. Stacking the books beside the nightstand and not seeing anything else, I close the drawer.

Heading into the bathroom, I make a quick sweep of the cabinets and toss Cole's deodorant, toothbrush, and razor, along with a half-used bottle of his medicated shampoo and body wash.

Moving up to the medicine cabinet, I toss a tube of athlete's foot medicine. I see two bottles of multivitamins and shake them both to see how full they are. They sound different, as though the tablets in one are smaller. When I open them, sure enough, one bottle has the large, beige, oblong tablets one associates with vitamins. The other has smaller, blue, oblong pills. Confused, I pour the two bottles onto the counter. One, I know is vitamins. The other must be some kind of prescription. My mind flashes to the pill bottle I'd found while tearing through the closet yesterday.

I run to the kitchen and fish out the empty bottle from my purse. I remember thinking yesterday I needed to research it, but I was too upset and decided moonshine was a better option. But I'm not drunk now.

Retrieving my phone from the bedroom, I shut off the music and open the web browser on my phone. I search the name of the drug, Verapamil, and read. It's listed as something called a calcium channel blocker and is typically used for high blood pressure. But from the best of my knowledge, Cole never had high blood pressure. And even though the prescription is in his name, there must be some other explanation.

I google other uses for the drug and my stomach drops when I read the words *hypertrophic cardiomyopathy*, the very thing Cole died from. I try to make sense of what I'm reading. Is it possible he knew he had it? Why wouldn't he have told me? How long had he known he had it? Deciding I need more information, I rush to my computer and boot it up. After what feels like ten years later, I type hypertrophic cardiomyopathy into the search engine.

A lot of the information I find is exactly what they told me when he died. His heart muscles had grown thick and it caused his heart to work harder and go into arrhythmia. Further research tells me a lot of times, people with HCM can not have any symptoms at all unless they begin to have issues like short-ness of breath, chest pain, and heart palpitations. And sure enough, one of the treatments is the drug he was obviously taking, as the date on the bottle was only a few months before he died.

As I continue to read, I'm convinced Cole must've known

he had it. And he kept it from me? Tears spring to my eyes knowing he most likely knew for years. Flashes of lines from his letters bombard my mind. *It was never gonna be me, Ada Mae. I've always known I was here for a good time, not a long time... You've always been my forever, even if I knew there was a good chance I couldn't be yours...*

I train my attention back on the computer screen to read more. My mouth goes dry when I read that HCM is usually inherited. Could Silas have it, too? Surely not, he's so athletic, he would've exhibited symptoms, right? And if Cole had it and they knew, Silas and Josie would have been tested, too, right?

I check the clock on my computer and see it's after eleven. I've been going through Cole's things for over eight hours? Shit. I know Silas should be home by now and he's got some explaining to do. No way he gets a call to prepare, either. I need to see his face because I'll be able to tell if he's lying. He's always been a terrible liar. But I need answers.

I grab my purse and the pill bottle and run to the car. I'm fully aware I could probably wait until tomorrow, but honestly, I don't know if my heart can take not knowing until then.

CHAPTER THIRTY-FIVE

SILAS

I'm just climbing out of the shower after coming home from the gym when I hear someone banging on the front door. Knowing how late it is, I'm unsure who it could be, but I still hustle to the door after dragging on a pair of boxers and sweatpants. I'm shocked to see Ada through the glass and I immediately throw open the door.

"Hey, I was getting ready to text you goodnight, but this is a good surprise," I say with a smile. She enters the house and I can tell by her body language she's tense. "Are you okay? Did something happen?"

She thrusts the pill bottle toward me, her tone accusatory. "He knew, didn't he? And don't lie to me, Silas."

I sigh and nod, resigned. "Yeah, he knew."

She backs up and when her knees hit the edge of the sofa, she drops. "How long?" I can't read her expression and her eyes are dry and I'm not sure if I should be nervous.

I cross the room to sit beside her. "Since we were seventeen."

Her head snaps in my direction and her mouth falls open,

all the color draining from her face. "Seventeen? *Seventeen?* He knew pretty much our entire relationship and he didn't tell me? What the fuck, Silas?"

"I can't answer that. It's not something we agreed on. I told him you should've been made aware from day one."

Her eyes fill with tears. "Why didn't you tell me?"

I shake my head, regret filling me for all the opportunities I've had to spill this truth to her. And in spite of the guilt I feel for keeping it from her, I answer as honestly as I can. "It wasn't my place, Ada. It was his body, his diagnosis, his choice. He asked me not to and I respected his decision. Regardless of the fact I disagreed with him. But it wasn't my decision to make."

"How could he let me be oblivious? I could've watched for signs. I could've made sure he went to the doctor. I could've—."

"Could've what, Wednesday? Could've suggested he undergo open-heart surgery and have risky procedures done? Could've asked him to try a lot of different medications whose side effects were almost as bad as the HCM itself? Could've watched him like a hawk and become his mother instead of the woman he loved?"

Anger flashes in her eyes. "That's not fair. You could have told me anytime since he died. I deserved to know."

"Yeah, you did. But I promised him, Ada. And would it have changed the way you felt about him? Would you have loved him any less?" Her jaw clenches and fat tears roll down her face and she shakes her head. "Exactly. Would knowing he was possibly going to die have made you love him less or more?"

"No."

"No," I repeat. "It would've only made you watch him and hover and wonder if today was the day he was going to die. It would've stolen all your joy. It would've become your focus instead of the way he loved you. And, fuck, he loved you. You know that."

"I'm guessing your parents and Josie knew, too?"

"Yeah. He started having heart palpitations the year he played soccer. They found it when they did an EKG. He tried a lot of different meds and that one is the only one that didn't do more harm than good for him. It was one of the reasons he never got drunk and always took good care of his body. His HCM was under control for years, until last year. They kept having to up his dosage, but even the safe maximum dosage wasn't working well anymore. But all the other available meds didn't work for him. One made him faint. Another caused his arrhythmia to be worse and made his blood pressure drop too low. Another caused liver damage.

"He was adamant he didn't want to pursue surgical options until there wasn't another option. He was probably almost at that point, even if he didn't want to admit it."

She clutches the pill bottle in her hand and looks down at it. "I can't believe he didn't tell me." Her head snaps in my direction again and fear is evident in her eyes. "It's inherited, right? You and Cole were twins. Do you have it?"

I shake my head. "Not identical, remember? I don't have it. Josie doesn't have it. It's a fifty-fifty chance you can get it if one of your parents is a carrier. Mom is, even though she doesn't have it. We all got screened and had genetic testing done. I'm not a carrier. Josie is. She'll have to decide if she wants to have kids since they'll be at higher risk for HCM.

"It's why Cole didn't want kids. He said he wasn't going to play roulette with his genes like that. It was why he didn't want to get married. He said if his HCM got really bad and he needed to undergo a lot of treatments or had to have a transplant, he wasn't putting that medical debt on you."

"So, all the tasks, you knew about them? He planned it all for a long time?"

I reach for her hand and she starts to move away, but finally lets me take it. "He mentioned something right after his diagnosis. I already told you he made me promise to take care of you if something happened to him, remember?" She nods. "I had no idea about the tasks until the package was delivered. But I guess, looking back, he hinted.

"When we'd go to the rage room, which, we started going last year after they told him his HCM had gotten worse. He was angry and didn't want you to see it. We'd go out and have a drink after and he'd remind me of my promise. He told me he had two life insurance policies and I asked him why. He said one to take care of you and another for me, to help follow through on the promise. And I've used it for whatever was required on my end for the tasks. The rest is in savings."

"I just don't see how couldn't tell me."

"If it had been me, I would've told you. But he and I weren't the same people. He only wanted you to see him as the strong, healthy man you thought he was. If I were to guess, he felt like you'd had enough to deal with during your life. He didn't want to be something else you worried about. He wanted to share his life with you and not have the cloud of HCM hanging over y'all. He wanted to see your face every morning when he woke up and know you never worried about him. He wanted you to be carefree and simply enjoy whatever time he had with you. You were the love of his life, Ada."

Her chin quivers and her eyes well with tears. "I know. It's just not fair. I would've wanted to know."

I wrap my arm around her and pull her against me and she comes willingly. "I know. I'm sorry." She leans her head against my bare chest and cries and I hold her, my heart aching for her. I rub her back and wish I could take this pain from her.

Once her sobs subside, she pulls back and sniffles. "I'm sorry I came in guns blazing."

I huff a laugh. "You didn't. You have every right to be angry and it's a lot for you to process. I've had almost fifteen years to process it and his death still hit me like a truck. You're processing his HCM on top of your grief and all the shit that went down with your dad. It's been a fucked up year, Peep."

She nods. "Yeah. It has." She levels me with a gaze. "You're not hiding any life-threatening medical conditions, are you?"

I shake my head. "Nope. Fit as a fiddle. I must have hit the genetic lottery, because other than some markers for type-two diabetes and high cholesterol, I don't have any issues."

"Must be those mountain man Campbell genes," she deadpans.

"Must be," I agree. "So, how's the organizing going?"

She shrugs. "About as well as can be expected. I thought you and your dad might want to go through his clothes to see if there's anything y'all want since you were all the same size. I picked out a hoodie, a tee-shirt, and one of his hats, along with his landscaping sketchbook. I set some pictures aside for your parents and left the ones up of you and him and you, him, and Josie. The rest, I'll pack away."

"That's only four items."

Ada nods. "I know. Other than that stuff and the letters and the pictures, I don't think there is anything else I want."

"Okay. Well, you still have almost two weeks."

"I think I'm good. Can you call tomorrow? I'll have every-thing ready. They can also take the bedroom furniture."

I frown. "What, your bed and stuff? Why?"

"You said you can't sleep with me in the bed I shared with Cole. I'll get a new bed."

I shake my head. "You don't have to do that."

"I don't want to give up the option of having you stay over at my place when it's an easy fix, Silas. I know I loved Cole. I know he loved me." She puts her hand on my chest. "I also love you enough to respect what you need. I think we both know Cole would be fine with it."

"Are you sure?" I ask. "I don't want you to have any regrets. Take the time."

"I'm sure." She sighs. "Will you take me to bed? I'm sad and tired and want you to hold me."

"Of course. It's been an emotional day for you." I stand and extend my hand to her and she takes it and follows me to my room. We climb under the covers and I pull her into my arms.

CHAPTER THIRTY-SIX

ADA

Over the next couple of weeks, I adjust to only having my things in the apartment, as well as the new furniture Josie went with me to pick out. The closet seems too big and the bookshelves seem too empty. But the things I kept are the things I know I was supposed to keep and have no regrets about any of the things I let go.

We enjoyed Thanksgiving with Ingrid, Miles, Pap, and Josie at the farmhouse and it was lovely. Not the same without Cole to eat his weight in sweet potato casserole, but it was still a good day. We all shared what we were thankful for. I said I was thankful for Silas's friendship and his love and also for the years of happiness Cole gave me. And if we all teared up, no one has to know, right?

Today, I awoke to find Silas already gone from bed with a note on his pillow.

Wednesday,
Be ready to go by four. I have a birthday surprise for you.

Before you text me a million questions, there is no dress code.
Dress for the weather. That's it. I'll pick you up.

Love you,
Silas

And so, here I sit on the couch, a few minutes before four, waiting for Silas. Right on time, he enters the apartment using his key—because it stopped being Josie's a long time ago, apparently—with a smile on his face. He's dressed casually, in jeans and a flannel over a tee-shirt and pair of work boots. "You ready?"

I glance down at his shoes. "Do I need to wear boots? Are we doing some work today?"

He shakes his head. "What you have on is fine. I had some prep I needed to do." I open my mouth to ask and he points a finger at me. "Don't even ask, you know I won't tell you."

I roll my eyes. "Fine. Let's go."

He takes my hand and leads me out to the Bronco and opens the passenger door. After I climb in, he pulls something out of his back pocket. "Put this on."

I look down at the blindfold in his hand skeptically. "Kinky. So, I don't even get to know where you're taking me?"

He shakes his head. "All will be revealed. Come on, be a good sport and play along. It's nothing bad."

I take it from him and after fastening my seatbelt, slip it over my eyes. He wastes no time starting the car and pulling out of the parking lot. And try as I might, I can't determine which directions we turn half the time.

About fifteen minutes later, he pulls to a stop. "Don't take it off yet." I hear him exit the vehicle and a few seconds later, he opens my door and unbuckles my seatbelt. "Okay, turn in your seat and I'll help you out."

"I still can't take it off?"

"Nope. Just trust me. It's a good surprise. I promise."

I obey and once I climb down, he wraps his arm around my waist and guides me through what feels like grass. But then, he stops. I raise my hands up and he pulls them back down. "Not yet. Damn, Wednesday, have some patience."

I huff a laugh. "Sorry. I'll try to be good."

"Good." He presses a kiss to my cheek. "Okay. So, I know this has been the year from hell. You've faced things no one should ever have to face. And thanks to Cole, and his relentless need to plan everything to the last detail, you've been able to come back to yourself. And thanks to Cole, we were able to fall in love. Granted, I've always loved you. But thanks to Cole and his tasks, we were able to spend time together and get to know one another, and develop a wonderful friendship that evolved into more. Some people might find it strange or unorthodox, but those people don't matter. What does matter is the love we have for each other and the love we had for Cole.

"When you were many years younger than you are now, you sketched a house. About five years ago, Cole had plans drawn up for that house and bought a piece of land. He knew he would never get to ask you to marry him or allow himself to give you children, but he did want to give you this one thing."

Tears begin to well in my eyes, even behind the blindfold, and Silas's voice grows thick with emotion. "And then, when he found out his HCM had progressed, he sold it to me on the condition I finish what he started. I think he always knew we'd get to this point, or at least, that was his hope. His design needed some modifications to incorporate rooms for the kids I wanted and the ones he suspected you'd want, too.

"Now, keep in mind, there's still a lot of work to be done, but it's far enough along for you to get the idea." He pulls the blindfold off and I gasp. It's my house, exactly as I sketched it, with a few modifications. But the two-story, white farmhouse with a wraparound porch and wooden columns stands proud and tall and mostly finished. And to top it off, colored Christmas lights are wrapped around the columns shining into the waning sunlight of the evening.

"Silas, this is..." I can't even finish the sentence as I burst into tears.

He swipes my tears off my cheeks and presses a soft kiss to my lips. "You think you can handle more?"

I let out a sound that's something like a mix between a scoff and a watery laugh. "More?" I ask, incredulous. "Isn't this enough?"

"Come see for yourself." He takes my hand and we walk up the porch steps and he pulls out a set of keys and places them in my hand. "Go ahead." I take a deep breath and unlock the door and he clicks the handle and we step inside. "Now, we'll still have to pick out flooring and paint colors. I know you said dark floors and light walls, but I want you to be able to make those choices." He tugs me to the right, where the living room is located. "As well as the stone for the fireplace. I knew I wanted one, but when you mentioned stone, I held off on doing the hearth or mantle until you got to look at some samples."

I'm still speechless as he guides me back the way we came and past the front door into the kitchen. "We'll also need to talk cabinets and fixtures and appliances and stuff, but I did some outlines on the floor in painter's tape so you could kinda get an idea." He points to the middle of the room. "Large island there." He turns and points to a large window. "Huge table over there. Big enough for the whole family and a few guests. You know, in case Josie ever finds a guy to put up with her."

He gives me a big grin. "I have one more room to show you." I follow him back toward the front door and he starts up a set of stairs. Once we clear the landing he wraps his arm around my waist and guides me straight back to a door. "Ready?"

I huff a laugh. "I'm not sure, am I?"

He gives me a quick kiss. "Go ahead." I twist the knob and walk in, only to be greeted by a wall of windows along the far wall. Silas comes up behind me. "It's north-facing, just like you wanted."

I look at him, dumbfounded. "This is my studio?"

He nods. "Yeah. And it'll have the drafting table and easel, but I wasn't about to pick that stuff out for you." He walks over to a corner and picks something up and brings it back to me. When I take it, I recognize the framed drawing of this house.

"I thought I'd lost this. I couldn't find it for years."

He grins. "Cole found it and took it to the architect for inspiration. Then he had it framed. I figure once the fireplace is finished, we can set it on top or hang it, whatever you want to do."

He takes my hand in his. "This is your house, Wednesday. Well, ours, if you'll let me live here with you. I know it's soon. I know people will probably think this is some strange grief bond, but I love you and want to build a future with you. Someday, I want to marry you and give you babies and even a big dog. I want to have family holidays and gatherings here. I want to grow old with you here."

I open my mouth to say something, but nothing comes out and Silas laughs. "Don't worry, this isn't a proposal. You'll know for sure when I ask you to marry me. That day is not today. I'm simply asking you not to renew your lease and move in with me. I don't want to spend another day not waking up beside you. I want to fall asleep next to you every night."

"I can't believe all this."

He shrugs. "Call it fate or kismet or whatever you want, but you were always meant to be part of our family. Cole was meant to be your first love. I'd be honored to be your last, Ada."

My chest tightens with emotion and for what feels like the tenth time in as many minutes, my eyes well with tears. "You sure that's not a proposal, because damn, Ass."

He laughs and kisses me. "Yeah, I'm sure. I do have something else for you, though."

I shake my head. "I don't think I can handle any more."

"Well, just one more thing, and then we go home and watch *Grey's* and have Mexican and margaritas and strawberry pie."

I blow out a breath. "Okay. Lay it on me." He reaches into his back pocket and pulls out a small box and hands it over.

"It's not a ring. Like I said, not a proposal."

I can't help but laugh as I lift the lid on the velvet jeweler's box. Nestled inside is a necklace with a small gold pendant with a diamond center. I lift it closer to my eyes to see better and look up at him. "Is that a compass?"

He nods and lifts it out of the box and gestures for me to turn around. "Yes. And the diamond in the center was made from Cole's ashes. So you'll always have him with you." I gasp as he closes the clasp and turns me back around to face him. "What was it he said, 'whether you needed the stars or a compass to help you figure out where you were going, as long as you were together, you'd never get lost'?" I nod, tears in my eyes again, and he gives me a smile.

"That day I had to bail on *Grey's*, it was to meet with the designer. I was supposed to meet with them the next day and they had an emergency and were going out of town and wouldn't be back for weeks. To get the piece done on time, I had to meet with them then. I wish I could have told you back then, but I didn't want to ruin the surprise.

"I knew from the beginning I wanted to have some of his

ashes turned into a diamond because Cole would've thought it was just too cool. And I wanted you to have something with you forever, regardless of what happened between you and me. And when we were at the cabin and I saw your star tattoos and you mentioned his compass tattoo, it hit me later that's exactly what I wanted to do."

"Silas, this is amazing. I love you."

"I love you, too. So, is that a yes on moving in with me?"

I nod and throw my arms around his neck for a tight hug. "Yes. A million times, yes."

He laughs and returns my hug. "Thank God. I also have this for you." He pulls back and fishes something out of his back pocket.

"Okay, you got Mary Poppins pockets or something? Are those bottomless pockets, because everything you have has come from those."

He shakes his head, his expression softening, and holds it out. My smile falters when I see the envelope. "Oh."

Silas nods. "Yeah." He gestures out the window. "There's a rocker out there if you want to read it now. Or you can read it when you get home."

My brow furrows and I look down at the letter, a sense of finality washing over me. "It's the last one, isn't it?"

He nods again, his voice quiet. "Yeah."

My breath catches and when I swallow, my throat aches from the tears threatening to spill again. "Okay. I'll read it here." He tugs me down the steps and out the front door and around the porch where a single white rocker sits.

He gives me a kiss on the cheek. "I'll be down in the car. Take as long as you need. When you come down, would you care to unplug the lights from the porch? I'll go ahead and lock up the house."

I nod, unable to say anything as I take a seat, the letter in my lap. Silas retreats around the side of the house and I look around. The yard is level and mature trees dot the landscape and will provide ample shade during the summer. This really is my dream house. And the two men who've loved me more than I could hope to ever be loved made it come true.

Fingering the compass necklace, I blow out a deep breath. After a final moment of hesitation, I run my finger under the flap of the envelope, breaking the seal. And even though I know I'm not prepared to read the last words Cole will ever have for me, I still pull the folded sheets of paper out and straighten them to read.

Ada Mae,

If you're reading this letter, it means I don't get to call you <u>my</u> Ada Mae anymore. It means you and Silas have found your way to one another. You've fallen in love exactly as I hoped when I set out for you two to complete the tasks.

Tears burn my eyes as understanding finally washes over me. Knowing I wasn't imagining things when I thought Cole was trying to play wingman and hype Silas up for all those months.

In case Si hasn't told you, he's loved you for as long as I have. I was just quicker on the dibs. I promise it wasn't some weird thing between us where I shared stories about our sex life or anything. It was an unspoken agreement that we didn't talk about you when we were alone. I didn't want to hurt him. Because even though I loved you more than life itself, he's my brother and my best friend and he loved a girl he couldn't have, so I tried to minimize his pain.

But now, I hope the two of you are happy. I hope you'll get married and have lots of babies and fill up that house he's building for you. I might have started it, but when I knew I wouldn't be able to finish it, I gave it over to him.

I'm sick, babe. You might've already figured it out; you're a smart woman. But on the off chance you haven't, I have something called hypertrophic cardiomyopathy and it's progressed. The meds I'm on aren't working. If I'm still around in January, they're likely going to press me to do surgery, but honestly, I'm not sure I want to do it. I'm sorry I kept it from you. In hindsight, I never should have. I didn't want you to worry, though, so I'd like to think my reasons are good, even if they're not.

Personally, I'd rather be remembered as the man you know and love. I don't want to possibly go out on some surgeon's table and the last memory you have of me be whatever I said when they were wheeling me away. I want my last words to be some everyday, ordinary conversation we share. Because I know without a shadow of a doubt, I never left anything unsaid between us. I hope you always knew how much I loved you. I hope you know how much I still love you.

It's a bittersweet thing to think about Silas finally getting to love you. He finally gets his happy ending. As his brother, I couldn't be more overjoyed for him. But for him to get this happy ending, I simply have to end. And the bitterness comes from the knowledge that I will have to leave you. It's a hard pill to swallow, Ada Mae, knowing for him to be happy means I won't be around to see it.

Please know I was never happier in my life than those mornings I was privileged enough to get to wake up beside you. Please know that you were the best thing I ever had. Please know, even as I took my last breath, you were the only thought I had. I know that's how it will be and no one can convince me otherwise.

I hope someday, there is only joy when you look back at

our life together. That the wonderful years we shared outweigh your grief. I don't want me being gone to be something that makes you sad. I want you to revel in the knowledge that every day I lived, I lived with the love of my life. I had the privilege of never having to know what it's like to lose the person I love. And I suppose, in that, I'm selfish and self-centered.

I know you'll survive losing me. Not only because you now have Silas; although, don't get me wrong, I'm so very thankful you have him. I know you'll survive because you're a survivor, babe. You'd survived more in the first fifteen years of your life than anyone should ever have to endure. And even if it doesn't feel like it sometimes, you are the strongest person I know.

If I know you and Silas, in spite of how much you might feel for one another, you're still butting heads and fighting. I hope when you fight, you always make up just as quickly. I hope the making up is just as much fun as the fighting.

I hope you know I would've given almost anything to never have to write any of these letters. To only be focused on our future together and the life we wanted to build. But if you're reading them, it means life had other plans for me. And for you and Si.

Take care of each other. Love him more than you loved me. I told Si I felt like I was quicker to call dibs because somewhere deep down, I knew he'd be the one you ended up with. I only wanted to get to call you mine for as long as I could.

And, oh, did I call you mine, Ada Mae. I'm fortunate to get to say I've only ever loved one woman my entire life and she was the only one I gave every part of myself to. I have no regrets about any of it. The only regret I'll ever have is that I won't get to see your face when you see the house. I'll regret I couldn't entertain the idea of marriage and kids with you. I'll regret I won't get to watch you and Silas be parents or grandparents. I'll regret I won't get to see you with gray hair. I'll regret I'll never get to make love to you again.

Even though this is technically goodbye, I'll be around. I hope you and Silas will still share anecdotes about me and laugh about all the things we did together. I hope your children will know about their Uncle Cole. I hope those kids have their mother's beautiful gray eyes and dark hair. Because let's face it, your eyes and hair are a lot nicer than Silas's, even if he's an okay-looking fella.

I hope you'll think of me when you see the waves at the ocean or someone mows grass and you smell it. I hope you'll occasionally still dream of me. We don't have to tell Si. I hope, when you miss me, it's not with longing, but just the general way you miss a friend when you haven't seen them in a while. My hope is Silas and the children you hope to have will fill up every nook and cranny of your heart. It's okay if there's no room for me anymore. Just know that loving you gave my literal hard heart a reason to beat.

I will forever love you, Ada. Thank you for being my family, my confidant, my lover, and my partner. You made my short life worth living.

You will forever be my always.

Love, Cole

The front of my shirt is soaked with tears. Tears of sadness, pain, love, and joy. I draw my knees up to my chest and sob knowing I'll never get to hear Cole's voice ever again, even if it's only in his written words. I let the loss of him wash over me like those waves, knowing they will recede, even if it's not immediate. I look out toward the tree line as my sobs turn into hiccups. The sun is just beginning to set and I'm reminded that even on bad days, the sun goes down. But it always comes up again.

I wipe my eyes and nose on the cuff of my long-sleeved tee-shirt and take several cleansing breaths. I bring my fingers up and lay them against my new pendant. "You will always be with me, Cole. Thank you for loving me so well."

I rise and walk around to the front of the house and unplug the lights. As I descend the steps, Silas starts up the Bronco and headlights illuminate my path back to the vehicle. When I open the door and slide into my seat, he gives me a soft smile. "Ready?"

I nod. "Yeah. Let's go home."

"You've got it, Wednesday."

AUTHOR'S NOTE II

Dear Reader,

If you've made it thus far, you are a ROCKSTAR and I love you. Just a heads up before you delve into the epilogue. It contains content related to pregnancy and birth. If you're not in the right headspace for that kind of subject matter or have no desire to read about those things, I've got you. You can rest easy knowing Silas and Ada are safe and happy in their forever.

With respect,

Rachael

EPILOGUE
SILAS — FIVE YEARS LATER

"Daddy, why's Mommy's face look like that?" Our four-year-old, daughter, Bea, asks.

I huff a laugh. "Well, Mommy's going to have a baby and it hurts some. And as soon as Aunt Josie gets here, I'm going to take her so we can meet your baby brother."

Bea runs over to where Ada is swaying, hands on hips, trying to breathe through her contractions. Our little girl places a tentative hand on her mother's belly. Even through her pain, Ada grins down at her. "Hey, sweet girl."

"Can I talk to him?"

Ada blows out a breath and nods. Bea presses her ear to the bump. "Hi, baby brother. I hope you like marshmallow peeps. I saved some for you from my Easter basket. Mommy says they're good, but I don't really like them. So you can have them."

I watch as another contraction hits her and she groans. I close the distance between us and swing Bea up into my arms. "Hey, honey, why don't you go pick out a movie for you and Aunt Josie to watch? Hopefully something with a lot of singing.

She loves those." I press a kiss to the top of her dark head and nudge her toward the stairs and she takes off.

"Come on, Brutus," she hollers at our lab mix currently lounging in his bed. At Bea's command, he hops up and trots over to her. The two scramble up the stairs and a moment later, they're in her room.

I rub Ada's lower back, hoping to help ease her discomfort. "Remind me why we decided to do this again," she demands through gritted teeth.

I huff a laugh and take her hand in my free one. "Come on, let's walk a little, see if it helps. And I don't know that it was a choice. I was just too irresistible on the plane ride home from New York. Good on you for marking off three of my bucket list items in such a short period of time."

"I blame the first-class mimosas. I wasn't thinking clearly."

"Hey, you were the one who suggested we finally join the mile high club."

She winces and breathes through another pain. "Like I said, not thinking clearly. I hope you remember how great it was because it will never happen again."

"If you say so, but I think we both know I'm pretty good at getting you to do things."

"Don't remind me. Last I checked, it was also your idea to skinny dip in the river when it was twenty degrees outside. It's a wonder we didn't die."

"Yeah, but getting warmed back up was pretty nice. And the little girl currently stomping around her room was the product of that, so can you really be all that upset?"

"I'm in labor, Silas, I'm allowed to be cranky."

"Oh, I know. It's the only reason I'm not giving you shit."

She narrows her eyes. "You still give me shit, even when I'm ten centimeters dilated and pushing these babies out. Who, might I remind you, have those giant Campbell heads."

I can't help but laugh. "You don't know what kind of head he has. He's not been born yet."

"Call it a hunch," she deadpans.

The front door swings open and Josie comes in, breathless. "Okay, I'm here. Sorry it took so long. I was at the farm when I got your text. Pap was showing me something in the stillhouse." She looks around. "Where's Bea?"

I start shuffling Ada toward the door. "In her room. We're out. Ada's contractions are already three minutes apart. We'll be lucky if we make it to the hospital before this kid decides to join the party."

I pick up the duffle bag and Ada's purse and Josie waves us off as she closes the door. "Okay. Y'all be safe. I've got the girl."

Four hours and extensive amounts of swearing later, our son is placed onto Ada's chest. I'm forced to wipe the tears from my eyes to be able to cut the cord. Directly after, I'm peppering her face with kisses as the nurses wipe the baby down. "You did so good, Wednesday. Fuck, I'm proud of you," I whisper in her ear.

She grabs the back of my neck and pulls my mouth to hers for a long kiss. "I hope you enjoyed that because I'm not doing it again, buddy."

I huff a laugh and press my forehead to hers. "Sure. Whatever you say."

I look down at our son, whose fine hair is lighter than Bea's was when she was born. Ada shifts him in her arms, where he's currently swaddled, blinking slowly. His pudgy face gives him the look of some cranky old man, but he's beautiful. She lifts him up to me and I take him, making sure to support his neck and head. I lift him to my face and breathe in that sweet, newborn baby smell and brush a kiss across his forehead.

"So, do you all have a named picked out for this big boy?" The doctor looks at Ada. "Nine pounds, Mama. You're a trooper."

Ada and I share a smile. "His name is Cole." I glance down at him. "Happy birthday, little man." I close my eyes as tears threaten again. *Thank you, brother. For everything. For letting me love her. For giving me the opportunity to let her fall in love with me. I hope you can see we didn't waste the precious gifts you gave us. This little boy is proof. He'll always know you're the reason he's even here.*

Cole begins to fuss, so I place him back into my wife's arms and he hungrily latches to nurse. I press a kiss to Ada's cheek. "Thank you for marking off the final item on my bucket list. Thank you for giving me these beautiful babies."

She smiles. "You still have one more item."

"What's that? I have everything I could ever want."

"You're supposed to grow old with me."

"Couldn't stop me if you tried, Peep."

ABOUT THE AUTHOR

At the age of eleven, Rachael discovered her grandmother's stash of clench-cover romance novels and she was forever changed. A lover of many, many fictional men and one very non-fictional one, she strives to write real and emotional characters who always get their happily ever after. Rachael lives in East Tennessee with her husband and two sons on their family farm.

ALSO BY RACHAEL OGLE

Until August (Until Book 1)

Until Forever (Until Book 2)

Fake It Till You Fall (Fall Book 1)

Falling Into Forever (Fall Book 2)